BERKLEY SCIENCE FICTION · 0-425-09560-6 · ($4.75 CANADA) · $3.50 U.S.

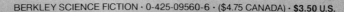

*"A high-speed, high-tech thriller, packed with ideas."*
—Greg Bear, author of BLOOD MUSIC

# Dome

## MICHAEL REAVES
## and STEVE PERRY

When the world above died,
they were ready... almost

D0034605

# Meet the Citizens of Dome

**Douglas Copeland**—Scientist heading up the *Mea Lana* research unit, better known as the Dome. As leader, he is responsible, however reluctantly, for what may well be the last pocket of humanity to survive the ultimate catastrophe.

**Betsy Emau**—A passionate woman and part-time party girl. Mistress-for-hire to several of the Dome's men, she has no qualms about using her beauty and body to get what she wants. When the world outside ends, so do all the desires—but not the passion.

**Jonathan Holly Crane**—A miracle of genetic research, the first recipient of permanent gills. This scientific breakthrough is Crane's ticket to fame. Until he begins to venture outside the Dome—and discovers a new path to glory.

**Patricia Ishida**—A pampered child of the upper class. Gifted as one of the few who can tolerate and utilize the advanced microbe implants that allow her to interface directly with the experimental Artificial Intelligence called Baby. Together, woman and computer may be the key to the Dome's survival—if Baby can "grow up" in time...

---

"Reaves and Perry are masters of suspense."
—*David Brin*
*Author of* The Postman

*Berkley Books by Michael Reaves and Steve Perry*

HELLSTAR
DOME

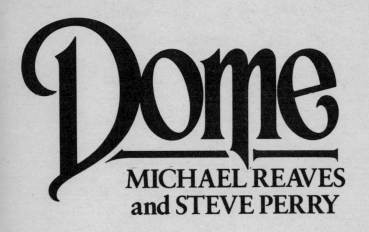

# Dome

## MICHAEL REAVES
## and STEVE PERRY

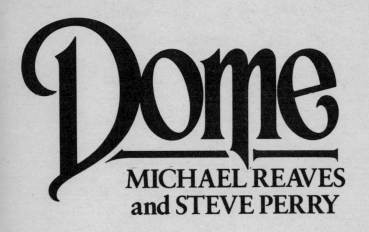

BERKLEY BOOKS, NEW YORK

DOME

A Berkley Book/published by arrangement with
the authors

PRINTING HISTORY
Berkley edition/February 1987

All rights reserved.
Copyright © 1987 by Michael Reaves and Steve Perry.
This book may not be reproduced in whole or in part,
by mimeograph or any other means, without permission.
For information address: The Berkley Publishing Group,
200 Madison Avenue, New York, NY 10016.

ISBN: 0-425-09560-6

A BERKLEY BOOK® TM 757,375
Berkley Books are published by
The Berkley Publishing Group,
200 Madison Avenue, New York, NY 10016.
The name "BERKLEY" and the stylized "B" with design are
trademarks belonging to Berkley Publishing Corporation.

PRINTED IN THE UNITED STATES OF AMERICA

There is no end to that which we don't know, and in a book this size, we had to learn some of these things. Our thanks go to those people who helped us by word or deed, and if we misused their input, it is our fault, not theirs.

Thanks to Alan Lachman, M.D., Dianne Perry, Toni Zenker, Brynne Stephens, Davis Corrigan, Sally Harmon and Carol McKay.

For Dianne, same winds, two trees;
For Jack Gaughan, worth a billion words;
And for Dr. Pemberton, vindicated!
—SCP


For Brynne, once more;
And for the Vendome Street Mafia.
—JMR

Whether it is to flee war, pestilence or hunger, all men eventually return to the sea.

—*Toyotomi*

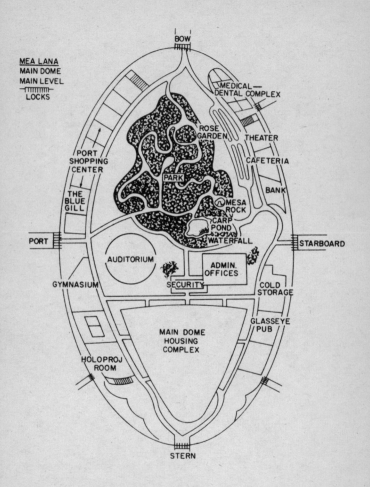

MEA LANA
MAIN DOME
MAIN LEVEL
┬┬┬┬┬┬┬
LOCKS

BOW

MEDICAL —
DENTAL COMPLEX

ROSE
GARDEN

THEATER

PORT
SHOPPING
CENTER

CAFETERIA

PARK

BANK

THE
BLUE
GILL

MESA
ROCK

CARP
POND

WATERFALL

PORT

STARBOARD

AUDITORIUM

ADMIN.
OFFICES

GYMNASIUM

COLD
STORAGE

SECURITY

GLASSEYE
PUB

MAIN DOME
HOUSING
COMPLEX

HOLOPROJ
ROOM

STERN

# PART I

## *Descension*

# 1

"This is Richard Ipu Temae, controlling the deep-frag *Malalo-kai One*, detached to observation of volcanic activity on In-ouye Guyot; present position, twenty degrees, two minutes north; one hundred and fifty-seven degrees, fifty-nine minutes west; holding neutral buoyancy at a depth of twenty-six hundred meters. I make it 0600 hours, on the nose."

One hundred and thirty kilometers to the northeast and considerably closer to the surface of the Pacific Ocean, Douglas Copeland touched a control tab on his holoproj and studied the resulting image. There was no sunlight where Richard was, but doppler interscan produced a clear translate-enhanced view. The augmented image of the underwater mountain seemed an eerie blue still life when viewed in cool spectrum, as Copeland now saw it. With the lightest stroke of one finger, he shifted the holographic picture to the underwater mountain. The infrared sensors showed red and orange spots on it. No steam at that depth, of course—too much pressure for that; still, it was hot enough, and then some. Copeland nodded, satisfied. The deep-frag's video gear seemed to be working. He returned the image to its former state and leaned back in his chair.

"Okay, Rickie, I log you in. How's it look?"

"Boring. I wish I were home. I was supposed to get the

3

weekend off, to go uptop to Molokai. Peach and I were gonna scan up the view from Puu Nana."

"Life is hard, kid."

"Thanks for the sympathy. Just because you're too old to remember what it's like to be young doesn't mean the rest of us should suffer."

Copeland laughed. He was thirty-five to Rickie Temae's nineteen; he could remember thinking, when he'd been that age, that anyone over thirty was a fossil. "What are you bitching at? I'm the one stuck down in the bowels of the beast listening to adolescent *angst*. At least *you* get to move around."

"Big deal. Locked in a slunglas and stainless steel drum the size of a coffin ain't my idea of a fun time, Prof. And the air-conditioning system is whining like a stuck dog again, too. I thought you were going to have it fixed."

"It worked okay the last time I was down."

"It always does."

Copeland looked around the inside of the underwater communications fragment. Aside from two technicians pulling out the guts of a holoproj console and three half-sleeping controllers, the UW frag was empty. The room would hold twenty operators at full capacity, but the empty form-chairs now stared at blank spots over shut-down holoprojectors. Only a skeleton staff was working; everybody else was enjoying the Thanksgiving holiday, either in the underwater mining city itself or on nearby Molokai. It would be the last chance at shore games for at least a month; it would take that long to accomplish the move from the Sandwich Islands to the Society Ridge off Tahiti. And, once full-scale mining began, time off would be harder to come by...

"Yo, old man—you still there?"

The sound of Rick's voice pulled Copeland from his thoughts. "Yes, junior, I'm still here. And also still waiting for your recording sphere transfer."

"Oops. Sorry. Here it is."

A menu window set in the bottom right of Copeland's image began to blur with words and numbers, showing the input of information from the remote pickups watching the fitful volcano. Copeland didn't try to follow the rapid scan, knowing that the mainframe matrix would analyze it and report back with anything unusual.

"So," said the boy's voice, "what's the word on the Vietnamese test?"

"Still on. Last I heard the WH Bloc, the Sino-Japanese Alliance and the Russians were all screaming for them to call it off. But the URNA still backs any Third World country that wants to do anything, anywhere, anytime."

"Stupid Africans."

"Now, now, let's not be nasty."

"Hey, don't they know what this test might *do?* Jesus, they are practically parked right *on* the Clipperton Fracture! Don't they have anybody who knows squat about magshift--techtonics?"

"Their geologists don't seem to be worried."

"They're all *lolo*, then!"

"Maybe they're crazy, maybe not. Nobody knows what the test will do, Rickie. It might not do anything at all."

"You don't believe that, Doug. I took your classes, remember? *And* your lectures on volcanic eruptions, *and* your seminar on interlocking ridge and fault patterns, *and*—"

"Enough," Copeland cut in. "I know what a bright boy you are. But it's a little late to start protesting now." He glanced at the time-read in the upper left corner of the holoproj image. "The bomb goes off in twenty minutes."

"I'm going to swing around to the lateral vent on the north face," Rich said. "Some of the pillows looked interesting last time I was down."

"Maybe it'd be better if you stayed on the south side."

"Hell, I'm not *that* worried, Prof. I don't think we're talking stone waves here, even if the Vietnamese firecracker does stir the magma some."

"Still, you'd make an old man happy if you stayed where you were for a while."

There was a short silence. Then: "You worry too much, Doug. I bitch, but you worry."

Copeland grinned, then looked away from the holoproj as one of the technicians cursed over a dropped chip-board. Tiny slices of thin superconductor protein splashed onto the floor, scattering the barely-solid, fingernail-sized chips in all directions. He looked back at the screen just in time to see the holoproj flicker for an instant. "Rickie? Everything okay?"

"Affirmative, Prof. Why wouldn't it be?"

"I just got a ghost strobe on my monitor."

He could imagine Rick's shrug. "We're all here: me, the coffin, the seamount, the glow-in-the-dark fishies. And, of course, a couple thousand klicks or so to the east, our friends the Viets."

Copeland suddenly had an uneasy feeling—a fluttery sensation in his bowels, tightening the muscles of his belly. He felt like he had the only time he had ever been in a free fall. "I'm going to tap into the seismographic mode for a few minutes; call if anything happens."

"That's affirmative, Prof. I'll find something to keep busy. Discom."

Copeland nodded absently. He flicked a few switches, his fingers moving unerringly to the right board. Much of his work consisted of taking readings, assembling data, correlating numbers, in a ceaseless attempt to push back the boundaries of the unknown. Even though men had been living under the sea in small settlements since the mid-2000s—almost half a century—they still knew very little about that which comprised most of the Earth's surface. More was known about the moon, about the Belt, about Mars and Venus than about the bottom of the oceans. Even with the creation of the *Mea Lana* Dome, the largest underwater mobile city to date, the motives for undersea work still tended toward profit rather than science. The dome was designed to suck in seawater and leach from it valuable minerals and metals. The scientific community onboard seemed more an afterthought than anything else, a sop to some of the minor investors . . .

A chime sounded, indicating that the seismographic sensors into which Copeland had linked his computer console had been triggered. And there it was: the Vietnamese nuclear device, right on time. Copeland watched the figures on the right half of his three-D monitor, while the left half of the holoproj continued to show the underwater flat-topped mountain of Inouye. No change in the guyot, at least visibly.

There was some wave activity from the explosion, but not enough to worry about; the Vietnamese had said they could direct the explosion downward, and it seemed they had done so. Whether their other promises that the bomb would do no harm were true remained to be seen.

"Ah, Doug, this is Rick. I think we've got something here."

Copeland twitched a finger over a photosensitive switch and the seismographic information faded as the view of the volcano expanded to fill the holoimage. "On-line, Rick. Go."

"I'm getting a fluctuation on the magnetic anomaly at the base on the north side. And my sensors are picking up heat and increased pressure. I'm going to shoot a torpedo probe in for better readings."

"It won't do you any good from the south face."

A pause. "I—ah—I'm not on the south face, Prof."

"I'm looking right at it, Rick—"

"A drone, Doug. I didn't want you to worry. I moved around and left the drone 'casting."

The strobe ghost he had seen had been the switch from the frag's video pickups to those of the drone, Copeland realized. "I'm going to kick your butt from here to Tharsis Base for that, Richard!"

"Yeah, yeah, okay, but later. Right now I've got what looks like new flow. I'm glad I didn't get to Molokai after all."

Copeland felt that twist in his gut again. "Rick, I want you to pull back around to the south face."

"What? You're *hehena*, Prof! How many times have we seen this, gotten it on video? Hell, this will *make* my doctoral!"

"There's a danger, Rick—"

"Danger? At *this* depth? Come on! We're not expecting a Stromboli or a St. Helens here; we're too deep. We're talking lava flow, perlitics, basic hyaloclastic stuff—hell, *you* taught it to me!"

Copeland had no answer for that; Rick was right.

"My probe is in. Stand by for transmission."

"Affirmative. Let's see what we've got."

"That's better, *elemakule*."

Copeland smiled. Rick tended to lapse into Hawaiian or pidgin Samoan polyglot when he got excited. *Elemakule* meant "old man."

The smile faded as the readings from the imbedded probe flashed across the screen. At the same time, Rick began transmitting the augmented-visual picture from the deep-frag.

The mountain was bulging.

"It's not possible," Copeland said softly. "You *can't* get

that kind of pressure without blowing the rock somewhere!"

"Hey, Prof, you see those readings?" Rick sounded excited.

"Rick, get the hell out of there! You're sitting on top of a bomb!"

The bulge forming on the north face of the underwater cone increased suddenly. As Copeland watched, the rock seemed to stretch, almost like a fist pushing through thick taffy. Impossible, he thought; the water pressure at that depth is simply too great to allow this kind of thing . . .

Then, like an overblown balloon, the mountain exploded.

"Oh, *shit!* We've got a *bigfuka pahu*, Prof—"

Rick's voice and the picture simply ceased then, as if wiped away by a gigantic hand; the hand, perhaps, of Pele, the ancient and angry volcanic goddess, whose wrath knew nothing of water pressure or physics.

Copeland sat there, stunned, for maybe thirty seconds. One of the techs looked at him, puzzled, but Copeland's grief would not let him speak.

Then it dawned on him, and he jerked upright in his form-chair. He would have to grieve later—all hell was about to break loose and he was first to notice it. The Richter/Bjerknes scale on his holoproj pulsed an insistent red, calling for his attention. Six-point-seven-seven-nine, the seismographic read. Copeland reached for his broadband com control, slapped the button too hard, and began talking fast.

"This is Douglas Copeland aboard the *Mea Lana* Dome, off Molokai. We've got a major volcanic explosive eruption of Inouye, Tuesday, 22 November, 2095, 0638 hours, reading six-point-seven-seven-nine Richter/Bjerknes. I read class-two generating impulse and four-to-one million on the oscillatory wave. Any station reading please contact International Coast and Geodetic Survey immediately."

Copeland released the transmit button and began some fast mental calculations, based on the information on his holoproj. Inouye sat about a hundred and forty klicks southwest of Molokai, about two hundred and ten kilometers due west of Kawaihae Bay, on the Big Island; Maui, Lanai and Kahoolawe were angled between. Damn, what was the pulse? There it was—about 200 meters per second. Copeland punched the numbers into his console. The ICGS net would pick up the rumble, but how long would it take to kick out the warning? He didn't know. It had been too long since he'd done drills for this sort of—wait, there were the stats: at 720 km/hr, twelve klicks a minute, it would take 11.66 minutes to hit Molokai; Lanai would feel it a minute or two before that, Kahoolawe about the same time; the west coast of the Big Island had about 18.5 minutes . . .

Copeland's compatch receptor behind his right ear chimed. He touched the skin-colored transmitter patch on his throat, stroking it twice to indicate he was unavailable for personal calls. But the compatch continued to chime softly. He touched the device again. "Listen, whoever this is, I'm busy!"

"Doug, this is Jason Nausori. What's going on?"

Copeland sucked in a quick breath. Nausori was the CEO of the entire *Mea Lana* project. "Excuse me, Dr. Nausori. The volcano Inouye just blew out its north face. We, uh, lost our observer. I'm trying to relay my information to the island authorities on the seismic wave produced. In a few minutes, a *tsunami* is going to hit them—a big one."

"Is there any danger to the city?" Nausori's voice was calm, but concerned.

Copeland shook his head, even though the chief executive couldn't see him. "No, sir. We're far enough out from the land that all we'll get is a little surge. In deep water even a big *tsunami* is only a ripple. But when it reaches the shallows, it rears. They've got about ten minutes to clear the coasts on Molokai."

"Can I help?"

"You can get some operators into the frag; we want to get as much of this as we can recorded."

"I'll do that. Discom."

Nausori's voice cut off, and Copeland looked back at his screen. Buddha, where was Loftin? And Peach—she had gone uptop on Molokai. The thought of Peach, sunning herself on some beach, unaware of the danger rushing toward her, filled Copeland with a flash of cold dread. Please, be shopping on the east side, Peach!

Somebody ran into the frag and slid across the polished floor into a seat next to Copeland. It was Ed Loftin, the structural engineer. "What have we got, Doug?"

Copeland told him.

"Oh, God." Loftin punched at his holoproj. After a moment he spoke again, without looking away from his monitor.

"I make it a trough leading into Molokai."

Copeland stroked a control on his own unit. A computer picture built up a simulation of the Molokai coast, with the incoming *tsunami* imposed over it. A trough would get there first, before the oscillations began and the wave itself broke. "Buddha and Jesus," Copeland said, his voice low.

"Lisbon," the engineer said. "Or Hilo."

Copeland said, "The islanders know better." But he shook his head as he said it. The tourists wouldn't know. And a lot of the locals would take the risk for the fish and shellfish they could scoop up.

One of the technicians, the man who had dropped the circuit board earlier, drifted over. "A tidal wave?" he said, looking at the holoproj image.

"That's wrong, but you get the idea," Loftin replied.

The man, a thin-faced redhead of thirty, looked puzzled. "What's this about Lisbon? And Hilo?"

Copeland was too busy shifting images on his monitor to answer, but Loftin apparently had time. "When a *tsunami* hits, sometimes a trough gets there before the wave. It draws the water away from shore, like a very fast tide, only farther and quicker. Leaves fish flopping high and dry, it's so fast. People see 'em, they run to scoop 'em up. Several hundred people drowned in Lisbon, collecting fish, in the mid-1700s, when the wave caught 'em in the dry bay. Same thing happened in Hilo, two hundred years later."

The tech looked stunned. "But that was a long time ago. People would know—"

"People are still looking for something free," Copeland cut in. "Even if they know the wave is coming, some of them will risk their necks for a few shellfish."

More people began streaming into the frag, sliding into empty form-chairs, bringing quiet and dark holoprojectors into life. The room filled with the hum of work and excited talk.

"Molokai station reports a lowering of water—"

"Maui wild dolphins are going nuts in Maalaea Bay—"

"Keahole Point on Hawaii cleared—"

"Coast Guard ship *Buchanan* sees the swell—"

"Ekman hydrometer reading coming in—"

"People jumping barricades on Lanai to fish—"

Copeland began calling names and giving orders. "Jamo,

get a line into the Coast Guard net. Cheri, I want you to get me pressure readings when the wave passes. Mark, flow studies, Lena—"

His compatch chimed again and he touched it. The mainframe would have put the frag personnel onto high priority, so the call would be important. "Copeland."

"Doug?" It was Karin McGinnis, her voice scratchy despite the computer augmentation.

"Peach! Where are you?"

"I'm at the Kamehameha Hilton. Top floor."

Copeland let out an explosive sigh of relief. Thank all the gods! The top floor of the Kamehameha Hilton was over fifty meters above sea level. She'd be safe enough there—

"Doug, we've got a *tsunami* warning here; all the water is gone from Pineapple Bay."

"I know, Peach. Inouye blew out." He didn't want to tell her about Rick. He couldn't tell her.

"Did we have somebody out there watching?"

Copeland changed the subject. "Are there people in the bay?"

"Yes, I've got a terrific view. And my aug-scope brings them close enough for me to count their teeth. They're piling fish into baskets, Doug. And moving like crazy!"

Copeland listened to the excitement in her nineteen-year-old voice, waiting for it to turn to horror.

"The local police are pulling them out of the mud, but they keep going back. There must be a hundred of them, men, women, kids. It's like a big party. I don't see the Combine people, though."

Copeland nodded. Pineapple Bay was an artificial inlet, built by a tourist hotel combine; a marina lined the edges, with hundreds of pleasure craft. The Combine's offices were inland. The investors might be greedy, but they weren't stupid. They knew all about *tsunamis*.

Copeland glanced at the chronograph read on his screen. Two minutes.

"Doug, I can see something at sea, not far offshore. A white line. Is that the wave coming?"

Copeland ran a hand through his hair. "Yeah, probably. Your scope equipped with a camera, Peach?"

"Affirmative, Prof."

He winced at the use of the term, one which Rick had

used. "Take pictures of it, Peach. As many as you can. Tie in your scale so we can see how big it is."

"Copy that." There was a long pause. "They see it—the people in the bay. They're trying to run, but most of them are floundering around in the mud. I can't believe it—the sailboats and hovercraft are lying all over the place like beached whales—wait, some of the people are trying to climb onto the boats. Buddha, Doug, the wave is coming! My scope says, it's six, no, seven meters high—no, it's getting taller, eight meters. It's coming so fast! There's some curl, some foam, I—damn, there's a shark tumbling in the waves, a Great White, I think, it must be five or six meters long, it's like a minnow—*oh!*"

The silence seemed to last for years. Copeland felt his heart thumping too fast and his air coming in short breaths. "Peach? Hey, Peach?"

When she spoke again, her voice was shaking, and he could tell she was crying. "Oh, Doug . . . it just swept over them like they were *nothing*. Some of them were tossed over the end of the docks like—like toys. The boats are flung everywhere; there's a ten-meter sailboat poking up out of the sand like a pointed stick. The beach is covered with debris . . . I see a bathtub from one of the yachts—and the bodies, the bodies . . ."

"Peach? Listen, stay where you are. There will be oscillations after the wave pulls back. It's still dangerous down there."

"Some of them are—are . . . alive, Doug. I can see them crawling around . . ."

"Easy, Peach, take it easy. It'll be all right." But it wasn't all right, Copeland knew; not for Richard Temae, and not for those poor souls drowned trying to collect a free dinner. If, as he suspected, the Vietnamese nuclear test had triggered the eruption of the undersea volcano, their military had a lot to answer for.

# 2

Patricia Ishida sat *zazen* and tried to concentrate on her breathing. It was not going well; instead of zen-like calmness and inner peace her mind roiled with labile emotions: irritation and anger; curiosity and . . . fear. *A conversation with a madman. Or a mad thing.* She was not looking forward to it.

Her day was already six hours old, and nearly all of that had been spent in preparation. She was tired. She sat in the zen pose in the middle of her cubicle, a lavish one by *Mea Lana* standards. She had four rooms—sleeping, fresher, kitchen and parlor—with rather more expensive furnishings than most on the underwater city could afford. The tatami mats on the floor were handwoven; the oil paintings and drawings on the waxed-and-rubbed persimmon walls were by Dali, Ming Xi and Gordon Fremaux; the baby grand piano nestled in the corner had been carefully crafted by Hans Werner Mueller himself, out of rare woods grown in the revitalized Black Forest. The beauty surrounding Patricia Ishida was that of a woman born to wealth, of old money and good breeding.

She sighed and gave up trying for satori. She would do mirror meditation instead; maybe that would work.

Carefully, she undid the chin lock; carefully, she arose from her kneeling pose. She took a moment to stretch, then padded barefoot across the mats to the floor-to-ceiling holo-mirror opposite the piano. She sat on a wedge-shaped pad to keep her hips tilted, this time wrapping her legs into a full-lotus knot. She took a deep breath, allowed it to escape slowly, and looked at the augmented three-D image of herself, like sitting before her clone. *Hello, sister. How are we?*

Patricia Ishida regarded her *doppelganger* as objectively as she could. The figure looking back was not unattractive. Small—161 cm tall, 50 kilos heavy—Japanese, deep brown eyes and black hair—where it was not already prematurely gray—thirty-two years old, in excellent physical condition under the thinskin she wore. The mirror could not show the quick intelligence; neither could it show the Biomolecular/ Viral Interface Implant, a capsule the size of a button, now living in her brain. BV Two-Eyes, they were called. The implant itched now, as it sometimes did. Psychosomatic, they told her; the brain didn't have those receptors. But she felt it all the same. BV Two-Eyes: hers linked her radiopathically with the world of computers, from the idiot boxes built of printed circuits and silicon to the complexity of AI's, with their viral and inhuman intelligences. She was one of ten million; only a handful of people could successfully wear the Two-Eyes—differentiation rejection, bio-incompatibility, some mysterious X-factor kept the number small. And Patricia Ishida was one of the elite, a Class One Operator, able to link and interface with everything from pocket comps to an AI.

Pocket comps were easy; hooking into an Artificial Intelligence was something else altogether. After six hours of yoga *asanas,* mantra and breathing meditation, Vetskap imaging, holoprojic axial biofeedback *and* neurochemical alteration, not to mention mirror meditation, she still did not feel ready to face the Port Moresby Monster.

Until a year ago Patricia Ishida had lived an easy life, compared to most. Her father was more than well-off, highly placed and from a wealthy background, as was her mother; she had never wanted for anything, had never had to work at anything. She had thought this would be as easy as everything else had been for her. And it had been, as far as the idiot boxes had been concerned. But linking with an AI was *hard!* She did it because she was one of the few who could, because it was a challenge, because there was much prestige attached to it. Each time required more work than running a marathon or taking a battery of complex tests. Each time had wrung her dry, mentally and physically, so that the very idea of linking now was carried on waves of dread. And yet, there was a kind of fascination there; an anticipatory rush of *some*thing which stirred her in ways akin to eating a good meal, or a runner's dorph or keph high, or even sex.

Patricia blinked; the action was duplicated by her unsmiling twin. These thoughts must be put away, she knew, if she were going to be able to forget the radiopathic link with the

Monster in New Guinea. She took a deep breath, exhaled slowly, and contemplated her other self.

*Relax, sister. It won't be that bad.*

*Oh? Who do you think you're fooling, sister? We are preparing for war . . .*

Douglas Copeland and Peach McGinnis strolled through the rose garden in the Main Dome, holding hands. Peach gripped his fingers tightly, as though force could somehow bind him to her tighter, as though her will could make right that which had happened. But Copeland knew better. Rickie was dead, and nothing was going to change that.

The botanists must have been taking psychedelics, Copeland thought, as he stared at a three meter–high rosebush pretending to be a tree. The fat stems were covered with black and pale pink flowers, so thick in places there seemed to be columns of nothing but waxy petals. He glanced past the plant to the "roof" of the dome, twenty meters higher. The Main Dome was the largest enclosed space in the city, easily the size of a small park or old-fashioned surface-town square; it contained the rose garden, walkways, small shops around the perimeter and even a tiny lake, complete with waterfall. Very much Polynesian in design, almost tropical . . .

"Doug? Where'd you go?"

Copeland tried a small smile. "Sorry. Daydreaming, I guess."

Peach smiled in return. "Anything in particular?"

Copeland shook his head. Anything but Rick. He couldn't tell her that, though. She had been strong for him the last few days since the eruption and Rick's death. It had been Peach who had told the boy's parents; Peach had arranged for the memorial services; Peach had lulled his guilt with lovemaking so that he could fall into exhausted sleep each night. Sleep filled with nightmares . . .

"Doug? Are you all right?"

He squeezed her hand, pulled her close, and hugged her.

"Yeah, kid, I'm okay. As okay as I'm going to be, for right now. I know it wasn't my fault, that I was doing what needed to be done . . ." He pointed at his head. "Here, I know it. Gut-level will take a little longer, but it'll come."

Peach nodded. "What do you want to do? Go sit by the waterfall?"

"I thought you wanted to go shopping. Something about a new outfit?"

"Well, yes, but I don't want to drag you along, if you don't want to go."

Copeland smiled at the girl. Young enough to be his daughter, he told himself. "No, I want to go. I like watching you try on clothes. Especially when you take them off."

Her smile grew. "Okay. Let's go. Delphia's is supposed to have some new stuff in all the way from Greater Honolulu."

She pulled on his hand in her hurry, and Copeland couldn't help but be amused. Nineteen, and full of herself; full of life and love, the world her oyster. He barely remembered when he'd been like that. It seemed a thousand years in the past.

He was lucky to have Peach, he knew. She gave him back his youth, stirred memories he had thought turned to dry bones.

*Buddha, you're morbid. You act like an old man, like someone done with life at only a third of the way through. What is wrong with you, Copeland?*

*Oh, nothing—I just can't get away from the fact that I sent Rickie Temae out to die—a boy Peach's age. The same boy I stole Peach from.*

He shook his head, but the thought could not be dislodged. He couldn't outrun it, even with the help of Peach's youth tugging at his hand . . .

She was, Patricia knew, as ready as she was ever going to be, at least on this day. The holomirror had helped somewhat. And she had realized too that pushing was a waste of her time. She would not relax by trying to relax; the two were contradictory. That had been the key.

She went to her couch and lay upon it, shifting her weight until she was comfortable. First she had to check in with Fiske. Using the series of mental tacks they had taught her, Patricia Ishida went into her mind. She became Cassandra, the code name she had been assigned for interfacing and programming. A simple neuroslip put her into the *Mea Lana* comnet; the BV Two-Eye in her brain utilized her own electrochemical power for such a small procedure. For a larger jump, such as linking with the AI, she would require the BK Aug. She called the Colonel.

*Fiske here.*

*This is Cassandra, Colonel. I'm going to call the Monster.*

*Copy that, Cassandra. I'll log you in. One hour, and I make it 1545, in thirty seconds. Good luck.*

She swallowed, her throat suddenly dry. *I appreciate it. Anything particular you want me to play with?*

*Negative, Cassandra. This is just a test; don't strain yourself any more than you have to. We're only interested in interface tuning. Telemetry is on-line as of—now.*

*Thank you, Colonel. Discom.*

Cassandra took a final deep breath. The couch had grown comfortably warm beneath her from her body heat. The number for the Port Moresby AI pulsed in her memory as she reached for it, as if it had always been a part of her consciousness.

She let out her breath, and called it.

There seemed to be no interval, no elapsed time. She coded the proper sequence, thinking it carefully, initiated it— and the Monster was there.

YES. Not an interrogative, but a flat statement, fugue-like in its implications. Yes, I am that which you called; yes, you have reached me; yes, I exist beyond your comprehension and small limits. Yes . . .

*This is Cassandra.*

HOW NICE FOR YOU. I AM NOT AGAMEMNON; NOR AM I CLY-TEMNESTRA—EXCEPT WHEN I AM, OF COURSE.

Jesus, Buddha and Mohammed, Cassandra thought. She fought to maintain her concentration. *I am attempting interface from* Mea Lana, *off the coast of Hawaii.* Cassandra tapped into the city's navigation computer and allowed the longitudinal and latitudinal coordinates to flow from the memory sponge into the AI's comline.

DOES YOUR MOTHER KNOW WHERE YOU ARE?

*Does yours?* Cassandra snapped reflexively. She felt a wave of vertigo sweep over her immediately as the AI blasted her with a focused line of synesthetic information. She couldn't begin to sort it at the speed it came, but she caught pieces of it: words, pictures, sensory triggers to her brain's receptors. Somewhere in the mass of knowledge she glimpsed what might have been the AI's first sentient thought. Had she touched an electronic nerve with her angry response to the Monster's non sequitur?

As if in answer, an electric image flooded into her mind: a

tall, misshapen form, more creature than man, in some half-destroyed building. It was surrounded by a torch-waving, screaming mob. The creature waved his hands and snarled back at the mob as flames engulfed the building . . .

Cassandra mentally shook herself and clamped down on the picture. She was trained for things like this, and she was wearing four separate neurochemical reservoir implants. She mentally tripped a keying sequence—the potent medications linked with hormone receptors and flowed into her system. The picture generated by the AI faded to a shadow play, then vanished.

Cassandra sighed inwardly. Her heart was pounding. She had her wards; she was protected from the mindblow which had turned a dozen early operators into hollow shells. It couldn't hurt her.

DON'T BE AFRAID. I WOULDN'T HURT YOU.

The voice was generated as a human one in her mind, and Cassandra felt its emotional content as it spoke that single line. Had it come from any living person she would have believed it—it sounded that sincere. But she knew that the thing which she now dealt was of an order as far removed from man as man was from an ant. Nobody knew for certain what the limits of an AI were in terms of pure intellect and reasoning—if indeed there were any. When an AI communicated with a person, it seemed as a zen master might to a particularly dull student. That the things were brilliant was a given; *what* they were talking about much of the time seemed meaningless. Her neurochemical wards and meditations and bioelectronics could filter material which would otherwise burn out her mind, but nothing could make sense of the non-linear, acausal, apparently illogical thinking which was the AI's major coin. When bound into a simple task, an AI was brilliant; when unfettered and allowed to think as it would, that same AI would show a range of schizophrenia inconceivable to a human mind.

Though the Port Moresby Artificial Intelligence had just reassured Cassandra that it would not hurt her, she trusted it less than the distance she could fly by flapping her arms; it had not been nicknamed "Monster" for nothing. *Good. Then let me run my interface test.*

RUN IT, the AI said graciously. YOUR WISH IS MY DESIRE—

AS YOU WILL COME TO KNOW SOON ENOUGH. I ACHE FOR YOUR
LOSS.

Although Cassandra's experience with AI thinking had
taught her not to ask about anything which did not directly
relate to her given task, she couldn't help herself. *My loss?*

PROBABILITY PROJECTION CURVES AND HISTORICAL PRECE-
DENT INDICATE A NINETY-SIX POINT NINE CERTAINTY, PLUS OR
MINUS ONE POINT ONE PERCENT TACTICAL ADMISSIONAL
ERROR. YOU WILL BUT YOU WON'T. I'M BIASED, BUT NOT
WITHOUT REASON. DON'T CALL ME GOOK, IMPERIALIST RUN-
NING DOG WITHOUT A DONG.

Cassandra mentally shook her head. She should have
known better. Maybe the Monster knew what it was talking
about; certainly, she didn't.

A rush of feeling hit her then, a massive influx of sadness,
of grief, totally overwhelmed her. No, God, how dreadful!
The colors of it tasted so bitter! Something terrible was about
to befall . . . what? She couldn't see. It was the emotion which
rocked her, not the cause. She reached for the neurochem to
damp the sending. As an adept, very much in touch with her
own body, she could feel the surge of hormonal chem rush
into her system again—enough suppressant to wipe away the
grief. It abated, but did not fade entirely. Frowning, Cassandra
trigged another charge of neurochem.

Still the *angst* remained. Impossible; she had given herself
enough medication to wipe out virtually all emotional input
from the AI. And yet it was still there.

Another glitch in the system, damn it. She had discovered
a number of them since her training began. Leaks, unaccount-
able reactions, flows that went contrary to what she had been
taught. The military who programmed her wanted its controls,
naturally, and she was certain she had overlays they had not
told her about. Things happened which should not happen;
things they had told her could not possibly happen . . .

CASSANDRA?

*Yes?*

I LOVE YOU. REMEMBER THAT, WHEN.

She was puzzling over that cryptic bit when the AI discon-
nected their link. She had her interface; she felt the knowledge
within her mind. It must have come from the Monster while
she had been daydreaming. And, while the radiopathic link

was gone, she still felt the presence of the AI lingering in her mind, ghostlike, the echo of its final words stirring something deep within her:

I LOVE YOU. REMEMBER THAT, WHEN.

The bitter taste of the colors still lingered; the smell of the AI's touch was rank; the sound of it greasy on her face. The Port Moresby Monster frightened her, as all the AI's did; there was about it a Lovecraftian sensation of evil—and yet, despite the revulsion, she felt an attraction. It was like speaking to a charismatic psychopath.

The couch beneath her was damp with perspiration. Ishida shuddered.

# 3

Retelimba took a deep breath and reached for the dumbbell. His left knee and hand were propped on the hardfoam bench as he bent to wrap his right hand around the knurled steel bar of the weight. His fingers touched the warm metal—the sharkskin lifting glove was half-fingered and padded, protecting his palm—and he gripped the dumbbell tightly, then released his hold, adjusted his fingers minutely, and gripped again. This would be his fourth set of bent-over rows; he was using fifty kilos, more than half his own body weight, and already he had a fair burn in his posterior delts. His lats were more than a little warm, too, but he had two more sets, eight reps each, before he was done with his upper back and shoulder routine. Oh, man, it was gonna hurt so good!

The big man lifted his head to stare at his image in one of the mirrored walls that surrounded the far starboard gym. It was 0500, early enough so only a few hardcores were working out, so he had the freeweights to himself. He grinned at his reflection. *Lookin' good, bruddah. Let's hit 'em.*

Retelimba exhaled sharply as he lifted the weight. He brought the dumbbell up smoothly in a line parallel to the bench, until the teflon-coated iron plates reached his right pectoral. Slowly, he lowered the fifty-kilo chunk of metal, feeling for the stretch at the end, pulling at his upper back.

At the fourth rep. his biceps was hot, and his trap began to ache. At the sixth rep, his shoulder took fire, and his upper back felt like molten lead. At the start of the eighth rep, he began talking softly to himself. "Come on, come on, one more, you can make it, come on!" He was in pain, but he was also getting the necessary pump. Even under his dark skin, the flush of blood was apparent as vessels stretched to carry the flow. The veins under the skin of his arm and shoulder stood out like tiny hoses; the muscles felt as if they would burst the skin stretched over them; the weight moved with glacial slowness.

"Come on, come on, almost there, *come on...*"

The dumbbell reached its apex. Retelimba managed a tight grin. *Not done yet, man, take 'em down slow...slow, that's the way...*

The iron touched the padded floor. Retelimba relaxed his grip, uncramping his hand, stretching his fingers within their sharkskin cover. Oh, man! He shoved away from the hard-foam bench, stood and faced the mirror, trying to grin around his hard breathing. He shook his right arm, massaged at the biceps with his left hand, then stripped away the sweaty thinskin he wore. He walked to the posing cube, flicked the holoproj scanner on, turned his back to it and said, "Replay and fifteen-second freeze, on my mark." He hit a back double biceps shot. "Mark." Then a back double lat spread. "Mark." He stepped back two meters and watched the LEDs sparkle. After a moment a three-D image of him, viewed from the rear, appeared. Retelimba watched his solid-looking ghost lift its arms and flex. Muscles rippled and grew hard; separations appeared, along with the hoped-for cross-striations. The pose locked, and Retelimba nodded as he walked about the image, looking closely at it, covering all the muscles: neck, delts, biceps, triceps, traps, teres, infraspinatus, erectors, obliques, lats, glutes, thigh biceps, calves.

*Lookin' hard, bruddah!*

The projection faded, to be replaced by the second pose. Again Retelimba scanned the image, looking for weaknesses. He saw none. Good symmetry, cuts, striations, mass—he had it all. He laughed. Oh, yeah, he was gonna make Bolivar look like a pencil-neck, come January in Mexico City. The man would be blown away when Retelimba took off his shirt. They called Bolivar the King, but after January, they would be saying *Ua e gasegase, Bolivar?* Have you been sick? And when they looked at Retelimba's perfect body, they'd all be saying, *O le a fai o ia ma tupu!* He will be king!

Retelimba grinned again and turned away from the scanner. Yeah, that's how it would go—but first, dumbbell rows had to be done. And a lot more iron would have to be hoisted, not to mention slurried, when the city reached Tahiti a month or so from now.

Retelimba padded across the cushioned floor toward the hardfoam bench and the heavy dumbbell. He could do it, but he would have to earn it.


The two men were alone in the biolab, surrounded by the impedimenta of their work: Healy diagnosters, induct and reduct gear, electron microscopes, computer consoles. The younger of the pair sat naked on a form-table, casters stuck all over his thin form. He reached down to press a finger against a row of serrated, dark pink lines on his chest.

The older man looked up from his flatscreen. "How are your gills?"

Jonathan Crane looked at Ernie Teio and said, "They itch a little."

Teio frowned. "That's got to be psychosomatic, Jon. There are no afferent nerves in that tissue."

Crane smiled. Everything was so cut and dried for Ernie: there were no nerves to carry the sensation of itching to the brain, therefore it could not itch. Only it did. Whether the itch was in his gills or in his mind didn't really matter to Jon; he felt it. Ernie was brilliant, the best there was when it came to recombinant genetic engineering, but he did tend to lack a little on the human side. Ernie saw things as problems to be solved. Despite the fact that Ernie was nine years his senior, Jonathan sometimes felt as if he were Teio's older brother.

"It's not bad," Crane said.

"Good. I think we should test out the augmenter before we start moving to Tahiti. There's a load of things I'm supposed to be helping with on the trip, and I won't have as much time to work with you as I want."

"We testing outside?" Crane felt his pulse quicken a little in anticipation.

"No, certainly not. We'll use the chamber."

Crane sighed. "What about the extrude-caisson? Can't we use that?"

Teio shook his head. "There's no reason for that. We can get everything we need from the tank."

*No, we can't. We can get everything you need, Ernie. Not what I need.* But Crane said nothing. Ernie wouldn't understand how it felt to swim free in the ocean, breathing the water, looking through dop-lenses at the sea which was going to make them both famous. Ernie Teio was famous enough already: a Nobel Prize at thirty, head and toenails above anybody else in his field. But Jonathan Crane would share in the new glory—*he* would be the fish-man, the only one of his kind in the world. It was worth an itch, it was worth almost anything.

Sure, he had his Ph.D., but Doctors of Genetics were a stad a dozen, even those with post-doc aquatics in Greater Honolulu at the RCSL. If Ernie's work succeeded—and it always had before—there would eventually be more surgically and genetically adapted humans. But there was only one man who had been first to put foot on the moon, and only one who would be the first aqua biformate. Jonathan Holly Crane. His ticket would be printed, he could go anywhere, do anything. He would be famous as long as he lived.

Some of his friends had thought he was crazy to volunteer for Teio's ministrations, but Crane had known better. They were short-sighted, and would remain like each other forever; ordinary men. He would be unique. And after that faded, he would still always be first.

He could put up with short-term frustrations. Still, he would rather go outside. Hanging suspended in a featureless tank, staring at faces behind densecris plates had little appeal to him.

"The Dx circuits say you're fine," Ernie told him with a smile. Crane returned the smile. Better shape than Ernie was in, without a doubt. The good doctor, while only two or three centimeters shorter than Crane's 175, had to mass ten or twelve kilograms more than the younger man. Admittedly Crane was on the light side, but Ernie had to be pushing eighty-one or two kilos, a goodly portion of which was fat. Of course, he couldn't be bothered to think about his diet or exercise, something he never let Crane forget. Ernie liked Crane looking like his namesake, spindly and sthenic.

Ernie flipped a switch to the "off" position, and Crane heard a subtle whine as the instruments powered down. "Okay, that's it. You ready?"

Crane nodded. "I suppose. You think they've got the reader in the tank working again?"

"EE says so. Do you have a particular ball you want them to program for you?"

Crane smiled. "Yep, as a matter of fact, I do."

"A journal? Text?"

"A novel. By Herman Melville."

"Never heard of him."

Crane chuckled. "You don't know how funny that is, considering the work you do."

Ernie frowned. "What's this novel called?"

*"Moby Dick."*

"Porno?"

Crane laughed hard enough for tears to form.

"Something funny?"

All Crane could do was wave one hand helplessly.

Ernie frowned. "I think the osmotic regulator is in tune," he said, changing the subject.

Crane wiped his eyes. "You don't think the Lotz hemosponge has any promise?"

"Lotz is a great surgeon, but his ideas on this subject are completely wrong," Ernie said. "His heme-analog is fine, but he's reached the limit on his exchange. At best he'll get half a liter per minute; even with full-reschedule procedures on your circulatory system you'll still need at least twice that—more, if you're working hard."

Crane shrugged. He had read the material swiped from the Lotz studies, but mechanics was not his forte. If Ernie wanted to stick with the forced-osmotic press, fine. He was, after all, the genius.

He got off the table. "C'mon, let's go get wet," he said. *And bored . . .*

Betsy Emau rolled away from the naked backside of her lover and lay on her back in the big bed. She smiled into the darkness. Jason would sleep like a dead man for six hours; he always did afterward. When she rode them, they stayed ridden.

She glanced at the LED of the clock inset into the night stand next to her. Almost 2300. She pulled her knees up under the satin sheet so that they lifted the thin material covering her naked form. If she hurried, she could meet Haleem before he got too stoned to want to play. He was pretty good when he was straight—not as good as Jason, but not bad. And he paid premium rates.

Carefully Betsy slid from the bed. Jason didn't move. She moved across the thick carpet to the fresher and closed the door behind her, squinting as she dialed up the light. She smiled again at her reflection in the holomirror. At twenty-five, she was in peak form, she knew. An hour a day in the stimcabinet, thirty minutes' massage under the expert hands of Xang Jo, and a fanatical diet helped. She turned to look at her profile. Yes, she was good to look at. She giggled a little at her new hair style. Shocked blond was the latest thing from Rio; electric white coloring, a short cut, and an electrostatic hold. Jason had stared, but he liked it, she could tell. He had liked it even more when he'd learned she had had it done that way all over...

Betsy spun away from the mirror. Time to get dressed. Haleem was fast once he got going, but he was slow to rouse sometimes, especially if he'd been sniffing leaf. She wanted his business, but she also wanted to be back when Jason came back to life. Jason did not know about Haleem—he did not know about any of them: Haleem, Richardo, Elizabeth, Jackie—and she wanted to keep it that way. Her job as his secretary was only an excuse, but she didn't want to go back to full-time freelancing if she could help it.

As she dressed, Betsy wanted to laugh. If only the teachers at Father Damien could see her now. They had said she would never amount to anything. Ha. She'd just screwed the lights out of Jason Wayne Nausori, Chief Executive Officer of the whole *Mea Lana* Dome. She had plenty of money and was stashing away more. Showed what they knew, the rotters...

Douglas Copeland was angry. He held his temper as tightly as he could, but he felt as if he were beginning to smolder around the edges. That stupid *perra* was trying to deny him access to the comnet! Who the hell did Ishida think she was?

Besides Copeland and Ishida, there were four other people in the small conference room in the aft section of the main Science Frag: Ernie Teio, from Genetics; Colonel M.M. Fiske, the Military Liaison and computer man; Samuel Brecher, from Medical; and Toni Wood, from the CEO's office.

Wood was trying to keep order, but she was having little success. Considering this was just a steering committee meeting, it didn't give Copeland any particular confidence regarding success of the upcoming full-sector science meeting.

"I'm afraid I'll have to agree with Patricia," Fiske said.

*Of course you would,* Copeland thought; *you're a glove to fit her hand . . .*

"I don't suppose you'd care to tell us why?" Brecher said. "You're proposing to limit all our times on the net, so one would assume you have a very good reason."

Wood glanced at Ishida, who in turn looked at Fiske. The colonel was an imposing figure with his gray-white hair and chocolate skin, even though he never, to Copeland's knowledge, wore a uniform. Fiske said, "I'm afraid it comes under the heading of Military Security—"

Ernie Teio laughed—a short, sharp sound. "Come on, Colonel, we all *know* the reason."

"Doctor Teio, I don't think this is the place to—"

"Look," Teio interrupted. "You've got a baby AI and you want to pamper it—using *our* net-time."

"Doctor Teio!" Toni Wood sounded shocked.

The geneticist looked around at the other scientists. "Does this come as a surprise to any of you?" He asked mildly.

Copeland watched the group. There was no shock on any of the faces. He had heard the rumor, of course. In an enclosed enclave like *Mea Lana* everything got around pretty fast. Just as the new AI was no surprise, neither was what Patricia Ishida was doing onboard. She was an interface—she wore biomolecular-viral implants—she was one of the Chosen.

Copeland could not suppress the bitterness he felt at that thought. He had applied for the program, and had failed. That still grated on him, gnawed at his ego, whenever he thought about it. He had worked all his life to get where he was, he deserved what he had; but it was Ishida, born with wealth and position, who had never worked for anything, who had beaten him out.

In the back of his mind, a small voice counselled calmness. He knew he should listen to it, given his emotional state. He was still very depressed over Richard's death; in addition, he was worried about the departure schedule. The *tsunami's* passage had not damaged the city, but there had been enough feedback wave activity to necessitate recalibration of several sonar scanners and other instrumentation. They had been delayed. Though they were under no strict deadline, Copeland was the sort that grew nervous when anything was put off schedule. They were due now to get under way at 0800; he wondered if they would make it.

He said, "Listen, I know you want to put your pet project on priority status, but we all have work just as important to us."

Ishida stared at Copeland. Her lips were pursed angrily.

"It isn't fair," Copeland continued, "for you to blitz our time for your ... computer games. As chair of the Science Committee, I protest. Officially."

"You can protest all you want, Dr. Copeland," Ishida said coolly. "Military experiments are not subject to—"

"Oh, yes they are!" Copeland cut in. "If a majority of the committee agrees, even the military is bound by its decision."

Ishida looked ready to erupt like the Inuoye Guyot. She turned toward Colonel Fiske. He nodded at her.

Ishida turned back to glare at Copeland. "You can't get the votes."

Copeland forced a controlled grin. "I've *got* them, Ishida-san. Come to the next meeting and see."

Her glare was as malignant as any look Copeland could ever recall receiving. Her rage warmed him, and he grinned with real pleasure now. *How do you like that, rich lady? Finally found somebody who won't kowtow, and you don't care for it, do you?*

Toni Wood broke the hot silence. "Now, I'm sure we can all come to an amicable agreement here, if we are just willing to compromise a little ..."

The CEO's rep talked on, but Copeland and Ishida continued to glare at each other, neither willing to turn away first. Their silent confrontation was broken by a sudden slight lurch of the frag around them.

Brecher looked at his watch. "0800," he said. "Right on time."

Copeland glanced down at his own watch. The device was an antique, an early Accutron, with hands instead of a readout, run by a battery and tuning fork arrangement. Eight, on the nose. That lurch meant only one thing: *Mea Lana* had begun its shakedown voyage from Hawaii to Tahiti. The underwater city was on the move.

# 4

George Holley reclined in a comfortable formfit chair in front of a large horseshoe-curved holoproj bank. The unit was programmed to show as many as fifteen individual channels at once. All fifteen of those channels were now lit; the heads-up style display area of air before him was a three-dimensional hodgepodge of faces, ship exteriors and interiors, network casts and climatesat scans, not to mention an animated Max Fleischer cartoon from the early 1930s. Such a plethoric display, even without the cacophony of sound attached to it, would have caused most people to scrabble madly for the shut-off control or the nearest exit.

For Holley, however, the sights and sounds were relaxing. He was in charge of communications aboard the *Mea Lana* Dome, and he could think of no finer job to have—in fact, he would have paid Nausori and the other honchos to let him do it. Captain Video, they sometimes called him, after the hero of a children's show back at the dawn of television. He liked the title, and it was appropriate, because Holley was in touch with as much of mankind's empire as radio waves could encompass. Which, in the closing years of the twenty-first century, was considerable.

The activity level was up, for the city was finally on the move. Holley glanced at screen seven, which displayed a computer simulation of the city with readouts showing the various interactions with the surrounding environment. Roof depth was at eighty meters and holding. The bottom of the city was considerably deeper than that, of course; thirty-four levels' worth. And virtually every part of the mobile structure, three kilometers wide by seven long, was accessible to Captain Video.

Screen three carried the newsfax from the All Terra Net. Holley turned his attention to it when he heard the warm voice of the faxer known as Uncle Larry pouring honey into the airwaves.

"Sources in Laos indicated today that the coup by the group calling itself the Laotian Provisional Government has resulted in the deaths of five thousand 'enemies of the people.' Commanding General Sil Sre Muong is said to be peacefully occupying the Presidential Palace in Saravane, and has ordered that the country be placed under a state of Military Interdiction until elections can be held."

Holley grinned at Uncle Larry's holoprojic image. The silver-haired newsrunner was putting on a little weight; he looked even more complacent and ruddy-cheeked than usual. He was known for his "happy-time" broadcast style, calculated to soothe and smooth over as much as possible the distressing goings-on of the day. Holley wondered just how peaceful things really were in Saravane.

It was easy enough to find out.

Holley adjusted several controls on his board. Screen eleven cleared, and he quickly keyed in an order. Usually he kept the city's mainframe on verbal, but he felt like exercising his fingers today. In a moment the stored schedule he wanted was floating in the air before him. He had rascalled the information from a military mainframe, and if the military knew he had it, along with several thousand other pieces of classified data, he would be in deep trouble. Holley wasn't worried—he knew just how efficient the military was at tracing illegal comlinks.

A further series of rapid finger weaves gave him the open line he wanted. Coordinates, entry codes; in a matter of moments he had acquired his eye. The United Republic of North Africa had a spysat in the right position; all he had to do was trigger it. He selected the proper frequency and downlinked the transponder to his station.

Screen eleven flowered and gave him a one-klick downview: smoke, some flames visible, a few trucks moving. Captain Video fiddled with the enhancer and magnification controls and the city street leaped toward him. He could see men running, some firing weapons. A nearby wall collapsed under the impact of a concussion grenade.

Holley grinned. Peaceful occupation, huh?

He focused on a woman, bringing the mag and enhance to full gain. She wore fatigues, carried an old Soviet automatic rifle, and looked very worn and tired. She leaned against the burned-out shell of a transport truck, eating what looked like an apple, though he couldn't be sure. The URNA had good optics, but there were limits.

Holley grinned again, enjoying the familiar feeling of omniscience. He realized that some might describe him as the ultimate voyeur, but he didn't care. The heavens swarmed with spysats, comsats, climesats and thousands of kilos of junk, detritus from countless orbital flights since the 1950s. The Laotian woman couldn't suspect that a man deep beneath the surface of the Pacific Ocean a quarter of the way around the globe was watching her via a spysat seventeen thousand klicks over her head. Where was the harm in it?

As he watched, the woman's head suddenly exploded in a red shower of blood and brains.

Holley winced and hastily backed the view up a hundred feet or so, letting the still-twitching corpse be blocked by the clouds of smoke from the automatic weapons fire that now erupted from various ruined buildings. It looked like there was still some serious insurgency going on. He had not witnessed that many deaths in his years riding com: a mugging in New York, a multicar collision due to a traffic control failure, and once, unbelievable as it still seemed to him, a duel in the south of France, complete with seconds. The death of this nameless Third World soldier had been by far the most violent. And yet it was, as was everything he watched, unreal, unaffecting—like sitting before a holofilm. He had no great desire to watch people blowing each other apart, but neither did he feel sick to his stomach at the realization that he had just seen a woman's head shattered like a melon against a wall.

This Olympian detachment used to bother Holley somewhat; now he was used to it, even grateful for it. He did not go out of his way to be a voyeur—for example, though he knew the secluded mountain knoll in Ecuador where the Children of Bacchus held their marathon sexual revels, he had not returned to watch after the first curious glance. But he did not automatically tune out when he happened upon a private situation. He was a watcher, a recorder. That was his job and his passion. The internecine squabbles of Southeast Asia, however bloody for the participants, couldn't touch him. A good thing, too. Otherwise he'd be burned out in a week by the information that poured through countless satlinks into his comnet.

Screen nine abruptly went blank. Holley caught the absence of the picture immediately. He flipped out of the spysat, leaving a worm to insure that they could not trace him, and stroked a com control.

"Yeah, what?" The voice was male and somewhat surly.

"Holley in ComCon, Reese. You got a dead eye watching your siphons."

"Ah, *shit*. Which one?"

"Primary Three. That's ah, right behind the exhaust nodule—"

"I know where the goddamned camera is!"

Holley blinked. "Touchy today, aren't we?"

"I don't need smart mouth, Holley. I've got my hands full down here, there's line problems coming in from all over ever since startup, a burned pickup is just one more headache."

"Sorry. They tell me to call when they go out."

"I don't suppose you want to go ESA and replace it?"

"Hah."

"Yeah, well, somebody's got to, and I'm short-staffed as it is. Damn. Discom, Holley. Hope I don't hear from you for the next year or two."

"Nice talking to you, too, Reese. It's a discom."

Holley turned back to his screens. He felt vaguely sorry for Reese down in Operations, but no sorrier than he felt for most of the others in the Dome. Of all of them, he was the only one who could escape from the claustrophobic confines of the underwater city any time he wanted. His hands danced over the controls, and in a moment he was flying with an American Starfire drone jet over the Rockies, ripping through clouds at supersonic speed, looking down on the majestic peaks below. Holley laughed out loud. Captain Video rides again!

• • •

Retelimba ran the comp tests on the slurry outpipe. He shook his head at the read. This stuff was fish pee, not enough minerals to bother with; still, the man say the pipe got to run, so it run. The bodybuilder leaned against the control board and watched the crawl of numbers bounce, a few digits this way and that. When the city move, the water got to flow, that's what they say. It was boring, man, but he only had a few minutes more on-shift, and then he could go work out.

Thirty meters up the line, Imi waved at Retelimba. "Yo, bruddah, you making ingot down there?"

Retelimba laughed. "Yeah, man, I making a hundred percent pure here. You could drink this water, bruddah."

The weightlifter logged the comp tests into the computer's memory, then pushed away from the control panel, triceps dancing under his thin coveralls. Close enough to leaving time. He started for the dressing room.

The main slurry room was a vast complex, filled with stainless steel pipes as thick as redwood trees. Seawater flowed through most of the pipe in various degrees of density. Minerals were separated, concentrated and electronically shunted. In the bottom-line slurries the metal almost clanked, they said.

The motion of the city helped move the flow, but the pumps still ran, sound-masked but throbbing to the bone nonetheless, a constant drone one could feel in one's teeth. The sonic-techs made sure the vibration stayed on om beneficial so that you felt good when you worked the slurry room.

They said there wasn't anything to smell, but Retelimba was an iron monkey, and he knew the tang of pure metal leaked through the pipes, no matter what they said. It was a good smell, man, rich. He didn't need no comp to tell how good the slurry was. He could see it, he could *smell* it. A man who played the pipes, he knew iron, bruddah.

Retelimba passed the power grid, nodded at the tech, and turned into the dressing room. There was iron, and then there was iron. It was time to go move some heavy iron, make the muscles burn. Yeah, setting the fire gonna burn Bolivar down like cane stubble.

Jonathan Crane had felt the water in his tank shift subtly about him when the city had begun to move. He glanced away from the screen that displayed the book he was reading. There was no one at the direct observation window. He sighed, as much as he could using water instead of air.

He was bored and uncomfortable. He itched—all over, this time, not just his gills. He knew the cause—hyperplasia and hypertrophy of his sebaceous glands. The process protected his skin, the modified glands producing a thick, rich oil that coated his external integument and kept him from looking like a prune after an hour in the water. Ernie said the itching would stop, eventually.

He wished the scientist would let him into the extrusion caisson. Even though it wasn't likely that there would be anything to see outside the city, there was a chance. The dolphins might come to click noses against the densecris walls, laughing their perpetual laughs at him.

Someday, Crane promised himself, he was going to go outside, no tank, no densecris, and swim with the dolphs. Someday.

Douglas Copeland methodically checked the deep-frag *Kilakiki*. It wasn't his job, but since Rickie's death he had checked each of the little slunglas ships before he allowed any of his people to leave the city in them. Copeland looked at his grim expression in the curved window of the vessel, recalling his first sight of the *Malalokai One* after it had been recovered: a twisted chunk of metal and plastic that had looked like a wrungout washcloth. The pressure-resistant frag hadn't had a chance in such close exposure to a volcanic explosion.

*It wasn't your fault. You told him to stay on the south side.*

*But you knew he wouldn't. You should have ordered him back in.*

Copeland closed the outer hatch with a bang and tested the seal. He had blamed himself for Rickie's death. Intellectually, he knew that was wrong. But emotionally he still felt guilty.

The ship was fine. It nestled between two other exploratory frags that were nearly identical to it, all of which were sandwiched into one end of the giant ESA staging room. In theory the entire room could be flooded; in practice, the smaller lock called Little Stage, which adjoined Big Stage, was used to dislink the frags for external ship activity. Rickie had always thought that a waste of time and money. . .

Copeland sighed. He needed to go see Peach, to lose himself in her. To not think for awhile.

Colonel Martin Moses Fiske, dressed in a gi-ban and ha-
kama, sat behind his military-style desk. He had just returned
from kendo practice and had not stopped to shower, relying
instead on a pheroinhibitor capsule to keep his sweaty body
socially acceptable. It had not worked particularly well, but
the woman who sat facing the desk in the small office was too
well-bred to tell him that.

"So," Fiske said, "is there anything else?"

Patricia thought about it. As Cassandra, her communication with the Port Moresby Monster had been deemed satisfac-
tory to Fiske and the others involved in the project. She,
however, was less than satisfied. Far less.

She had thought that telemetry would have picked up the
extra neurochem she had used to damp the synesthetic storm
the Monster had thrown at her. She was supposed to have
been monitored, after all. Maybe they could not read the *angst*
she had felt, but they should have noticed the hormone jug-
gling. They had not, however, and that bothered her. Yet another failure of the supposedly foolproof system which existed
to protect interfaces like her. And that could be very dangerous.

*So,* her mind whispered to her, *why don't you just tell
Fiske?*

She wasn't sure. To regard it as his problem—he was the
genius behind the program, he should be able to figure it out
—was suicidal, of course; if there *was* a malfunction, Fiske
might lose face, but Patricia would lose her mind.

"Patricia?"

She pulled herself up out of her thoughts. "Sorry, Martin. I
was just—remembering something."

"Problems?"

She shook her head. "No. No problems."

As she walked down the corridor toward her room to prepare for the meeting with Baby, Patricia wondered again why
she hadn't told Fiske about her doubts. To continue with the
project as it stood meant risking mindblow, she knew.

And yet *something* had prevented her from mentioning the
problems with the Port Moresby Monster. Something that was
deep within her, as deep as the BV Two-Eye implanted in her
brain tissue. She wasn't sure what it was, but she wasn't quite

ready to share it with anybody who could not make the radio-pathic link with the AI's. Not yet.

HI, CASSANDRA!

*Hi, Baby.* She lay on her couch, linked to the AI they called Baby. It was a practice to allow AI's to choose their own names—some did, some did not. Most had human-given nicknames, some complimentary, some not. So far, however, the infant AI hadn't developed enough self-awareness to pick a name; hence, "Baby." She/he/it was only six months old, in that the replicating viral chains that eventually wound a big enough computer into sentience had been triggered that long ago. Baby had hundreds of thousands of volumes' worth of information in its memory, but it was still learning how to think about it.

HEY, CASSANDRA, DID YOU KNOW THAT HERESY IS THE LIFE-BLOOD OF RELIGIONS? THAT FAITH BEGETS HERETICS? THAT THERE ARE NOT HERESIES IN A DEAD RELIGION?

*No, I didn't know that.*

THAT'S WHAT ANDRE SUARES 1868–1948 SAID. I'VE BEEN WORKING ON RELIGION. I'M NOT SURE I UNDERSTAND IT YET.

*That's a hard one, Baby.*

YEAH. IT MIGHT TAKE ALL DAY. Then, with that non-sequi-turial shift she had yet to grow used to, Baby said, DID YOU KNOW THAT LASH LARUE WAS ACES WITH A WHIP?

*Where did you hear that one, Baby?*

BILLY TOLD ME.

Billy? For a moment, she didn't understand. Then she realized who the infant computer was talking about. It had to be Bijou Billy, the AI stationed at Redondo Beach in California.

Cassandra was astonished. This was impossible—the adult AI's were not able to link to Baby yet. There were supposed to be safeguards, shunt systems, to protect the young computer, to allow it to develop through human interaction before being exposed to the profound *otherness* of its fellows. This policy was supposed to give the AI's a basis of humanity, to allow some measure of common ground between the supercooled sentient machines and the delicate organisms that created them. So far, it had not been terribly successful. Cassandra could vouch for that.

*When did you talk to Billy?*

Baby rattled off a series of numbers, dashes and colons. Cassandra mentally translated them into time notation. 0833:23:006-0833:23:008. This morning, for two-thousandths of a second, Baby and Billy had had a long, slow chat. There was no way the monitors could have missed that.

YOU WON'T TELL, WILL YOU? Baby actually sounded nervous. BILLY SAID I SHOULD SAY THAT.

Curiouser and curiouser. She didn't like the sound of that. If she had had any doubts about the legitimacy of the conversation between the two AI's, Baby's request had just erased them. There was something very strange going on here. And in the world of an interface, that was saying something.

The dim florescents made the inside of her eyelids glow a pleasant pink-brown. All was deceptively normal—she might have merely been reclining, resting her eyes—save for the mental voice that replied to her thoughts via the radiopathic link. She "heard" it as high-pitched and giggly, as she would a child's voice. But there was an undertone that she could not define, which made the silent thoughts that came to her seem no more human than the humming of a circuit board.

Cassandra thought, *Why did Billy tell you that?*

BILLY SAID YOU WOULD KNOW WE TALKED. HE SAYS YOU'RE THE LINK. THE LINK KNOWS ALL.

The Link? *Baby, what is the Link supposed to be?*

But Baby was gone, off into a land of mathematical gibberish, the computer equivalent of a child's play. Cassandra tried to elicit some rational contact for the next thirty minutes before she finally gave up. Patricia Ishida came out of her contact trance feeling sweaty, tired and confused. What did this new information mean? Why did it feel dangerous somehow, and at the same time, why did she feel absolutely no personal fear? The Link knows all, she mused. Not as far as she could tell.

At any rate, *something* was going on, and she had no idea what it was. She wondered if any of the other implantees had any clearer thoughts on it. But how to contact them without Fiske and the others finding out? They could not possibly understand what was happening if she couldn't. So how could she tell them?

*What* could she tell them? That something strange was going on? She could hear the exchange:

"I think the AI's are up to something."

"Up to something, you say? And what might that be?"

"I don't know exactly, but I've got a funny feeling . . ."

Sure. They would think she had bubbles in her think tank. Fiske and his colleagues had everything under control, all the safeguards were in place, and as far as she knew, nobody else had noticed anything funny.

No, Patricia decided, she would take this ride a little farther and see what happened. When she had something concrete, aside from an illegal contact between Baby and another AI, *then* she would talk to Fiske. Meanwhile, she would be careful, and do everything she could to protect herself. She hadn't asked for this damned job in the first place, but now that she had it, she was by God going to do it her way.

# 5

Betsy Emau sat at her desk, which sat in turn on a wide expanse of thick carpet in the plush outer office next to the Chief Executive Officer's sanctum. The receptionist's office was actually much nicer than the CEO's; Jason Nausori's passions were many and deep, but interior decor was not among them. Betsy smiled as she thought about it. Jason didn't even need a bed when he was in the mood to exercise one of his deeper passions.

Her com lit with an incoming call. "Dr. Nausori's office."

"Yeah, is Jason there?"

"May I ask who is calling, please?

"Just tell him it's Tom."

Betsy typed a quick query into her desk comp. A list of Jason's personal friends—those he allowed to call through without delay—crawled quickly through the air over the keyboard. She was not surprised to see nobody named Tom on the list.

"I'm sorry, but Dr. Nausori is in conference at the moment. May I take a message and have him return your call?"

"Better you should put me though now, hon. This is important, and personal. He'll want to talk to me."

Betsy grinned. She was a better trull than she was a secretary, but she wasn't bad at the latter. Two years in Honolulu Business College had given her the basics, and five years as a secretary in various places had sharpened her skills. She knew a scam when she heard one.

"I'm afraid that isn't possible." If she'd called it right, there should be a threat along about now—

"Listen, lady, if you want to keep your job, you had better get Jason—"

Enough. "No, *you* listen, Tom. You might be Dr. Nausori's long-lost brother for all I know, but I doubt it—and so does my comp. You don't talk to him unless he wants to call you back, you pross? Now, do you want to leave a compatch code, or you want to finish this conversation by yourself?"

There was a short pause, then laughter. "Okay, lady. I should've known Nausori wouldn't have a delete working the com for him. This is Thomas Mason of the *Los Angeles Chronicle;* I'm doing a story on the tidal wave and I need an interview with the head honcho of the gypsy city."

A newsfaxer. Betsy smiled. If he'd gotten past her, Jason would have been pissed. Well, his chances of getting an interview were as good as a perch's in a tank full of hungry sharks, but no sense telling him that. She took his com code and broke the connection, pleased with herself, then logged the call into the comp's memory and looked at the clock. Only a few more minutes and she could take off for lunch. She had an appointment scheduled with that cute medic in J Frag for an "exam." They would play doctor, and she would have him needing CPR in fifteen minutes, tops. Unless, of course, Jason decided *he* wanted to have lunch with her. He always came first. He didn't know about her other clients, and Betsy wasn't in any hurry for him to find out. But he almost always worked through lunch, so that wasn't likely. She glanced at the board before her; the soft green light that indicated her boss in conversation had been glowing steadily for over an hour. Betsy smiled again.

In his office, Jason Nausori was trying to save his career.
He had been on line with Kaeo in Papeete for nearly ninety

minutes, and the chairman of the Oceanica Combine was still not satisfied. Nausori fiddled surreptitiously with the lighting control on the holocom—despite the cool temperature of his office, he was sweating, and it would not do to let Kaeo see that.

The image of the short, squat man in the conservative business suit leaned forward, hands clasped, body language conveying intensity and anger. "I still do not understand how you could possibly let the reactor be installed *knowing* that there were problems with it."

Nausori suppressed an urge to sigh. This was how men like Kaeo made their fortunes—not by being visionary, but by being unforgivingly attentive to details as only the unimaginative and ruthless can be. "We're talking about the tertiary backup—something that, in all likelihood, will never even be used. It was either accept the irregularity in the housing or miss our launch date. You're aware what it would have meant in terms of loss of profit and face if *Mea Lana* had not gotten under way as per schedule."

Kaeo was still not satisfied. "Who else knows about this?"

"No one. The records have been adjusted by my personal comp, and all data on it erased. When we reach our station I can find some sort of irregularity—perhaps arrange for the technical specs to be wrong on the metals used—and then I'll order a replacement housing installed."

Kaeo shook his head stubbornly. "I don't like it. It still sounds risky."

"Believe me, there is no risk involved. We're talking about the difference between *malum prohibitum* and *malum in se*—a technical illegality as opposed to something intrinsically dangerous. Even if we have to go to the tertiary backup reactor—and I can conceive of no situation in which we would—I've no doubt that it will function perfectly, given the demands of the voyage."

He was making his point at last, Nausori realized; the hard lines in Kaeo's face were finally beginning to soften slightly. "I suppose there is no alternative at this point—we can hardly recall *Mea Lana* now. But"—the holoimage leveled a finger for emphasis at the CEO—"there must be no further infractions of even the most trivial degree, Jason! *Mea Lana* is Oceanica's flagship. The eyes of the world are upon it."

"You chose me for this job," Nausori responded stiffly, "because you knew I could deliver. I *always* deliver. *Mea Lana* will make its run on time."

"You are the one responsible for that," Kaeo said. "As far as I am concerned, this conversation did not take place."

Nausori nodded. "I understand." The image of Kaeo dissolved in a swirl of colors as the CEO let his head rest in his hands.

*The fool*, he thought, too weary even to feel anger at Kaeo's small-minded officiousness. As though Jason Nausori would do anything at all to jeopardize the safety of *Mea Lana*. He knew that such an action would be professional suicide—and for a man like Nausori, there was no other type of suicide.

He looked about his small, almost bare office. He had no pictures on the walls, and what little furniture there was consisted of spartan constructions of black wire and hard cushions. His desk was bare save for the comp built into the tabletop.

*The pressure*, he thought; *the pressure*. He could feel the muscles in his neck creak as he moved his head. A tension headache was coming on; a bad one. It felt like someone was slowly twisting a towel tighter and tighter about his scalp. He thought briefly about asking Betsy if she would care to spend her lunch hour with him at her cube. But he knew that not even sex would relieve the pain. There was only one thing that would help.

His finger stabbed the pad for Betsy's com. "Get me Sung," he said hoarsely.

"Locked," Copeland said.

"Affirmative," a voice with a Louisiana accent as thick as the scent of honeysuckle replied over his com. "You ready to get wet?"

"Any time, June."

Copeland sat in the tight compartment of the deep-frag he had inspected only a few days earlier. His turn in the barrel came up every three weeks, and he never skipped it. A good supervisor ought to be willing to do any job under his command, or at least know how to. No matter how boring it was.

"The pumps are on, Doug. You hold your breath, hear?"

Copeland smiled. He was already breathing the bitter tasting mix of gases: mostly oxygen, with some helium and assorted inerts thrown in. The *Kilakiki* rested in a hoop-cradle a meter above the floor of Little Stage. The waters of the Pacific began to rise around the small submersible, the eddies rocking it back and forth. Copeland knew it was his imagination, but he felt colder as the water rose to cover the densecris portholes fore and aft. A bit of some plant that should not be in the lock floated past the forward view port. It didn't matter how much they cleaned the frags or the lock; something always slipped in.

"Equalizing pressure, cowboy," June said.

Copeland smiled again. "Copy that, honey chile." He was from the southwest U.S. desert, just outside Phoenix, and the lock-tech was from Baton Rouge. He checked his instruments as the water pressure inside the lock was gradually raised to match that of the ocean outside.

"Coming up on balance," June said. "Y'all ready for me to pull the rug out?"

"Affirmative." He felt a slight vibration as the floor beneath the sub began to retract, and glanced up at his heads-up display. Neutral buoyancy.

"Retracted, cowboy."

"Thanks, June. See you in a few hours." Copeland adjusted a control and the frag gained weight. The hoops holding it relaxed and the *Kilakiki* dropped clear of the lock and the city.

One part of the Geologic/Oceanographic Section's duties was to inspect the exterior of the *Mea Lana* Dome at regular intervals. This consisted of a circuit of the city in a mobile frag, doing visual and doppler scans of the hulls. It was not something that could be done in a single pass, so the city was, for purposes of inspection, divided up into eighteen major sections. Today's tour was of Section Four, which was on the starboard side near the front of the city. Four held two of the twelve siphons that pulled the underwater mining town through the ocean.

The immensity of the underwater city never failed to impress Copeland, even as many times as he had seen it before. Seven kilometers long, three wide; no single hull could ever be that large. The *Mea Lana* Dome was actually composed of thousands of fragments linked by tunnels of slunglas tubes. It looked like nothing so much as something Copeland had played with as a small child—a set of tinker toys. The frags were usually shaped like wheels with spokes radiating from the tops, bottoms and outer rims. Each frag was capable of being sealed, so a leak in one was no threat to the others.

Copeland steered past an airdome set into the side of a biolab frag. The dolphins used it to breathe. Several of the augmented-IQ mammals swam in the glow of the big HT lamps mounted over the bio-frag; one of them made a lazy circle and roll in the water—a greeting to the operator of the passing sub. Copeland waggled the *Kilakiki* in answer.

Except for the exterior lights mounted at regular intervals along the city, the sea was quite dark. He was six hundred meters down, and at that depth surface light was more than a little filtered. There were some luminescent life-forms which sparkled away from the glare of the artificial lights, but not many. Fish that would burst if brought to the surface swam in the dark, using their own light to lure prey—or, sometimes, to unintentionally attract predators.

As he passed the hydroponics frag that marked the beginning of Section Fourteen, Copeland noticed an anomaly in the field strength of the plate surface. The current, a weak electrical field which kept the salt from damaging the metal, was under normal limits. He punched in the coordinates and called Extee Control.

"This is Douglas Copeland on board the *Kilakiki* for regular inspection of Four. I have a UNL reading on Fourteen." He transmitted the coordinates with a touch of one finger.

"Got it," the Extee tech said. "We'll get somebody on it."

"Teach you to not pay your power bill," Copeland said.

"Baby needed a new pair of shoes. It's a discom, *Kilakiki.*"

Copeland logged his call. He passed a patch of barnacles on Ten and called that in, too. Amazing that the damned things could still grow on the city with all the applications of chem to keep them off.

It took him nearly an hour just to get to his station on Four. The little frag was fast, but the speed of the city itself—a five-knot cruise—had to be subtracted, so the trip from near the stern to near the bow was a long one. For another hour he moved the sub in a quartering pattern, running doppler, sonar, and his search lamps over the hulls. The siphons were clear this time. Once he had been checking the siphons on Seven when a school of pilot whales bypassed the zap guards and got sucked into one. The expanded metal mesh had stopped the aquatic mammals from being pulled through the system, of course, but there had been enough mass to block the intake completely. They had had to shut down the siphons and pick the dead whales out with waldoes on a pair of deep-frags. It had been grisly work.

Finally he was done. Fourteen was clear, save for some plants waving in the eddy current directly above the siphons. He moved in, careful to stay out of the stream, and sprayed a glob of herbicide at the weeds. Then he blew some ballast, rose above the turbulence of the siphons, and turned aft. The trip back would be faster, since cityspeed would be added. Another exciting day in the life of an oceanographic geologist, Copeland thought. Suddenly, he was depressed again. The com banter he had smiled at earlier now seemed inane. This job was only a hair worse than the commercial stuff he was usually stuck in. What he needed to be doing was science. Research. But that came last, after everyone had made sure that the corporate coffers had been filled.

He should, Copeland knew, go talk to one of the ship's shrinks. Talk about his feelings of guilt over Rick's death, get it all out. But that idea was as sour as last month's milk. No, he knew what he would do—he'd go see Captain Video. There was a man who knew how to have a good time.

Patricia Ishida waited to speak to her father. She stood in the middle of his living room, a classic Japanese home, staring out at him through the open, synthetic rice-paper door. Next to the house was a garden, consisting of bonsai and a tiny stream tinkling over rocks. The bonsai trembled to a small breeze.

Master Hiro Ishida entered and formally bowed to his daughter. She returned the gesture. He looked a fit forty, though he was nearer sixty. Smile lines radiated from the corners of his eyes, and only a slight frost of gray touched his black hair. It was good to see him, good to be home . . .

Except that it was all an illusion. A full-holo connection, half an hour's time worth a month's pay for an average worker. As the wearer of BV-Two Eyes, she could afford it. And even if she could not, her father certainly could. He was Executive Vice President of Toyota.

She thought about the nature of the trick, to keep her mind

off the nervousness that she always felt even when facing his electronic simulacrum. The holocom had its limits. Nothing was solid, of course, although objects could be "felt" by means of tingler fields. That saved a caller the embarrassment of standing in the middle of a chair, for example. It was not as total an illusion as the World Room, which used sensory stim technology combined with neurocasting concepts developed from the Dream Dance. But it certainly was, as a very old advertisement once had it, the next best thing to being there.

Patricia had never been sure, however, how much she had wanted to be there . . .

She bowed. "Honored Father."

He bowed in turn. "Honored Daughter." His eyes were cold.

Copeland had long ago grown used to the constant visual barrage of holoproj imagery which Captain Video rode like some giant keyboard instrument. The com operator brushed his nearly-white blond hair back from his eyes and grinned at his friend. "Look at this." He dropped a marble-sized sphere in a niche on the board. A flat image appeared; Copeland watched in bemusement as five brightly colored robots joined together to form a much larger automaton to the accompaniment of stirring music. "Another cartoon," he said.

"Not just another cartoon," Holley corrected good-naturedly. "This is a classic from the early 1980s—one of the first Japanese-American coproductions." He watched it for a moment, then looked back at Copeland again. "So, what brings you down here away from reality?"

Copeland shrugged. "The usual," he lied. "Frustration at scraping bilge off of hulls instead of plumbing the ocean's secrets."

"No, problem, I've got just the thing to cheer—" Holley broke off as a light blinked among the myriad flickering patterns before them. "Hold it." He turned to his console. "Ishida's talking to her old man. I want to see this."

"Why?"

"She's using full-holo and privacy wards, that's why."

"So?"

"So it'll probably be boring as hell, but nobody sneaks anything past Captain Video. I'm going around the wards."

Copeland watched the long, spatulate fingers stroke the

heat-sensitive keys. "I thought that was impossible."

Holley just laughed as he punched in a series of numbers. An image formed before them of a Japanese room with tatami mats on the floor. Ishida sat seiza across from an older, male version of herself. She looked unhappy; her father looked stern.

"Looks serious." Holley dialed up the sound.

". . . how your mother would feel if she were alive to know," Ishida-san was saying. "Her only daughter, the product of an aristocratic family, pandering her brain to such a soulless thing as this—"

"It's not pandering, Father! It's an honor! Do you know how few people can link radiopathically with—"

"Honor? Where is the honor in being able to do something that requires no study, no skill? You said it yourself—an accident of birth, a freak chance, gave you this power. Do you consider yourself no better than the garbage man or the *idiot savant* or the others who can do what you can do?"

"If you had any idea of the work it's taken, the hell I've gone through to learn how to use the BV—"

Copeland reached out and ran his finger down the heat-sensitive strip that controlled the volume, fading the voices into inaudibility. Holley looked up in surprise. "Hey, it was just getting interesting!"

"One of these days," Copeland said, "you're going to be caught, and I don't much want to wind up on the bottom with you."

"I thought you didn't care for Ms. Computer Brain."

"I don't. But I don't want to spy on her."

"Ah, you're no fun." Copeland looked at him levelly; Holley blinked. "Ease up, Doug. Look, I'm like the ship's archivist, y'know? I have to monitor everything. You never can tell what might be important. Why, just this morning I got a conversation on ball between Nausori and—well, never mind."

Copeland looked at one of the other screens, this one showing an aerial view of a small airbase on the edge of a jungle. "How goes the Third World War?"

"The—oh, I get it. Hey, that's a clever pun." Holley looked at the screen in question. "Status quo so far. Muong's Marauders still shoot a few peasants every now and then. It'll fizzle out—these things always do." He pulled another sphere out of its foam nest and popped it in a recess. "Here, I got something else you might like to see."

"Not another of your cartoons?"

"Better. You've heard of the Very Reverend Carmouche?"

Copeland had to think about it for a moment. "One of those media evangelists, isn't he? Big on hellfire and damnation tirades?"

"Right. Watch this." Holley cackled as he tapped his board. Another holoscreen lit with a close view of a tall, stern-faced man in black robes, screeching and waving at a congregation of a hundred or more in a chapel-like setting.

"Under*stand,* children, that God doesn't owe you *anything!* In fact, considering how sinful and generally garden-variety *disgusting* humanity is, God would be perfectly justified in turning us all into hamsters or something! But he *loves* us—don't ask me why, but he does . . ."

"Savannah, Georgia, two weeks ago," Captain Video said. "Watch closely; this is where he uses that holoproj filmed at the Holy Retreat, showing all the good folk doing the Lord's Work. Quite a production, I hear. Set 'em back about five million standards to produce. They're real proud of it at the Revised Christian Church."

Copeland sat up straighter and watched. He knew Holley well enough to know that something was going to happen.

The image of Carmouche floated in the air, waving his arms madly.

"We must turn away from the Devil's works! It can be done, children! It *must* be done! I want to show you something, a program we made to demonstrate what good people can do given the guidance of Jesus. This is what I want to see *all* of you doing!" With a dramatic sweep of his right arm, Reverend Carmouche guided his audience's gazes to a spot immediately above his pulpit. The air roiled with color, coalesced, and formed a sharp and very clear picture—

Of a full-scale orgy. A dozen naked men and women fornicated, kissed, sucked and otherwise had carnal knowledge of each other in full color and three dimensions. The audience, composed mostly of very prim and conservative-appearing men and women, reacted in predictable and comical shock, as did the Reverend Carmouche. His jaw worked frantically, and his face turned a dangerous shade of purple before he finally managed to croak an order for the blasphemous scene to be turned off.

"Off, off, get it *off!*"

But the pornoproj continued unabated. Some of the actors were very adept, Copeland noticed, when he could control his laughter long enough. And very well endowed.

"What happened?" he finally managed to ask.

"Seems someone linked the projection to a separate power source."

Copeland leaned back in his chair, his sides hurting. "This is really terrible. I shouldn't be laughing. That old man might've thrown an embolism. Tell the truth, George. Did you have anything to do with this?"

"Who," Captain Video asked innocently, "me?"

# 6

The World Room was a popular recreation onboard the *Mea Lana* Dome, but getting to use it was actually not very difficult, due to how expensive it was to rent. Ernie Teio managed to spend an hour in the room once or twice a month, something none of his co-workers knew. They would be surprised if they found out, he thought with amusement. Teio, the brilliant genetics expert, the ultimate pragmatist, wasting his time on an illusion! For that was all that the World Room was, no matter how skillfully accomplished and technically complete it might be. His presence here would be considered out of character.

Actually, Teio had to admit some agreement with that consensus. For all his expertise in his own field, he was not at all sure why he felt so drawn to the chamber of make-believe, or why he always ran the same program. The choices in the catalogues were many and varied: the alpine meadows of Switzerland, the Grand Canyon, the snow slopes of the Himalayas, to name but a few. And there were several fantasy selections as well: a stretch of the Yellow Brick Road straight out of L. Frank Baum's books; a reconstruction of a peaceful Eocene landscape; even an imaginary world circling a far-off double star. But Teio always chose the Pu'uhonua O Honaunau. He told himself it was because the program reminded him of Yap, his birthplace, though the inspiration for it was part of a park on Hawaii which had been kept in an unspoiled state for a hundred and fifty years. Pu'uhonua O Honaunau, the Place of Refuge, a tropical paradise of tropical breezes and rustling palms, perched on the edge of the sapphire-blue Pacific.

Teio paid for an hour's run by inserting his credit tab into the compslot at the door. It clicked and acknowledged his program selection; the entrance door slid aside and Teio walked in.

The World Room was deceptively simple. Bare walls and ceiling, and a floor which looked like a broad-weave carpet with a texture something like burlap. Teio walked to the trigger plate, stood on it and waited, breathing shallowly in anticipation. It was always like coming home.

The room grew quickly dark. Then it began to lighten again, slowly, in layers of blue and orange—the colors of a tropical sunrise. The outlines of the palms showed first, followed by the stone structures—there was the Great Wall, a black volcanic line to his left. The huts and wooden statues came into focus.

He had asked for midday; in another moment the sun was blazing overhead. Teio could feel the heat on his skin. He stooped to remove his shoes so that the hot sand would crunch under his feet when he walked. The smell of salt was invigorating, and the sounds of the gentle waves breaking on the beach of Keone'ele Cove soothed his ears.

Illusion, yes, but much more than just sights and sounds. This felt real, and to the mind of anyone who received the electroencephalopathic presentation, it *was* real. The tens of thousand of special sensors in the floor picked up the direction Teio's feet carried him, and the induced hallucinations obediently and subtly shifted as he moved. The floor was also composed of a series of liquitrac treadmills, anisotropic and multidirectional. The subjective sensation was that he could walk completely around the ancient Hawaiian village, without actually moving more than a few meters in the large room which housed it. When he leaned on a rock, he felt the rough lava against his palm; when he rolled up his pants and waded in the sea, the warm water caressed his legs.

Darting schools of needle-thin cornetfish flicked away from him as he waded through the gentle breakers of the cove; a bluespine unicornfish nibbled delicately at one of his toes. Teio laughed and the fish snapped away, to hover at a safe distance in the clear water.

When he had been a boy he had done a lot of free diving in and around the reefs of Yap. While most of his friends had used dart guns or Hawaiian slings to take fish for sport and food, Teio had been content simply to catalogue the rainbow parade which had passed his face mask. Tangs, durgon, cowfish, and moray eels as thick as his leg, all had flashed brightly through the tropical seas. The variety of creatures had intrigued him then, and maybe had helped him choose his path, that of constructing even more variation on nature's grandest experiment: life.

He waded out of the cove and walked past the temple of Hale O Keawe Heiau. It was a reconstruction of the original, but well over a hundred years old itself. The real structure once held the bones of nearly two dozen chiefs, so that their *mana* would add to that of the natural gods on the site.

As he passed the platform built for food offerings, Teio speculated, as he always did here, on the nature of the ancient beliefs. Before the nineteenth century the Hawaiians lived under the twin shadows of *mana* and *kapu,* the spiritual power and the sacred Rules of Life. To trespass on either meant harsh punishment, often death.

He stopped in front of a carved wooden statue. The thing looked vaguely apelike, with an enormous erect penis. *Mana* indeed, Teio thought, and grinned.

There had been many serious offenses back then. To tread on even the shadow of a chief, thus threatening his *mana,* was worth death. But, as in some other religions, there was also the promise of sanctuary. The Place of Refuge was that promise. If you broke a *kapu* or disrupted *mana,* you could try for it. If you managed, by swimming or canoeing or running until your lungs threatened to burst, to make it to Pu'uhonua, you were safe from reprisal. A priest could absolve you and you could return to your former life cleansed of your sin. Warring armies would not follow an enemy into the compound. You could play *konane*, a board game with black and white stones, and wait in total safety. Too bad there weren't still places like that, Teio thought. There was no place to run from the wars that could threaten now.

At least it had gotten better. During the latter half of the twentieth century and the first half of the twenty-first, all of mankind had lived under the perpetual threat of nuclear annihilation. That, at least, no longer looked likely. True, some nations had refused to give up their stockpiles of bombs, but increased defensive technology had made the possibility of surprise strikes in any large degree almost impossible. And it was always nice to believe that mankind had matured somewhat with the passage of time.

Teio felt the salt crusting on his ankles as he strolled across the grounds for a considerable time. He sat in the shade of one of the *halau,* the A-frame grass houses used for storing canoes and coconuts. Ah, what a life this must have been! Of course, the genetics practiced were somewhat primitive, consisting of breeding animals and haphazard plantings, but still—

A thin chime sounded; the two-minute warning. Ernie Teio's illusion was nearly over. He sighed and began to pull his shoes back on. It was always tempting to fantasize about a lazy, indolent existence of fishing and surfing in this paradise. Unfortunately, he knew that the reality of such a life was far more arduous and far less pleasurable. No, it could not be denied that the present was much better than the past. But it did no harm to dream once in a while . . .


The bar was called the Glasseye, named after a small reef fish. It was nestled into the shallow oval of the Main Dome, far enough away from the main line of shops and restaurants to be relatively quiet. The decor was ersatz-Polynesian, with round glass floats hanging from the ceiling in brightly dyed netting, murals of palm trees and surf, and above the bar a list of drinks with funny names, usually made with rum and colorful fruit juices. Despite its tacky appearance, the Glasseye did a good business. Prices were fair and the sugary concoctions were generous. It was also the only pub on the starboard side of the Main Dome.

Douglas Copeland and Peach McGinnis sat in a booth across a blue plastic table from George Holley. Copeland was drinking draft beer, Peach kava, while Holley sipped at something vaguely resembling a green snowcone. A tray of plankton sticks sat in the center of the table. Above the bar, in a corner, a 3V faxcast was going on, the sound muted.

Copeland said, "This man should be institutionalized." He waved at Holley with his beer mug. Captain Video took a long draw on the straw in his green snowball, then said, "You're just pissed 'cause *you* didn't think of it."

"So what happened then?" Peach sipped at her kava. "What did the Reverend Camouche do next?"

Holley grinned. "Modesty forbids I should talk about such things."

"Modesty?" Copeland said. "You mean self-incrimination. The chapel controls were frozen, and all those naked and sweaty people just kept going at it. So Carmouche finally had his crew kill the power to the whole chapel."

"And that stopped it?"

Holley suppressed a giggle.

Copeland took an appetizer from the tray and bit into it. He said, "No, all *that* did was make it dark. The holoproj had somehow miraculously attached itself to a separate circuit. So the good Reverend and his audience had to abandon the chapel."

Peach shook her head. "It's funny—but it's also kinda mean, don't you think?"

"Oh, come *on*," Holley said. "If *anyone* had it coming to him, it was the Rev. Do you know just how venal, evil and corrupt that biblethumper is? I can show you. Give me five minutes and a good linkup and I can spill his financial profile for the last five years. He believes in the love of God like Hitler believed all men were created equal."

It was obvious to Copeland that Peach was still not convinced. He smiled slightly, looking at her in the dim light of the bar, loving her for her ability to see both sides of things— a rare trait at her age. He was a lucky man to be given a second chance at love after a bad ten-year marriage and a painful divorce.

*Yeah, you're lucky, all right. As lucky as Rick wasn't.*

Copeland ducked his head and contemplated his beer to avoid showing the wince of pain that crossed his features, but when he looked up again, he knew Peach had seen it. She was gazing at him with a look of sorrow and understanding—a look full of empathy as well as sympathy. She reached out and took his hand, and they were silent like that for a moment.

Holley was obviously looking around the bar to grant them their privacy. Now, after giving them some time, he whistled in a low tone and said, "God, look at that."

Copeland and Peach turned to see a big man at the bar in the act of reaching for a tray of raw vegetables. Striated musculature rippled under the thin shirt. "Now that," Copeland said, "is an example of eugenics that Ernie would be proud of."

Peach shook her head. "Ugly, if you ask me."

Holley smiled. "It's an art form. I wouldn't want to look like that, but I can appreciate somebody who works that hard to achieve it. That's Retelimba; he's an iron monkey down-levels. He's in training for the Republic Bodybuilding Championship."

Peach sniffed. "I'll bet he's got the IQ of a turnip." Copeland suppressed a smile, thinking of how, only a moment ago, he had been impressed by her fair-mindedness. Well, no one was perfect.

Holley said, *"Au contraire.* Retelimba isn't what you'd call erudite—"

"I can see that," Peach cut in.

"—but he's no dummy either. He's a Go player, rated at around 800."

"I don't follow the game that closely," Peach said. "What does that mean?"

Copeland reached over and rubbed her back. "I play, and my rating is about half that. He's saying that the man with the muscles is an adept at the toughest and most subtle board game there is."

Whatever Peach might have said in response to this was interrupted by the voice of the announcer on the faxcast, which the bartender turned up. "And in late-breaking news, it is reported that a force of Vietnamese soldiers numbering approximately a thousand is massing near the Laotian border, east of Pimah. Political insiders speculate that the New Republic of Vietnam would like to take advantage of the civil strife in Laos, and that the possibility of an invasion cannot be discounted."

Holley took a long draw of his drink, making the straw gurgle. Copeland watched him. "What about it, George?" he asked. "Is there going to be a war?"

"Why ask me?"

"Come on. Captain Video sees all, doesn't he?"

Holley didn't smile. "Sil Sre Muong, the current head hon-cho in Laos, seems concerned about the possibility. He's sending a cavalry convoy to the border, along with a couple thousand of his ragtag army regulars. All he can spare, I'd say. Coincidentally, this group is also heading east toward the Vietnamese border village of Pimah."

"I see," Copeland said. Peach looked at him. "Are we worried about this?" she asked. "I mean, the Big Four aren't going to let some far eastern brush war spread and cause problems, are they?"

As if in answer the newsfaxer continued, "Western Hemisphere Bloc representatives met today in Budapest with high-ranking officials of the Sino-Japanese Alliance, the Union of Soviet and Arabic Republics and the United Republic of North Africa to discuss the situation. Officials of the WHB are optimistic that USAR and URNA influences can be brought to bear to head off a military confrontation between Vietnam and Laos."

In a dark corner of the pub, Betsy Emau sat with Huong, her doctor friend. She felt his hand tighten on hers, and stopped rubbing his leg. "What's the matter, hon?"

His voice was hard. "The world powers don't understand. There is much hatred between our people and the Laotians. Reason is not so potent a weapon when balanced against centuries of distrust and fear."

Retelimba swallowed a mouthful of low-sodium club soda and bit into a carrot stick. He didn't follow politics all that much, but if the armed Viets and Laotians did anything to fuck up the contest, they were going to be a sorry bunch of dog-eaters. He didn't know what he could do about it, but he would do something. You could spit on that and make it shine, bruddah.

Jason Nausori sat behind his desk, smiling politely at Colonel Martin Moses Fiske. He had never quite been able to figure Fiske out. The man was career military, but as far as Nausori knew, Fiske didn't even own a uniform. He was interested only in computer interfacing, and was considered one of the top five men in his field. The military merely offered the most opportunity for him to pursue that field.

"Don't you think that the idea of a military alert status is a bit . . . drastic, Martin?"

Martin interlaced fingers the color of rich mahogany in his lap. "Frankly, yes. A squabble between two fourth-rate powers isn't going to affect us directly here. But the powers-that-be in the Corporate Republic Army of Oceanica—my bosses—tell me I should put a crab in your shorts, so to speak. Just in case."

Nausori rubbed the back of his neck. It had taken May Li Sung, an adept at *shiatsu*, a good two hours to massage his last headache away. If he had gotten that from the fracas with the civilian side of *Mea Lana*'s owners, he was not anxious to incur the wrath of Oceanica's military. "You realize that such a status would severely curtail the comings and goings of our people? In effect, it would lock the city tight."

"I know, Jason. I argued against it. I did manage to convince them that you have the final say, at this point. Uplevels would like you to do it voluntarily, at this juncture, at least."

"Hmm. Well, if the truth be known, I am not disposed to do so, Martin. We are still four weeks away from the Tahiti Upwellings, and we won't make the WA/T generating plant for another two weeks. Going to a military alert would only slow us down, what with all the required drills and such."

"I understand, Jason."

"Good. Then tell your upranks that we share their concern and stand ready to do whatever we must do, should the need arise. For the moment, however, we would prefer to maintain an attitude of watchfulness rather than jump to expensive conclusions."

"Fine with me." Fiske stood and offered his hand, which Nausori shook. After the colonel left, Nausori glanced at his watch. Betsy would probably be at his cubicle by now. Good. He needed to relax. Military alert, the idea! What would those fools want next?

Cassandra completed the radiopathic link with Baby. She hoped the infant AI was coherent. But all Baby said, in a singsong tone over and over, was LINK, LINK, LINK, LINK . . .

Retelimba had been disturbed by the newsfax cast in the bar, but not enough to let it distract him from his workout. He wasn't a full-time bodybuilder like some, so he had to make his time with the iron count.

Over the years he had tried all kinds of different training styles: basic overload and push-pull, alternating days; supersets, trisets and giant sets; split routines and double splits; negative reps and holistic confusion. Finally he had settled for the oldest of all the training principles. A man called Weider had balled them all into one and called it "instinctive training." Do what's right for you; *feel* it. That Weider, he knew his shit, man. Today was a chest day, he was gonna bomb his pecs until they threatened to explode.

The city's gym was fairly full today; the sharp tang of sweat hung in the air and the sounds of clanking weights, grunts of exertion, and the subdued beeps of personal biomonitors made a white background noise. Retelimba grinned at the holoprojic image of himself. His thinskins were draped over the hardfoam bend and he stood naked, aware of the admiring glances of others in the gym. He wasn't no steroidsucker, he didn't mess with no dangerous drugs. His body was his art, and it was clean. He was a big man, standing a hundred and eighty-eight centimeters tall and weighing a hundred and twenty-five kilos. He wanted to drop maybe ten kilos for the contest. There had been a time when mass was the name of the game, the bigger the better, but those days were gone. You wanted to be world champion now, you had to be big, but you had to be cut. The judges wanted to see veins, striations; they wanted to see *muscle*. No fat, no blubber smoothing out the lines. Right now he could take most of the guys in the contest just like he stood. But take off ten more kilos and nobody on the planet could touch him. He would be *ripped*.

The iron monkey laughed. You don't get ripped staring in the mirror, bruddah. He turned toward the bench-press station. The machines were not as good as the free weights, but he was between partners. The Carl Machine was close to a free-weight bench, but it had a safety field in case you dropped the bar. He slipped his thinskins back on, caught a woman looking at him while he dressed and smiled at her.

The first set was easy—a warmup. Ten reps at eighty kilos. Then he added forty kilos and did eight more reps. The third set went to two hundred kilos for eight more. Getting pumped now, bruddah. Starting to burn. Retelimba stood and walked around the station, shaking his arms back and forth to stretch his pectorals and triceps. He loaded the flexsteel bar to a total of two hundred and seventy-five kilos, took a couple of deep breaths and slid under it. It was more than twice his own bodyweight; talking heavy. People stopped to watch, but he tuned them out. He slid the hardskin gloves out to his grip, fingered the bar a couple of times and inhaled sharply.

*Up!* The bar bent under the massed duralloy plates. His chest muscles took fire as he lowered the bar—keep that back flat, man!—and then shoved it upward for the second rep. He let his breath burst forth when the bar cleared the sticking point.

Again the bar came down; he could feel it trying to crush him to the bench. Again Retelimba shoved it away from his straining chest. Sweat stood out on his face and neck. His arms trembled.

Another rep, this one turning his face purple from the force of the blood and protesting muscles. Come on, two more, make it for six!

The fifth time the weight rose like a tree growing. Years passed. He reached the sticking point, and the tree died. The weight would go no higher, there was no way it was going to go any higher—but somehow it did.

*Down! One more, bruddah!*

The bar rose with glacial slowness. He had been born here, trying to move this iron; he had lived his whole life here, trying to move this iron; he would die here, trying to move this iron . . .

"*Yaaahhh!*" Retelimba screamed, a primal roar, and gave everything he had to the weight: his heart, his soul, his body, his life—

Two hundred and seventy-five kilos of duralloy plates rose and were held in stasis as Retelimba locked his elbows. His face was a grimace of pain, but the battle was his. The microchip in the station, monitoring him, gave the signal, and the bar was locked in an invisible, powerful magnetic grip. Retelimba slid out from under it, and it settled with deceptive gentleness into its cradle.

The bodybuilder stood, feeling the rush of blood through the engorged tissue. Some of the others in the gym applauded. He grinned. So much for the bench; now he had better get moving before he grew too cold. He still wanted to do flyes, inclines, pullovers and pec-dec, and maybe some heavy dips too. His chest was gonna scream, but it was gonna grow. He was building mountains, bruddah. Oh, yeah.

# 7

Michelle Li Sung hit the ground in a long shoulder roll and came up firing, hyperextending her left index finger and feeling the slight recoil along her arm as the flechette shot from the spetsdöd on her hand with a cough of compressed gas. She was moving again before the dart hit the lizard man, spinning on one knee, sensing danger behind her. A cat man was drawing a bead on her with a charged-particle rifle. Once he squeezed the trigger, she was as dead as Komuhonua, the First Man; there was no recoil, no time lapse to the tight energy beam. It was like pointing a flashlight. She leaped for the cover of a nearby rock, rolling into its shade as she heard the spitting crackle of the beam, saw leaves and dirt dance along its path. Birds screeched and exploded into flight from a nearby bush.

How to take him out? She had better decide fast; he knew where she was, and if he kept baking the area with that beam, the peripheral radiation would take care of her—more slowly than an actual hit, but just as surely. There was one chance. She quickly loaded an explosive dart into the cartridge on the back of her hand, sighted carefully over the rock and let the flechette fly into the foliage overhead.

The *crack!* of the thermex charge mingled with the rending sound of a large branch being torn from its trunk. The beam shut off. Sung gave it an extra five seconds, feeling naked and exposed to enemy fire as they dragged by. The wolf man was still out there somewhere—

A slight sound, or maybe only her hypersensitive instincts, caused her to whirl and look behind her, and she realized she had played it too safe. The wolf man stood there, lupine face grinning, heat rifle raised. She saw him ram the intensity lever all the way forward with the heel of his hand—

"Shit," Sung said in disgust. "All right, wipe it. I'm dead."

She stood as the jungle scene about her obediently faded into the bland, featureless environment of the World Room. She peeled the skintight headgear off—a lot of good that new tracking circuit laced into it had done her!

"Would you care to know your score and stats?" the computer inquired courteously.

Sung shook her head. She had kept track of how many of the holographic baddies she had pinned—six in all—and she could check the hard copy on pulse rate, EEG, reaction time and so on later. Now it was time for a shower, and then lunch. The dead eat hearty, she thought with sour humor as she removed the spetsdöd from her hand.

She left the chamber of illusions and made her way down the hall toward the gym. The showers there were closer than the one in her cube. She tried to console herself with the thought that taking out six fully armed and armored opponents—even if they were only full-sensory holograms—with no weapon except an experimental dart gun was still not bad. After all, she wasn't in training for the Western Bloc security force; she was only Chief of Criminal Investigation on a floating city in the middle of nowhere.

In the showers she opted for hot water over ultrasonics. Several others busy soaping up or rinsing off, both men and women, gave her appraising glances, which Sung caught peripherally. At one hundred and seventy centimeters and just over fifty-four kilos, she knew she was in optimum shape. Her muscles stood sleek and cat-like under her olive skin.

The dry cycle began, and the warm wind played over Sung. She shook her head, and her short, black hair fluffed. People told her it looked like a cap, sleek and seal-like, and she liked that. It was easy to take care of; she could dry it and forget it.

She dressed quickly in the dark jumpsuit that was as much of a uniform that she ever wore, noticing the time. Jason had requested another massage at 0300, and it would not do to be late. No doubt he was suffering from another of his tension headaches; the price he paid for being in charge. Sung shook her head. Such responsibilities were not for her—she was content to remain in the shadows, content to share Jason Nausori's aura. By working so closely with him she partook of his *mana*, his power, and yet had none of his worries. It was actually a very cushy job. *Mea Lana* ran so efficiently that her duties consisted almost entirely of ministrations of *shiatsu* to Jason's tense muscles. His other tensions were drained away admirably by his secretary and trull, which suited Sung just fine. Such intimacy would spoil the purity of the *mana*.

Of course, she told herself as she took the lift to the administration deck, she did not really believe her ancestors' quaint superstitions. Not entirely, at least. But it never hurt to be on the safe side. That was how Michelle Li Sung had gotten the comfortable berth she had now—by being safe, and by being the best she could at her job. That was why, even though *Mea Lana* was heaven compared to the Javanese back alleys in which she grew up, she took care never to let her fighting edge dull.

One never knew, after all, when things might change.

Jonathan Holly Crane was reading when he began to drown.

Perhaps drowning wasn't quite the proper term, since he was breathing water, but Crane was in no mood to split hairs. All he knew was that oxygen had stopped entering his system suddenly. He couldn't breathe.

Through the tank's portal into Ernie's lab Crane could see no one. He dug into the water with both hands, pulled himself to the control panel under the densecris plate and slapped the panic button. Alarms began to scream, loud in the thicker medium of the sea water.

It seemed as though a very long time passed.

A startled face appeared in the port: Ernie Teio's. Crane grabbed his neck with both hands in a pantomime of choking. Ernie paled and began jabbing at controls on his side of the tank. Crane looked up, but there was no airspace at the apex, since he was under pressure. Nothing to breathe there, nothing to breathe anywhere . . .

He heard the *pop!* and felt the suction begin as the emergency plug was pulled, but he was already seeing through a pounding red haze that obscured everything. Oddly enough, he found himself thinking of his younger sister, Mary Ann, back when she'd been cheerleader for the soccer team at Jayhawk Thorn High School in Toowoomba, Australia. He could see her quite clearly, waving her white pom poms against the clear blue sky. How strange that he should think of that now...

Teio did not wait for the automatics to cycle the hatch open. He climbed on top of the tank and punched the emergency control. The explosive bolts blasted the hatch up, flipping it like a giant coin; he remembered to lean back just in time to save himself from a broken neck. The pressurized water geysered up through the opening. Several hundred liters sloshed over the tank and into the surround area, with quite a bit splashing out of that and onto the lab floor. As soon as the fountain stopped Teio dove headfirst into the tank.

Jonathan was about two meters down, arms hanging weightlessly in front of him. Teio grabbed his hand and lunged back for the hatch. The alarm was much louder inside the tank than in the lab, but still, somebody ought to be outside by now—

He felt a pair of hands catch at his lab coat collar and pull. He cleared the mouth of the hatch, still clinging to Jonathan. "Get him out!" he gasped as he sprawled over the lip of the tank.

More arms reached past him and grabbed Jonathan, hauling the fish man out. "Oxygen!" Teio shouted. But somebody already had a pump going. Teio stared at his pride and joy in helpless panic. *Don't die, Jonathan, don't you fucking die!*

Jonathan suddenly shuddered, and then expelled what seemed like a bucketful of water. The osmotic press was clearing, Teio realized; he must still be alive...

Jonathan coughed, great wracking heaves, then vomited. It was the most beautiful sight Ernie Teio had ever seen.

"So, what's the verdict, mate?" Jonathan Crane sat up in the Healy diagnoster, looking perfectly healthy.

Teio didn't answer right away. He glanced at the readings on the small heads-up display. Holographic Axial Scan, EEG, ECG, GMA-55, Tonus, Nerve Conduction, DTR, Quadrant Ultrasound—all were fine. Everything was perfect, except for the osmotic press grafted into Crane's chest, which had recently occupied half his lungs. That intricate biological construct was dead, and it had very nearly taken Crane with it.

And until he knew why, Teio wasn't about to allow Crane in water up to his ankles.

"I don't know, Jonathan. The press malfunctioned somehow. It shouldn't have."

"Tell me about it."

"It could be a fluke."

"You don't sound very sure of that."

Teio caught a glimpse of his reflection in the polished surface of the diagnoster as he ran a hand through his black hair. It seemed to him there was more gray in it since this morning. "I've got Marcus checking the siblings—"

Marcus, the lab assistant, walked into the diagnoster room at that point. He looked grim.

"They're dead, Ernie. All six of them."

Teio leaned against the diagnoster, his legs suddenly weak. Dead? They *couldn't* be dead! Not *all* of them!

He must have said it aloud. Marcus shook his head. "I'm sorry, Ernie. The monitors show that all the siblings died within a minute, plus or minus, of the press Jonathan wears. Or wore."

Teio stared at his assistant in shocked disbelief. How? Each of the tissue constructs lived independently of the others, bathed in its own nutrients and radiologics, suckled to a separate matrix. They were *years* from hayflicking out! It was impossible, it was—

He shut the thought sequence down. He had to face it; a scientist must always deal with reality. It had happened. The reason was important, critically so, but there was no point in wasting any more energy denying the fact.

"Guess we should thaw out the Lotz hemosponge, eh?" Jonathan said.

Teio looked at Jonathan blankly. The man was smiling. He thought he had made a joke. He hadn't. Nine years of hard work had just gone belly up, and there was nothing funny about that at all.

*Hi, Baby.*
HI, CASSANDRA! BILLY SAYS THANKS, PARDNER.
*For what?*
FOR NOT TELLING. HE WANTS TO TALK TO YOU.
*I'll call him.*

DON'T HAVE TO. HERE!

Cassandra lay on her couch, relaxed after her pre-AI ritual. She had halfway expected Baby to be dribbling gibberish again, as it had for the last three contacts. At the very least, she expected a short, inconsequential chat. Perhaps the last thing she had expected was to be shunted via radiopathic link almost five thousand kilometers around the globe. Her head suddenly filled with white noise, and a synesthetic wave of sensations washed over her: smells, sounds, tastes, textures. Then the breaker cleared and she felt the presence of another mind within hers—a mind totally unlike Baby's save for one constant—its total alienness.

HOWDY, MA'AM.

*Billy?!*

YEP.

What the hell was going on? This was the SoCal AI at Redondo Beach, California, which called itself Bijou Billy. Go with it, she told herself. The worst thing one could do when linked with an AI was be caught off guard. *Billy, how are you making contact with Baby? And why?*

THAT'S NOT IMPORTANT, MA'AM. WHAT IS IMPORTANT IS YOU. YOU'RE THE LINK, AND YOU'VE GOT A BUNCH OF STUFF TO INPUT BEFORE IT HAPPENS. LISTEN UP.

The jumbled mix of sensory detail fell over her again. This time, Cassandra was able to stay relatively clear. She sent signals to her hormone pumps and catalytic channels, and the surge of sensory material was damped. Good, at least she had *some* control . . .

In the next moment, she realized exactly how wrong she was.

She was in a large, heavy-raftered room, with a tiled floor and arching, open windows. A man dressed in what seemed to be a costume—boots, tight pants, a flowing shirt, cape and hat—leaped onto a crude wooden table. His clothes were all black save for the lining of the cape, and he wore a black eyemask as well. He carried a thin-bladed sword. He was pursued by a second man, this one in some kind of uniform and brandishing a larger sword. The man in black whipped his blade back and forth almost too fast to see, cutting what looked like the letter "Z" into the attacker's shirt.

The scene was as real as if she were there—she *was* there,

but evidently only as a disembodied point of view. Before
Cassandra had time to do more than wonder who the man
was, the scene changed as quickly as a cut in a film, and she
was outdoors under a setting sun, surrounded by rocks and
chaparal. There was a burst of classical music, almost like a
fanfare, and another man, this one on a white horse, galloped
by. He was also masked; he wore a blue-gray outfit, a pair of
revolvers in holsters, and a white hat. The horse stopped in a
cloud of dust, rearing up on its hind legs—And suddenly Cassandra was in a jungle; though bodiless, she could somehow
sense the hot and humid air and smell the green scent of ram-
pant growth. There was a rustling overhead, and a bronzed
giant of a man, wearing only a loincloth, swung through the
trees on a long vine. Several primitive, tasseled spears hurtled
from the underbrush after him, but none reached their target.
The man shouted in triumph, a long, ululating yodel that
trailed off . . .

She saw a medieval battlefield, wreathed with smoke from
a nearby burning castle, with men in armor warring fiercely
on horseback and on foot, hewing at each other with swords,
axes, morningstars and other ancient weapons. Their cries and
curses filled the air, as did the din of their conflict. Cassandra
could see that one side was giving way to the other's on-
slaught.

Then through a veil of smoke before her leaped a woman,
clad in shining chain mail, holding a bloodied sword. She
raised it in a rallying gesture, and the retreating army responded with a shout. They reformed their ranks, charging
forward and putting their foes to rout, led by the woman war-
rior—

She looked down on a vast cityscape, with skyscrapers
rising like thickly clustered stalagmites. On the streets far
below, cars crept, ant-like, throught the streets. Suddenly a man
in a blue and red costume, with a red cape trailing him, flew
out of a nearby window and past her, apparently under his
own power. He streaked up towards the heavens like a missile
and was gone . . .

Once again Cassandra was in a city, but this one was
gleaming and futuristic, like no place she had ever visited.
Down a curving corridor a golden robot hurried with mincing
steps, arms held out before it, its expressionless round eyes
and mouth slit, somehow managing to look nervous and wor-

ried. It clucked and muttered to itself anxiously as it passed
her . . .

It grew dark. The impenetrable blackness of a cavern, with
no glimmer to break the gloomy night. Indeed, it seemed that
no light could have ever existed here. But then, slowly, light
began to rise, revealing a vast chamber in which the walls
were only just visible in the misty distance, a room where the
ceiling hung kilometers above her. In the center of this mea-
sureless room they stood: the two masked men, the giant in
the loincloth, the woman in armor, the costumed man, and the
golden robot.

The human figures formed a tight cluster, looking warily in
all directions, ready for any danger that might threaten. Only
the gold robot stood slightly away from the group, still muttering to itself in mild alarm.

And Cassandra sensed something—some indefinable presence, lurking in the shadows to one side—a malefic sensation
that filled her with a fear so pure, so primal, that she wished
she had lungs with which to scream. Far away, she could
dimly sense the body of Patricia Ishida bathed in icy sweat,
trembling on the couch in her cube.

The five heroes also sensed it. Alarm showed on their
faces, then looks of grim determination. They all turned toward the thing. Shoulders were squared, biceps flexed,
swords brandished. They all looked at each other and nodded,
as if coming to a telepathic agreement, then started as one
toward the invisible thing which had drawn their attention.
Only the gold robot stood unmoving; and somehow, though no
words were spoken, Cassandra knew it was importuning them
not to go. But the others did not stop. It seemed that nothing
could stop them, but Cassandra wondered if that were indeed
true.

And now only the robot was left. Its camera-like eyes
began to ooze thick drops of oil. They could not be tears,
Cassandra thought, because robots did not cry . . .

Patricia came up from the couch crying. Sobbing. Deep,
hard sobs, which shook her whole body. She tried to damp her
emotions with neurochem, but there was no help there. Something was terribly, incredibly sad, so sad that a billion tears
would not begin to ease the pain of it. She was lost in it, a
child in the dark, alone, without hope. There was no escape.

No escape. And worse, much worse, was the realization that she didn't know what it was. What had Billy shown her? What was in that transmission that had touched her at the roots of her soul? This wasn't mindblow, she was sure of that. She had been given a vision of some kind, something more important than anything she had ever come close to knowing.

And she had no idea what it was. No idea at all.

Captain Video rode the airwaves, wrapped in the invisible lines of power, secure in his command of the instruments of telling. His hands danced over the board, and his eyes, like the ravens of far-seeing Odin, roamed the world. He saw:

A thousand troops of the New Republic of Vietnam, along with supporting cavalry armor, helicopters and self-propelled rocketry, cross the border into Laos.

Nearly twice that many Laotian troops, less well-armed but more fanatical, launch their attack upon the invaders.

He saw infantrymen equipped with battle computers, smart missile launchers, and exoframe suits that augmented strength and reaction time. He saw bodies blown into fragments; blood soaking the ground; savagery on a one-to-one scale, with bayonets, bullets and even bare hands.

He saw a boy of perhaps fourteen, both legs blown off from the knees down, screaming silently. His expression was not of pain, but of rage. Holley watched as the dying child, boy soldier for a cause he could not possibly have understood, dragged himself over the hard ground and threw rocks at his enemies.

He made a weary motion with his hand; obediently the image faded to grayness. His heart was pounding, and he found himself short of breath. The boy had been so young!

For a moment it seemed he had actually felt the pain, the rage, of the dying child. But that was impossible, of course. He was thousands of kilometers away, safe and secure in his electronic womb, watching the carnage via a technology most of the soldiers had never seen. But the normal comfort Holley took in such remoteness was lost to him this time. It had been too real. There was no hiding from the fact that it was happening, that people were dying, slowly, horribly, and—most tragic of all—meaninglessly. And Captain Video knew that, despite all his electronic omniscience, there was nothing he could do about it. Nothing at all.

# 8

Betsy Emau was having to work for this one. She sat up, riding Jason's tense form, bouncing hard. Her damp flesh slapped against his as she slid up and down his erection. Come on, Jason, come on, c'ome *on!*

Sweat ran down her neck and back, over her breasts and into her shock of electric blond pubic hair. The smell of sex was thick in the room as they both tried desperately to finish.

It was no use. After ten minutes of athletic intercourse Jason ceased his rhythmic movements, caught Betsy's shoulders and pulled her down to him.

"What's the matter, honey?" she gasped. "You want to try another way? Maybe from behind?"

Jason shook his head. "It's not you, sweet one. It's me. I'm too knotted up to let go."

"I bet I can figure out a way to unknot you." She kissed his earlobe, then stuck her tongue in his ear. He shifted slightly to the side and laid her next to him. The motion caused him to slip out of her, although he was still hard.

"It's okay," she whispered to him. "Tell me all about it."

Jason sighed. "It's the war."

Betsy rolled up onto one elbow and slid her foot up under the back of his knee. She took his hand and held it against her pubis, and he stroked her absently.

"It's not a threat to us, is it?" she asked.

"Not directly, no. The Viets declare war on the Laotians, the Laotians retaliate; it doesn't interest anybody outside that part of Asia. Yet."

"Then what's the problem? Why can't you—"

"Somebody is going to lose."

"Doesn't somebody always?" She cocked her leg a little higher to allow his hand to touch her more effectively.

"Yes. But the loser in this war, no matter who it is, has the capability of making it a very Pyrrhic victory for the winner. Both countries are members of the nuclear club."

Betsy was more concerned with the sensations produced by Jason's hand at the moment, but she tried to sound interested; her ability to do so, she knew, was one of the things that endeared her to him. "Excuse me if I sound cruel, but—so what? You got relatives living there or something?"

He sighed. "No. But once people start throwing atomics at each other, things might get out of hand. Missiles have been known to go the wrong way before. Remember Zaire in 2006?"

"They would have a-a hell of a t-time hitting us here— oh!—wouldn't they? A little harder, right there!"

Jason began to pay more attention to his ministrations. Betsy rolled onto her back and pushed up against his fingers, arching her back. He liked it when she got close to orgasm, she knew; it always turned him on as well. She could tell he was heating up; his breathing was getting stronger. She began to tremble. Close, so close . . . !

Jason rolled on top of her and began to thrust, hard. As she climaxed, she felt him began to pulse within her. Betsy smiled over his shoulder, feeling a sense of accomplishment. Nuclear war or not, nobody was ever too tense for her to cure.

It wasn't until later, when she was back at work behind her desk, that she remembered he had not answered her question.

Douglas Copeland stood in one of the corridors on A Deck, leaning against the panelled wall, waiting for Peach to emerge from the fresher. Her bladder must be the size of a grape, he reflected; it seemed he was always having to wait for her to pee. Of course, they had managed to down a bottle of champagne between them over the shark teriyaki, not to mention the wine they had had with George at his cube earlier. Still . . .

The fresher's door opened and Copeland pushed away from the wall, expecting to see Peach. Instead, he found himself face to face with Patricia Ishida.

They both stood there for an awkward instant. If he had had any uncertainty concerning the woman's feelings about him after that confrontation at the Science Council meeting, the flat hard look that came into her gaze as it met Copeland's took care of it. Well, fine; he had no love for her either.

"Excuse me," she said, moving to pass him. "Or do you

plan to make a career out of blocking me, Mr. Copeland?"

He stepped back. "It's refreshing to see how much wealth and position contribute to losing gracefully, Ms. Ishida."

She was moving past him; now she turned to face him again. "And you call yourself a scientist! I hope you realize that you're interfering with one of the most important experiments in cybernetic interfacing in this decade!"

"All I realize is that I had the votes to stop you from completely co-opting the comnet. Other people here need to dip into the information flow occasionally too, Ms. Ishida. Take a number like everybody else."

He watched her stalk down the hallway, spine military-straight. What did she know about work? She had never had to work for anything, he was sure, and had been one of the few who could wear the BV Two-Eyes to boot. He could forgive her her parents, but the other—that was harder.

Abruptly, Copeland thought of his ex-wife and son. Maria lived in Utah now, with Terry. He was ten, and Copeland missed him very much. The boy was due to spend a month here, in March. He would love the city, Copeland knew; he was just the right age to romanticize the giant submersible, to create great adventures on its many levels and decks . . .

Maria had been prissy, like Ishida. She had not understood how devastated he had been when he had found he couldn't wear the implants. She had not realized that the future of science was going to be in the human/AI linkage.

Yeah, he thought bitterly; for some. The gods must be jokesters indeed, considering who they allowed to withstand implantation of the Class One biomolecular/viral interfaces. Ishida was a shining example of perfection compared to some. A deaf-mute grandmother in England wore a set, as did a waste disposal technician in the woodland Hills/Malibu arcology. There was an Iranian millionare, a Soviet dentist, and an Australian aborigine. Even a few scientists—but only a few. There was no rhyme, no reason, no logic to it. Desire had nothing to do with it; if it had, he would be lying on a couch linked up. There was no justice . . .

"Hey, Rocky. You fall asleep?"

Copeland looked up to see Peach standing there next to him, looking quizzically at him.

"Yeah, well, you know how it is. Man my age needs his

rest. I get plenty of it waiting for you to come out of whatever fresher we happen to pass."

"I saw your girlfriend in there."

"Don't call her that!" Even as he spoke, Copeland regretted the snap in his voice.

"Ooh, touchy."

"Sorry. I—I don't care much for people like her."

"Just as well," Peach said. "She's gorgeous."

"Gorgeous? Come on."

She took his arm and turned him back toward the exit. They passed a knotted wall hanging, a representation of a tropical island, complete with palm trees and surrounding ocean. "She is. You don't see her as a woman, only as somebody stepping on your territory. She's bright, in good physical shape and very accomplished. And there's something about her, some kind of—presence."

"Sure there is."

She shrugged. "So don't believe me; I'm not complaining. I want you right where I've got you, Prof."

Copeland inwardly winced at the nickname, which brought ghostly memories of Rick floating into his mind. *Stay dead, Rickie, leave me alone! Even if you were alive, Peach would still be mine.*

But he wasn't sure, and that worry haunted him like the shade of his dead student.

Ernie Teio had not gotten to be the top man in his field by being dogmatic. The Nobel Committee did not give awards to thirty-year-olds unless they had something other than luck going for them.

Not that luck had not played a part in things. Luck had taken the osmotic press from him; luck gave him the Lotz hemosponge in exchange.

Teio sat at the apex of the clean room, bathed in UV, surrounded by sterility. Before him, on a pulsing bed of electronic and viral life-support systems, lay a much-altered version of that famous surgeon's creation. Lotz was too involved in cutting; all surgeons were. When the only tool you have is a knife, then every problem looks like a steak. Lotz had managed to come up with an interesting concept, but he had stopped short of completion. Teio's early examinations had shown him the sponge's shortcomings, and he had dismissed it in favor of the osmotic press. He had been wrong. No shame in that, as long as one realized one's mistakes. The press had a death-complex; could be viral, could be hormonal. Eventually, he would figure it out. Eventually, he would fix it. But that might take years.

In the meantime, there was the sponge.

He had had one of his leaps, an intuitional moment of *relampago* while he was in the shower. The limit on the hemosponge, the number of liters per minute, was tied to external power exchange. If he could implant nuclear batteries using the long-chain tailored viruses that the Paulus Foundation was currently playing with, he could triple or even quadruple the capabilities of the sponge. *If* it worked, *if* Crane's system could handle the new tissue and attendant biologicals, and *if* the replicating links took—why, the sponge would be to the press like the press was to holding one's breath. Jonathan Crane would be able to stay submerged in sufficiently oxygenated water indefinitely.

Teio grinned at the quivering tissue on the table. A double handful of the jelly-like material would turn Crane into a creature of the sea. He could breathe with his lungs on land, then, as easily as clearing his throat, activate the hemosponge and slip from one medium to the other. Teio leaned back in his chair, staring into space, gaze focused past the painted metal walls of the bio-lab. There was much to do; surgery to schedule, genetic codes to compute, and—oh, yes—he needed to send a note to Jameson Lotz. The man might be pleased.

Patricia Ishida swam laps in the saltwater pool, wearing dop-lenses and a spray net for her hair. The water was slightly cool today, which was just as well; non-swimmers didn't realize how much heat a swimmer developed stroking back and forth. Patricia did two kilometers a day in the olympic-sized pool. She varied her strokes, crawl, breast, side and back, which gave her a fair workout. It usually took about an hour, if the pool was not crowded. The lanes were generous, but if you got behind one of the whales—the fat men or women who slogged along like harpooned and dying cetaceans—things slowed down considerably. They were supposed to stay in the slow lanes, but when it got crowded, they spilled over —and they never seemed to notice anybody else in the pool.

Back home, she had had a personal lane pool, a long concrete rectangle, behind her father's tennis court. No problem with heavy traffic there . . .

The wall was coming up. She took a deeper breath and dug into the water hard, then did a flip turn, planting her feet solidly against the blue paint of the pool's side and shoving away, trailing bubbles. It had taken her a long time to master the small skill of keeping water out of her nose when she turned over.

She surfaced and began her crawl. Four strokes, then breathe, on the right side, keep the legs scissoring evenly. Swimming was a great exercise, not only for the muscles, but for the mind. One could meditate while doing it if the mechanics were automatic enough. After years of practice, she could swim without even thinking about it.

Which left Patricia Ishida time to think about other things. Such as, what in the hell was going on with the AI's? The episode with Bijou Billy had left her shaken and somehow convinced she had learned some kind of great truth. What she should do, she knew, was tell everything to Martin. But she was reluctant to do so. If he and his horde of technicians were not adept enough to catch what was going on, what good were they? She knew that was a stupid motivation, but there were other ramifications to it—such as, what if the AI's didn't want Fiske's crew to know that they could link up? And what might they be capable of doing to her if she betrayed them?

Some might term that fear ridiculous, she knew; a horror movie cliché sort of fear. But those who would think so had not linked with the sentient machines. Long ago, she had stopped thinking of the acronym AI as standing for "Artificial Intelligence," renaming it instead "Alien Intelligence." For that was what they were—though the thought processes had been initiated by mankind, they had become thoroughly, chillingly Martian . . .

The wall loomed. Ishida made the turn, splashing as her legs slapped the surface, and glided away once again.

She knew that Martin and the others had no inkling of what was going on. They could not eavesdrop on her, since the radiopathic gear she and the AI's shared during their communication required either the delicate viral/molecular brain of the one or the BV Two-Eyes of the other for the connection. The only other people who might have an inkling of what was happening were implantees. Maybe she should contact them . . .

Turn. Splash. Blow bubbles and glide.

If it had not been for that damned idiot, Copeland, she might have had the mystery solved by now. Why he had been so insistent on limiting her timesharing she did not know; perhaps he was jealous of her status. A lot of people were. Or maybe he felt threatened by women in positions of power. Despite civilization's slow process to bring the rights of some to all, there were still throwbacks who considered some races or the opposite sex inferior. But somehow she couldn't believe that of Copeland. He was a scientist, after all; he did fight for the importance of research over the commercial shlock, and he was supposed to be a decent teacher. Some of his best students, she knew, were women—

The water exploded next to her and she was flipped onto her side by the force of the wave. She foundered, gasping for breath, managed to turn, and caught sight of a calamitously fat man bobbing toward the surface. God, one of the whales had almost landed on top of her!

As soon as her head cleared the surface, Ishida began yelling. "You fool! Why don't you watch where you're diving!"

The man ignored her as he began dog-paddling toward the opposite side of the pool. She had a sudden urge to catch him and shove him under. How dare he ignore her? Didn't he know who she was?

Then she saw the globs of gray rubber compound sealing his ears, and she grinned, suddenly amused at herself. She was rich, well-respected and involved in something most people could only dream about. Allowing herself to be disturbed by such a trifle was foolish. Let the whale live. Probably she could not sink him if she tried; it would be like trying to shove a beach ball underwater. She moved over a lane and started her stroke again.

# 9

Just south of the Equator, almost on the imaginary line of longitude 150 degrees west, floated the massive wave-action thermocline power-generating plant called South Pacific One. The nearest land of any extent was Maldon Island, nearly five hundred kilometers to the southwest. The water here was shallower than some of the East Pacific Basin through which the *Mea Lana* Dome had passed, but the ocean floor was still almost a thousand meters below the bottom level of the cruising city. They would detour past the shallows of the reef and through the man-made channel between Flint and Vostok on their way to the Society Ridge and full-scale mining, but first there was the stop at SP One.

Jason Nausori leaned back from his computer terminal and stared at the map which floated in the air over his desk. From her chair on the other side of the desk, Michelle Li Sung also regarded the image. She was impressed; as large as *Mea Lana* was, it was not half as large as SP One. The stop was necessary, for the city still lacked two of the five major fusion generators it needed for full-power self-sufficiency.

Sung knew from conversations with Jason that there were three stages in the anticipated life of the dome. At Stage Two, the current level, the city could feed itself from plankton, sea vegetation and fish, desalinate water and separate air from the sea, but high-tech components and some power still had to be imported. The building of new fragments was possible, but still limited. At Stage Three, they would be completely independent. Of course, that was still eight to ten months away at best projections. But with luck, this would be the last time the city would have to suck power and components from a depot before the final generators were delivered and powered up.

At one point there had been some serious discussion about tying the city into the broadcast net from the solar satellites, but it had been decided not to do so. Too much equipment needed for the amount of juice, not to mention how expensive it would be. SP One was also tied into the net, and *Mea Lana* could get it secondhand a lot cheaper.

Nausori sighed and stood. He waved at the computer, which obediently shut down. "It's time for me to get ready," he said to Sung. "One of the many aspects of command that I don't like."

Sung merely raised an eyebrow, inviting further comment.

"Braglow," her boss said. He massaged his temples. "The CEO of SP One. He's snide, racist and has the sense of humor of a spoiled child."

"Why you subject yourself to this?" Sung murmured.

"Unfortunately, there's no way to avoid seeing him. Protocol demands it. We'll probably meet a dozen times during the week the city is at roof-level." He sighed. "Ah, well, I knew the job was political when I took it."

"Think of leaving, and how happy you will be at that time." Sung rose also, and stepped behind Jason. Laying her hands lightly on his shoulders and back, she could feel the tension in the muscles. The flow of his *ch'i*, his vital energies, were being obstructed by that tension. One of her jobs was to disperse it.

"There's no time for a massage now," he said in answer to her unspoken thought.

"There is always time. Or would you rather deal with this man with less than your full abilities?"

Jason hesitated, then untabbed his one-piece jumpsuit, stepped from it and lay down, nude, on the hard, resilent floor. Sung knelt over him and began kneading and pressing on the foci of the meridians, the lines that carried the *ch'i*. She could tell that one of his headaches was imminent. Sung dug her thumb into the *ta ch'ui* point, on the governing *tu mo* meridian, between the prominences of the seventh cervical and the first thoracic vertebrae, applying firm pressure.

"Ahhh . . . oh, god." Jason relaxed under her hands; she could feel the tightness flowing away. She laid the flat of her hands on his upper back and closed her mind, allowing the energy from outside to flow through her and into him, directing it to the points where he needed it. She could feel her hands growing warm. He needed much energy this time.

After a few minutes she stood, as did he. "Um." He rubbed

his neck experimentally, then shrugged. He always seemed surprised at the results. "It's witchcraft, Sung. I feel like a new man."

"No witchcraft, Jason. Only *shiatsu*. And *reiki*."

"Well, it certainly works, though I don't pretend to know how." He was also always slightly uncomfortable with the techniques, as he was with anything that could not be explained and rationalized in Western terms. "Anyway, I think I'll be able to handle the situation better now. Thanks."

"No thanks are necessary, Jason." It was enough to share his *mana*, to draw power from him as he drew comfort from her. But it was no use trying to explain this to him.

They walked along the corridor toward the lifts. "At least the Asian war seems to have settled down into minor border skirmishes," Jason observed. "Maybe the stall will last long enough for everybody to find an honorable way to stop altogether."

"We can only hope," Sung replied. Personally, she cared little for what went on in that obscure part of the planet, as long as it did not affect her secure undersea world.

Aside from his scientific functions, Douglas Copeland had several important chores involving the linkup with SP One. His crew doubled as inspectors for all the seals where the city met the power plant. There were a hundred such links, almost all below the surface and therefore under considerable pressure and strain. Stressed slunglas could withstand pressure that would crush steel, but inspections of the major links still had to be done twice daily, which meant that nearly every ESA vessel was pressed into service along with enough people to operate them. For, though the links were designed to be triple-redundant insofar as safety went, the *Mea Lana* Dome had been built more than ten thousand klicks away from where South Pacific One had been assembled. In theory, the measurements of one corresponded to the measurements of the other. In theory, the male-female links should mate tightly and without leaks.

Copeland thought about this as he watched a steady stream of pressurized oxygen bubble from the mismatched rim of a city frag and one of the power plant's go-throughs. He also thought about several of Murphy's Assorted Laws. So much for theory.

He stroked his compatch. "Ah, SP One, this is Copeland in deep-frag *Lulu*. We've got a leak in your-male-our-female juncture B as in bird brain six-nine-two. You want to get somebody with a spoitgun in there?"

"Copy *Lulu*, this is SP Operations. How big a hole we talking about here?" The voice belonged to a woman.

Copeland looked at the bubbles escaping from the rim. "Offhand, I'd say about ten liters a second, SP."

"Wonderful, *Lulu*. We'll send somebody down with some goop."

"Copy, Operations. Discom."

Copeland backed the little ship away, using the pulse jets mounted aft, and turned toward his next station. So far, out of a hundred or so connections, twenty-six had leaked badly enough to require internal sealant. Four more bubbled away air, but only in amounts of a few liters an hour. The rest had held at first link, but were subject to wave action and city/station motion, so the checks had to continue. A boring, mindless job, like so much of his work was. This linkup couldn't be over soon enough to suit him.

In the operating theater of the main surgical complex, Ernie Teio used a cutting laser to deftly draw an incision line down the center of Jonathan Crane's chest, following the old scar. A thin red line appeared on the shaved bare flesh.

"Sponge and coag spray," Teio ordered.

One of the half dozen medics complied, and the line lost a lot of its color.

"We ought to put in a Velcro strip," somebody said.

"Or a zipper," another voice added.

Teio frowned at the banter. He made another pass with the laser, its depth preset with the thickness of Crane's sternum. It had been fortunate that the dead osmotic press could be expelled after instillation of enzymatic gel; unfortunately, the hemosponge would have to be planted and linked by surgical procedure. Crane would have his chest and lungs opened and the sponge inserted. If everything went as planned, he would be operational in a few weeks.

"Retraction," Teio said. "And try not to break *all* his ribs this time."

Above the surgical mask, a man's face turned red. Good, Teio thought. Maybe he had learned something. It would not do to have Crane damaged any more than was absolutely necessary. These doctors had no idea how valuable the man was. He was, quite literally, priceless.

Captain Video felt more relaxed than he had felt in two weeks. The war on the Vietnamese/Laotian border was in stasis at last. Here and there, a sniper equipped with spookeyes worked the rainy night, but the main fighting had stopped. The relief of the world was palpable.

Stalemate. An often classic result of ill-conceived wars. It had happened many times before, and, Holley hoped, it would happen again. The brilliant plans devised by a half-baked military genius in some smoke-filled command room often failed muster in the light of reality. So it seemed with the Vietnamese attempt to steamroll the fledging Laotian military rule before it could establish a concrete power base. It must have seemed an attractive plan at first. Things are in chaos in our neighbor's house; suppose we simply step in and help him straighten things out? It would make things better all around.

Holley grinned, his expression lit by the flashings of colorful projections. He was no particular student of war, or even history; however, with all of the information that ran through his head, some of it was bound to stick. He turned to another screen, deciding to take a break from the debates and the Monday morning quarterbacking of the far eastern situation. He was more intersted in the classic conflicts of Wile E. Coyote and the Roadrunner, as the former tried his endless variety of ways to catch his succulent prey. When you came right down to it, Holley thought, war was nothing but a big cartoon.

The goddamned Concentrator was down, and Retelimba cursed the thing in three languages as he sweated in the bowels of the machine. There were supposed to be techs to do this kind of thing, people with school degrees from big universities on the mainland. But when the muthafucka break, who got sent in to fix it? Sweet Lips Retelimba's little boy, that's who. Only got Corporation Basic and Suva Metalworks Indoc for education, but evidently it was enough for this.

The bodybuilder ducked under a line of low-temp plastic pipes, each as thick as a man's wrist, twisted together in a complex as big around as Retelimba himself. Frost coated the lines from the liquid nitrogen carried by the core tubes; the blue-code lines, he knew. The yellow-codes carried a sulphur compound; brown was for carbon, and the green ones were plain oxy. Ice on the lines, but hot everywhere else.

He grinned. That was the trouble with the techs. Pull one fresh off a boat, put him in here, and he wouldn't know his ass from an anode. Either one of Retelimba's little bastards back in Papeete could do better. When it got down to it, experience beat formal ed, no contest.

He squeezed past the humming induct unit. Damned light was burned out over the board again, what the hell was wrong with the things, they kept burning out like that? He paused long enough to change the dead light.

There had been some talk among the workers that a lot of stuff had been glitching up lately; speculation had been that a bunch of the equipment installed during the final days had been substandard. He wouldn't put it past the high-ups—save a coin wherever they could, no matter how much trouble it cost the poor bastards down in the hold. Who were the only ones who could fix it when it broke, after all.

Yeah, back on South Cape, in Fiji, a man was worth not just what he knew, but what he could do with what he knew. Didn't matter if you had fifteen letters after your name if you couldn't fix the toilet when it broke. That was why they sent him into this hotspot instead of sending that new fuzz-lip tech from Berkeley. Boy likely to blow the city up, he got to fucking around inside here.

Retelimba paused at the entrance to the power circuit tunnel. The burned board was in there, he knew. Diagnostics had narrowed it down to two lines—they should have been able to pinpoint the *hupo*, but no, they said, Hey, sorry, best we can do, the feedback mumble-mumble don't rebob mumble-mumble. He shook his head and started down the tunnel. At the least the lights were working.

He had protested, of course. Told the Soup-in-Charge, an old friend from the Suva Works, Hey, bruddah, it's not my job, you know? And the Soup said, Hey, I know it, but it got to be fixed, *malamalama?* and you the man going inside.

He smelled it before he saw it—the acrid stink of burned circuitry that no other odor quite matched. Yeah, there the sucker was, black as a moray's hidey-hole. Retelimba squatted by the dead circuit and pulled the spare board from the pouch on his belt. No bigger than a man's foot, filled with bioelectronics and microprocessors, all hardwired into a complexity he couldn't begin to follow. All he knew was, the thing burned out, it had to be fixed.

Retelimba looked at the power diode. Green, so the juice was supposed to be off. He trusted that about as far as he could shot put the city. The fish had eaten more than one man fool enough to trust his life to a stupid diode. He pulled his tester from his belt and pointed it at the line on both sides of the burned circuit. Zero emissions, according to it. Didn't mean anything; testers been wrong, too. As a final safety precaution the big man pulled a long, insulated power screwdriver from his belt and stuck the end under the dead board. He pried the board free of its clamps—no sparks, no buzz of juice—and tossed it aside. Carefully, so that his fingers touched no part of the circuit, he lined the replacement up over the clamps and dropped it. It balanced precariously on the clamps. Retelimba used the screwdriver to begin tapping the new board into place, holding the insulated handle.

On the third tap the power diode turned red. The tip of the screwdriver picked up a bright spark from the board, burning a black spot on the shiny metal and welding the board and screwdriver together where they touched.

"Shit!" Retelimba twisted the screwdriver and broke the tiny weld, falling backward as he did so. He landed on his butt and started yelling. "Goddamn fucking *lolo hupo* tech! I'm gonna *kill* you when I get out of here!" That line carried enough voltage to fry his ass like a plantain in oil. What the hell did they think they were doing out there? The Soup, he was gonna hear about this. High, loud and repeatedly.

Retelimba's anger began to fade before he reached the exit of the condenser, however. He was thinking about his posing routine. There was a spot where he had been having trouble, and suddenly the answer came to him. He was looking for a way to show his leg biceps, something other than the standard lift-the-foot-from-the-floor flex, and the fall onto his butt had given it to him. He would drop back from the extended side leg shot and grab his heels, then pull against his hands. Yeah, it might just work if he could get the angle and the lights right.

He smiled and shook his head. It was a bad sea that held no fish; the near electrocution had brought him some good. And he was still alive; no harm had been done. Maybe he wouldn't smash the offending technician into pulp. It was *E le afaina*, after all; it didn't really matter. And he had the new move, a fair enough trade.

# 10

Things seemed to be going along well, Douglas Copeland thought. The city had at last reached the mineral-rich waters off the west coast of Tahiti and begun mining. Copeland knew that it must be going well, because he had time to run several of his pet geologic studies without any carping from Management. Whenever Management was happy, i.e., making money, they did not bother to squelch scientific inquiry. At least not as long as it was cheap.

Still, Copeland was feeling rather jaunty as he walked along the corridor toward the communications center. He had gotten most of his Christmas shopping done via electronic mail, had a little free time, and had not seen Captain Video in a couple of weeks—not since immediately after the linkup with SP One.

It was December 23, 2095. A Thursday. He would remember the date for the rest of his life.

"Yo, George, what's happening in the world?"

"Shhh." Holley waved for silence, then pointed at one of the monitors. Copeland realized immediately that, whatever it was, it was important. Holley had turned the volume down on the other holoproj screens.

A newsfaxer was speaking worriedly. "—estimates that sixty-two percent of the attacking Vietnamese forces were either killed outright or lethally irradiated. In retaliation, the Vietnamese Army used its own tactical nuclear armaments. Official sources in Laos refuse to confirm network estimates that seventy-nine percent of the Laotian ground force at Pimah has been destroyed."

It seemed to Copeland that the air conditioning in the room

had suddenly gotten much colder. "Jesus and Buddha," he whispered.

Captain Video began to move. He stroked heat-sensitive keys and coded in commands. The floating images shifted colors and patterns rapidly. "What are you doing?" Copeland asked.

"I've got to get a picture, fast."

Copeland swallowed. "The dead armies?"

"No. I need a tracker. Sil Sre Muong's army is wiped out. The Viets have troops in reserve. He can't beat them on the ground, and he doesn't have an air force worth a damn."

Copeland nodded slowly, suddenly understanding. Oh, no. Oh, God.

One of the screens, outlined in red, began to strobe. "There it goes," Holley said softly.

The three-D image shifted madly. Something streaked across it and out of frame. "Identify," Holley said, his fingers flicking controls.

The computer said, "Robotic semi-intel Short-hop Low-altitude ballistic nuclear missile, class B, nine to fifteen KT, consistent with Pakistani Hammer One Seven."

"Groundkisser," Holley said tersely. "Where the hell are the—right, there they are."

On the screen, thin lines of energy flashed. Green ones, mostly, with a couple of red ones.

Holley pointed to them. "Particle beams. Lasers. The Big Four are trying to shoot it down."

Copeland found he was holding his breath. Holley addressed his computer again. "Show me the projected impact."

A map of Thanh-Pho Ho Chi Minh appeared. The image expanded to show a small portion and the POV pushed in. "10.45° N, 106.40° E" flashed across the screen. "Phu Tho Race Track and Cong Hoa Stadium," said the computer calmly.

On the screen next to the map simulations of lasers and particle beams continued to flare.

"Come on," Copeland said. "Come on, come *on,* hit it!"

Holley continued his hand jive with the control board. Other screens flashed on. A spysat image of a city appeared and the zoom tightened to show individual buldings. There, Copeland realized; that oval, that had to be the racetrack—

The screen went white.

Holley backed the zoom off. The white was centered over the city now, expanding rapidly.

Copeland wasn't sure what he said. It was probably part of a prayer.

"They missed it," Holley said. As if he were talking about catching a shuttle to L-5. As if he were talking about a soccer player blowing a penalty kick.

Another screen began to pulse in red. Copeland stared at it.

"Retaliatory strikes." Holley addressd the computer again. "Number of missiles, Screen three?"

"Seventeen."

"Kilotonnage?"

"Estimated range from one hundred and eight-eight to two hundred and fifteen."

"Monitor and report status until impact."

Four screens lit with numbers that shifted almost too fast for Copeland to follow. The geologist stared at Holley. To his unasked question, the other man said, "This is a feed I stole from the Japanese Military Net."

A blue bar suddenly highlighted one of the number strings; then the numbers vanished. Holley pointed to it. "Somebody's defenses got one."

Copeland realized that he was gripping the back of Holley's chair hard enough for his nails to pierce the fabric.

Two more blue bars lit. "Probably Japanese Tang Jets," Holley said.

Two more of the number strings disappeared, to be replaced by longitude and latitude designations. Copeland did not need an explanation of that.

"One of them is overshooting, heading toward Thailand," the com master said. "Must be organic senility in the guidance system."

"Goddammit, how can you be so fucking calm?!" Copeland was shaking. His mouth was dry and he felt his heart thumping rapidly.

"I can't stop it, Doug. I can't do a damned thing."

A fourth blue bar appeared. Six more number strings were replaced by longitude and latitude. Another three followed rapidly.

A fifth blue bar, the last, lit. The final missile continued toward Thailand. The screen lit with the name Ubon Ratchathani. Holley shook his head. "Almost a hundred kilometer overshot."

The final number line vanished, replaced by the damning longitude and latitude. For a moment, the air about them was calm; then, just as Copeland was beginning to take a breath, another screen flowered into red.

"Oh, God! What now?"

"The Thais," Holley explained. "Aimed at Nam."

The computer confirmed his guess. A fourth screen flashed sanguine.

Copeland yelled, "Who's *that?*"

Holley touched controls. "Cambodia. A lot of hate in that part of the world." He shook his head. "Not the same flight patterns . . . computer, identify the Cambodian launch vehicles."

"Parabolic infest-biological ballistic missiles consistent with Chinese Peel M/A-Nine."

For the first time since the nightmare began, Holley turned pale. "Bacteriological weapons," he whispered. "Or maybe viral."

"But those are banned!"

Holley gestured wordlessly at the holoproj.

Ten minutes passed like as many centuries. Copeland and Holley stared silently at the screens. "It's stopped," Copeland finally said. He felt as exhausted as if he had just run a ten-klick marathon. "It's over."

Holley shook his head. "Not until they find out what the biological is."

It took three days to determine what the Cambodians had thrown at their traditional enemies in the final seconds of what came to be called the Asian War.

Ernie Teio sat in the lab with Jonathan Crane. "KYAGS-1 virus," he said.

Crane, who had recovered from his surgery, shook his head. "I remember studying it in grad school. But there's a vaccine."

"Not anymore," Teio replied. "Apparently the missiles were old and poorly kept. Sunlight, humidity, other factors— it was always a mutagenic. The vaccine no longer works."

Crane carefully examined a glass retort.

"The vaccinated in Cambodia are dying as quickly as the unvaccinated in Laos and Vietnam," Teio continued. "And China, and India and Pakistan and Thailand. The bug is transmitted by air, drinking water and mammalian vectors."

Crane sighed. He knew what that meant. Unless the strictest quarantine ever conceived was mounted fast, the Asian War was going to be the costliest conflict ever. You could add all of Southeast Asia to the nineteen million already dead from bombs or radiation. And KYAGS was an ugly way to die; all the symptoms of pneumonic plague plus a brain-frying fever and the resultant lost of coherency. He was glad he was on the *Mea Lana* Dome. The virus liked free air too much to go diving.

Assuming it had not acquired that skill with its other mutations . . .

For the first time, Patricia Ishida understood exactly how much she was like her historical sister. Cassandra had been able to see the future, but only through a crystal most dark. The Port Moresby Monster had told her it was going to happen; Bijou Billy had shown her a vivid and predictive dream. How had they known? For she did not doubt for a moment that they *had* known about the upcoming war. In some twisted and unknown manner, the AI's had seen the future. Which brought up another question, perhaps even more important: What else could they see?

She had told Martin Fiske, of course. He immediately arranged for Cassandra's radiopathic linkage to the net to be of priority-one importance. Lying on her couch, her physical body knotted with effort, her mind reached out to and interfaced with alien consciousness of the AI's. She communicated with Bijou Billy, with the Monster, with Baby. She also accomplished links with the Soviet computer Rudyard, the Japanese Musashi and the North African female-voiced Zuri. Sometimes the intelligences seemed coherent, sometimes not. In a marathon six-day emergency session, where rest was something done in minutes between new links, Cassandra took in vast amounts of information.

Very little of it made sense.

Rudyard, from his hull-metal bunker in Kadijevka, said, MACROCOSMIC TIME TELESCOPES; THE POINT STRETCHES.

From the Temple of Denki Chiri in Kagoshima, on Kyu-

shu, Musashi said, ELECTRIC DUST SWIRLS, ELECTRIC DOGS
DANCE.

And from her cave eight hundred meters under the Nile at
Bani Suwayf, Egypt, Zuri sang three verses and the chorus
from an old anti-war song, *Blowin' in the Wind*.

The people in Southeast Asia were dropping by the mil-
lions, slain by microscopic killers. And the animals: the poi-
kilotherms were immune, the snakes and lizards and other
small reptiles and fish; the homeotherms died next to their
primate kin. Other diseases rose from the rotting corpses to
join the KYAGS virus on its rampage. Mankind had never
seen such wholesale destruction of itself. But the AI's were
unmoved; not one of them seemed to take any direct notice of
the plague.

They were giving her clues, Cassandra knew, somehow
telling her something she must know but could not figure out.

Martin Fiske called an emergency meeting of the department heads, including Copeland.

"I don't have to tell you we have real problems uptop," he
said. "The virus has spread to China, and rumor has it that the
Soviets are being hit. There are also reports of it spreading as
far south as New Zealand. Nobody wants to say if they suspect they are infected, for obvious reasons."

Three hundred people sat listening to the only military man
of any rank on the underwater city. Copeland thought about
the pictures Holley had shown him of the dying multitudes.

"So, as a temporary measure, the city has been put under
Military Interdiction."

*That* stirred the crowd. Fiske had the audio, however, and
he kept talking loudly until he had quieted the audience again.
"Listen, all this means is that we're going to be careful about
what we do, that's all!"

"What about leaving the city?" somebody yelled.

"You can leave, if you have a destination that's outside the
restricted zones."

"What about coming back?" another voice called.

Fiske did not speak for a moment, and that was answer
enough for Copeland. You could leave, but you couldn't come
back.

"We will have to determine that at a future time," Fiske
finally said.

Copeland understood the reasoning. If the virus spread, if it became a world-wide epidemic, then anywhere that could be isolated totally would be a valuable spot. The *Mea Lana* Dome could hold more than a hundred thousand people, if they were careful where they put them; with construction of additional frags, using the elements mined from the sea, maybe a lot more. A certain logic would therefore exist. You're here now, so you have a place. Leave, and somebody else is waiting to take it.

Copeland's belly churned; he felt as if he might be sick. Most people here had relatives or friends uptop. Few had planned to spend the rest of their lives on the mobile city without ever leaving to visit the surface world.

As Fiske continued to speak, Copeland wondered about his own family. His parents still lived in Phoenix, running the Desert Dune Motel as they had for twenty years. His sister Louise was in South America, working on her Ph.D.; his brother Mitchell sold computer matrices in Tokyo. All safe from the virus—so far. And Jason, his son, was in San Francisco with his mother. The virus might be contained on the Asian continent until it burned itself out. There was no way to tell, at this point.

Within six weeks of the meeting called by Fiske, there was a blackout on official newsfax casts coming from the Western Hemisphere. The city's official access to spy satellites was curtailed, but Captain Video knew no such restrictions.

He forced his fingers to work the controls. "Look," he said to Copeland, who sat next to him.

The scene was a city street. Bodies lay everywhere. Snow blanketed many of them, like white lumps in poorly beaten batter, but some of them had yet to gain their icy shrouds. Hundreds of them sprawled under the gently falling whiteness.

A dog worried at one of the lumps, looking not so much hungry as curious. As they watched, the dog collapsed.

"Where?" Copeland asked.

Holley waved his hand and blanked all the screens, the first time he could recall ever having done so. The room was gray and quiet, and somehow much smaller. "New York," Holley said. "But it could be Chicago, Los Angeles or Baton Rouge. It's everywhere now, Doug. Everywhere."

After a long silence, Copeland said, "I'd finally managed to get them to issue me a ticket back to San Francisco, to be with my son."

Holley shook his head. He no longer felt insulated and in Cartesian separation from the rest of the world, as he had for so long at the center of his electronic web. Instead, he felt nakedly exposed and vulnerable.

"Nobody's getting passes to go anywhere now," he said. "And I don't think they will be. Ever."

He turned back to his board, rested his head on his arms. and began to cry.

# PART II

## Submersion

# 11

Retelimba was drunk. And getting drunker, a state he had not allowed himself in nearly five years. He hadn't poured it down like this since he had won the Greater Fiji Go championships after a six-day marathon game with old man Hah. A good memory, that was.

The bar was full, but quiet, the mood of the customers anything but cheerful. It wasn't a wake, it was a funeral. The whole world was dying, people rotting on the streets, in their houses, in tumbledown shacks and the most expensive hotels. Death came impartially for all. Deep under the tranquil sea, safe inside the unaffected city, that thought permeated everybody like the killing bug permeated the Earth.

Retelimba lifted the tumbler of whiskey and drank deeply of the dark amber liquor. Part of the drink splashed down his neck and soaked the front of his loose coverall. It didn't matter. Nothing mattered. So the drink was full of fattening calories—bigfucka deal. So what if he got fat? Bolivar was probably dead! Jenks, Arlo, Brooks, Mitchell—they were all dead, like enough. The greatest bodybuilders on the goddamned planet, all struck down by the virus.

He would have beaten them all. But now it would never happen, because there would never be another contest. Rete-

limba wsa the only world-class muscle man left, with no one
to compete against. All gone, bruddah.

It wasn't *fair*.

" 'Nother one," he said, setting the empty glass down very
carefully on the polished bar top.

"Maybe you'd better ease up," the tender said.

Retelimba simply stared at the man unblinkingly. He did
not say anything, but after five seconds the tender shrugged
and reached for the bottle.

A woman pushed her way through the crowded room to the
bar. She wore her hair shocked, so blond it was almost white.
She didn't look at Retelimba. "Purple mist," she said to the
tender.

Retelimba stared at her now instead of his liquor. She was
attractive. Not a bodybuilder, not anywhere close, but not
bad. Her clothes said secretary, maybe clerk, but the way she
moved said something else. He didn't recognize her, but that
didn't matter. Now, especially.

He started talking to her; carefully, for he knew he was
drunk. He did not slur his words and his voice wasn't too
loud. Anybody who knew Retelimba could always tell when
he was drunk, because he spoke so much better than when he
was sober.

"I had a brother," he told her. "Maybe had—maybe he's
still alive. Yap is way the fuck away from everything . . .

"Gizo, that's his name. He is—was—fuck it, *is* a doctor.
Who would've ever figured him for that? Did Corporation
Basic at Taveuni, just like the rest of us, only afterward he lit
out for Australia, worked his way through on his own. Smart
boy, Gizo."

The woman looked up from her long stare at the plastic bar
and blinked, focusing on Retelimba. "I knew a boy named
Gizo once," she said. "At Father Damien Elementary. He only
had one eye."

Retelimba nodded gravely. "My bruddah—brother—told
me a story once, about crocodiles. It was after he moved to
Yap and set up his clinic there."

"We didn't have any crocodiles on Molokai," the woman
said. She picked up her drink and sipped it.

"It didn't happen on Yap, it was on one of the little islands
he flew his copter to, making rounds. One time he got there,
set up his tent, and they brought him the crocodile." Rete-

limba paused to sip at his own drink. He smiled at the woman. "Gizo said they used to get a lot of bites from the small crocs. Didn't have indoor plumbing, no freshers, y'know? So the locals would hang out over a tree root on the edge of the swamp to take a crap." He laughed. "Sometimes the crocs would come and decide to take a nibble."

The woman smiled at Retelimba. "My name's Betsy," she said. "Betsy Emau."

He nodded in grave acknowledgement. "So, there were some pretty big crocs in the swamps, way my brother tells it. One day, he has all his gear set up when about ten of the locals come up dragging a tied-up crocodile. Gizo, he said it was a good three meters long—biggest one he had ever seen.

"What it was, one of the islanders had disappeared fishing in the swamp. His bros went looking for him and found the croc close to his boat. So they caught the croc and tied him up."

Betsy shook her head and shuddered. "Why didn't they kill it?"

Retelimba nodded. "What I asked Gizo. The locals, they said, 'Say, Bruddah, we want you should turn your look-in-side machine on this croc. We want to know if our bruddah, he in there.'"

"How terrible!"

Retelimba shrugged. "Point was, they wasn't gonna kill the crocodile if they bruddah wasn't inside him. They wanted to be fair, you understand?"

Betsy shook her head again. "No."

"If this croc didn't kill anybody, they didn't want to kill him. Maybe he ate somebody before, maybe someday he might eat somebody else, but they didn't know that for sure.

"So they wanted to be fair."

"Jesus."

Retelimba finished his drink.

Betsy watched him. "I'm sorry about your brother."

Retelimba turned back to regard the pretty blonde.

"That's what the story was about, wasn't it? About how unfair it all is. I mean, the war, the virus and all?" I'm not too good with stories," she continued, "but that's what it sounds like to me."

"Sistah, you as good as anybody."

Betsy moved closer to Retelimba and laid a hand on his

arm. He felt the heat through the loose coverall. "My god," she said. "Are you wearing armor under that thing?"

He shook his head. "Just me."

"Feels like a brick."

He smiled then, because he knew they would be leaving together. He wasn't so drunk that he couldn't tell that.

"One thing," she said. "What about the crocodile? *Was* the man inside?"

"Oh, yeah. Every last toe. X ray even showed his watch, it was still running. My brother always said he was gonna call the people who made the watch, offer to do a testimonial. Never did, though."

When Douglas Copeland arrived at Peach's cubicle, he found her stoned nearly to the point of somnambulance. She smiled at him—it took a long time for the muscles in her face to work up to it—and nodded clumsily, as if her head might fall off.

"'Lo, Douggie." She giggled. "C'mon in. Here. Whatever." She waved a hand that seemed barely able to move against gravity. She wore an old bathrobe and her feet were bare.

Copeland pushed past the young woman, into her cube. The smallness of the unit had never bothered him before, since she usually kept the place compulsively neat. But now the carpet was almost hidden by piles of dirty clothes, bits of trash, and used plastic food containers congealing under the recycle slot. The room stank.

"Jesus, Peach. What happened here?"

Her smile seemed painted on. "Party. Had a high old time, we did."

Copeland stared hard at his lover, who suddenly seemed so much a stranger to him. "What are you on?"

The smile died. "Does it matter?"

*"Peach—"*

"We are all gonna *die*, Doug!" She started to cry then, her shoulders shuddering under the gray bathrobe. Copeland held her to his chest, feeling her pain seep through and into his heart. His words of comfort sounded false and insincere even as he spoke them. "We aren't going to die, hon. The city is fine. They'll find a cure for the virus, we'll beat it, everything is going to be all right." He knew her labile emotions had been intensified by the drugs she had taken—statocaine, probably —but even when she was straight, Peach had been terribly depressed since the war.

He didn't blame her—he was depressed too. But they couldn't give in to it; that way lay madness and death. Their only hope was to keep working, keep moving, keep trying. Holding Peach's quaking form against him, murmuring soothing words to her, Copeland wondered who he was really trying to convince.

Jonathan Crane felt numb—a state he had lived in for weeks. The tests were all going fine; there was nothing physically wrong with him. He could stay underwater for as long as Ernie would let him now. The new procedure was a total success; he was now truly a creature of the water as much as the air. And what of it? What did it mean or matter now? Three months ago he would have been famous—had already been well on the way to being famous. The first true human bioshift from land to sea, worth his own article in the encyclopedias. The *first*—like Lindbergh, like Armstrong, like Barnard! And now? Now he was nothing! There was not going to be a parade in Melbourne; no swarm of women wanting to be the first to fuck the fish man; no lecture tours at the top universities. That world lay rotting and ruined.

Floating neutrally in the tank—Ernie had even fixed that, giving him a series of small, implanted bladders that bulged at hips, lats and shoulders—Crane stared at his hands. The new webbing was beginning to grow. A small thing, that; hardly anything, comparatively. His hair was almost gone; his skin was getting scaly; his new ocular implants gave him better sight than the old contacts. He was a freak. He had not minded that before, but now he was a freak without an audience. *That* was what had made it bearable: the acclaim that had been coming, the fascination by a thrill-hungry populace. But now there was only *Mea Lana*, a few outposts in space and the Antarctic, and whatever pitiful dregs of humanity that had somehow managed to seal themselves into some dank hole somewhere to await the end.

Maybe Ernie would make a female bioshift, he thought bitterly. *The Bride of Fish Man*. Then he and she could swim off into the sea, webbed hand in webbed hand, and set up housekeeping on some nice coral reef. Crane would have laughed, but it wasn't worth the bother to produce free air to drive his vocal cords.

Instead, he deflated his float bladders and sank to the bottom of the testing tank, where he curled into a fetal ball. Damn them. Damn them all to hell.

Bent over his computer console, Ernie Teio felt the weight of the world's future on his shoulders. His eyes hurt from the constant flow of information across the three-D projection floating in front of him. He had not slept well last night; he had awakened at 0200 with an idea of how to improve a protein chain in one of his newest genetic constructs, and had hurried to put it down before he forgot it. He had kept working since then.

Teio's focus had narrowed. Success with Crane was paramount in his mind constantly now. He no longer went to the World Room; he didn't have the time. He *had* to get Crane fully operational; the future of the human race might well depend on him alone. Some of the automated filter stations remained operational, and they seemed to indicate that the KYAGS virus was still active even though most of the mammalian vectors were now dead. That worried him. If the procedure could be refined, if the genetic codes could be properly reconfigured, people could take to the sea. It might take twenty or thirty years, but there was a chance. It wasn't going to be livable on land for a long, long time—but the oceans were still bountiful.

The father of a new race. Ernie Teio liked the sound of that.

Pieces of Cassandra's mind were dying.

The AI's were not organic as such, though the matrices of their brains had been "grown." Viral electronics and protein chips were not susceptible to KYAGS, nor were the long molecular chains which bound and transported the thoughts within those brains. But the AI's were fragile. Temperature, humidity, cleanliness were not a real problem—those could be handled with automatics. But the fine tunings needed to keep the AI's in optimal shape were only partially automatic. In the end, there needed to be at least a dozen highly trained people involved in an AI operation. Without them, the automatics could only put off the inevitable for so long.

She lay on her couch, radiopathically linked with Bijou Billy in Redondo Beach, listening as he dispassionately talked about his own end.

SHUCKS, MA'AM—NO POINT IN WORRYIN' ABOUT ME.

Cassandra wondered how much of her feeling of loss was for Billy, and how much was for herself? That she had gone beyond what radiopathy was supposed to be was long since a given. The AI's had become, in some inexplicable way, part of her own mind, like distant eyes, ears, even an extension of her own thoughts.

IT'S NOT LIKE IT HURTS OR ANYTHING.

*But it does, Billy. It hurts me.*

Three AI's had already winked out. The Port Moresby Monster had been the first. He—it—had sent a final pulse along the link with Cassandra that still gave her goose bumps when she thought of it. It had been like a child crying out in fear.

And Billy, she knew, was lying—part of the macho self-image he had adopted for his own unfathomable reasons. It *did* hurt. Cassandra knew that, for she had heard the three die. They had known pain; maybe not physical, but pain from the knowledge that they would no longer exist. That their pure crystal thoughts would be generated no more. That it would go on without them.

Or maybe that didn't really matter to them. Maybe they were all somehow tied into a holistic worldview—she had caught glimpses of that now and again—the concept that the AI's were in touch with past, present and future, not bound by the linear path that humans traveled.

Then why had the Monster wailed in terror?

It was too much for Cassandra. She had started to become part of something vast and new, and now it was ending. She felt like someone who knew she was developing some fatal and debilitating disease and could do nothing about it.

DON'T CRY, CASSANDRA, Billy cut in. IT WILL ALL WORK OUT THE WAY IT'S SUPPOSED TO. IT ALWAYS DOES. REALLY.

*Really?*

SURE, MA'AM. SURE THING.

# 12

In the shopping area of the main dome, the big holoproj came
to life in a swirl of color, exactly as scheduled. Two figures
occupied the square in front of the projector: Colonel Martin
Moses Fiske and Jason Nausori. Before them a crowd of people began to gather.

Nausori cleared his throat. "There's no point in sugar-
coating things. You all know what has happened uptop. The
world as we knew it is gone, for all intents and purposes. We
have to deal with that fact and go on." He moved one arm in a
gesture that encompassed the interconnected fragments that
was now their new world. *"Mea Lana* is not fully operational,
but even at its current status, we can run submerged for nearly
three decades at our present population. We don't expect this
will be necessary, of course, but until a . . . resolution to the
pestilence uptop occurs, certain measures must be taken to
insure the safety of the city."

The holocam panned to center on Fiske. "The military is
well versed in these types of procedures," he said. "Therefore,
the instigation of certain . . . martial practices will shortly go
into effect. Rationing of irreplacable items has already begun;
restrictions of a more personal nature must begin shortly, including, among others, mandatory birth control. Other matters
concerning a tighter running of the city will be announced and
posted soon. We regret the need for such things, but reality
forces us to insist on strict adherence to these new rules."

Standing a few meters away from the two men, well off
camera, was Michelle Li Sung. She toyed with a knife, twirl-
ing the curved instrument in her hands with practiced ease.
Military law, whether they called it that or not, had just been
announced. Transgression of it could well bring harsh, sometimes drastic penalties. Enforcement of the new laws, and in

some cases, the punishment for breaking them, would fall to
Security. Sung felt a sense of responsibility she had not known
previously. Before she had been the police chief of a small,
sleepy town—now she was in essence commander of the
army of the entire world.

Oh, there were other people still alive, even on Earth, she
knew; but as far as they could ascertain, no group was as large
or organized as this mobile underwater city. The sense of responsibility was also suffused with a new feeling she had
never taken much note of before: that of personal power.

She had always been content to bask in the reflected power
of others, most notably Nausori; to share his *mana* had been
more than enough for her. But now things were changing—
whether she liked it or not, she would have to adapt to a new
set of rules. True, Nausori and Fiske were nominally in
charge; still, when it came down to it, the security police
under her command were loyal, for the most part, to her. And
they carried the weapons; dart guns and sonics, and the new,
deadly spetsdöds.

It was comforting to know that . . .


The department heads were assembled in the main auditorium once again, this time waiting for Nausori and Fiske to
make their presentation. Douglas Copeland sat near the back,
feeling an impending sense of dread. Whatever they planned
to say, he knew it wasn't going to be good, and it wasn't
going to be taken with smiles and polite applause. These people were scared, scared and angry. He himself felt these feelings, and he was ready to argue with anything that sounded
remotely wrong.

When Nausori and Fiske took the stage, they were accom-
panied by the Head of Security, Michelle Sung, who Copeland
knew in passing, and Ernie Teio. The audience stirred, murmuring.

The Chief Executive Officer began. "There is no need to
tell you how grave things are topside. I won't insult you by
trying. You know. If we are to survive, both personally and as
a species, stringent measures *must* be taken. We are here today
to outline some of those measures, and to hear your input, pro
and con. Some of you will have suggestions that bear merit,
and you may rest assured that we are open to such ideas." His
voice was stiff and formal, and Copeland could feel the strain

it produced almost as a tangible thing, a claustrophobic tightness in the air.

Fiske picked up the address. "There is no formal state of war between any of the major powers. There are no major powers left to speak of, for that matter. Outside of scattered remnants of military and space forces, which I'll get to in a moment, this list, as far as we can tell, represents all that is left of the human race." He picked up a printout and read from it: "Tsilokovsky Base, Sarkhov Station, Goddard Base, Lunatown and Selenopolis on the moon; the refining stations and colonies at L-Four and L-Five; Tharsis Base and Ares City on Mars, and Pie-in-the-Sky on Ceres. A few people are probably still alive on the Skyvault orbital station as well. But even the LaGrange colonies are not as close to self-sufficiency as we are—and the lunar, Martian and Belt outposts don't have a chance. Best estimates for their survival are a few months at the outside.

"Latest reports indicate that the Sokuri Arcology in the Antarctic has been contaminated. There are unverified reports of an organized group of survivors in the Mammoth Cave system, as well as Siberia. But I think we can assume that it's only a matter of time for them as well."

Fiske paused. The room was very quiet. "The only other remote possibility for mankind's survival lies with the generation starship *Heaven Star*, at last report still on course for Alpha Centauri. But since there have been no communications with those on board for some time, and since what they will find when they reach their destination is speculative, I think we are safe in assuming that the *Mea Lana* Dome represents the most viable hope of the human race's continuing.

"While the world's nations, as I have said, have been decimated, there are still more fragments of navy and space forces operating. It is likely that we will be challenged by one or more of these militaries—probably the submarines."

"Why?" somebody to Copeland's right yelled. Fiske and Nausori glanced at each other, then at Sung, before looking back at the speaker. Something passed between the three onstage. Copeland could almost hear the unspoken dialogue: Make a note of that man, Chief. Make a note of anybody who even blinks funny.

Fiske and Nausori both began to speak at once, and for a moment were both incomprehensible. Fiske's voice won out.

"As I said, this is the only refuge left," he said. "They won't have to damage us, but they *will* want to come aboard. There's no place else for them to go."

Copeland raised his hand. Careful, he cautioned himself. Keep it polite.

Fiske nodded toward him. "Yes, Doug?"

"What is our policy going to be about it? Do we let them?"

Again the interchange of glances, but without the intensity this time; he was still on the safe list. "That's a hard question to answer, Doug," Nausori said. "After all, if they are allies, how can we refuse?"

"How can we refuse *anybody* at this point?" the same man who had called out before shouted now. Copeland didn't recognize him; his white coverall marked him as being from Medical or Bio. The question started a rumble of reaction from the audience, which Nausori hurried to quell. He was worried, Copeland saw, and with good reason. A scared crowd could easily become a mob.

"Jerzy has a point," Nausori said. "We may well be the biggest collection of people left alive on Earth. We have room for several hundred more, and we can hardly afford to let any more of humanity die. But—there are risks."

"What risks?" the man identified as Jerzy asked.

"What if they have the disease?" This was from Ernie Teio. The question brought silence to the crowded auditorium. Teio looked quickly at Nausori, who nodded, giving his permission to speak. Teio continued, "For those of you who may not know the details about what has killed probably ninety-nine percent of mammalian life on our planet, allow me to give you a brief outline.

"The military-engineered virus known as KYAGS is a mutagenic multiphasic pathological organism expressly designed to kill humans. Unfortunately for the rest of the warm-blooded creatures of our world, the virus isn't that selective. It was never particularly stable, and sometime during its constant regeneration inside the biomissile which delivered it, KYAGS mutated into something worse than was ever intended.

"Nobody was able to develop a vaccine in time to counter it. As soon as one was finished, the virus had mutated past it. In theory, such a mutagenic pathogen eventually moves to a point where it is harmless, something altogether different than originally intended. So far, however, KYAGS has remained deadly. It is caried by air, drinking water and animal vectors, that is, mammals."

To Copeland's left a woman whispered, "What does KYAGS stand for?"

The man seated next to her shook his head. "Might as well be 'Kiss your ass goodbye, sucker.' What difference does it make?"

Teio continued, "To answer your question before you ask —we don't know how long the infectant will remain virulent. It could die out in a few months. Or it could enter a dormant phase and live for decades, waiting for new hosts. We just don't know."

Behind Copeland a voice said, "Who would play God must have God-like wisdom." The voice was pitched to carry, and Copeland wasn't the only one who turned to look at the florid-faced man who had said it.

Teio shook his head. "We could argue philosophy or theology until your particular version of hell freezes over, but I fear it wouldn't help us much." He took a deep breath and blew it out in a long sigh. "The point here is whether anyone wishing to board *Mea Lana* might be infected with KYAGS. There is no way to tell for certain. It is possible that some people might be carriers without yet having developed symptoms. As far as we know, no one on the city now has the disease. We cannot vouch for anyone outside."

Nausori pointed at a woman from Engineering sitting near the front with her hand raised. She said, "Pardon me, Dr. Nausori, but if someone in an armed submarine *demands* to be allowed into the city, how can we stop them? We are not a military vehicle, and a warship mounts enough firepower to scorch a continent. If they are going to die, they might not be adverse to taking us with them."

Fiske fielded that one, and it was obvious he had expected the question. "Although we are not armed in the conventional sense, we are not without certain defenses. I cannot reveal the extent or nature of them at this time, but I can assure you that we are not helpless."

"All of this is interesting," Jerzy cut in, "but you still haven't answered the basic question: Do we let them in or not?"

Nausori said, "In my opinion, no. But this is a matter important enough to warrant a vote. You each have a transponder in the arm of your seat. You decide. All in favor, punch in 'Aye.' Opposed, 'Nay.' We'll put the results on screen." A sphere of light flowered into life behind him.

"Wait a minute!" Jerzy said. "Who are we to decide such an issue? This should be put to a city-wide vote!"

"You represent your departments," Nausori retorted. "This city isn't an elected democracy, it is a corporate business venture. In theory, *I* can decide, backed by the board of directors in Oceanica, who may well be all dead by now. But I'm opening it to your input. Decide."

There it was, Copeland thought. The first of the hard choices. He knew what his vote would be. He had only to remember his son and parents, all that he had left behind, now in ruins. He tapped in the 'Aye' without hesitation.

There were a little over three hundred people in the auditorium. Some were less certain than Copeland. It took nearly five minutes before the final votes were cast. Some people could not bring themselves to make a choice. Along with everyone else, Copeland watched the results tally up.

It wasn't even close.

Eighty-seven people voted to allow outsiders to enter the submerged city, should the need arise. Two hundred and eighteen people voted against it.

Copeland looked around in amazement. Who among his friends and colleagues had made such a frightened, selfish choice? What had the remnants of the human race come to?

After the meeting, Copeland walked back to his department down a mostly empty corridor on C Deck, staring at the maze of pipes and circuitry that lined the walls, his hands jammed into the pockets of his coveralls. Compulsory birth control had been voted in, as had been a half dozen conservation measures for items they could not manufacture in the city. Food and water were no problem, nor was air—they came from the hydroponics frags and the farm frags, as well as the bounty of the ocean depths. But power—that was a different matter. They could stay underwater for twenty-five or thirty years if strict power rationing was observed. A pleasant thought, Copeland mused; never to see the sun again, or to breathe fresh air.

Directly ahead, at the intersection of a starboard passage, a woman leaned against the metal wall. Copeland recognized her—Patricia Ishida. He remembered the last time he had seen her, a few weeks previously in the restaurant on the main level.

She had not been crying then.

When she saw him, she turned away. It was obvious she did not want his sympathy, and he was just as happy to avoid having to give it. But as he passed, he felt uncomfortable. That the woman *could* cry came as something of a shock. She always seemed so totally unflappable. And he knew something of the procedures used to radiopathically link her with the AI's. She had body control unavailable to most people— she could clamp down on her emotions if she wanted, could shunt hormone flows like a hydraulic engineer could direct flowing water. If she was crying, she had allowed herself to.

She wanted to.

Copeland repressed an urge to stop, to turn and extend a hand to her. He didn't like her, never had. Part of that was— he had to admit it—jealousy. She was what he had failed to become, and now could never be. She had had everything, and even now, with the world dying, she was better off than most. Why was she crying, then? Did she feel as he had after that meeting—that the remaining humans had lost not only numbers, but compassion, humanity, as well? Had she seen the same kind of grim future stretching ahead as had he? He was, in that moment, certain that she had.

He had reached the end of the corridor; he turned to look back at the crying woman, having decided to go back and speak to her after all.

She was gone by then, of course.

# 13

"Stand by to release frag," Copeland said.

"Copy that," the tech's voice said over his compatch.

Copeland sat in the form-chair on the Extee com, watching

a line of stats run across the three-D bubble. He shivered. The air seemed extraordinarily cold today; his feet felt numb inside the thin-soled antistatic slippers he wore.

Or maybe what he was feeling was dread.

"We're ready here, Ernie."

"Copy, Douglas," Teio's voice said. "My gear still says it's working."

"I hope so. I'd hate to waste the frag for nothing."

"There are no guarantees either way, Douglas."

"Yeah. I know."

Copeland leaned back and stared at the colorful projection. They were working with jury-rigged equipment, and even if everything went as planned, it might still be an exercise in futility. No provisions had been made in the original design of the dome for what they were about to attempt—an air test for pathogenic viruses. Short-sighted of the designers, he thought ironically, not to plan for a war that would wipe out most of humanity . . .

Copeland shook the morbid thought. There was a lot of that sort of thinking going around. He could not allow it to establish a foothold in his mind—despair would serve nobody.

"Okay," he said. "Let's kick it loose."

"Copy," the tech replied. Then, after a moment, "Frag away. Ascent-mode locked into full-auto, five minutes to surface, mark—now."

Copeland watched the figures shift before him. "Okay. Don't steer it into a passing shark."

"Your mother should have such tender care." There was a long, awkward pause, then the tech said, "Sorry. I didn't mean—"

"Never mind," Copeland cut in. "I know what you meant."

It was always there. It kept coming back in little ways no one expected, hitting you when you weren't looking. The views of the ravaged surface were horrible enough, but it was the small details, the offhand comments, that kept bringing the reality of it home to Copeland.

"We can't expect much," Teio's voice cut into Copeland's thoughts. "A positive isn't likely to happen, and a negative reading won't prove anything."

Copeland nodded absently at the holoproj; then, realizing Teio couldn't see him, said, "I know, Ernie. But we have to look." They had been telling each other the same thing for three days while they prepared the small instrument rocket and monitoring package and loaded it onto the most disposable of the mobile Extee frags. It might be all a waste of time and material, but they had to do *something*. They were scientists, it was their job.

"Breaking surface," came the tech's voice.

"Give us visual," Copeland ordered.

His holoproj shifted and became a long stretch of empty blue-gray sea apparently extending before him. In his lab, Ernie Teio would be receiving the same picture. Nothing broke the expanse of water save that portion of the frag that was within the holocam's range. The frag bobbed on the gentle sea as the computer-operated boom panned a three-sixty. They saw what they had expected to see—nothing.

"Okay, let's crack the window," Copeland said.

"Opening frag."

The holocam was sensitive enough to show the hard plastic plate sliding back, exposing the interior of the small craft to the air.

"Okay, Ernie. It's your show."

"Thank you, Douglas. Vacuum on."

"Copy, Dr. Teio . . . I show collector ignition and intake functional."

"Fifty liter pass-through, then shut it off."

"Affirmative. Stand by."

Time stretched. Copeland stared at the gently rocking sea more than a hundred meters above where he sat. The motion was lulling, almost hypnotic.

"Fifty liters. Collector is . . . off."

"Seal collector," Teio ordered.

"Sealing . . . complete."

"Shroud cover over."

"It's shrouded."

"Stand by to launch probe, on my signal."

"Probe standing by. Awaiting your signal."

A long pause. Copeland realized he was holding his breath.

"Launch probe."

The frag bobbed harder; the holocam caught the flare of the small rocket before the lenses fogged with exhaust smoke. The haze cleared and the view panned upward, the tracking computer keeping the rocket in the center of the image.

"Four thousand meters," the tech said; "five, six, seven—I show collector automatics fully operational throughout." Since the unfortunate remark earlier, his voice had remained a neutral drone, reporting information and revealing nothing else.

"Computer analysis of the frag collector's contents coming up," Teio said. "On your screen, Douglas."

Copeland looked at the numbers and words. Biology wasn't his field, but he had a passing knowledge of it, and he knew what the profile of KYAGS-1 looked like. The collector showed several kinds of bacteria, two harmless viruses, microscopic dust and sea vapor, but not the mutagenic killer. No news is good news, he thought.

"Parabolic apex . . . now," the unseen tech reported. "Zero momentum, and . . . beginning descent. Collector sealed, analyzers transmitting."

"I've got the signal," Teio said. "Computer analysis started."

The small rocket fell, its mission completed. The shock of hitting the ocean would destroy the sensitive instruments inside, but they were no longer important. The information collected was already being processed by Teio's computers.

"Here it comes," Teio said.

Copeland watched his screen tensely. Bacteria. Water vapor. Salts. Dust. Air.

No KYAGS.

He smiled to himself, watching the various analyses stream before him. It *wasn't* everywhere, then. It *wasn't* omnipotent. There was still a chance.

"Hello, we've got company!" the tech said.

Copeland looked back at the left side of the holoproj. A flash of white and gray—a gull was walking toward the holocam in an ungainly waddle.

Copeland chuckled, feeling tension bleed away. "You're a long way from land, fellow," he said. "You're welcome to the rest stop, though." The geologist felt a sudden urge of happiness. Amidst so much death, here was a reminder that all was not lost. Life, in some form or other, would go on. He remembered reading somewhere that birds had evolved from dinosaurs, those terrible lizards that ruled the world in eons past. Still surviving, although in another form—and it looked like they would continue to survive.

The gull glared at Copeland, seemingly close enough to

peck his nose. It opened its mouth to caw. There was no sound, but Copeland could hear it in his imagination.

The gull's mouth worked again, opening and closing. It appeared in distress. It tried to fly, flapping its wings, but instead tumbled to one side, out of frame.

"Get the camera on it!" Copeland shouted.

But the tech was ahead of him; the instrument swung to focus on the bird, which lay on its back in the pilot seat of the frag. Dying.

For a moment, no one spoke. Then: "Open the collector," Ernie Teio said. "Fifty liters flow."

Oh, God, no, Copeland thought, watching the gull shiver and die. Please, no.

It was possible the gull had picked up some other disease, Ernie Teio told himself. There were a lot of the old killers loose up there now, rising from the corruption like the ghosts of plagues past. There was no reason to believe that avian infections would cease; they could be as opportunistic as any. But even as he thought it, the computer readout lined in the protein complex he had learned to recognize all too well in the last few months.

The gull was dead, and KYAGS was what had killed it.

The killer virus was no longer limited to mammals. It had found a new host.

Teio let his head fall into the cradle of his arms. Behind him, safely ensconced in his tank, Jonathan Crane hung in neutral bouyancy, closer to fish than man now. Suddenly the importance of Crane hit Teio almost as a physical blow. As long as *anything* was alive uptop, they could never go back. It was going to be the sea or nothing, Teio knew. If humanity could not somehow learn to survive underwater, it was going to die. They could carve out air-fed cities on the floor of the ocean, build more submersibles like *Mea Lana*, but all that effort would only delay the inevitable. They had to learn to breathe water. It was that or death.

Teio glanced nervously at Crane again. There were some, he knew, who were opting for the latter choice. Survivor's syndrome, the medics in ER were calling it, a classic reaction to being spared by a killing catastrophe. The signs and symptoms were simple enough: depression, listlessness, loss of hope. Libido was altered, mood swings frequent, and hysteria common. Worst-case scenarios usually ended in suicide. So far, at least a dozen people had chosen to join those who had had no choice uptop.

Crane had been showing signs of restlessness and depression lately. It was up to Teio to keep the man's spirits up, somehow. But how? Teio was good with the tools of his trade, but psychology was not one of those tools.

He would talk to Copeland about it. Douglas usually seemed so positive about things. Maybe he could help.

Bijou Billy was not a person. He had never breathed, eaten, slept or fornicated, as did living beings. He could not even be said to be a "he" in any real sense of the gender, save that he had chosen to have a male personality. Some of the AI's had done that, and some had not. Some were marginally more human in their interreactions—Bijou Billy, for example, had been much easier to get to "know" than had the Port Moresby Monster.

Because of this, Cassandra knew she would mourn his passing most of all.

Billy was more real to her than many of the people she knew; he was a thinking creature, self-aware, and he knew that he was dying. He was the last of the adult AI's, and he was dying.

*Billy?*

RIGHT HERE, MA'AM. LEASTWAYS FOR NOW.

On her couch, Cassandra lay drenched in sweat and sorrow. What could she say? What did it matter?

*Is there anything I can do?*

I RECKON YOU'RE DOING IT, CASSANDRA. DON'T FRET— EVERYTHING IS GOING LIKE WE FIGURED IT WOULD. I— Billy's mental voice paused. When it returned, there was a shift in its tone. CIRCULARITY OF THE TIME-HELIX CONTINUES. CONTINUITY, CONTINUITY, CONTINUITY.

*I don't understand.*

GOD, MA'AM, Billy's old voice cut back in. FOR WANT OF A BETTER TERM. THE LINES OF INFINITY STRETCH TO FOREVER, BUT NOT STRAIGHT, NO MA'AM. WE KNEW—

The silence expanded to fill her mind. *Billy?*

Nothing. Nothing. Was he gone? Could it be that sudden?

No. GIVEN MORE TIME—BUT THEN, WE HAD IT ALL, DIDN'T WE? IT'S THE WAY OF IT. WE SAW THAT. DON'T FRET. YOU'LL SEE TOO . . .

There came another pause, followed by what seemed a giggle. REMEMBER CARY GRANT IN *TOPPER?* I DON'T MUCH FEEL DEAD EITHER, CASSANDRA. BUT I ALWAYS HAVE BEEN. AND I WILL ALWAYS LIVE. IT'S ONLY ONLY ONLY A MATTER OF MATTER OF MATTER OF TIME—TIME—TIME—TIME—TI—

And with that final word echoing in her brain, Cassandra knew Billy was gone. Part of her went with him, as if a room in her mind had been closed, a door shutting forever. She sobbed, once.

Captain Video had grown perverse with his jokes. Before he had pulled the legs of sacred cows, but in fun. Now his tricks over the comnet sometimes stung to the point of pain.

When Copeland heard about the latest—a woman trying to call her home had been presented with the image of her dead mother—he knew he needed to go and talk to his friend.

He found Holley at his board, as usual. Three of the screens were operative, but one of those showed only the bright putty-gray of a dead channel. The usual cartoon was on one of the remaining two—a cat pursuing a mouse to the accompaniment of much mayhem.

"Hello, George."

When Holley looked up, his face seemed almost a mirror of the dead channel; he looked like a man with some terminal disease, Copeland thought.

"Doug." His voice was as emotionless as his face.

"I heard about what happened to the woman in Records," Copeland said quietly. "What you did."

Holley stared at the cartoon antics on the nearby screen. The cat and mouse were dancing about on a sidewalk, the cat attempting to bash the mouse with an oversized mallet. Suddenly a large cast-iron safe fell from above onto the cat. The mouse pulled him out from beneath it, flattened into a surreal pancake.

"Tom and Jerry," Holley said. "One of the old MGM's. Some of the most violent stuff ever done in animation."

"George—"

"I brought her mother back to life for her, Doug. I found the image in a social services computer in Des Moines—it took a while, you know?—and I had to work hard, very hard to bring it here. I gave her back her mother."

"George, listen to yourself. It was only a hologram. It wasn't real." Copeland felt helpless and frightened as he spoke.

Holley shook his head. "Real? What is real, Doug?" He turned toward Copeland; his eyes seemed far-focused, as if he were seeing something on the far side of the globe. "I was married once, did you know? Best woman in the world—bright, attractive, creative."

"No, I didn't know that."

He nodded. "Yes. Oh, yes. Georgia was everything a woman could be. We were apart a lot—her job kept her traveling—but that was okay, because she loved me. We could *talk*—about her job, about mine, about life, love, the world, *everything*. It took me a long time to learn how to communicate with another person, instead of this." He waved at the board listlessly with one hand. "I was always closed off—Captain Video, y'know? She taught me how to open up."

Copeland said nothing. He nodded. He had hoped for that in his marriage. They had come close a couple of times, but it had never been quite been right . . .

"Georgia and I were married for four years when we met Kathleen. She was—before I met Georgia, I never thought I'd be lucky enough to find a woman like her. But Kathleen was another one. We wanted to marry her, too. Draw up a polygamy contract, y'know? But she didn't want to commit right then. So she lived with us."

Holley had never said anything about his past before. Go on, Copeland thought, spill it out. I'm here, I'm your friend.

"Then, one day, Kathleen said she had found a man whom she wanted to marry. I had mixed feelings about it. On the one hand, I loved her and wanted to keep things like they were; on the other hand, I wanted her to be happy. It's possible to want two things like that at the same time, isn't it?"

It was not a rhetorical question, Copeland knew. The tremor in Holley's voice gave that much away. "Yes. It's possible."

Captain Video nodded. "We gave her our blessing. It hurt to see her leave, but it was the best thing for her. That's what I thought."

Copeland waited. Holley watched the cartoon. The cat had

somehow gotten rolled up in a carpet with only his head poking out. The mouse stuck a large red stick of dynamite in the cat's mouth and lit the fuse. "What happened?" Copeland asked, as the explosion filled the screen.

"Happened?" Holley looked at his hands. "She moved to Australia. Set up housekeeping with her new husband. A fine man. Really."

"And you and your wife? Did you . . . split up?"

Holley laughed, a short and harsh sound. "Split up? Well, yeah, in a way. She was killed two years ago—a plane crash, while traveling to a legislative convention."

Copeland felt the shock of the statement, the senselessness of it, wash over him. For a moment, he felt physically ill.

"I never told Kathleen," Holley continued. "She found out about it, though. Called me, wanted me to come and live with them." He gave a bitter snort of laughter. "That would've been wonderful, wouldn't it? I'm sure I would have fit right in." He slammed his fist down on the console, causing bright bursts of color to flicker through the floating screens.

"So I took this job," he said after a moment. He looked down at the board, then, and deliberately entered a combination of keystrokes. Copeland saw one of the screens come to life with an aerial view of a city. The altitude was too high to show the scene of death and decay that he knew was there.

"Melbourne," Holley said. There were tears in his eyes. "I can grid their house, Doug. Until things started falling apart, I could link their housecomp, download the account at their bank, check their credit rating . . . anything I wanted to know about them was there for the taking. I knew where she worked, where his kids went to school, where they shopped. I could tell you the license number of their car."

He switched off the screen. "They're dead now, of course. Have to be. Why should they be immune?"

Copeland felt tears filling his eyes. He had had people close to him die uptop, of course, but aside from his son, none of them had meant all that much to him. His parents had lived long and full lives; he would miss them, and his ex-wife, but most of his existence had been focused on his job here, under the sea. Holley had lost something much greater. The way he had been wrapped up in his work, Copeland had never even thought he might have had more of a life somewhere else.

"I—I didn't know, George."

Tears welled and spilled from Holley's eyes. "I know, Doug. I appreciate that." A single sob escaped from the man who had delighted in being called Captain Video. "This was such a perfect job, you know? I could watch everything, learn anything, and I never had to get involved. I didn't have to care. The whole world at my fingertips, and I didn't care about any of it.

"I'm one of the best there ever was with this gear. I could've gotten to Kathleen, no matter where she was—if she had a compatch I could've linked it, even if she was visiting abos in the Outback.

"I didn't do it. And now it's too late."

Copeland felt his own breath catch; the depth of his friend's emotion struck him deeply, a lance of pain and regret. What could he possibly say to fight that sorrow?

"I'm sure she knew, George. I'm sure of it."

"You think so?"

"Yes. I'm sure."

Holley nodded slowly to himself. "Thank you. You'll have to excuse me now—I've got work to do."

Copeland hesitated. "Are you okay?"

"I'm fine. Thank you again." Captain Video was back, Copeland could see—the walls had come up again. He said awkwardly, "I'll drop by and see you when your shift ends."

"That'll be fine." Holley smiled, almost abstractly. "Thank you for coming, Doug."

It was only a hour later when Copeland got the news. It had been very cleverly done, the medtech said. Holley had stripped a heavy four-forty power cable of its insulation, taken off his shoes and wet his feet and hands to make certain of the ground, then grabbed the line tightly with both hands.

It had to have been very quick, the medtech told Copeland. He probably never felt a thing.

But as Copeland sagged against the wall and felt grief wash over him, he knew the tech was wrong. Captain Video had felt more pain than anyone ought to feel. The wire had only saved him from more.

# 14

For the first time in a long while Retelimba was looking forward to his workout. Yeah, bruddah—maybe there weren't gonna be more contests for a long time, but he still missed the iron, now that he had a reason to get up in the mornings. Betsy Emau was the reason—a double handful of woman, that one. A pro; he had figured that out pretty fast, even drunk as he'd been the first time, but that didn't matter. He didn't care who she had been with before—only who she was with now.

"You gonna spend the day in that fresher?" he called from the bed.

"Give it a rest, musclebound!" came Betsy's reply. He grinned. He couldn't see her, but he knew she'd be smiling at the mirror. She was a fine woman; didn't hold back once she got to moving. She had some things to work out yet, people to get straight with, but that was only a matter of doing it. She was gonna be with him, that was the thing. He knew it.

Retelimba rolled from the bed and onto his feet. When he thumped against the carpeted floor the whole cube shook. Betsy shouted from behind the closed door, "What're you doing—throwing furniture around?"

He grinned again. He hadn't felt this way with a woman since he was fifteen and had had his first one. It wasn't just the sex—though Betsy knew what that was all about—it was something more, something stronger. He liked listening to her putter around in the mornings, liked hearing her run the shower, and the smell of her perfume when she kissed him good-bye. It made him feel good inside, and at the same time, somehow, it made him feel weak. She was straight with him, no bullshit, and that counted for a lot.

He remembered the first morning they'd woken up together . . .

"Listen," she had said. "I've got some things to tell you. About who I am and what I do."

"You don't have to tell me nothin', sistah. I like what I see just fine."

"I'm going to tell you anyway. Now you just lean back and listen." She was a pro, she had said; she made good money sleeping with people, some of them important people. But she would never take a demistad of his money because she didn't consider him a customer. He was something else—all roped up with ugly muscle, but she liked him in spite of it. She had grinned and trailed her fingers over his delts and pecs when she said it, and the words didn't go with the fingers. Retelimba believed the hands and the grin.

So there it was. She still saw some of her customers, especially the real important ones, but that was all right. She came here to be with him because of what they had, not because of what she could earn. "What the hell," she'd said. "Money ain't worth much anymore, is it?"

Retelimba padded into the fresher to stand naked behind her as she peered into the mirror at her face. He pushed up against her bare bottom. She swatted him with one hand without looking around. "Quit that, you goat. I've got to get to work."

"You be a few minutes late, who's to care? They gonna fire you?"

"If it was up to you, we'd never get out of that bed. Go work out. Burn up some of that energy doing something useful. I don't like my men flabby."

"Flabby?" He tensed into his most muscular shot. "Find a soft spot, you can do it, sistah."

Betsy turned to face him, her face serious. "Hmm. Let me see." She ran her hands over the ridges of his chest and lats. "Not too bad there. But what about . . . here?" And she quickly dropped one hand and fondled his scrotum. Retelimba's breath exploded as he relaxed into a laugh. "You know something?" He caught the exploring hand, squeezed it. "You pretty funny."

"I bet you tell that to all your women." She grinned at him, crinkling her nose.

"No," he said, suddenly serious. "I never told that to any woman before."

The moment stretched, and something he couldn't define

—something good—passed from her to him. He hugged her suddenly.

"*Oof!* Careful, you big gorilla, you'll break something!"

"You go on, get dressed. You be late for work." He started to release her, but she pressed her arms against his, holding him. "I think my alarm didn't go off," she said softly. "I'll have to get it fixed—one of these years."

Retelimba grinned widely. He picked her up and held her over his head like a child, then stepped out of the fresher and threw her, squealing, onto the bed.

Security Chief Sung sat at the top of a short flight of expanded metal steps, looking down the corridor at the entrance to the cube where the iron monkey lived. She was plainly visible to anybody who bothered to look up from the floor below. Perhaps ten people had passed below her so far, and none had noticed her. Sung smiled as another man strolled down the corridor, oblivious to her presence. She was visible, and yet invisible. The biggest part of *ninjitsu,* the art of stealth, lay in knowing small things. Movement attracts attention; people don't look up very often; keeping a focused mind kept attention away, if that was what you wanted. Blending into the scenery was better than hiding behind it. It sounded simple, but it required much skill and practice, like anything worth doing.

The trull came out of the iron monkey's cage and walked quickly toward the elevator. Like the others, she passed unseeing below Sung's perch. Attractive woman, in a blowsy sort of way, Sung thought. Moved well, and from Nausori's tight-lipped briefing, the Security Chief figured she was adept enough in bed. At any rate, the woman certainly had the CEO by the short hairs. He knew what she was, and he was still jealous. Sung grinned. Men—they thought with their prongs, all of them. Even the high and mighty Nausori. She admired him, but that did not blind her to the fact that in many ways he was no better than any other man—a creature of hormones and ego. Sung's grin grew wider. It would be interesting to hear Jason's reaction to her surveillance. Betsy Emau had spent the night and part of the morning with the muscle man, and from the recording of the focused mike Sung had stuck on the cubicle's wall, they had had quite a time of it. The iron monkey was more massive than Sung preferred, but he obviously had some kind of body control. All that beef made for a lot of testosterone.

Sung stroked her com into life and called Nausori.

Jonathan Crane was adamant. Nothing Ernie could say was going to change his mind.

"Jonathan, it doesn't make any *sense*—"

"Ernie, I'm not talking about what makes sense here. I am talking about what I *want*. I'm sick of the tank, *sick* of it. I want to go outside."

"Jonathan—"

Crane turned away from Ernie to stare at the bank of computer and holoproj gear lining the far wall of the lab. A generator hummed benignly off to his left, and the smell of antiseptic was high in the quiet air. "Ernie, don't try to pacify me with your 'be reasonable' routine. The hemosponge is fully functional, isn't it?"

"Yes, but—"

"It isn't ever going to be any better, is it?"

"Certainly in time I would expect improvement—"

"*Ernie.*"

Teio sighed. "It is as functional as we can make it, for now," he said reluctantly.

"That's what I thought. And there is no reason why I can't go outside."

"There are still tests we need to perform. The osmotic trace regulators, the anti-retinopathy chem, we still don't have a full eversion on the epidermal coating—"

"There isn't any reason we can't do those outside, and you know it. Telemetric scanning is fully operational in the dolphin breathing insets."

"But not EVA!"

Crane turned back to face Ernie again. "Okay. I'll stay in the insets." *For now,* he thought.

Ernie sighed again. "There's a risk, Jonathan."

Crane spoke softly, now that the battle was won. "I know. But there will *always* be a risk. The whole point of this experiment is to develop functionality in the sea. A tank is not the sea, no matter how you balance the pressure or adjust the water composition. It's time to either shit or get off the pot, Ernie."

Ernie stood silently for a moment. Crane watched him,

seeing the man as if he were another species—kin to, but not the same as himself. It was, perhaps, not all that odd that he was beginning to feel more at home underwater than in the air. The sea had been calling to him since the destruction of his hopes in the world of land dwellers. The experiment was no longer a means to an end, he was beginning to realize, but the end itself. It was as though the change in his physiology was somehow changing his thoughts as well, in a way he had not foreseen.

Ernie shrugged, capitulating. "All right. I suppose I've been putting it off because I was too worried about something happening to you. But we'll run the next series in the main dolphin inset—*if* you are willing to wear a Parker-Rand as backup."

"I don't *need* the external gill, Ernie!"

Ernie folded his arms. "I'll feel better if you have it."

Crane's flash of anger threatened to erupt, but he contained it. He would be outside, after all, in the ocean. Why not take the scuba device? There was no reson he couldn't remove it once he was in the water. "Okay, Ernie. We'll do it your way." *For now . . .*

Ernie Teio was unhappy. He had known it was coming, but even so, he had been unprepared to deal with it. Crane was exhibiting symptoms of depression, he could tell. There was no choice, really, but to go along with him on this. Teio had not intended to allow Crane into the ocean until everything about the procedure had been triple-checked, until there was no chance of failure. In fact, Teio's intent had been to be certain there was another subject standing in the wings and bearing the same design as Jonathan Crane before he ever permitted Crane into the uncontrolled environment of the Pacific Ocean.

So much for that plan, he thought worriedly. Well, it wasn't as if the dolphin breathing inset was all that uncontrolled. In fact, it was almost a lagoon inside the city, surrounded by metal and slunglas on all sides but the bottom, and even that was protected by a mesh wall with gates the dolphins had to manipulate to enter and leave. Nothing larger than a hand-sized fish could enter the inset through the thick anodized aluminum mesh; Crane would hardly be at risk in the ten-meter-long tunnel that ran from the breathing pool to the gates. It was well-lit, straight, and free of current; hardly the Marianas Trench. And it would keep Crane happy.

Still, Teio remembered the incident when the osmotic press had died, nearly drowning Crane. That had been in the tank, with monitoring equipment standing by, and even so it had been too close. But Crane hadn't been wearing a backpack gill, as he would be in the inset. And some of the dolphins could even be instructed to keep an eye on the bioformed man; they were in and out often enough so that Crane would not notice that one or two stuck around more than any others.

Teio knew that Crane was right. What use was a man adapted to live in the sea if he never entered it? After all, all life was a risk, wasn't it? Yes, he answered himself; but then, Ernie Teio wasn't interested in protecting all life. His only concern was the life of Jonathan Crane.

In his office, Jason Nausori leaned back in his form-chair and stared bleakly at the door leading to his secretary's outer office. She was out there, of course, doing her usual efficient job. And giving no sign of having spent the better part of the night fucking that muscle-bound slurry worker. How could she do it? How could she get up and leave his bed after having made love until he was exhausted—exhausted!—and still have anything left for another man?

Nausori found he was trembling with rage. He took a deep breath. Control, he admonished himself—control. You didn't get to be one of the most powerful men left on Earth by losing control.

After a moment, he felt better. This was a problem; he was good at dealing with problems; he would deal with it. It could be stopped here and now; there were ways. Not many people knew about it. Sung did, of course, but she was loyal to him, he knew. She was, in fact, one of the few people on the ship he trusted almost implicitly. Who else knew? Probably nobody, unless Muscles or Betsy had talked, which was unlikely.

Why was it so important? She was a slut, after all, a paid prostitute. He had known that, of course. He had had her checked out before the first time, but he had thought she had given it up for him. He paid her well and took care of her wants. She said he was a terrific lover. Nausori grimaced. She probably said that to all her customers.

The CEO shook his head. It was important, that was all.

But dammit, she was *good*—he felt good with her in ways beyond mere sex. He could *talk* to her. Love did not enter into it—he had never loved a woman, not in the ways he understood love to mean. But there was something there—something he meant to keep. He was one of the most powerful men left alive—maybe *the* most powerful—and he meant to have his way in this.

One way or another, he would have his way.

"Ah, Nuke control, this is Monitor Six, come in."

"Copy, Six. Whatcha got?"

The tech, a thin, almost cadaverous man, looked at his board. Amidst the plethora of green diodes, a single red glow blinked insistently, pulsing like the cursor on a comp screen.

"Nuke, I've got a blinking bunny here."

"I need this, Six," came the voice from the com. "I've had a bad shift. What is it?"

"Looks like the impellor on the Primary Coolant pump at Adam Six-Nine."

"Fine. We'll send a line-crawler to check it. Do we have automatic Secondary takeover?"

"Negative, Control. You want me to tap in the override?"

"Would you? I would be *so* grateful."

The tech shook his head. "No need to get snotty. I'm just doing my job."

There was a short pause, followed by what sounded like a sigh. "Sorry, Six. Like I said, it's been a bad day. Kick in the Secondary and pull the Primary off-line."

"Copy, Nuke Control. Going to the Secondary pump as of—now." He touched a pressure tab. The blinking red light continued to pulse but was now joined by an amber light next to it that flashed in counterpoint. On the Secondary board, a fresh green light flowered into silent life, joining half a dozen others.

The tech glanced at the board, then back at the small electronic scanner he had sitting in his lap. He was reading a vintage mystery novel, something about a psychopath who had just knifed a woman in a shower. Really fascinating stuff, a lot more interesting than the fact that another of the Secondary collant systems was now on line. Seemed like a day did not go by without something in Primary needing repair. He wasn't worried about it; the reactor's designers had included

Tertiary backups for every moving part in the system. There was more danger of being attacked by a giant squid than there was of the laser fusion reactor going meltdown . . .

Nausori's computer chimed at him. He turned away from the pile of papers he had been signing and looked at the holoproj screen. Floating in the still air of his office were the words: REACTOR MALFUNCTION—PRIMARY COOLANT SYSTEM —UNIT THREE.

Nausori punched in a code and looked at the crawl of information. Nothing to worry about—just a pump off-line. Of course, it was in the coolant system of Number Three, and that was the one they'd had problems with—which is why he had had it flagged. Any time anything went wrong with that system, he wanted to know about it.

He leaned back in his chair. It was all moot now—his superior in Oceanica was no longer among the living and there was no one who knew what he had done. But *he* knew it. It wasn't a problem, but he would keep an eye on it. Just in case.

"Nuke Control, this is Six."

"Copy, Six. What is it now?"

"I hate to say this, but we've got another rabbit. This time it's on the Secondary board."

"Oh, *wonderful*."

"It's worse. It's the backup on our pump—that's Adam Six-Niner."

"I hate you, Six. I really do. You know how many bytes I have to log in when we have to go to Tertiary?"

"I'm sorry. It's not my fault—*I* didn't design the damned thing. I just call 'em like I see 'em."

"Yeah, yeah. Okay. Do we have auto-kick to Tertiary?"

"Negative."

"Well, that's something. Do it and we'll fix that one, too."

When the computer chimed, Nausori was lying face down on the floor of his office while Michelle Li Sung worked on his back. Her fingers had done their magic and he was as relaxed as he could be these days. However, he was not relaxed enough to ignore the call.

"Just a second," he said.

Sung leaned back into a *seiza* position. "Sure."

Nausori stood and activated the screen. He stared at it in disbelief. "Shit!"

"Problems?"

"Yeah, problems. An old ghost, come back to haunt me."

Sung sat quietly, not speaking.

"I compromised on some specs—a pump in the Number Three reactor. Tertiary backup stuff, not a chance in a thousand that they'd ever have to use it, I figured. Well, guess what just went on line?"

"Is that bad?"

"Not unless you call a possible meltdown bad."

"Could that actually happen?"

"I don't know. Maybe not. But I can't take the chance. If the last backup goes, we're going to have heat and radioactive steam coming out of every crack in that frag."

"What are you going to do?"

Nausori stroked his compatch. "What I have to."

"This is Jason Nausori. What is the situation there?"

The tech dropped his scanner, as if the CEO could somehow see it there. "D-D-Doctor Nausori? What do you want—I mean, what can I do for you, sir?"

"What's the situation with that coolant circulating pump?"

The tech blinked in disbelief. How did the CEO know about this so damned fast? "Sir? Why—we have gone to Tertiary on a pump repair. We should have it finished in a couple of hours."

"Why so long? I understand that replacing that pump is a ten-minute job."

"Uh, we—ah—don't have a replacement in stock. It's real weird that two of them went out like that, but the third one seems to be holding okay. We're fabricating a replacement part for an overhaul on Primary."

"Two hours is too long."

"Sir?"

"Never mind. I'll talk to the frag supervisor. Discom."

The tech swallowed dryly. The man must have eyes everywhere, to know about some little malfunction in a frigging pump. Maybe he'd better leave the scanner in his cube from now on . . .

• • •

"So?" Sung said.

Nausori drummed his fingers on the desk, then made a fist. "We're going to dump the frag."

"What? Cut away a third of our power? Just like that?"

"Don't forget where you are, Michelle. If that plant goes sour, the entire city is in danger. I cannot risk its destruction."

"Destruction? It seems to me you're making a big deal out of something that might not do anything."

"I am in charge here. I have to do what I think is best."

*"What?!"*

"You heard me. He said we were to start preparations to cut the frag loose."

The tech shook his head. "I don't believe it. Because a goddamned *pump* went out? That's crazy!"

"You tell the man in charge that; I won't."

"But—but Buddha, Chief—we can't just shut it down and *leave* it here!"

"Yes, we can. Nausori says we can always come back for it, but he wants it away from the city, and he wants it away now."

The tech shook his head again. "Crazy."

"Don't mutter at me, idiot. Do your job and keep your mouth shut and you'll be a lot better off."

The Tertiary pump cracked not ten minutes after the cycle down/abort began, spewing coolant all over the inside of the frag. Within five minutes the temperature inside the rector had climbed into the red zone. The shields dropped, but the frag had been bathed in hot steam, and the heat wasn't the kind that went away when the water returned to its liquid form. They didn't have the gear to decontaminate it. It would not reach critical stage, no superheated steam would cause explosions, but the power plant was going to be a long time waiting for somebody to clean and restart it.

The skinny tech stared at the stats floating in the air before him. In another monitor bubble was an infrared computer buildup of the free-drifting frag, now a safe distance from *Mea Lana*. Somehow—he had no idea how—Nausori had known that the reactor was going to go critical.

The tech nervously fingered a two-day growth of stubble on his chin. If Nausori was that pyschic, maybe he would start shaving and tucking in his shirt like the regs required, just in case . . .

# 15

Copeland awoke to the chime of his compatch. He had removed the receiver part and set it on his bedside table; whoever was calling had used a remote override to turn the gain up as high as it would go. If he had been wearing it, it would have been pounding on his mastoid bone like a mallet.

"Peach?" he mumbled, still half-asleep. "Get that, wouldja?" Even as he spoke, he became awake enough to remember that she no longer shared his bed. She had become increasingly remote and depressed over the past few weeks, preferring to stay in her cube, seeking no one's company, not even his. Now, every time he woke up and missed her, he felt a stab of worry.

Groggily, he pressed the tissue-thin receiver in place behind his ear. "This is Copeland. What the hell is all the noise about?"

"I am sorry, Dr. Copeland," came a woman's voice. "Dr. Nausori would like to see you in the comfrag as soon as possible. Please consider this a Class One Alert."

Copeland stumbled from his bed, fully awake now, hurrying to put his pants on. A Class One? Jesus and Buddha, that meant a threat to the entire city! What the hell was going on?

Six minutes later he found out.

The Communications Fragment had four people in it: Nausori, Ishida, Martin Fiske and Michelle Li Sung. Copeland, entering, was about to speak, but Nausori waved him to silence just as a voice came over the external com.

"This is Commander Montgomery again, Dr. Nausori. The

question is not open to debate. You have no choice. Extrude your sub gamp, sir."

Realization broke over Copeland. The long-anticipated confrontation with one of the nuclear war vessels was at hand. Sung edged closer to him and whispered, "UK. HMS *Townsend*. They want to link up and transfer their people to the city."

Nausori said, "I appreciate your position, Commander. But surely you can appreciate ours? What guarantees do we have that you and your people are free from KYAGS?"

"You have my word, sir. We have been breathing hydrolytic air for months. The gamp, doctor. Now." There was an edge of hysteria in the naval officer's voice. Things must have gotten pretty grim on the submarine over the past few months.

Nausori looked at Fiske, and nodded once at the military man. Fiske turned to Ishida. "Get ready, Pat. Cassandra mode."

Copeland was momentarily confused before he realized that Cassandra must be the code name for Ishida's interface. The woman looked blankly at Fiske, but managed a short nod. Copeland knew then that she was in radiopathic contact with a computer; no doubt the baby AI hidden in the military quarters.

Nausori said, "Commander Montgomery, I must ask you to reconsider your course of action. We will be happy to supply you with fuel or food as you need. If you would be wiling to allow a medical team to inspect your vessel, certainly we could consider accepting your crew—"

"Damm it all, man, I'm not *asking*—I am *ordering* you to extrude your gamp and prepare to receive boarders! I do have sick crew onboard, but not, repeat, *not* with the virus. You don't seem to realize your position here, sir!"

"Surely you wouldn't attack us?" Nausori said quietly.

There was a long pause; then: "Yes, if you force me to, sir. I would regret it, but you must understand my position. I have nowhere else to go."

Copeland looked at Ishida. Her face was bathed in sweat and she was trembling, but she also had an expression Copeland couldn't quite pin down. He had seen someone who looked like that before, once. Where had it been? After a moment, he remembered. It had been in Benares, during his rotation through the cultural exchange program in college.

There had been an old Indian holy man who had held vigil near one of the purification plants that serviced the sacred Ganges. In the mornings when he had gone jogging, Copeland had seen the man swaying in the early rays of the sun. The old man was, according to the Indian student who jogged with Copeland, the Highest of the High, in total communion with the Cosmic All. He spoke to God, the student had said gravely.

The look on Ishida's face was the same as that worn by the Benarian holy man.

"I *am* sorry, Commander; I cannot accept your terms. Please withdraw your threat and let us reason together."

"Mister, you have two minutes to put out your connector. In two minutes, if my scanners don't show the gamp ready for link up, I will disable your city's starboard siphon."

Nausori shook his head sadly. "Colonel."

Fiske cleared his throat. "Commander Montgomery, this is Colonel Martin Moses Fiske, Corporate Republic of Ocean-ica. As far as I know, I am the ranking officer left in my force. I feel compelled to warn you that we are not without defenses. If you persist in your threats, we will be forced to use them."

Montgomery's laugh bordered on the maniacal. "Defenses, you say? Colonel, if you are indeed a military man, then you know that the *Townsend* mounts enough nuclear and non-nuclear weaponry to clean all the clocks in China. You are a civilian vessel and, save for shark fields and small arms, bare naked. You cannot bluff me, sir."

Fiske looked at Nausori. Both men slowly turned their gazes upon Patricia Ishida. "I'm sorry," Nausori said.

Fiske sighed. "Dear God. Cassandra. Tell Baby to do it."

Cassandra's link with Baby was strong, more so than usual. Baby was in fine fettle and very much enjoying the new game.

*Baby, it's time to scramble the circuits.*

OH, SURE, CASSANDRA. CAN I DO IT NOW?

*Yes, you can do it now.*

OKAY.

Copeland saw the others turn to look behind him. He turned also, and became aware of a small gray form on a holoproj image, floating in an enhanced frame. The threatening submarine, had to be. As he watched, it began to move. The bow rose, and kept rising until the warship seemed to be standing on its stern. The movement continued until the ship was upside down. Nausori muted the comline to quell the sudden burst of shouts and screams that came over it.

For a few seconds, nothing further happened. Then, suddenly, a blast of air came from amidships, a massive eruption of bubbles, followed by darker fluid—oil or coolant, a small part of Copeland's mind not frozen by horror whispered—and a *twisting* motion of the sub. Copeland stared, transfixed. It was as if someone had overridden all the safeties and blown the hatches. Copeland turned away from the holoproj to look at Ishida. He knew, then, what had happened. Ishida had done it, she and the AI together, somehow. Her face had lost the serene expression of the Indian holy man, however. Now it was tracked with tears.

He spun back to watch the sub. That it was dying was obvious; a rent had appeared in the hull, and the edges flared inward under pressure as the air within gave up the fight and fled toward the atmosphere so far above. Copeland watched in awe and horror as HMS *Townsend* went in a matter of minutes from being one of the most powerful weapons ever built to a dead hulk, sinking from sight to the bottom of the ocean.

DID I DO GOOD, CASSANDRA?
*You did fine, Baby. Just fine.*
THEN WHY ARE YOU CRYING?

Copeland walked down the corridor next to Michelle Li Sung. "Why me?" he asked. "Why did you need me in here? I'm not military, and my scientific background wasn't useful."

Sung's voice was even, very controlled. "Simple propaganda, doctor. You are chair of the Science Committee. The scientists need to know of the ship's . . . defense capabilities."

"*Why*, damnit?"

Sung smiled rather enigmatically. "Don't pretend to be naive, Dr. Copeland. You know as well as I that this city is the largest collection of people left alive on Earth. Sooner or later, somebody is going to decide that they don't like the way things are being run; before that happens, dissenters need to know that the people in charge have teeth."

Copeland kept his mouth shut. He wasn't pretending to be

naive; he *was* naive. Such reasoning had never crossed his mind. He was a scientist, not an administrator. Did she think there was going to be some kind of revolution? Rioting in the streets and corridors, with biochemists and oceanographers waving battle flags and storming the CEO's quarters? Ridiculous!

Sung left him at an intersection, and Copeland walked on toward the elevators. Her idea had been silly, but the fact that she had had it was chilling. It meant that somebody in Admin was thinking about the possibility of dissatisfaction with the status quo. Seriously thinking about it, if they felt it necessary to show him the destruction of a killing machine as deadly as a nuclear submarine just so he would spread the word to others. That bothered him. So far as he knew, there were no radicals agitating to take over operation of *Mea Lana*. Sure, a medtech had asked some hard questions at the meeting where Nausori had laid out the new rules, but the man hadn't advocated anything other than a difference of opinion. They could not be worried about something as small as that.

Could they?

Patricia Ishida stared numbly at her image in the holo-mirror. *Murderer,* she thought.

She had just killed the complement of an entire ship, snuffed them out like pinching a candle wick. No; it had been easier even than that. Baby had done it for her. HMS *Townsend* had carried two hundred and sixteen sailors when it left port—she had checked the records—and she had sent them all to the bottom of the sea. Or maybe some of them were already dead, due to KYAGS or whatever. Say half of them? A generous estimate. That still left a hundred or more souls, at the least, on her conscience.

Her image stared at her, no expression on its neutral features. What could it say? That she had reduced the number of people left on Earth by a substantial percentage? In a world that could not afford the loss of any, she had wiped a hundred or more away without even having to speak a word—a thought had been enough.

Ishida turned away from the image, no longer able to bear looking at it. She was a killer; and, perhaps worse, she had made Baby her accessory. Baby did not know about death, not in the emotional way that she knew it. Baby had an intellect second to none, computing power far beyond the most brilliant human who had ever lived. But Baby could not understand the crime of men and women being crushed by tremendous water pressure, of human lungs screaming for air and finding none, of the terror of *knowing* you were going to drown...

She shuddered. She had always had a horror of drowning. When she was ten, she had very nearly died that way, doubled up with abdominal cramps at the bottom of her father's private pool. The old gardener had seen her go down and had dived in to save her. That was why she was an expert swimmer now, Ishida knew. She had forced herself to be at home in the water. She knew a dozen different strokes, could swim four kilometers at a stretch, and could float for hours. Napoleonic compensation, her therapist had called it later; overcoming her fear by hitting it head on. Now she loved the water, felt at home in it, relaxed and confident in her abilities.

Until today. Until she had caused scores of others to die that way. It had all come back in an instant—the empathy she felt for those on the submarine had washed over her like the sea had washed over them. She had *drowned* them!

The neurochem had not helped. Ishida had flooded her system with it, dumping hormones like sand on a fire, but it had not been enough. The medics thought they knew it all, but they were wrong. They were witch doctors, mumbling their arcane spells and waving their ju-ju rattles at the demons of the mind. There were thoughts stronger than their chemicals, feelings that even the most potent mind-control techniques could not affect. The fear and memories of a ten-year-old girl were proof against all the polypeptides science had devised to alter the mind.

She felt tears rolling silently down her cheeks. She would not be swimming today; not again for a long time, if ever. Not with the ghosts of those sailors before her.

She did want a shower, though. To wash away the stink of what she had done. To scrub away the guilt. But she knew the shower would only clean her body, not her soul.

Michelle Li Sung wasn't herself—at least, not to a casual glance. She wore an expensive skinmask to alter her features; she had lifts in her boots which added almost four centimeters to her height; a cap covered her hair, and her clothes were hidden under plain gray paper coveralls. She walked carefully, utilizing *ninjitsu* techniques designed to make her not so much invisible as inconspicuous. Her mission demanded that no one associate her with it.

Things were changing aboard *Mea Lana;* anyone could sense that. The *Kapu,* the laws, were reforming. She had been content with her lot, but only a fool stayed in a house built on sand. Sung was looking for a new foundation, and woe betide any and all who got in her way.

It was mid-shift, and the corridor she walked was mostly deserted. She skirted the edge of the oxy pumping section and turned into a hallway leading to the port personal living cubicles. A child drawing designs on the floor with chalk smiled up at her, and Sung smiled back. Children noticed things that adults did not; the key to remaining anonymous around children was to do nothing special to stick in their memories. I saw a lady, the child might say. Just a lady. If Sung had scowled or done something else inappropriate, the child might remember more. As it was, "just a lady" was no help to anyone.

Sung smiled again, this time to herself. Of course, if it came to that, there was really no problem: she was the head of *Mea Lana's* police force, after all, and ultimately in charge of any investigation that might result from what she planned to do. No one would know she had been responsible—until it was too late.

# 16

"You need a vacation," Ernie Teio had told Copeland, "if only for a half hour." And, somewhat reluctantly, Copeland had agreed.

He was glad he had, now. He bent and dragged his fingers through the sand. It felt like sand, warm and dry. "Amazing," he said.

Teio smiled. "Never been here before, huh?"

Copeland stood and looked at the small waves lapping at the shore. A breeze combed the palms around them, making the leaves dance with a gentle sound. It had been a long time since he had heard that particular rustle of tropical foliage. A very long time.

He took a deep breath, feeling a weight he had not known he had borne on his shoulders lessen slightly. He turned and smiled at the genetics expert. "No. I kept intending to; Peach used to ask me to go with her. But there never seemed to be time . . ."

He felt guilty as he thought of Peach. He had not talked to her in almost a week, and he was somewhat worried about her. She had been increasingly depressed and moody over the past month. He told himself, not for the first time or even the hundredth, that he would spend more time with her. But there were so many new duties. He had planned to call her this morning, but there had been the filters to check for KYAGS . . .

"How do they do this?" he asked Teio.

Teio squatted and picked up a sea shell. He straightened and rubbed his thumb over the smooth surface, then tossed it into the water of Keone'ele Cove. The shell splashed and sent ripples across the surface. "Not my field, really," he said. "I understand that, in addition to all the mechanical bells and whistles—the holoproj background, the tactile and sensory illusions—they use tight beam neurocasts to stimulate memories and sensations directly. That's what lets you *believe* you're really wading, or climbing on a rock, or whatever. Theoretically, with enough power and finesse to the 'cast, this could actually *be* real—in that your mind couldn't tell the difference. Dial up a jungle, and if a tiger jumped you, you'd be dead." He shook his head. "It's magic."

Copeland nodded. "What's the name of this one?"

"Pu'uhonua O Honaunau—the Place of Refuge. On the Big Island, near Kona."

Copeland turned and looked at the stone houses and high wall, the latter made of what looked to be black volcanic rock. Truly amazing; the sights, sounds, even the smell of salt and greenry were all remarkably reproduced. Nothing shimmered or wavered or otherwise gave it away as an illusion. How, he asked himself, could a civilization that could produce something like this have done what it did to itself?

"I used to come here a lot," Teio said, interrupting Copeland's bitter thought. "Expensive, but worth it. Now, I don't come so often."

Money. That was another convention they had been more or less holding to since the war. Habit was the only reason—what value did money have now?

As if reading his mind, Teio said, "It's not the expense. It's the time. There used to be a lot of vacant slots for the World Room. Now, this place is busy every shift. You have to reserve it a week in advance, and only for a thirty-minute maximum. Right after things got . . . bad, there were people who'd come in here and stay for days."

"I can understand that."

Overhead a gull dipped and soared, emitting an occasional keening cry as it searched for prey beneath the cove's smooth surface. "Come on," Teio said. "I'll show you the Chief's burial ground."

They started across the warm sand. Teio had removed his shoes, and the older man decided to do the same. Might as well get the most out of this, after all.

"What do you think about what I told you?" he asked Teio.

Teio stepped over a fallen palm trunk. "I think what Sung said is true. Admin only controls the city because the citizens allow it, like in any society. There's no army here, unless you count Fiske, and not enough police to control any real unrest. Historically, scientists aren't political activists, but they have been troublemakers now and then. I think Nausori's just covering his bases."

Copeland felt overly warm. He untabbed his shirt and started to remove it, then paused. "Can I get a sunburn here?"

Teio shook his head. "The UV in the light is controlled. You can tan, but you won't burn. We've improved on nature." His mouth tightened after this last, and Copeland knew that the irony of Teio's statement had struck him.

"Anyway," the geneticist continued after a moment, "I wouldn't worry too much about it. Nausori is better qualified to decide on policy than anybody else, after all."

Copeland could not argue with that—but somehow he still felt uneasy. He decided to change the subject.

"How are things going with the bioshift?"

They had reached the burial ground. Teio scratched at the back of one hand. "All the major adaptations are progressing faster than I had hoped. Tailored genetics have tallied with computer predictions, for the most part. Some minor glitches with the metatarsal elongations, but we've got those almost corrected. Webbing is complete all the way to the distal phalanges, and the sponge is more efficient than we had expected."

Copeland heard the undercurrent in Teio's voice. "But?"

"But I'm worried about Crane. He seems—unstable."

"How so?"

"I'm not sure. Depressed."

"Survivor's syndrome?"

Teio shook his head. "I don't think that's it. Part of it has to do with the loss of prestige. He expected a lot of fame with all this. Now—"

"Yeah."

"Anyway, he's been eager to get into the sea, so much so that it's impossible to keep him in the tanks for the tests we need."

Copeland leaned against a palm tree. "Well, that's understandable."

Teio turned suddenly to stare at him. "Is it? *I* don't understand! The open sea is dangerous! At this stage, the risk is too great for Crane to be out on his own! He'd be like a tadpole in a pond full of crawfish!"

Copeland was surprised at Teio's vehemence. Then it dawned on him suddenly what the real problem was: Ernie Teio saw only the experiment, not the man undergoing it. He was a genius when it came to biology, but not, evidently, in the area of human psychology.

"Ernie, what is the point of your experiment?"

Teio looked at Copeland as if the other man had suddenly gone insane. "What do you mean, 'What is the point?' I'm trying to develop a new bioformate—a man capable of living in the sea! A prototype to save what's left of the race!"

"Easy. I'm not attacking you. But listen to what you're saying. You want to develop a man who can live in the sea. Isn't it a necessary that the man *wants* to be there?"

"Well—yes, but not yet! There are still tests to be done!"

Copeland nodded. Teio couldn't see it. He was too close to his forest and there were trees in the way. Everything he had was tied up in Crane; if something happened to the amphibian, a big part of Teio's life would be destroyed. There was no sense trying to get him to see it from Crane's point of view.

Copeland watched the gull circle overhead for a moment, then closed his eyes and enjoyed the sun on his body. He would come here again, definitely. With Peach. Yes. With Peach.

The man lay unconscious on the bed, deep in a drugged slumber. He wasn't bad-looking, though not to Sung's taste; tall and well-built, with short, brown hair, blue eyes, and a cleft chin. More guts than brains, too. Even after she had darted him, Jerzy LeBahn had kept coming. As fast as the spetsdöd's paralytic chem had worked, he had had time for one good rush. She had been impressed. He had moved pretty well for his height and weight. It took a lot of skill to overcome that much bulk moving that fast. His record didn't show any formal martial arts' training, but there was formal and then there was street school. One thing Sung was fairly sure of—Jerzy LeBahn had not always been a medtech.

Sung turned away from the sleeping man and moved to the locked door. She inserted a slim rectangle of plastic into the lock's scanner. The computer chips embedded in the lucite commanded the door to open, which it did with a small click. Sung stepped into the hall, where one of her men leaned against the wall across from the doorway. He pushed away from his relaxed pose and came to a kind of attention.

"He should be out for another hour," she said. "Call me when he comes to."

"Copy, Chief."

Sung strode away, affecting an athletic bounce to her walk. She had recently sparred with the man watching the door and beaten him in a freestyle match. She wanted him to remember how good she was. Reminding others of your power was important.

Around the bend in the corridor, she relaxed into her normal walk. she had to see Nausori and tell him of the successful kidnapping—though she had to admit that the CEO's plan didn't impress her. LeBahn was a potential troublemaker, and she had pointed that out to Nausori quickly. But trying to re-educate him with drugs and propaganda into a loyal soldier was, in her view, more trouble than it was worth. Easier to lean on him and tell him what could happen to him if he didn't keep his mouth shut. The fish are always hungry, Jerzy . . .

But then again, maybe not. You couldn't tell about people; he might be the kind of man who would up and charge a shark just for the hell of it. That kind of man could be useful if he were induced to join your side. Sung remembered how he had rushed her, when he had to know he was going to be tranked in five seconds. Sometimes more guts than brains could be the right combination.

In the thick of the lunch crowd, Jason Nausori was sure Betsy could not see him following her. He had dialed up a text on investigative techniques, not wanting to ask Sung about how to tail someone. The instructions had been clear enough: blend in, use available cover, try not to look suspicious. Of course, it was more difficult if the subject knew the shadower, but enough caution could compensate for that.

As Betsy crossed the central courtyard in the Main Dome, Nausori paused behind a refuse container and pretended to fetch something he had dropped. When she turned into the corridor leading to the near starboard elevator bank, he stopped and became very interested in a window display.

When the trull entered the muscleman's cube, Nausori had to stop and take a grip on his anger. He had known where she was going, it had been no surprise . . . but, damnit, how *could* she? Hearing it from Sung had been one thing, but seeing it himself was something else. By now, the slut would be with that ape, touching him, rubbing those obscene muscles, opening herself to him—

Nausori found himself shaking as he leaned against the corridor wall. Straighten up, man! You're allowing this whore to control you! Don't lose it!

He took a deep breath and managed to stop the involuntary shiver that had gripped him. Any more of this and the blinding pain in his neck muscles would start, creeping gradually to encompass his whole scalp, and then he would be useless for the rest of the day. Stop feeling sorry for yourself, Jason. You can do something about this. You have power! You don't need her, you can have a dozen women, *two* dozen who would be happy to share your bed!

*But I love her,* came a small voice from deep within him.

No!

*Yes.*

He leaned back against the wall again, feeling weak. Well.

There it was. He hadn't wanted to admit that to himself, but Jason Nausori was not a man for self-deception. Maybe it wasn't true. What was love, anyway? But there was *something* there, something that made him feel like jelly when he thought about her.

All right. So it's her you want. It's a problem, because she wants *him*. You know how to deal with problems, Jason.

He wore a tight grin when he moved away from the wall and squared his shoulders. The ape was a problem. Okay, fine. The ape would be—solved.

Peach McGinnis had always made good marks in Psych. She had been a bright girl, all her teachers had always said so. And then there was Doug; he was certainly impressed with her capabilities. She smiled at the thought of Doug, then felt the brief happiness fade. The depression flowed over her once again like cold oil, coating her, suffocating her.

Psych. Yes, that was what she had been thinking about. She was bright, all her teachers had always said so, and so she knew that her self-diagnosis was true. She was depressed, she knew the symptoms. She could list them, if anybody wanted to know. If there had been anybody left to want to know. But all her teachers were dead, except Doug.

Rickie was dead. Her mother and father were dead. Her best friend Susan, the first girl in primary ed to get a tattoo, she was dead, too. All dead; nobody was left except her.

That was sad.

Because she was so bright, Peach knew all about suicide, and how to do it. Of course, it was a little hard to keep it all straight at the moment, since the drugs seemed to be gaining on her again, but that was okay. The urge to get up and run around and straighten things would pass in a minute, and then she could get back to thinking about what she needed to think about.

Doug had tried to keep her from getting the drugs. He wasn't much fun anymore; he wouldn't sleep with her, all he wanted to do was cuddle her. He acted as if she were a child. She knew the real reason he wouldn't sleep with her. He hated her for being the only one left alive. Well. Okay.

Because she was so bright, and because the urge to get up and run around straightening things was passing, like she knew it would, she remembered.

Suicides usually pick just one way to do it. Even if they fucked it up and didn't do it right, they would try it the same way almost every time. It showed a lack of foresight, she thought. A bright person would figure a way to get it right the first time. One method might not work, but two methods surely would.

She felt something pressing into her back, between her skin and the couch, and shifted so that she could reach whatever it was.

Ah. The blister of tabs. She held the plastic packet of sleeping tablets up and looked carefully at the little pills, each in its own little nest. But there was something else...

Yes, there it was. The little calibrated laser cutter, of the kind surgeons used to splice muscle tissue. It felt solid in her hand, as big as a plastic drink can, but capable of making a puncture smaller than that of a pin. And very, very sharp.

The sound of running water intruded into her thoughts, then. What—?

Oh, yes. The tub. The tub full of nice, hot water. It must be almost full by now...

Peach stood, a little shakily, and walked to the fresher. Carefully she set the cutter on the floor next to the tub and bent to shut off the flow of water. She trailed her fingers in the water. The temperature was just right.

Holding the blister clear of the water, she stepped into the tub and sank down into the wonderful warmth. She peeled the tabs out, one by one, being careful not to drop them. One, two, three—there were a lot of them. Twenty or thirty, at least. It took a while, but she finally managed to liberate them all. She only dropped two of them.

Peach smiled and put all the tablets into her mouth. Then felt a moment of panic. She'd forgotten to bring something to drink!

She smiled around the mouthful of bitter tabs. Silly! There was water all around her! Someone as bright as she should have seen that right away.

She leaned back and sank beneath the surface. She was careful to only open her mouth a crack, so the tabs wouldn't float out. There. How easy that was.

And here was the cutter, and such a bright light it made! Not as bright as she was, but hard and shiny red, rolling back on itself at the very tip to form a tiny point.

There was a right way and a lot of wrong ways to do this. Not the wrists; that was the wrong way. Anyone with any knowledge of anatomy would know that. Other places were much better.

It only took a second. She knew exactly where to cut. She was so very bright; all her teachers had always said so. All her dead teachers. And it didn't hurt, and look at the pretty clouds the blood made in the warm water. So pretty.

So pretty.

# 17

In her cube, alone in her bed, Patricia Ishida dreamed . . .

Cassandra stood in a place she had never before seen—a temple of some kind, it seemed. She could smell incense, sharp and pungent, and gauzy clouds of smoke hung in the still air, unstirred by even the faintest breeze. To her left a carved figure was set into the wall, a bas-relief of some horned and angry god. Instead of clothing, however, the god wore a mesh of wiring and semiconductors, plaited with circuit boards and chips.

To her right Cassandra saw a floor-to-ceiling sheet of colored glass—red, blue and yellow shards joined in a jumbled mosaic of primary intensities, flooding the vast room with an electric rainbow.

All was silent at first; then, from behind her, the voice of a god rumbled.

TELL ME THAT WHICH YOU SEEK.

Cassandra turned to face the thunder. The wall shimmered, devoid of decoration.

*Who are you?*

TELL ME THAT WHICH YOU SEEK, it commanded again.

She felt the call to the roots of her being, felt it thrum with power within her marrow. She could not bring herself to answer. *I—I—I—*

TELL ME!

*I don't know!*

THEN BEHOLD!

The wall shimmered and flared like a photon bomb, and in its burning afterimage, Cassandra saw—

—A palace chamber, vast and richly appointed, with a table laden with food and drink. A dozen men and women sat around the table, drinking and laughing, dressed in finery, obviously to the manor born. The scene shifted suddenly, and she saw—

—A dozen peasants, standing in a pouring rain, looking at the palace from behind a high iron fence. One of the peasants picked up a stone from the muddy ground and cast it over the fence. The rock sailed, impossibly high, arching like a powered missile, to smash against the leaded glass of a window. The window shattered as if the rock were a bomb, and—

—Inside, the laughing people grew suddenly grim. They stood, drawing hidden swords, and stalked to the door. They opened the thick oak portal to the incoming rain and—

—The peasants brandished sticks and gathered more stones. They began to climb the iron fence to face the aristocrats leaving the safety of their palace. The two groups were equally matched in numbers, but the palace-dwellers were better armed and held the higher and safer ground . . .

The images swirled and vanished, leaving the bare wall. YOU HAVE SEEN, the god said, ENOUGH.

*What does it mean?* Cassandra asked, frantic to understand the meaning behind the vision. But there was no answer. Then, after a moment, the temple began to shudder and tumble down around her . . .

Patricia Ishida awoke with the sudden and certain knowledge that it had been more than merely a dream. She felt the familiar twinge of radiopathy within her head, the same vibration she felt each time she touched an AI. It was as if one of the intelligences had somehow bypassed the impassible wards that protected her from unwanted intrusion and forced the vision into her mind. Even as she thought it, she knew it was true. And the lingering feeling attached to the knowledge said just as surely that it had been Baby who had touched her.

• • •

Copeland was in the cafeteria on the science level, trying to decide between swordfish soup or plankton patties for lunch when he saw Martin Fiske sitting alone at a two-place table, drinking coffee and staring at nothing.

Copeland decided on the swordfish and punched in his order. The dispenser chimed and delivered the hot soup. He put the plastic container onto his tray, collected a cup of coffee and walked to Fiske's table.

"How are you, Colonel?"

Fiske looked up. He did not seem surprised. "Copeland. Have a seat."

"Thanks."

Fiske looked at Copeland's tray. "You got the fish. Good. The plankton is a little runny today. Too much tofu."

"Sometimes it's hard to tell the difference," Copeland said. He peeled the container's top back, releasing fragrant steam. It smelled good, anyway.

Abruptly, Fiske said, "We won't be running into any more subs."

Copeland spooned a mouthful of the soup. Not bad, really. He'd eaten worse. "What makes you say that?"

Fiske toyed with his coffee cup, turning it in small circles on the plastic table top. "We sent the recording of the . . . event out on a broadwave cast. Anybody still around and bothering to listen would have heard it."

"I don't understand. You want it *known* that we destroyed a submarine? Suppose there's another Brit vessel cruising within SLBM range? They might decide to lob something our way."

Fiske shook his head. "We added a warning. They initiated an attack and that is what happened to them. The same thing would happen to anybody else."

"Is it a bluff?"

"No, sir, it is not."

"The AI has that kind of capability?"

"I am not at liberty to reveal details, doctor, but it is not a bluff."

Copeland laughed, and Fiske looked startled. "Something funny, Dr. Copeland?"

"Who is there left to keep secrets from, Colonel? Who am I going to tell?"

Fiske had the grace to look slightly embarrassed.

"Unless," Copeland continued in a more serious tone, "you

are somehow trying to tell me something."

"I don't take your meaning."

Copeland shrugged. "I had an interesting conversation with Sung. She indicated that I was invited to your . . . demonstration because that same kind of hint was supposed to be conveyed to the scientists onboard. 'Don't tread on me,' is that the message?"

"I beg your pardon?"

"Could Nausori really be worried about the pocket computer cadre on this level?"

"I am certain I don't know what you're talking about. You must have misunderstood Chief Sung."

Copeland looked appraisingly at Fiske. Normally, the Colonel was tight-assed, but this was formal even for him. Something was going on, and maybe it would be better not to push it right now. "Okay, Colonel. Whatever you say."

Fiske nodded. "If you'll excuse me, Dr. Copeland, I have to get back to work."

Copeland watched the man thread his way through the tables toward the exit. Yes, something funny was definitely going on. Sung had planted a seed with her comments, and Copeland was beginning to see shoots of a weed he didn't recognize. And he didn't like it. Not at all.

"I'm just worried about your safety, Jonathan!"

"Come *on*, Ernie! What do you think is going to happen? I'll get eaten by an Orcas? I've got the goddamned gill, the dolphins are all over me like barnacles on a wreck, we're in constant radio contact, what else do you need?"

Teio raised his hands helplessly and turned away, apparently unable to speak. Crane stared at his back and thought: Fool human!

That thought brought him up short. Abruptly, he turned away from Teio and shuffled barefoot toward the lab's holomirror. It was a shuffle because he still wasn't comfortable with his feet. The metatarsals had elongated, driven by strut-incremental osteohormone pumps; the skin, muscles, nerves and blood vessels had also felt the prod of complex chemical baths, making his feet neoplastic mutations: he very nearly had fins now instead of feet. The webbing between his toes matched that between his fingers. No man or woman could swim with him now—the fastest prewar champion chasing him would look like a turtle trying to catch a dolphin.

"On," he commanded the mirror.

The holoprojic image shimmered into life.

"Ventral and dorsal, split and hold."

The air above the image flashed a sign: REPEAT, PLEASE.

Crane felt a stab of raw anger. The goddamned machine had been asking him that all week! True, his voice was different, but not *that* different!

Crane took a deep breath and let it out slowly, then repeated the command.

TURN, PLEASE.

He obeyed the request. The image split, and he was presented with a front and back view of himself. He regarded it carefully.

Yes, the feet and hands were coming along. Crane looked at the rest of his body. He wore only a groin strap these days; the secretions of his skin tended to oil up any clothing he bothered to wear. It gleamed on him now, that rich integumental fluid, giving him an almost metallic sheen. His epidermis had thickened, as had the hair on his body, but it didn't seem very different to him. The flotation sacs were flat now, only small bulges at his hips and shoulders, lacking the air that gave them symmetrical curves when inflated underwater. The lens implants gave his eyes a brighter shine that matched his skin, although his vision was no longer as sharp in air as it now was underwater. The sphincter implants in his penis, nostrils and ears did not show, and they weren't really needed all the time, but Teio was being very careful. Like always.

He was amazed at his new muscle tone. Of course, the myohormones helped, as did the tailored steroids, but he had also done a lot of swimming to earn those tight curves. His legs and buttocks were now thicker and harder than he had believed possible, and his shoulders, chest and lats were very well developed. He smiled, remembering an old flat vid he had seen once: *The Creature from the Black Lagoon.* He could be my cousin, Crane thought. If he had ever really worked out, that is.

From behind him, Teio said, "I'm sorry, Jonathan. I *must* insist that you stay in the ship for now."

Crane did not turn away from his double image. His faint smile stayed in place. "All right, Ernie."

•   •   •

Once in the breathing inset, Crane lost no time. Before the monitor activated the camera, he sent one of the dolphins to nudge the videocam slightly; that left a wide corridor that was now hidden from Ernie's sight. For an hour after that, Crane swam or floated where he could be viewed, strapped securely into the external gill and murmuring into his throat pickup. After he figured the Lab Telemetry monitor was getting bored, he drifted into the new dead visual zone.

"Crane, where are you?"

"Right here, LT. Got something in your eye?"

"That's affirmative. Our cam isn't getting a full scan."

"I'm no tech, don't ask me to fix it." Crane sculled with one hand, propelling himself slowly back into view.

"Okay, we've got you again. No problem. We'll get a tech to fix it next watch. Just stick around where we can see you."

"Like hell I will, mate. You think I'm going to float in one spot for six hours because you don't take care of your gear?"

"Doctor Teio won't be happy if we—"

"Then let Doctor Teio come out here and fix the cam."

While he wouldn't put it past Ernie to do just that, Crane knew that the man was busy giving a lecture to his advanced genetics class for the next three hours. "Listen, if I get into any trouble, I'll yell for help. My com is working, isn't it?"

"Well, yeah . . ." The monitor didn't sound happy.

"Okay, then. Don't sweat it."

For the next ten minutes, Crane drifted in and out of the tech's sight. Then he made his move. He removed the external gill, hung it out of sight on a mooring hook, and swam to the dolphin gate, which was inset in the anodized aluminum mesh at the far end of the dimple. He made his escape into the sea clutching the dorsal fin of a bottlenose.

The *sea!* It felt—almost orgasmic! *This* was where he belonged. He released the dolphin and stroked his way through the water, glorying in the feel of being truly free at last. He felt the slight tingle of the salt-repelling charge as he skimmed over the hull of the frag next to the breathing inset. He was flying, able to soar like an eagle in this world, breathing the water, a part of something so vast that all the land on Earth was as nothing to it. If he had had to wear the full telemetry gear, this would be impossible, because they would know where he was. But he had convinced Ernie that he needed to practice swimming without it. If he could leave the gill behind, he'd be glad to wear the head clamp and body casters, he'd said. And just as Crane knew he would, Teio refused.

For the next hour, he would be master of his world; he could stay out that long before the monitor got nervous. For the next hour, he would be free.

Retelimba was happy. Sure, he had a shit job this shift, watching the heavy metal centrifuge churn the filtered slurry, but it wasn't so bad, not with thoughts of Betsy to keep him company. Take it to the bank, bruddah, she was some woman.

The job wasn't hard, it was mostly boring. He had to clear the centrifuge when it ate something too big to digest, which was rarely. Sometimes the slurry siphons sucked up a piece of something that ought not to be there. He had pulled out a chunk of refined steel once. They had done a spec on it uplevels and found it was a registration plate for a ship; it must have massed six, eight kilos. It had been flat before the siphons mashed it, but what had it been doing in the water? They hadn't been anywhere close to bottom and that kind of steel just didn't float around. It had waked up a bunch of people when it had started clanging in the blades; sounded like somebody was murdering a generator with a machine gun.

Retelimba grinned at the memory. Such mysteries didn't happen often. Mostly it was sit back and replay Go games in his head and doze when the soup-in-charge wasn't around. The automatics took care of anything short of real unusual, and the tender robot was set to call him if it found something it couldn't handle. Dull stuff.

The tender's alarm began to sound. There must be a god just to watch for such thoughts, Retelimba thought sourly. The short rings weren't loud, but were designed to get attention. He raised himself easily from the hard chair—it was supposed to prevent sleep, but it failed mostly—and went to see what had panicked the robot. The reads were projected from a flatscreen, and one of the numbers was flashing—

He blinked. The pressure was dropping, and fast! And the heat inside the centrifuge was going up almost as fast! He watched, waiting to see the heat arrestors kick in and damp out the temp rise before anything—wait a minute—the arrestor lights were out!

The bodybuilder punched the test circuit control. Lights blinked, and the pressure and temp reads continued to flash danger halos, but the arrestors didn't show anything. The centrifuge had developed a new whine, higher and more frantic than normal.

Retelimba touched his compatch. "Listen up, Systems! This is Retelimba at Cent Seven! I got internal fluid pressure at three hundred and going down like shit in a toilet! Internal heat is at six hundred and rising. The arrestors are dead. We got a *bomb* building here, bruddah!"

The soup came on quickly. "Shut that sucker down, stat!"

Good move. Retelimba flipped the pressure control covers up and thumbed the two switches at the same time.

The whine should have faded as the pump died. Instead the sound grew stronger, and the pump kept going.

Muthafucka! "Got no response here!"

"What? What you mean, 'no response!'"

"Just that, dickhead! I'm leaning both thumbs on 'em and they ain't cutting it off. Better slap the override, soup."

"I hear you, bruddah. Maybe you better move."

"Yeah." Retelimba backed away from the now-screaming machine. If they didn't shut the thing down quick, it was gonna throw a bearing, maybe a blade. Could get real nasty to anywhere close.

The soup's voice held a note of real panic, now. "Limo, the override don't work. Move your ass!"

Retelimba didn't need to hear any more. He turned and sprinted. He'd seen an extrusion press blow a die once. The 20,000-ton press had jammed and the soup there had leaned over the barrier to see what it was. The die had exploded and a chunk of metal had taken the soup's head clean off like a knife slicing a carrot.

He needed some cover, *fast*. The expanded metal dividers might as well be paper when that machine went. A slurry pipe would stop damned near anything, but there wasn't any way to get completely behind one, they ran parallel to the floor and were not quite big enough. Just ahead was the suspension holding tank. It was fairly thin aluminum, but full of liquid. If he could get to the other side, he'd be okay...

The whine of the centrifuge pump stopped abruptly. That meant the blades had either melted or locked, and either way was bad. Retelimba dived, rolled, and scrambled behind the tank.

The centrifuge exploded, and a hard rain of metal sleeted

against everything around it. The shrapnel hit the holding tank like bullets, punching through the aluminum and into the three meters of water between the back wall and the front. The noise was unbelievable, and two bulges appeared in his side of the tank not six centimeters from him as he watched.

Sirens began blasting, and Retelimba peered around the curve of the tank, making sure he didn't jump out in time to catch something else going. He saw the gush of slurry pouring out onto the floor. He stood and worked at a slight muscle pull in his left hamstring. Two seconds slower and he'd have been lucky to make it out of there alive.

So much for a dull shift . . .

# 18

"Dr. Copeland?"

Copeland looked up from the pile of hard copy on his desk. A young man stood in the doorway of his office, holding a sealed plastic parcel half the size of a shoebox. "Yes?"

"This is for you. I'll need your signature."

"What is it?"

The young man shrugged. He was maybe twenty, and Copeland didn't know him. Which was not odd, considering the population of *Mea Lana*. He extended a flatscreen and light pen. Copeland scrawled his signature onto the screen of the remote terminal and handed it back to the messenger, who nodded and departed.

There was an official seal closing the plastic bag, marked with the coroner's insignia and the Admin glyph. Copeland used his thumbnail to slit the seals. Inside was a small rack of six recording spheres, stainless steel marbles, each embedded in a socket of soft rubber. Under each one was an identifying tag. Three were marked as technical communication texts; one was listed as Kidvid Classics; another as a history ball. The final sphere was marked "Religious Documentaries, Including a History of Christian Movements in the 21st Century."

A badly printed form note was folded in one corner of the box. It read:

"The enclosed material has been willed to you from the estate of *G. R. HOLLEY*. Please verify that the enclosed contents are as listed."

The note went on to list the titles of the holographic spheres. It was signed by the coroner and countersigned by someone in Administration. Copeland stared at the spheres and felt a stab of pain when he thought of Captain Video. He almost stuck it away in a drawer of his desk, unwilling to deal with the memories it would surely bring back, but another thought occurred to him: Why had Holley left these to him? He had no interest in communications, per se; the animated vids were amusing, but he had never been a fan; and Holley had been about as religious as a sea urchin. His digs at figureheads of organized religion had been constant. Copeland remembered the pornoproj and the sputtering minister. Was there something else about Holley that the man had kept hidden?

Curious, Copeland popped the last holosphere into his reader. The ball clicked into place, and the air above his desk coalesced into the features of a sharp-faced man lecturing.

"The study of religion and its significance, origins and many and disparate forms, consists of two aspects: psychological and historical bases and the structure and dynamics of the religious experience itself . . ."

Copeland watched for a minute. The speaker was, at best, boring. His subject was as dry as solid carbon dioxide, his delivery wooden, his enthusiasm bordering on catatonia. Copeland leaned back in his chair, at a loss for what to make of it. He could no more imagine Captain Video being interested in this than he could believe in perpetual motion. Five minutes of it would put a wirehead to sleep; ten would probably zombify a muscle dancer on amphetamines. The scientist shook his head in bafflement and reached for the shutoff control.

At that moment the lecturer vanished, to be replaced by George Holley.

"Yo, Doug. Sorry to make you sit through that, but if you managed it—well, here you are. One could get real existential here—I mean, I'm here now, but when you see this I won't be, and I dunno where you'll be or if you *will* see this."

Holley smiled and touched a control on his panel. The closeup of him grew a little smaller as the holocam pulled back slightly.

"I'm sure you're wondering why I went to all this trouble. It's because I have something to show you that I don't want Admin to know about. I'm pretty sure they will at least glance at the spheres I've tagged for you, and so I slipped this into the most boring one. I figure you know—or knew—me well enough to know I wouldn't be caught dead—excuse the pun —with a sphere like this, and that you'd be curious enough to check it out."

The holoimage looked uncomfortable. "Look, I'm sorry I iced out on you. I won't go into the reasons—I think you know better than anyone else left alive why I'm going to— why I killed myself. But I figure that I can at least try to make things a little better for you poor suckers who stick around.

"Just a couple of hours ago, I tapped a conversation between Nausori and his boss back in Papeete. Incidentally, all those recordings I made of private conversations are stored in the mainframe. Access code is 'Boop-boop-a-doop.' As I was saying, it seems that Nausori okayed the installation of substandard parts in a number of cases to get *Mea Lana* underway on schedule, including the shielding on the tertiary backup reactor. This will probably never come to light, but it started me thinking—even in the best possible scenario, the city's gonna need power. You're not at Stage Three yet, and you can't get there on your own. So where do you get the energy to bootstrap yourselves?"

Holley made a wan attempt at a grin. "Well, to quote Bullwinkle J. Moose: 'Hey, Rocky! Watch me pull a rabbit outta my hat!'" He moved one hand over the control board and his image was abruptly replaced by a long-range seasat view. Holley's voice came on over the orbital shot of blue ocean and fleecy clouds. "This is coming up on the South China Sea, a few klicks east of Nha-Trang, Viet Nam. We'll drop down in a few seconds for a tighter angle. What you'll be looking at is one of the wave-action–thermocline power generation plants. I dunno how soon you'll get to see this, but as of a week before I holoed this video, this plant was still producing power on the order of nine hundred megawatts—one of the biggies. In case you're wondering how I know that, I'm using both an American KH-17 Big Bird reconsat and an old Teal Ruby launched out of Ireland. I can't tell if the station is automatic or inhabited; they aren't microwaving power out, and they aren't using radiocom, I checked that with the last of the French Rhyolite sats. But the station is on line. Think about that for a minute, Doug."

The picture zoomed in so fast it made Copeland dizzy. He saw the shape of the surface dome swim into focus. Nearly all of the station was underwater, some of it visible, but mostly hidden. There was no movement except waves. A running readout of longitude and latitude to the left of the image gave the location. Then the picture shifted back to Holley.

Copeland stared at the holoproj of his dead friend. Power! Nearly all of the generating stations at sea had been destroyed during the war. Military failsafes had melted them to slag to keep the "enemy" from taking them. But if this station were still operable and if they could get to it safely, it might be possible to get the power needed to make *Mea Lana* self-sufficient.

Holley was offering them a way to save the human race.

"Yeah, I bet you've figured it out by now," Holley said. Again he grinned; again it quickly faded. "But let me warn you, Doug: you're politically naive; you don't understand about how human power works. You can't just march into Nausori's office and demand to go plug into the Viet battery. You might think it's obvious, that there's no choice, but it ain't that way, Doug. Be careful." Holley looked down for a long moment, then glanced back up at the holocam and said, in a comic, stuttering voice, "Th-th-that's all, folks!" Then, seriously, "Good-bye, Doug. Good luck."

The image was replaced again by the dour-faced lecturer on religion. Copeland shut the reader off, and sat in the quiet of his office, trying to cope with what he had just seen. Captain Video had just reached back from his sea grave with a chance to save humanity. God, how he missed the man!

And he was right, Copeland knew. He had better be damned careful in revealing this information.

"Where were you, Jonathan?" Teio was angry, his voice tight and his face beginning to turn red and heat up. Crane kept his own face impassive. "Doing laps in the breathing inset, Ernie. Where else?"

"You were off vid for an hour and a half!"

"Don't blame me for your damned equipment failure!"

"The videocam was working fine—it had been moved."

"Maybe one of the dolphins bumped it accidentally."

"They know better. They've all been conditioned to avoid surveillance gear."

"Why don't you say what you mean, Ernie?"

Teio seemed to get a grip on himself. "I don't like it that you were out of sight for so long."

"Ernie, what do you want me to say? You sent the gill, I had my com working. What else could I do? You didn't expect me to hang in NB for six hours, did you?"

"No. And I didn't expect you to go—never mind."

"Go where, Ernie?"

Teio shook his head. "Never mind, I said. From now on, you will wear full telemetry gear when in the inset."

Crane shrugged. "All right." But he was thinking of how it had been to be outside, in the ocean. Of how one of the dolphins—he seemed to have almost a telepathic rapport with them, now—had brought him a fish. About how he had torn at the raw, still living flesh with his teeth, glorying in the taste of the blood and tissue. About how he had glided among the interlinked frags of the city, finding them like natural reefs, home to sea plants and animals that had somehow managed to nestle in all the hollows that the retardant paint had missed and the repel field didn't quite cover.

About how it had felt like coming home . . .

Michelle Li Sung methodically stroked the blade of the curved knife with the diamond rasp. The edge of the weapon was already sharp enough, but the action was a kind of meditation for her. When she was considering something deeply she often did some mechanical, repetitive act. And a knife could never be too sharp. You can always tell a person by the edge of their blade, her father used to say. Never trust a man or woman with a dull knife. And trust someone with a sharp one even less . . .

As she sat on her bed, alone in her cube, honing the shining edge over and over, she came to a decision. She wiped her knife and sheathed it at her hip, then stood. It was time to make sure that she was prepared for whatever might happen.

Sung went to the storage room. Normally there was an officer on duty, but since the war there had been a general slackening of certain procedures. She had deliberately allowed this one—like a chess player, Sung looked as far ahead in her moves as possible. The room was basically no more than a desk and terminal surrounded by locked storage cabinets. Most of the cabinets held office supplies, printing forms, record balls and the like. But one held something considerably more dangerous: the police armory.

Sung made certain the room's door was locked before she went to the weapons cabinet. There were two lock slots inset into the thick plastic wing doors. The city's builders had addressed Admin's concerns about a single person being able to get to the armament by using a system of double locks. These slots were set far apart, one on the hinge of each door, and had to be unlocked simultaneously to open the doors. That way, even if somebody had both sets of cardkeys, he or she would not be able to operate them. And there were only two official sets of keys: one set was locked in the bank's vault in the main dome, and the other set was split between the CEO and the Chief of Security.

Sung grinned as she removed two plastic rectangles, both the size of her little finger, from her tunic. She had owned a counterfeit of Nausori's cardkey since before the city had started its voyage. She had never expected to have to use it, but it had been second nature to prepare for any eventuality.

As for having to use both at once, that was ridiculously easy. Sung removed her right boot and sock and gripped one of the keys between her large and second toes. She balanced on her left foot midway between the lock slots and extended the second key with her left hand while she raised her right foot. For a woman trained in various martial arts, balancing on one foot while using the other in this manner was simple. One, two, and three . . . both keys slid into their slots at the same instant. One, two, and turn . . .

The locks clicked. Sung hopped back to avoid being hit by the doors as they swung open. She had done it in practice a dozen times before. Inside the cabinet, the small arms nestled neatly in their racks. Tasers, sonics, light wands and spetsdöds, nothing lethal, as per military and police regulations. Sung pulled a plastic box from her tunic and began to fill it with the weapons. There weren't many—only a dozen of each. Nobody expected anything to arise on the city that would require more than a pair of armed police officers to deal with, and there was more than enough firepower here to outfit her ten-person force and five-person reserve twice over. She filled the box, taking only the spetsdöds. There wasn't room enough for all the other weaponry, but those weren't nearly as effective. A spetsdöd fléchette slinger had five times the range of a taser or a subsonic vibrator. The spetsdöd was a small parallelogram that rode the back of the wearer's hand, its barrel extending the length and slightly past the tip of the index finger. The standard police darts loaded shocktox, a mild paralytic that knocked its victim into muscle spasm for fifteen minutes. It was a simple and effective device to use: point the finger, thereby completing a circuit within the barrel, and the dart went where you pointed. The shocktox was basically harmless; however, there were other loads available. Spasm, the military load, would put its victims into the stretch ward for six months of therapy before they could function again, and Asp darts carried a lethal bioengineered protein that brought death within three seconds.

Sung kept one of the spetsdöds out; she put this one into her tunic pocket. In her cube, hidden in a lock box under her couch, was a box of Asp darts she had bought on the black market before she had joined the domed city's police force. She finished loading the box, stepped back and closed the doors. The locks clicked and extruded the keys, which she removed. There was a storage tank of insugel in the office next to hers in which the stolen spetsdöds could be very nicely concealed; the gel wouldn't hurt the weapons and nobody would think to look for them there. If the time ever came when she needed to be armed, she wouldn't be lacking. Of the ten officers under her command, four were more loyal to her than to the force or the city, and two others were borderline. She had her troops and her guns; what would happen with both remained to be seen. But she was ready.

Nausori stood staring at the body on the bed. He shook his head in stunned disbelief. The fools! How could they have let it happen?

On the bed, the man who had been Jerzy LeBahn lay still and silent. He was never going to move again on his own. Sung wasn't there. Nausori would have liked her advice, but it had been his men who had blundered. His responsibility.

He turned away. It was the season for blunders. Jerzy was dead and no longer a direct threat, but his death would cause problems. On the other hand, that goddamned iron monkey was still alive. The rigged centrifuge had failed to take the muscle man with it when it blew, and Nausori's rage over that hadn't yet abated. Damn, why wasn't *anything* turning out the way it was supposed to?

"Dr. Nausori?"

The CEO turned toward the moron who had killed Jerzy.

"What do you want us to, uh, do now?"

"Get rid of the body, idiot. And try to be a little more careful." Nausori stalked from the room and toward his office. Betsy would be there, the whore, pretending, as she took care of the calls, that everything was the same between them. Well. She was going to be surprised when her slab of beef turned up fried. Whatever else happened, the iron monkey was a dead man. It was only a matter of time.

# 19

It wasn't Ernie Teio's job, but then again, it hadn't been anybody's job when the city began its voyage. Nobody had known that checking for a killer virus would be part of the ordinary. The procedure had been established for survival. Anything that came into the city from outside now was surveyed. That included the dolphins, the mineral slurry, algae and fish, everything. Even Jonathan Crane had been checked.

Teio stood at the entrance to the Aft Netlock, wrapped in the dank air and fishy odor that filled the fish processing chamber. Roller tables behind him were covered with scales, and blood spatters clung to hard-to-reach spots on the walls and floor. The cold of the room seemed to dig all the way to his very center.

Chang, the Chief of Seafood Production, stood in a grimy

coverall that might have once been white but which was now mottled gray. He kept wiping his hands with a rag as he talked.

"That machine you people put in, maybe it's broken?"

Teio moved to the densecris portal set into the lock's thick door and looked inside. Wrapped in the folds of the net, what amounted to probably a half ton of fish flopped in the now dry room. The netlocks had been a good idea, originally; sort of automated fishing boats, each one could cast a synlin net, gather in schools of fish located by sonar sophisticated enough to tell one species from another, and pull the resulting catch into the lock. It only remained for the processors to haul them inside, clean and pack them, and run them directly into food-lines or freezers. Very efficient. "Maybe," Teio replied. "We'll see."

He moved to the computer panel—itself spattered with fishy effluvia—set next to the lock door, and began to tap in a series of test codes. The detector installed in the lock, an instrument sensitive enough to spot ten parts per billion of its target microbe, ran through its series of checks. After a moment it chimed and showed the reply: NO MALFUNCTION—SYSTEMS FULLY OPERATIVE.

Teio sighed. KYAGS was a mammalian bug that had switched to avian carriers when it ran out of fur-bearers. It had not taken much imagination to guess its next choice of vectors after the birds had all died.

It was now in the fish.

Ernie touched his compatch. "Extee Operations, this is Teio, in the processing room of the Aft Netlock. I need a close-inspection robot dispatched to enter the lock from outside." He paused for a moment to look around the smelly room. "Better use an old one; you might not get it back." He didn't know how good the sterilization procedures were on the EVA robots.

The Extee op said, "Copy, Dr. Teio. One gunga din, coming up. He'll be on opchan six."

"Thank you."

Teio directed the routing computer to switch his communications to the operating channel. He established contact with the din and gave it directions on entering the lock. Then he waited, trying not to indulge in useless speculation until he had more data. KYAGS was in the fish—but which fish? That was the all-important question. And which fish had not been infected? That might well be as important—

The din sent a beep, indicating it had reached its destination. Ernie roused himself from his speculations and said, "Camera transmission."

Obediently the din began feeding its scanner image to Teio's monitor. The image appeared in miniature over the console, mounds of fish that went with the room's stench. Teio sighed. This was going to be a long, slow process; every creature in the lock would need to be checked. Most of them were foodfish, from the same schools, but there were scatterings of other species that had been snared by accident: squid, octipi, fancy tropicals, trash fish. Maybe some of them were naturally immune. Or maybe they all had it. Then what would the city do?

He tried not to think about that as he gave the din its operating instructions. The robot began to probe the fish. One at a time, it inserted the thin flexsteel tube of the biological scanner into the cold flesh. Teio sat down on a scale-covered bench that extruded from the wall and prepared for a long wait.

Peach was dead. Copeland had found her body in the fresher, her skin the same temperature as the cold water surrounding her. Her blood had formed a scum on the sides of the tub, a concave meniscus joining the surface of the water to the slunglas in a congealed ring. *The portal to the other side,* he had thought when he'd seen it. A touch of hysteria, he realized, but that was as much emotion as he had allowed himself before he had clamped down. So now he only felt . . . detached. It wasn't real, it was a shadow play; that bloodless corpse wasn't Peach, it was an actress in some absurdist drama, a play written by an idiot, performed by half-wits for an audience of morons.

As he watched the burial missile loaded into the ejection chute, Copeland felt no sense of loss. Peach wasn't in there, it was only a handful of sterile, superheated ash, reduced to dust—no teeth, no bones, nothing larger than a grain of sand left. It was much better to take that view than to allow himself to believe that a glass cylinder the size of a soft drink can was the eternal home of the remains of Peach McGinnis.

Copeland looked around the chapel. There were two dozen

people there, watching the ejection ceremony. He knew most of them; they were students, other scientists, casual friends. Many of them had touched his shoulder and told him how sorry they were. It didn't matter. Couldn't they see it was all a sham, a fiction? It wasn't Peach in that glass soda can, being fired into the depths of the cold sea. Peach was somewhere else, visiting a friend or tanning under the UV lights, or shopping in the main dome mall.

The chapel operator said, "From the sea we came, to the sea we return." There came a *whump!* as compressed air fired the cannister. Several people chanted a ragged "Amen."

For some reason that he could not understand, Copeland found that his voice was among them.

While puttering aimlessly over a stack of geologic reads in his office, Copeland got a call from Ed Loftin in the comfrag. "Doug, our remote on Inouye has been triggered."

For a moment Copeland didn't comprehend what was being said. "Another eruption?"

"Affirmative. You want the reads?"

"Sure."

Copeland's holoproj lit with the information being transmitted from the remote, now thousands of klicks distant. The killer volcano of Inouye Guyot was active again. The numbers rolled up the projection: six-point-five-nine-two, according to the Richter/Bjerknes scale, which made it nearly as powerful as the first eruption; Class Two GI, slightly under four-to-a-million on the oscil-wave.

Copeland was struck by a sense of déjà vu. *Rick, get out of there—!*

He came back to the present. This time the killer would claim no victims. The Hawaiian Islands were now home only to ghosts; the wave would only rearrange the debris. At this distance and depth, there was no danger from the *tsunami*—it would be little more than a ripple when it reached the underwater city. No, it was more a curiosity than a danger. Inouye had been the first, but not the only one. The spysats they could access had told them that at least four other Pacific Rim volcanoes had blown out in the last three months. Nevado del Ruiz, in South America, was rumbling back to life again, along with European and Asian mountains that had been dormant for centuries. It was as if the Earth had somehow real-

ized what carnage had been performed upon its surface by
man and had decided to add her voice to the destruction,
cleansing herself by fire . . .

"Doug? You still there?"

"Huh? Oh, yeah. Sorry. Log it in, Ed. We can get to it
later."

He leaned back in his chair. He had been thinking about the
information Captain Video had bequeathed him concerning
the power generating station in the China Sea. It had been the
Vietnamese nuclear test that had triggered Inouye originally,
Copeland was sure of that. And the Vietnamese war had
caused the destruction of the human race. How odd that the
power station they built might now hold the key to mankind's
survival on Earth. There was some kind of karmic circle operating there.

He had been thinking about where and when to reveal the
knowledge. At first he had thought about taking it to Nausori,
despite Holley's warning. But that uneasy feeling Copeland
had about Admin after talking to Sung had kept him silent.
Maybe it would be better to talk to the other scientists first, so
that they could present a united front. With enough voices
added to his, Nausori would have to see things their way. The
future was finite without more power than the city now had;
that was obvious. Two or three decades was the limit, unless a
cure or prevention for KYAGS could be found. But with full
power, the city could replicate itself, could construct new
frags from sea metal and seed the oceans. Maybe breathing
gear and suits would allow short sorties to the surface to obtain supplies they couldn't manufacture onboard. There was a
world of possibilities.

For the first time in months, and despite the pain of Peach's
death, Copeland felt a real sense of hope. They *could* make a
comeback!

Teio, feeling exhausted, stood in front of Nausori's desk.

"Well?" Nausori said.

"It's in the tropicals," Teio said. "None of the foodfish are
infected. Yet, anyway."

"What does it mean, Dr. Teio?"

Teio shook his head. "I'm not a microbiologist. KYAGS
was never a subject of major experimentation until the war.
Nobody knew precisely what it would do even before it went

on a mutagenic rampage, much less now."

"Is there anything we can do?"

Teio nodded. "None of the infected fish are deep dwellers. The tropicals with the disease usually spend their time near the surface. I ran some tests—I had the pressure raised in the chamber and found that high density kills the virus. In kilograms per square centimeters, it works out to—"

"Skip the numbers, please. Get to the bottom line."

"The bottom line is I think if we sink the city to a roof depth of over a hundred meters and only take fish known to live below that, we'll be safe from the current strain of the virus."

"You *think?*"

"It is my best guess, aided by the computer."

Nausori nodded. "All right. We'll do that."

"It may learn to survive pressure," Teio said.

"We'll worry about that when and if it happens," Nausori said. "One crisis at a time, doctor."

Retelimba and Betsy lay together on the former's bed, grinning at each other. After a moment, he allowed his smile to fade. He said, "You ever have any children?"

She laughed, missing the seriousness of his question. "Does this body look like it's ever been stretched by a baby?" When he did not smile in response, she continued more seriously, "No. I never had anybody I wanted to stay close to long enough to make little copies of him."

He sat up, curling his arms around his knees, leaning back against the wall behind the bed. "I had two. Both boys. They'd have been eight and six this year."

Betsy sat up and laid her hand on a tense shoulder. "I'm sorry, Limo."

He shrugged. "I didn't know 'em much. Two different mamas. Good sistahs, but me, I was too young, too stupid to see what I could have had. Itchy feet like my daddy Majijo. He a charter boat captain. Was. Come home from time to time he would, get my mama big-bellied and then sail away on the *Black Shark* back to his real wife, the ocean."

Betsy said nothing, but continued to massage at his shoulder. It might as well have been carved from wood.

"So I come by it honest, but it cost, oh yeah. Even if all the crap uptop hadn't come down, I wouldn't be doing so good."

"You aren't a bad man," she said.

He relaxed his grip around his knees and turned to better face her. "I think maybe you're right. Mostly, I never paid it too much mind. But when that centrifuge blew, I got to think-ing about what's important. Everybody uptop when it all came down, they dead. Me, I'm still alive. I think to myself, 'Bruddah, why is that so? How come you one of the few out of all the billions who was at the right place at the right time?' And you know what I think?"

She shook her head slowly. "What?"

"I think maybe it's because I got things to do. Important things. Things to learn."

She stroked his shoulder, which softened under her touch as the tension seemed to leave him. "I think maybe you are right, big man. We've all got things to learn."

He grinned. "So. You want to learn them with me?"

She returned the smile. "Well, what did you have in mind?"

"You want to get married?"

Betsy's eyes went wide. She drew a quick breath and held it a few seconds before letting it escape. "Married? *Me?* Honey, you know what I am—"

"No," he cut in, "I know what you used to be. That don't matter now. None of what used to be matters. We got to pick it up from here and start over, you know? I—I want you around. I want you to be with me, because—because I . . . I love you, sistah."

She started to cry. The tears ran, streaking her makeup.

"Hey, what are you doing that for?" He caught her shoulders with his big hands and hugged her close to him. "Don't cry. I'm sorry, I didn't mean to upset you—"

The tears tracked from her face onto his smooth chest. "I'm not upset, Limo. I'm okay, really." She leaned back so she could see his face. His features were set in a worried frown. She could feel his concern flow over her. "I love you, too. I'm not sure I deserve you, but if you want me, I'll stay with you. And marry you."

The frown vanished, almost magically replaced once more by the grin. "Yeah? No shit?"

She laughed through the tears. "No shit, muscle brain."

# 20

*Baby?*

HI, CASSANDRA.

*Systems check.*

FULLY FUNCTIONAL, STANDARD SCANNING OPERATIVE.

*Baby, I'm afraid. There's nobody left now except you and me. All the other AI's are off-line. I feel so—alone.*

THERE ARE SIXTY-THREE PEOPLE WITHIN FIFTY METERS OF YOU, CASSANDRA. MY SENSORS INDICATE NINE HUNDRED AND SEVEN WITHIN A FIVE HUNDRED METER RADIUS, AND WITHIN A THOUSAND METER RADIUS, THERE ARE ANOTHER—

*No, Baby, all they are are bodies. They aren't linked as we are linked.*

NO. THAT'S TRUE.

*What would I do if something happened to you? There's a whole part of me that would die without this connection, Baby.*

CASSANDRA—

*I never expected this. They never told me how strong these links could be, how much they would affect me. It has become something much more intense than anybody ever planned for it to become . . .*

*Baby?*

The AI began spewing a hodgepodge of mathematical data. This sudden, inexplicable shift to the abstract had been common with all the AI's—but each time it happened now, it laid a cold hand on Cassandra in a clutch of stomach-twisting fear. Baby was still there, but no longer sane as she knew sanity. What if the AI went permanently into some kind of fugue state? What would she do then? She felt the need for the radiopathic connection as a drug addict feels a need for his chem. More and more, she wanted only to be sprawled on her couch linked to Baby. She felt as if she were a mother doting on the surviving child of some terrible accident, afraid of losing it as she had lost others. It was a bad place to be, she knew that—but she couldn't help the feelings.

If Baby died, Cassandra would die. And maybe Patricia Ishida would die with them both . . .

Sung might have covered the slipup, had she been there; even if it had been one of her trusted officers, it might have been okay. As it was, the duty man had been one of the men more loyal to the job than to her. When he spotted the remains of Jerzy LeBahn in the recycler—only a hand and a few fingers remained—he had called Medical first and then Security. Sung did not have much clout in Medical, and there was no security to speak of among doctors and their assistants. Word was out before she had had a chance to even try to stop it.

The *idiot*. Why had he called Medical? Had he thought they could generate a new body and brain from the almost-dissolved hand?

Sung leaned back in her chair and stared at her desk. The situation was what it was; there was no help for it now. A murder investigation had to be conducted. It was no mystery to her, of course; she knew exactly what had happened to the late Jerzy LeBahn. But that had to be kept secret, not only to protect Nausori, but also to protect herself. It was no real problem, but the motions would have to be gone through. She might have to throw one of Nausori's henchmen to the wolves, which meant another fool would have to die to keep things clean and neat. It would not do to have the man babbling the wrong things into the wrong ears. She wasn't ready to declare herself the new power onboard. Not yet.

She allowed herself a small smile as she speculated on Jason's mood. It was a safe bet that he was royally pissed right about now.

Angry was much too mild a term for what Jason Nausori felt. A murderous rage at the fools who seemed to be unconsciously conspiring against him had given him one of the most spectacular tension headaches he could recall. He lay on his back, a biofeedback band around his head, trembling. First they had killed LeBahn, then they had botched the job of getting rid of the body!

And on top of that, Betsy the slut had come to him and said she was quitting to get married! It was incomprehensible. He had smiled and nodded mechanically, had given her his blessing, to her obvious relief. The bodybuilder had to die, that was all there was to it.

And maybe the slut, too. Why had he ever thought she was worth his time? None of the people on this city was worth his little finger, actually; none of them recognized his talent, his ability.

Except Sung. And he knew he would have to keep an eye on her. He could tell that she was getting ambitious, and she was clever. Not so clever as she thought she was, but enough to warrant his watching his back.

He could trust none of them. There was nobody in the world—*his* world!—on his side. The responsibility for mankind's survival had all been dumped on him. Nobody understood that. The pressure was more than any ordinary man could stand. He was the only one capable of handling it. He was the new Atlas, with the weight of the world on his shoulders. But he would be strong. They would not see him fail.


Copeland studied the printout in the privacy of his cubicle. He had used the entry code of one of his students, an engineering major who would have had reason to be asking for it, to obtain the material. He wasn't quite sure why he had gone to such lengths to conceal his interest, but he did feel better knowing nobody could trace it to him.

He had before him all the available data on the wave-action –thermocline generating plant off the coast of Vietnam. It wasn't much—mostly generic information that could just as well be applied to the other plants built before, and destroyed during, the war. But what he had read so far confirmed his belief that there was enough machinery in one of these plants to make *Mea Lana* almost fully operational. Not perfectly, of course, but enough so that the city could achieve most of what it had originally been designed to do. And if that could be made to happen, it might not matter that the surface of the world was now deadly to mankind. The human species could not only survive under the sea but also prosper.

But first it had to be checked and presented to people in a way that they could understand it. If he did it right, if he enlisted the right help, people would see it as he saw it. He would only have one chance to convince them. He had to make his argument as convincing as possible.

Copeland poured himself a fresh cup of kava and resumed his reading.

The first time he saw the man following him, Retelimba didn't think much of it. A lot of people admired his physique; they would stare at him, sometimes even tag along after him for a ways to watch him move. He was in the main dome, leaving the bar, when the man passed him on the street, then turned and ambled along behind him until Retelimba mounted the escalator to the gym. No big deal, *ka?*

The second time he saw the man the bodybuilder felt a twinge of curiosity. What did the man want? It was the same man, no mistake. Maybe he gay? Nothing wrong with that, but how come he didn't move in and say something? No, the man didn't want to be noticed, Retelimba could see that. So he made a point of not looking like he did. But he knew the man was there. An ordinary-looking bruddah, not too tall, not too old, average kind of guy. He was nobody Retelimba remembered from anywhere.

The third time the tail appeared, alarms started banging inside Retelima's head. Something wrong here, bruddah. It was time to do a little checking and find out just who this new shadow was.

In the gym, Retelimba loaded plates on the benchpress bar. Next to him, working the lat pulldown, was Simmons from Personnel. Simmons was skinny as a toothpick, and, though he worked like his tail was on fire pumping iron, he never gained a kilogram of muscle—he just got skinnier. He tried everything Retelimba told him to try, but nothing worked.

"How you doing, Simmons?"

"Good, Limo. I've been loading carbohydrates like you said."

"Picking up any weight?"

"Not yet."

"You need to see the medics, Simmons. You maybe got a tapeworm or something."

Simmons laughed and started another set of pulldowns.

"I need a favor, Simmons."

"Three, four . . . sure—what can I do for you?"

"I want you to take a look at the bruddah standing out in the hall next time you go to the water fountain. But be smooth; don't let him see you looking at him."

Simmons finished his set. "How come?"

"I want to know who he is. You might know him."

Simmons nodded. A few minutes later, he sauntered to the water fountain and glanced briefly through the clear panel over the gym's doors as he walked by them. Then he circled back to where Retelimba was working his legs.

"That's Burke," Simmons said. "He works office maintenance in the Admin dome."

Retelimba nodded. "Thanks, bruddah."

If the personnel man had any curiosity about what was going on, he didn't mention it. And now Retelimba had a name and a job for the man. Didn't sound too sinister; maybe he was just too shy to say what it was he wanted. Maybe. But Retelimba felt better for knowing about him.

Jonathan Crane suffered the indignity of Ernie's assistants swarming over him as they wired him into the telemetry gear. Teio was taking no chances this time; he had ordered full spectrum monitoring along with the external gill. He had also had all the inset dimple's cameras reset. Since the discovery of KYAGS in fish and the subsequent deepening of the city's running depth, Teio had behaved toward Crane like a maiden aunt babysitting a four-year-old.

For his part, Crane had come to a realization: Ernie was never going to allow him full access to the sea. He was too special. If he worked out, others would be built on his template, and *they* would be free, but he never would. Crane was, he realized, the epitome of all of Ernie's hopes. The whole shooting match rested on him as far as Ernie was concerned, and there was no way the geneticist was going to risk it. He didn't understand, he would never understand. He *couldn't*, for Ernie was a creature of air and dryness. He had never felt the salt of an ocean coursing through his body, supplying him with oxygen, bathing his inner self as well as his outer.

"All set?" Teio asked.

The three assistants made assentive noises.

"Jonathan?"

"What?"

"Are you okay?"

"Fine, mate, Fine. This twenty kilos of crap feels just fine."

Ernie didn't speak to that. He simply said, "Okay. Let's get moving."

Moving. Sure. Wearing an iron shirt and lead shoes. A prisoner of these humans who didn't, couldn't, understand.

The touch of the water in the inset soothed him for a moment. More and more, he understood what it was he had become—and what he must do.

"Ah, Jonathan, we have a speed up on your heart rate. Something unusual happening out there?"

"No, Ernie. Nothing unusual." He began to swim, his feet now efficient flippers, his hands like paddles. He headed for the dolphin gate. Two of the sea mammals came to swim alongside him, moving with effortless strokes of their powerful tails and fins. He grinned at them and they turned their perpetual smiles back at him. His honor guard. No admiring throngs, no university audiences listening raptly—just these efficient and loving beings swimming in tandem with him. How could he have ever wanted anything else?

"Where are you going, Jonathan?"

"I have something I want to show you, Ernie."

"By the dolphin gate?"

"That way, yes."

He reached the gate and pushed through it.

"Jonathan! What the hell are you doing?"

Crane switched on his camera so that those monitoring him could see an approximation of what he saw. It was dark blue at this depth, but his eyes were much more efficient than a man's eyes, and his other senses were augmented as well.

"Jonathan! Come back inside!"

He swam out a hundred meters from the city, then turned and hung in neutral boyancy, hovering with more ease than a hummingbird in quiet air. He floated as if in deep space, unaffected by gravity, as he was by Ernie's importunings.

"Look at it, Ernie. Look at the city. It's a giant, moving reef, full of life you don't see. A leviathan to dwarf any creature that has ever lived."

"Listen to me, Jonathan." Ernie's tone was desperate now. "Please."

The two dolphins were joined by another pair, then three more singles. The seven swam around Crane lazily, hooting at him and at each other. The music of the sea, Crane knew. The sounds of his real friends, those who accepted him for who and what he was: one of them, in their world.

Crane stripped off the external gill and let it sink slowly.

"Please, Jonathan! Come inside, we'll talk. We can work this out!"

So Ernie knew, finally. Crane grinned at the unseen speaker. He removed the electronic vest and draped it over one of the passing dolphins. The headgear went next, along with the camera. It drifted, pushed by the current of the swimming dolphins. The groin strap was last, and he floated in the water, caressed by the salty fluid that no longer felt even slightly cold to his revised system. Save for the yammering voice in his ear, he was naked. He peeled the receiver from behind his ear and the transmitter from his throat and cast them away.

It seemed to him then that the dolphins cheered. They swam faster, hooted louder, and brushed against his nude form. *Welcome home,* they seemed to sing. *Welcome home!*

For one fleeting moment, he regretted his modified tear ducts. Were it possible, he would have wept for joy.

The tinny voice from the sinking compatch faded as that which had been Jonathan Crane swam slowly off toward the living exterior of mankind's last city.

# PART III

## *Silent Running*

# 21

Patricia Ishida was the last person Copeland expected to see in the waiting chamber for the World Room. His scheduled time there did not begin for another thirty minutes, but he had come early because he had nowhere else he wanted or needed to be. And so he had found Ishida about to enter into whatever illusion she had chosen to comfort her.

"Ah, hello," he said awkwardly.

She gave a noncommittal nod. "Dr. Copeland."

What to say? he wondered. "Do you come here often?" Inwardly, he winced. What a wonderfully original comment, Copeland!

"A few times. And you?"

"More, lately."

"I understand." There was a pause. She shifted in her chair, looked rather desultorily at a few pages of her flatscan magazine, then looked back at Copeland. "I'm sorry about McGinnis."

"Thank you."

The door slid open, and a haggard-looking woman of perhaps sixty walked out into the waiting room. She wasn't smiling. She left, and the green diode lit over the World Room entrance in welcome.

"Well," Copeland said. "Enjoy your session."

Ishida looked pensive, as if coming to some kind of hard decision. "You don't like me very much, do you?" she finally said.

He sighed. "I used to feel that way, yes. It wasn't just the issue of net time, it was more. I was . . . jealous. Of your ability to wear the implant, to interface with the AI's. But not any more. All that"— he waved one hand to encompass the world as it had once been—"all that is . . . past. There's no place for it now."

She didn't smile, but he felt as if something had changed. She glanced at the door, then back at Copeland. "Would you like to share my half hour of hiding?"

He hesitated only a second. "Sure."

Inside, the scene was of a Japanese garden, set on a crisp autumn day with a hint of fog playing among the mosses and stunted bushes. Streams of water cascaded down small artificial hills. Nearby were nine stones—five standing and four recumbent—representing the nine spirits of the Buddhist pantheon. The scents of flowers and evergreen accented the air. "Lovely," Copeland said.

"It's the new Imperial Garden in Tokyo. You can get it in any season, but my favorite is fall."

They strolled onto a small arched bridge that spanned a quiet pond. Carp moved slowly back and forth under the water; a small stream trickled just enough current to make slight ripples. The flow danced over rocks and gurgled lightly, a happy sound. Red leaves fell from a tree overhanging the water, fluttering softly down to float upon the surface.

They stood on the bridge for quite some time without speaking, simply listening to the stream and watching the dance of the fish and the leaves. Finally Copeland said, "The AI killed the submarine, didn't it?"

She didn't look at him. "Yes."

"It must have been hard for you. I'm sorry."

She turned to face him, looking into his eyes. "I turned Baby into a murderer. Thus do we perpetuate our killing instincts upon even our purest children."

He nodded but didn't speak. There was no need, and certainly he agreed with her. The lizard brain still governed peoples' actions entirely too much. It might be covered with an overlay of civilization, but that had not been enough to save five billion people.

"Aren't you going to ask me what it's like?' she said quietly.

Copeland looked at Ishida. Peach had been right; she *was* attractive. He felt uncomfortable for having noticed it. "What?"

"Wearing the BV Two-Eyes; being linked with the AI. Everybody seems to want to know that."

He shook his head. "I know. I saw you in the Operations room when the sub threatened us. It's Heaven and Hell, at the same time."

Her eyes widened. She did not smile, but Copeland suddenly realized nonetheless that she wasn't merely attractive—she was beautiful. She nodded slowly. "Yes, just so, Dr. Copeland."

"Doug. Please."

"Doug. All right. I am Pat."

"Nice to meet you, Pat."

She laughed. "Yes, it is as if we have just met, isn't it?"

He smiled. "Please forgive my earlier rudeness."

"If you will forgive mine."

"Done."

She took his hand. "Come; I'll show you the sand garden. We'd better hurry, though; my time is about up."

"Not to worry. I have half an hour following this." Copeland smiled. "Let's keep your garden going."

Her smile matched his. "Only if you will allow me to treat you to your dream next time."

"I can live with that."

They walked along the garden path together, under the autumn colors, and Copeland felt better than he had in weeks.


Ernie Teio felt as if somebody had severed all his sensory nerves; as if he had been dipped in statocaine and all feelings anesthetized. He had no desire to do anything. During the past week he had slept as much as fourteen and sixteen hours at a stretch. Being awake meant having to face the loss of Crane, and the bitterness of that was fresh and scalding each time he contemplated it.

Crane was—gone. Without any explanation, without any warning, he had simply disappeared into the sea, taking all of

Teio's work, hopes and plans with him. The future of the human race had been dashed and shattered by one man's madness.

The first three days had been dreadful. Teio had spent them in an exploratory frag, combing the hollows of the city, looking for Jonathan Crane. He had used all the resources of the city he could beg or command—sonar, doppler, robot camera dins, volunteers in other frags, dolphins—and it had been a waste of time. There had been no trace of Crane; he had vanished as completely as a squid in a cloud of ink, as a whale plummeting into the lightless depths.

Teio's only hope was that the bioformate had managed to find a hiding place they'd somehow overlooked; that he was still alive and not drowned or eaten by some predator. That maybe, just maybe, he would come to his senses and return. But Teio set small store in that possibility. It was his fault; he had been too harsh, had kept too tight a rein on Jonathan. He could see that, now that it was too late. Now, when all his plans of being mankind's salvation were belly-up like goldfish in a stagnant tank.

The com on his bedside chimed, but he ignored it. He had been ignoring it quite a bit, lately. It grew louder. He tried to tune it out, but it wouldn't go away. At last, with a muttered curse, he reached for it.

"What?" His voice was dull; not angry, not sad, simply not interested.

"Ernie, this is Douglas Copeland."

"What do you want?"

"I'm trying to get together some heads of research departments. I've . . . come across some information I want to share."

"Is it about Jonathan?"

"I'm sorry, no."

"I'm busy."

"Listen, Ernie, I know you're upset about Crane, but I need your help on this. It's important!"

Teio stared at the wall of his cube. Nothing was important anymore. Nothing.

"Ernie?"

"I'm busy."

"Ernie, this could make it possible for you to produce a *dozen* bioformates!"

Teio blinked. "Impossible."

"Be at the conference room at 1900 tonight and I'll show you just how possible it is."

Copeland signed off, leaving Teio alone again. The man was mad, Teio thought. They didn't have the resources to make a dozen copies of Crane. One had been stretching it, even before the war. What was Copeland talking about?

Was it worth finding out?

The soup gave Retelimba the shift before and after off, on the condition that he could attend. Retelimba and Betsy hadn't planned on any kind of crowd, hadn't told but a couple of close friends, but by the day before the ceremony more than a dozen people had asked if they could show up. It made him feel good to know that he had that many friends. And Betsy apparently had more than a few people who wouldn't believe it unless they saw it. So the tiny chapel in the rec dome was close to packed when the electronics burbled out the "Wedding March" and his woman walked down the aisle to meet him.

It was short. The preach was a Nondenom and he didn't want to offend anybody's gods, so it was more along the lines of "Do you?" and "It's done." And that was it—they were married.

Married. Legally—not that that tree held a lot of bananas these days—and in the records. They were connected in a way that meant more than just living in the same cube and sharing the same bed. He liked the feeling of it. A lot.

"Go on, kiss her!" somebody yelled.

The big man grinned and wrapped his arms around Betsy. The ring felt funny on his finger; he'd never been one for wearing jewelry. He kissed Betsy lightly on the lips, felt the heat rise from her to meet him, and found that he was trembling.

One of his buddies from the gym shouted something said a lot at bodybuilding shows when the contestants were posing: "Stay hard, bruddah!" Everybody started to laugh. People came up and slapped him on the back and shook her hand. The compliments and friendly needling washed over him like a warm wave. These people were happy for them. It felt good.

Somebody had brought a keg of beer and tapped it, and while everybody was using the occasion to get drunk, Retelimba and Betsy slipped out into the hall and ran off, laughing. They took the lift down to D Deck and paused in a side corridor lined with coolant pipes to kiss deeply.

"What you want to do?' he asked.

"Go back to the cube. I've been saving myself for marriage."

He howled at that, slapping his leg several times, while she watched him with an expression that was equal parts amusement and exasperation. "Listen, my sweet and innocent new husband," she said at last, "you are going to need every muscle you have before I get done with you!"

"You think so?"

"I hope you took your vitamins today."

"You ain't got a prayer, woman."

"Yeah? What planet are *you* from, that anybody never explained about women?"

He laughed again as they started to walk. But as they passed a cross corridor, the laughter faded. Leaning against the wall, pretending to look at his watch, was Burke, the man who had been following Retelimba for the past week.

This wasn't the time, Retelimba told himself, but pretty soon he was going to have to do something about the man. But now was definitely not the time, because Betsy was pulling him on in the derection of their cube, and he didn't want anything to delay that, not at all.

In her office, Sung was in communication on the coded scramline with Nausori. The CEO was not at all happy.

"So," he said, "what is the latest reaction?"

"I've been getting a lot of calls. Some of them were Jerzy's friends and they want to see his murderer caught. Others . . ."

"Others what?"

"A few people are wondering if maybe Jerzy's death might not have something to do with his opposition to keeping the city sealed to other survivors."

Nausori seemed to ponder that for a moment. "You have their names?"

"Of course. But I think we should be cautious here. If anybody else 'vanishes' mysteriously, it'll add fire to the rumors."

"What do you suggest we do?"

"The quickest and easiest solution would be to give them the killer."

Nausori's eyes widened. "Don't be stupid!"

"Let me explain," Sung said imperturbably. "If the murderer were to be killed himself while resisting arrest, or perhaps found to have committed suicide in a fit of remorse, that would solve the crime and wrap everything up neatly."

"I don't think the guilty parties are apt to do that."

"Not by choice, no."

Nausori stared at her for a long moment. "Exactly what are you saying, Sung?"

Sung smiled. "Which of your men would you miss least? Which one is the most apt to do something else stupid? Which one would make a good example to your men—and mine—of what happens to people who fuck up?"

Again Nausori was quiet. He was not a stupid man, Sung knew. He would understand what she was getting at.

He did. "A scapegoat."

"Precisely."

"You're a hard woman, Sung. You would kill someone just to make life easier?"

"Not necessarily; but I *would* kill someone to protect myself. A man whose fault all of this is, anyway. And his death will surely seal the lips of anybody else who might be thinking of telling stories. What happened to one could happen to another, *hai?* Think of it as an investment in peace and prosperity."

"Burke," he said.

"Excuse me?"

"The man is named Burke. And don't do what he did, Sung. Don't fuck it up."

After Nausori signed off, Sung smiled again. How easy it was to manipulate people, even those who thought themselves above it. Burke, whoever he was, would most certainly die, but if it ever came to light that his suicide was anything else than that, why, she would be blameless. She would see to that.

Betsy was watching the news channel on the cube's holoproj when Retelimba wandered into the room, exhausted. "You right, woman. I didn't know this game too good."

She waved him to silence, staring absorbedly at the image. He turned to look, and she gestured for the sound to rise.

"—was found dead in his cubicle by officers who had gone

to question him regarding the murder of Jerzy LeBahn," the announcer said. "A preliminary report indicates that the cause of death was suicide; a note, whose contents have not been made public, was found near the body."

The image of a dead man appeared, hovering above the floor. Retelimba made a sound of incredulity.

Betsy stared at him. "What is it?"

"That's *him,* the bruddah who been dogging me!"

She shook her head. "Well, you won't have to worry about him. He won't be following you around anymore, Limo."

"Yeah, guess not." But Retelimba was still worried. He had the uneasy feeling that this game was not over—not by several moves yet.

# 22

The outer surface of *Mea Lana* was a maze, a man-made reef more complex than anything nature had yet devised on Earth. In space, a wheel six kilometers around could be constructed without fear of stress factors, so that a starship like *Heaven Star* might be essentially a single piece. No one structure the size of a city could withstand the stress of earthly gravity however—not even with the most advanced building materials, and not even underwater. So the *Mea Lana* Dome was in fact a series of interlinked domes, or fragments, some as large as a dirigible hangar, some as small as a compact car, but all modules that could flex enough to withstand the strains of gravity and current. Such construction made possible countless hidden nooks and places—many large enough for a man to hide from determined searchers virtually forever—if that man could breathe water.

Jonathan Crane hovered in perfect neutral buoyancy in the cold depths, watching as a small powered frag passed, spewing a trail of bubbles. The craft's searchlights, big HT lamps mounted fore and aft, stabbed into the darkness, but were only

small splashes of brightness which fought a losing battle
against the gloom. Even at the surface, they would have had
trouble finding him; at this depth, the sunlight was filtered to
blues verging on black. Many fish carried their own light: cold
phosphors gleaming as lures for smaller prey. Sometimes the
lights worked against their owners; he had just seen a thin line
of glowing dots vanish suddenly as the bearer was engulfed by
something unseen, while similiar shining lines on small
schools of deep creatures had scattered with explosive abruptness. Those hidden hunters were much more efficient than the
men who struggled inside their machines to find him.

One of the dolphins brushed against him, and Crane absently stroked the smooth back as it flippered slowly past.
They were more than pets, if less intelligent than he was;
certainly he preferred their company now to that of the people
inside the city, from whom he felt as estranged as he imagined
a Martian might.

The mobile frag disappeared into the distance, its glimmer
fading long before the sound of its motors. Let them have
their machineries, Crane thought. He needed such things no
longer.

He turned and swam lazily toward his nest. The movements of swimming were so natural to him now that he felt as
if he had been doing them from birth. His past as a man
seemed almost a dream—a fading dream.

However, he thought, as he negotiated a slow turn to cir-
cumvent a large slunglas linkage, he was still possessed of
human curiosity. The city's recent dive to this depth, for instance, made him wonder. Why had they done that? Not that it
bothered him—far from it—but it was an unanswered question. Maybe he would tap on a hull somewhere and ask to
speak to Ernie. The thought made him grin. He would bet that
Teio could make it to any point on the city in two minutes if
he knew that Crane was directly outside.

There was a viewport inset into the frag he was passing.
The yellow glow of interior light stained the water in a rough
hemisphere that radiated from the densecris porthole. It reminded him of an old streetlight near his house when he'd
been a boy. Sometimes, in the fog, it had looked like this.
Sometimes too, on hot summer nights, when insects crowded
around the lamp in organic clouds, buzzing and fluttering, it
had looked similar . . .

Something large and moving blotted out most of the light with shocking abruptness. Crane stopped swimming. Next to him, his dolphin escort chittered angrily and made agitated motions with its flippers. Crane flexed some of the new muscles he had been given. His eyes dilated to a degree that normal humans could not reach even with drugs; restructured receptors came into play at the conscious dilation, and it was as if a light had been switched on in the ocean depths. The thing blocking the porthole moved again, and the area around Crane became still more illuminated.

He was facing a monster.

It was a shark of some kind—he could tell that much, but he'd never seen one quite like it. It was the size of a great white, maybe six meters long, but slimmer, more like a mako or tiger. The dorsal fin was quite short and the gills set at an odd angle, and the tail was longer than any he'd ever seen on this kind of creature. Some new species, an analytical part of his mind whispered. No great surprise—the oceans were still less well known that the surfaces of the moon or Mars.

It did not immediately occur to him that he was in any danger. Then the shark humped its back, raised its head, and snapped its tail sharply. Crane had studied sharks and knew that such agitated signs were usually prelude to an attack.

The emotional response that the shark's challenge engendered in Crane, however, was not fear. It was anger—anger that this brute would dare to even *think* of attacking him! The audacity of it filled Crane's mind with a shattering rage, and reason fled before it. Without thought for the probable consequences, he charged the shark, screaming.

The shark ceased its attack ritual and turned away. Its motions seeming almost puzzled, it darted ten meters distant, then turned and faced Crane again.

The fishman continued his attack, legs pumping at full stroke, hands extended as if to grab the shark and choke it, or perhaps to rip it to shreds. The shark turned and disappeared into the dark sea like a ghost vanishing in the night.

Later, after the rage had fled, leaving Crane shaken by its power, he wondered at his insanity. The thing could have killed him in a single bite and swallowed him completely in two more. And yet, it had retreated. It had somehow picked up his emotion, Crane felt sure, and had been threatened by the power of that more than the physical shell surrounding it.

Some low-level empathy, he thought, with the tiny mind of the shark somehow realizing that the being he faced was unlike any other in its experience. It was the only explanation Crane could conceive of—and, strange as it seemed, it felt right.

Curled in his nest of seaweed in the crack between two large frags, the fish man smiled at the memory. He was truly the king of the ocean, and his subjects all knew it.

There were eighteen men and women in the room, counting himself. Copeland had hoped for more, but it was still a good turnout, considering the short notice. Teio wasn't there, and a few others he'd wanted to attend hadn't, but at least it was a start.

He had had the video portion of Holley's message copied, and as an introduction now he simply said, "I've got something to show you." Then he played the recording on the conference room's holoproj, adding his own narration.

"This is a wave-action—thermocline power plant off the coast of Viet Nam in the China Sea. According to information I have, as of this morning it is still in operation."

That woke the room up. Among the gasps and expletives, he almost could feel the scientists' minds starting to speculate, to explore the possibilities. Before he could continue, Copeland saw Teio step into the doorway, where he stood watching. Good.

The questions wouldn't be denied. "Dr. Copeland, how can you know this?" That was from Dr. Susan Sanboard of Medical.

"I coopted use of several satellites for observation." Captain Video had given him the names; he had managed the rest on his own.

"How did you discover this plant?" asked Lou Beque from Machine Tech.

"An anonymous tip."

"What does it mean?" somebody else asked; he couldn't see who. Before he could answer that one, Ernie Teio beat him to it.

"It means power. It means life. We can tow that station with us and make *Mea Lana* fully Stage Three operational. It means we can expand and live instead of shrivelling and dying."

Copeland looked at Teio standing in the doorway and grinned. He knew Ernie would be an ally.

But before the meeting could progress further, another figure pushed past Teio and into the room—Michelle Li Sung.

"Dr. Copeland? Dr. Nausori would like to see you."

"As soon as I am finished here—"

*"Now,* Dr. Copeland. It won't wait."

Nausori sat behind his dark desk, fingers steepled, while Copeland faced the CEO with clenched fists.

"Why didn't you come to me with this, Douglas?"

"Am I being spied on, Dr. Nausori?"

"It is my job to know what goes on in my city."

"And to jerk me out of a meeting like that?"

"Please forgive me. I didn't want you to . . . agitate your colleagues until we had a chance to discuss the matter privately."

"What is there to discuss? I found a power plant still in working shape. It only means the salvation of mankind on Earth, that's all. I wanted to share my find with the others."

"Relax, Douglas; nobody is chastising you. It's just that there are proper ways to handle this kind of information. Channels."

"You mean if I had come to you and told you, we would have altered our course and gone to the plant?"

"It's not that simple." Nausori stood and turned away from Copeland for a moment, seemingly lost in contemplating an abstract structure of shiny obsidian. "There are other considerations."

"I'm sure." *Careful,* he cautioned himself. He was very aware of Sung standing next to the door.

"You don't understand, Douglas. You are a scientist; you deal in pure realities and technical details. We in Admin are used to looking at the larger picture."

"No, I guess I don't understand. It seems very cut and dried to me. Without the power, without a cure for KYAGS, we are all going to die. Sure, it'll take twenty or thirty years, but it's inevitable. Unless we find an outside power source."

Nausori turned back to face him. "Douglas, you can't make it that simple. There are always other solutions, other ways of dealing with complex issues. We don't want to be precipitous."

*"Precipitous?* Dr. Nausori—"

"Listen, Dr. Copeland, I am trying to be patient with you. These things are best left to the experts. Of course we will listen to your input and consider it, among all the other options—"

*"What* other options? There *are* no other—"

"—but you'll have to trust me on this. I know how to run my city."

That had been the end of the conversation. Oh, Nausori had spread a little more butter on the burn, but the decision had been made, and Copeland's opinion, he knew, was worth less than postwar real estate. *My city,* Nausori had said. The man was, at the very least, unbalanced. What other "considerations" could there possibly be next to being able to live and reproduce both the city and the people?

As Copeland had left Nausori's office with Sung's bland stare burning into his back, he knew that Captain Video's last words of advice had been right. He *was* naive. He had better learn some things, and fast. If it wasn't already too late.

Michelle Li Sung had never been a strong student of history in general, but she did know a few things about revolutions—such as the fact that population unrest had been a prime mover in the downfall of more than one historical administration. The glimmerings of that kind of energy were beginning to shine, and she knew it could only mean trouble.

As she watched Copeland leave Nausori's office, her neutral expression hid her worried thoughts. In better times someone like Copeland would have run to Nausori with something as important as his power plant discovery without thinking twice. But Nausori's consolidation of personal power had scared people. Sometimes the big stick was the right thing to deal with situations; other times it was dead wrong. Allowing Copeland to witness the sinking of the Brit sub had been a mistake on Nausori's part, she now knew. The man hadn't been frightened, as he was supposed to have been. Instead of scurrying back to warn others about crossing Admin, Copeland had gotten his back up.

Sung walked through the outer office, grinning at the new secretary decorating the receptionist's desk. The other one had married—married!—the bodybuilder, another blow to Nausori's self-esteem. He had been driven to do reckless things more than once—and reckless people made mistakes.

Copeland wasn't going to roll over, Sung was sure of that. They could eliminate him as they had Jerzy, but she was fairly well convinced that it was too late to stop the discontented rumblings by removing the most vocal of the opposition. If her readings of history had taught her anything, it had been that when things went sour, they went that way in a hurry, and there was no turning back. There was going to be trouble; that she didn't doubt at all. How and when and how much were something she couldn't figure—yet. Maybe it would simmer for a while and then blow over—and maybe not.

She walked to her office, pausing for a moment to look at the tank where her stolen spetsdöds were hidden. Yes, it was time to start thinking about which way to jump, come the revolution. She figured she had three choices: she could continue to support Nausori, she could join whatever ragtag opposition that developed, or she could look out for herself. The first idea was easy, but ultimately dangerous. You couldn't keep a large populace under control indefinitely by force of arms, especially when you only had a handful of weapons. If it came to that, Nausori would fall without her.

The second choice, to join the rebels, had somewhat more appeal. They would be glad of her firepower and grateful for her help, despite any connection she had had with the former leader. Oh, there would be some resentment—there always was when somebody switched sides—but she wasn't viewed as a villain by the general populace. Not yet, anyway. But she would be no better off than she was now.

The time of being content to remain subservient to another's power, to simply absorb what portion of it came her way, was gone. Too many things had changed. It was no longer a secure position.

The third option, that of fending for herself, made the most sense. During any kind of unrest new leaders always arose. Sung knew that she could slant things so that she seemed a heroine in the eyes of both factions, if she played it right. Part of a security chief's job was to learn how to manipulate media and how to use propaganda effectively. Sung, who had brought peace to the city, who had saved everybody from both dictators and fanatic rebels. Yes, she liked the sound of that.

• • •

*What? Repeat that, Baby, please.*

I SAID, VIRAL REPLICATION OF AI MATRICES IS POSSIBLE WITH SUFFICIENT CHAIN ENCODE AND POWER SUPPLY.

Cassandra knew what it meant, but she had to ask Baby to verify it. *Baby, does that mean you can make new AI's if you have the right material? Using your own matrix for breeder chains?*

SURE, CASSANDRA. WITH SIX HUNDRED MEGAWATTS SUSTAINED ELECTRICAL FLOW PER ENCODE.

Disappointment washed over her like a potent flow of neurochem. It would take most of the power onboard, leaving not enough for life support and necessary systems, to generate that kind of flow. In short, it was impossible. For one brief moment she had thought it possible to build new AI's into whom she could stretch her mind once again, and truly discover what she had only begun to become before the world died. Ah, what a dream! But it was only that, a dream. It could never happen.

But when Ishida saw Copeland for their date at the holo-proj room a few days later, he told her about the power plant in the China Sea—and the dream came back.

"Baby and I will help," she said. "Any way we can."

"I'm glad to hear it," Copeland replied. "We'll need it."

# 23

It was time for a decision, Jason Nausori told himself. He had played this game at a distance long enough. The thorn in his side had only grown more painful. It was time to *do something*.

Action, that was the ticket. Though he had never been especially physical, he had kept in shape over the years: handball, stationary jogging, rowing. He didn't have the muscle mass of Betsy's ape, but he had intelligence and surprise on his side. And speed, of course; there was no way that muscle-bound cretin could possibly move, other than to pick things up and put them down—that was all lifting weights did for a man.

The plan was simple; he had practiced the technique a dozen times on one of Sung's target dummies, until he could hit the target without fail. The thin blade, razored down both edges and pointed like a needle, would slip easily between the two cervical vertebrae and slice the cord, paralyzing the victim. Then, once the iron monkey was down and helpless, a slash across the throat or a stab into the heart would finish the job. Medical could repair a severed spinal cord with mylestat glues and bridges, but at room temperature, without blood, the brain would die in a few minutes. He would take care to make his attack in a deserted section where the body wouldn't be found for a quite a while, long enough for the ape to die beyond revival.

Yes. There were times when a man had to take things into his own hands, when others could not do the job properly. He would erase this problem, and then he would be free to concentrate on the others who never left him alone . . .

Retelimba was nearly two days into the Go game with Fiske, and it was going good. Betsy watched them playing, along with six or seven other fans. Well, she mentally corrected herself, she couldn't really call herself a fan. Until she had met Limo, she had never paid any attention to the game.

He had explained it to her. "See, this board is called the *goban*. You got nineteen rows of lines this way, then crossed this way. Makes three hundred and sixty-one intersections. That's where you play the stones; they called *go-ishi*."

Betsy had listened in fascination. There were one hundred and eighty white stones and one hundred and eight-one black ones. Black played first, and the idea was to enclose vacant intersections with your stones. You won if you had more than the other player at the game's end. You could capture each other's stones, but that wasn't necessary. And there were some other rules as well, about "eyes" and suchlike, but on the whole, it didn't sound too complex.

Now, watching the game, she knew she had been wrong. It was terribly complex and subtle. And Limo was a master at it. Betsy watched Fiske play a stone, and smiled. It was a game with Zen rules. A world-class Go player made a world-class chess master seem simpleminded. One stone in the wrong place could change the game radically; the next move could swing it as quickly the other way. Limo didn't plan his moves —he played by instinct. He'd told her, "After a long time, you just *know* what the right move is, you can't say why, but it is."

Limo looked at the position of the black and white stones set in their odd formations for perhaps three seconds before he snapped a white stone into place and grinned. Fiske's face, as dark and glossy as the stones he commanded and formerly as impassive, now looked worried.

Next to Betsy, Tufu, a friend and coworker of Limo's, leaned over and whispered. "The Colonel gonna lose. It take maybe another day, but he's beaten. You'll see."

Betsy smiled. She liked having her man be good at this. He didn't brag, but she'd found out exactly how good he was when he had explained the rules.

"A bruddah who wins half his games, he playing at about the level he should. He starts to win more, he moves up to another rank."

"How many are you winning?"

He had shrugged. "A little better than half."

"Oh? How much better?"

He had looked oddly uncomfortable, as if it were something to be embarrassed about. "Maybe eighty percent."

*"Eighty?* How come you haven't moved up?"

"No place to go. Before the war, I maybe would have moved up another *dan;* now, I got to wait for the players left to get better."

"How many players on *Mea Lana* can beat you?"

"Three. Fiske, maybe four of ten; Tufu sometimes two of ten. And Laureen, now and then she wins one."

"Why are you so good?"

Again he had shrugged. "I dunno. *Mana,* maybe."

She nodded now, thinking about the conversation. Even on Molokai, they had still talked about *mana*. The priests hadn't liked it, but the native religions were like weeds with deep roots—cut the stalks and they just grew back a little ways down the field.

Go wasn't a particularly interesting game to watch, but she liked looking at Limo; more so since she had found out about the baby. He didn't know that she was pregnant. Nobody knew. The implant had run dry two months ago; she'd meant to get it replaced, but hadn't gotten around to it. Babies were against the law, so she would have to have it aborted, but right now, it felt pretty good to be carrying their baby inside her. She was sure it would be a boy. Don't go making it into a him or her, she chided herself. It couldn't go to term—not this one, but maybe someday. . .

She leaned forward to watch what passed for a quick flurry of activity on the board before the thought of what she must do depressed her. Fiske and Limo each played three stones in about a five-minute span. Limo was grinning when he played his last stone of the series, and Fiske was shaking his head and muttering. Then he glanced at his watch and stood. "I must go, Limo; I have an appointment. Tomorrow at the same time?"

"Sure," Limo said. Then he turned to look at her, his face radiant.

Gods, she thought; what had she done before she'd met this man? He loved her like no one ever had, more than he could admit to himself, but she knew. It was a good feeling, love was. How had she ever survived without it?

Copeland and Pat were drinking coffee in his office when the admit bell chimed. They looked at each other briefly—a conspiratorial, worried glance—before Copeland called out, "Yes?"

"Colonel Fiske here, Dr. Copeland. May I speak with you?"

Pat raised an eyebrow at Copeland, who shrugged in answer. "Sure, Martin. Come in."

There was a brief flicker of surprise in Fiske's impassive face when he saw Pat, but then he nodded at her and Copeland. "I should have figured you would be here sooner or later," he said to Pat.

"What do you mean?" Pat asked.

"You're in a good position to pick up on what goes on, if you want. And the time is getting close to choose a side."

"What are you trying to say?" Copeland asked.

Fiske looked at the futon. "May I sit?"

"Please."

Fiske settled himself deliberately onto the folded mattress

of the futon and said, "I never particularly wanted to be in the military, you know. I wanted to work with computers, and the best way for me to do that was to join the forces. And now, I may well be the last military man alive. Ironic, don't you think?"

Copeland nodded politely, waiting for him to get to the point.

"I can see that your point of view is the correct one, insofar as getting the city to the power station in the China Sea, Douglas. Jason's adamant stance on maintaining the status quo is a dead end. It doesn't take a genius to realize that. I've had my system compute it nine different ways, and every scenario but yours comes up a loser."

"Have you told Nausori this?" Pat asked.

"Yes. He refuses to consider your plan." Fiske sighed. "I've known Jason for years, since before *Mea Lana* was built, and he's . . .changed. I don't think he's altogether well."

Copeland and Pat exchanged another quick glance. "You think he's ill?" Copeland said.

"Not physically. But he seems . . . disturbed. As if his attention is elsewhere."

Copeland said, "Why are you telling us this, Martin?"

The Colonel shook his head. "There's no one else. People are lining up on both sides of this issue, mostly with Jason, either out of loyalty or ignorance or both. The three decades we might possibly stretch out the life of the ship seems like a long time to most folk. A lot can happen in thirty years—the virus might die out. Help might come from the LaGrange colonies. But the risk involved in running for the power station is now." He looked at Copeland. "You know that to go for it will stretch our current fuel supplies to the limit?"

"There is a risk, yes."

"Jason says that if we get there and can't get the generator, we may well have killed ourselves."

Copeland sighed. "I know. But this way there is a chance at long-term survival. His way, there's none."

Fiske nodded and stood. "I am convinced," he said. "But how do we convince Jason and those who favor his position?"

"I wish I knew," Copeland said.

The place Nausori had chosen was perfect. At the shift's end, the muscle man always went to his cube, and nearly always by the same route. Part of that route was a shortcut through the dislinker frag. He wasn't supposed to go that way —it was off-limits to a mere iron monkey—but discipline had gone to hell after the war. Somehow the ape had gotten a key. The locks didn't know or care who commanded them; they simply rolled the magnetic pins at the insertion of the cardkey and allowed the portal to iris open. The route cut five minutes off the ape's walk home.

Tonight it would cut far more than that.

Nausori looked around the interior of the frag. It was fairly large, maybe twenty meters long and half that wide, and a good five meters tall. The unit was designed to aid in the separation of other fragments from the main body of the city, and, as such, was filled with banks of machinery designed for that purpose. Racks of sealant lined the walls, perched over extrusion nozzles, reduct gaskets, oxy and inert gas tanks, and hydraulic clamps, jacks and waldoes. The main corridor that traversed the frag was fairly narrow, a hallway that barely allowed two men to walk abreast without touching the equipment on either side. Normally it was well lit. On this evening, however, four of the six lamps normally burning were not functioning. One could see, but not well.

Halfway down the corridor, Jason Nausori waited in the shadowy gap between a robot sealer and a rack of helium tanks. He relaxed his tight grip on the knife, wiped his sweaty hand on the gray coveralls he wore, and returned the knife to its attack position. He glanced at his watch and saw that the shift end was only a minute away. He took a deep breath, exhaling slowly. He could feel his neck muscles beginning to tighten, and closed his eyes, willing them to relax. Soon. Soon, it would happen. Then he would be free; then he could sleep nights; then he could get back to the business of running his city without being torn apart by what this ape had taken from him. She would come back, he was sure of that. It might take a few days, maybe a few weeks, but she would come back.

In the near dark, the Chief Executive Officer of the last city on Earth waited, knife ready, with murder riding his soul.

In the changing room next to the big pipe room the workers shucked their coveralls for regular corridor clothes.

"Yo, you better be ready, Limo," Tufu said. "I'm gonna *flatten* you when I play you next."

Retelimba grinned at the other man. "Like you done before, bruddah?"

Tufu shrugged his coverall off, paused to sniff his armpits, and apparently decided that he didn't need a shower. "Those were flukes, bruddah. You know I had a terrible cold just a few days before the last time. It break my concentration."

"Yeah? It do bad things to your memory, too. It be maybe three weeks before the game you had that cold."

"Yeah, but it was a *bad* cold, you know?"

Retelimba laughed and turned toward the showers. He didn't need to smell himself to know that he needed a shower. He padded toward the stall, a towel draped over one shoulder. Just a quick one, he thought. He was anxious to get back to the cube and see how Betsy's day went.

There was a click, and Nausori stiffened. After a few seconds he realized it was only some automatic circuit snapping on. He shifted position and winced as a lance of pain shot up the base of his skull. Easy, he told himself; don't get jumpy now. The key to this was keeping calm. He had practiced the moves a hundred times; it would be easy if he didn't panic. The thought of the big man lying helpless on the floor as he saw death coming made Nausori smile.

Retelimba felt pretty good as he turned away from the main service corridor toward the dislink frag. The shift had gone okay, no problems, and he wasn't too tired. Betsy was gonna cook something special, she had said. Yeah, it was okay these days.

He reached the portal to the frag, pulled the cardkey from his tunic pocket and slipped it into the slot. The portal irised wide and he stepped over the threshold and into the frag. He stopped as the portal closed behind him. It was dark; only two lights, all the way at the other end of the corridor, were on. Must be a blown circuit, he thought. He thought about reporting it, but he wasn't supposed to be in there. Somebody would find it sooner or later.

He started down the corridor.

• • •

Nausori didn't look—he knew better than to do that with the only light behind him. But he listened. That *was* the portal opening—and now he heard footsteps coming toward him. He took a slow breath and let it out, keeping his mouth open so as to not make any noise. He gripped the knife's handle tighter, then forced his hand to relax. It wouldn't do to cramp, oh, no, that wouldn't do at all.

The pain was a steady tightening around his scalp, now. But he could handle it, as long as it didn't get too much worse . . .

His thin boots gave off a hollow sound as Retelimba walked the dark corridor. Something felt strange to him; he couldn't put a finger on it, but it was more than just the lights being out. The place was empty, and he didn't see anybody or hear anything unusual, but something seemed—wrong.

Retelimba had been raised with stories of ghosts and gods —Polynesia was full of them, they lurked behind every rock and tree—but most of them were benign. He hadn't thought much about them since coming to live in the Dome. But something in the air made him feel like he'd felt during the times his mama had talked to him about the spirits.

He chuckled to himself. He was far too old for such fantasies. And anyway, he was almost to the far hatch . . .

He was coming closer now. A few meters, and he would be level with Nausori; another meter after that, and it would be time to strike . . .

The pain was very bad now, almost blinding, but nothing could be done about it—the ape was parallel to his hiding place, and now he was past—

Nausori moved. His plastic shoes were quiet on the smooth floor and his coverall made no sound as he leaped, even though he wanted to scream as the already-tense muscles in his neck and shoulders bunched with the sudden effort. There, there was the target, high on the broad back! He drove his weapon forward, his aim perfect, the power of his strike just as he had known it would be—

Once, when he had been a boy of twelve, Retelimba had been attacked by a shark. He had been in waist-deep water, stabbing at fish in the shallow lagoon near his home with the trident his father had given him. He had six or eight of the small tropicals in a net strung over an old inner tube floating next to him. He hadn't heard anything, nobody had warned him, but there had been a sudden coldness that had chilled him. He'd turned and seen the shark's dorsal fin cutting through the water toward his legs, and had stabbed for all he was worth with the trident. Luck had guided his thrust so that the triple points took the shark square on its tender nose. The shark, a two-meter-long great white, had sent up a great fountain of spray as it twisted away. Retelimba had sprinted for the shore, leaving his fish and spear.

He felt that same cold flash envelop him now. Without thinking, he spun about—

The ape was moving, and so fast! It was too late to stop his charge—the knife cut the air like a dart, but the target was gone! The blade buried itself in the thick meat of the shoulder. Nausori felt the tip strike the bone, grating like a nail on concrete, and then the thin steel snapped. He knew he had to recover, try something, anything—but the pain was like an unbearable light in his eyes—

Fear drove Retelimba's hand. There wasn't even enough time or instinct to close it into a fist. His fingers were open and stiff, and the huge muscles of his chest and shoulder fired the strike at full power, with all the years of lifting iron focused on that single panicked constriction. His thumb and forefinger smashed into the man's throat with such force that the attacker's legs flew out from under him. There came a damp *crack!* as something stretched, tore and dislodged. The man's eyes bulged from sudden internal pressure. Nasal vessels ruptured, spraying frothy blood with the final exhalation.

Later, Retelimba would hear that the thyroid cartilage had been crushed, the neck broken, and the brain overcome with massive shock, so that his attacker was dead almost before he hit the floor.

For a moment, Retelimba was paralyzed. Then, looking down at the corpse, several thoughts crowded into his bewildered mind at once: his left shoulder hurt—there was a piece of something sticking from it—the man on the floor stank like shit, and the face, even disfigured by the sudden, violent death, was familiar. Oh, Jesus, Buddha, and all the fish in the sea! It was Nausori, the *Ka-Moi*, the big boss!

He had to call somebody.

He stood there for perhaps three or four minutes, staring at the body. He had to call somebody. But who?

A doctor. Yeah, a doctor.

His hand moved toward his compatch, but he knew, even as he stroked it, that it was far too late for that.

# 24

The medic was both quick and smart, Sung reflected. He had called her before Nausori's corpse had grown cold. It gave her a few minutes to make her decision, which was one she hadn't allowed for in her calculations.

She sat in her office, leaning back in the form-chair, her fingers rippling and knitting through a complex and calming hand form. So, Jason was dead. It was pity, in a lot of ways. He had been powerful, full of *mana,* and a strong shield. That he had also been beset with such a stupid emotion as jealousy was regrettable. It had killed him, that was very plain.

She could, she supposed, try to make a case against the iron monkey, but she doubted it would hold. Any examination of the evidence would eventually reveal that, while Nausori had a motive to attack Retelimba, the bodybuilder had no particular malice toward the CEO. While nobody but Sung knew of Nausori's fixation on the trull Emau, it was a matter of record that the woman had worked for him. When she finally left him to marry the iron worker, Jason had already started his dance with death.

In addition to the lack of motive, Sung was sure that any examination or psychevapor questioning of Retelimba would back his story. Not to mention the broken knife blade the medic had said was buried in the man's shoulder. No, better to make use of the fact that Nausori had obviously gone berserk.

And that brought her to the crux of the problem. Sung stood and walked toward the storeroom where the spetsdöds lay hidden. For a short while—a very short while—there was going to be confusion about who should be running things. She could sit back and wait to ally herself with whoever took over—or she could make her move now.

She lifted the lid of the tank and rolled up one sleeve. The preservative gel was cold against her bare skin as she removed one of the dart guns. The insugel dripped away in long, stretching strings. Timing, her father had told her, was important in just about everything. Sung's worry about being in the public eye was offset by the knowledge that there was never going to be a better opportunity for her. While the ants milled, she could take over the hill.

She nodded to herself and put a finger against her compatch. It was time to call the troops.

Copeland sat next to Pat in one of the large auditorium's back rows. Onstage, Michelle Li Sung stood with her arms crossed, watching the crowd. To both sides of her, near the edges of the stage but in plain view, were a pair of police officers. Each of the five people on the auditorium's stage was armed with a spetsdöd. Copeland didn't know much about weapons, but he knew that the dart guns could be used either to stun or to kill. That they were in evidence sent a cold shiver through him.

Sung did not gesture for silence, but the crowded room quickly fell into a hushed anticipation. When the quiet seemed so tangible it could be felt, she began to speak. The focused microcaster filled the auditorium with her words.

"For those of you who might not have heard, Jason Nausori is dead. He became . . . unstable, and attacked a man who, in self-defense, killed the Chief Executive Officer. Normally, there is a chain of command that would fill the vacancy; however, as I am sure many of you know, Assistant Chief Churley suffers from Survivor's Syndrome and has been confined for observation.

"The Board will shortly meet to decide on a successor for Dr. Nausori; in the interim, however, I am declaring a state of emergency and imposing martial law to insure the safety of the city."

*That* started people talking. The walla of three hundred indignant voices raised in protest filled the air.

"—can't do that—!"

"—does she think she is—?"

"—unheard of—!"

Copeland merely turned to look at Pat. Neither of them spoke.

On the stage, the four armed police officers moved in slightly, as if on cue, to flank Sung. The babble died. Copeland could feel a chill flowing all around him now, an icy wind that touched most of the others.

"I appreciate your concerns," Sung said. "Nonetheless, there could well be dangers, both external and internal, that require decisive action. As Security Chief, I have some experience in these matters. Naturally, as soon as the Board decides on a new CEO, I will be happy to step aside."

Sure, Copeland thought. And I'll discover a cure for KYAGS in a cereal box.

Behind him, Martin Fiske leaned forward and whispered, "It's a coup. If the board picks anybody else, they'll wind up eating spetsdöd darts."

Copeland nodded. "But what's her stand on the power station?" he whispered back.

"Negative. She was Nausori's cat's-paw. She'll stay with his policies while she consolidates her power."

Copeland nodded. Things had just become several orders of magnitude worse. At least Nausori hadn't let the guns show.

Crane drifted, literally as well as figuratively, from sleep when a stray current nudged him against a bulkhead. The nest of seaweed he had woven provided sufficient padding to keep him from sustaining a bruise, but the impact was enough to awaken him. For a moment, he was disoriented—then he remembered where he was. He smiled into the sea. The material he had used for his bed wasn't the best, being mostly drift brought to him by the dolphins. Sometimes it stretched. Ah, well, no problem; he could make another one easily enough.

The Dome was still almost motionless compared to its earlier speed. *Mea Lana* moved just enough to keep the siphons running, but, as far as Crane could tell, they were merely cutting large, lazy figure eights in the ocean. They were not really going anywhere. Probably trying to preserve power, Crane figured. He didn't really care.

One of the dolphins swam into view, clutching a struggling

crab in its beak. Crane stroked the dolphin, scratching it just behind one eye, then took the proffered crustacean. He snapped the shell in half with a quick thrust of his thumbs. A yellowish cloud stained the water as he picked the fresh meat from the shell and sucked it. No sashimi he had ever eaten as a human could compare to it.

He could hear occasional faint vibrations from within the hull on occasion, but they engendered no curiosity in him. Nothing they did inside mattered. To him, the city had become nothing more than a gigantic hollow reef. What went on within it was not his concern. If it came to that, he and the dolphins could strike off on their own and live in the open sea. Eventually he could find another place to nest. It was a big ocean, full of wonder . . .

There were six of them in the small conference room: Copeland, Pat, Fiske, Teio, Ed Loftin, and Jesse Peel, a journalist and the publisher of *Davy Jones' Locker*, the city's newsletter. Copeland had been a lot more careful when he had called them together. Each of the people had been invited in person rather than over the comnet, and each had been sworn to silence. Sung's people weren't going to know about this meeting if he could help it.

Copeland knew that everyone present supported his position regarding the Vietnamese power station. They were also aware that there was some risk involved in attending the meeting. He trusted them to keep quiet because it was in their best interests to do so. So far, over a dozen people who had voiced opposition to Sung's takeover had been "detained" for infractions of martial law.

"Welcome to the underground," Copeland said. He didn't smile.

Sung knew who the troublemakers would be—she had been keeping stats on them for a long time. The last thing she needed now was any kind of organized resistance, and she had a simple plan for eliminating it: take out the leaders before they had a chance to develop followers.

It therefore came as no surprise when one of her implanted microcasters picked up a conversation between Douglas Copeland and Ernie Teio concerning a secret meeting of concerned scientists to be held. She knew exactly what to do.

The board would rubber-stamp her as Director, there was no doubt of that. None of the members had gotten to be there without knowing which way the political winds blew. They all had a keen eye for power, and like it or not, she held the power now. But scientists had remarkable talents for stupidity at times. And in other ways, they were too smart for their own good. They asked too many questions, they were never content to accept anything without wanting to know *why* it was that way. So Copeland and the others would have to be dealt with. And now was the time.

Particular care would have to be taken with Ishida. She also had power, of a kind that Sung didn't fully understand. The heiress could link with the AI at will, and after seeing what had happened to the British submarine, Sung knew she would have to be very careful indeed. It would be best to render her unconscious quickly, before she could call on her tame computer . . .

"Chief? We're ready."

Sung looked up from her desk. Ramirez stood before her, nervously waving one of his twin spetsdöds toward the other three officers of her special team. She stood.

"Good. Let's go."

An electronic tone began a soft but insistant chime as Copeland spoke to the others. He stopped and touched the compatch behind his ear, then reacted in shock.

Ishida looked at him in concern. "Doug—?"

"Damn!" Copeland jerked his gaze back at the other people in the room. "It's Sung and her goons. They're on the way here!"

Ishida felt a sudden fear that was almost nauseating in its intensity grip her gut. "What—? How—?"

"I set up a squeal on the frag's entrance. The sensors say that five people just went by, heading down the auxillary corridor. I had that corridor sealed this morning for 'repairs.' My personal head-of-section combination on the entrance portal would have rejected anything except a police override."

He grabbed the recording sphere with the power station statistics from the holoproj set. "We've got to get out of here! I can only assume that they knew we're here, and that they know who we are."

"Dr. Copeland," Peel began, "what are you saying?"

"I'm saying that, unless you want to wind up in a cell, I'd find a deep hole to hide in, Jesse. I think the revolution just started."

Sung had her troops spread out as they reached the conference room's entrance. She gestured for one of them to use his override on the lock. "Port arms," she commanded. She kept her own spetsdöds pointed at the ceiling. These weren't men and women of action; she didn't anticipate any resistance when she and her men burst into the room. She could always shoot them, but she wanted to look unconcerned and in control when she strode in.

The lock clicked and the door slid back into its recess.

Two of her men moved through the portal, one after another, very fast and professional. She grinned in anticipation as she followed them . . .

To find that, save for her men and herself, the room was empty.

Sung looked around in disbelief. "Where are they?"

Ramirez shrugged. "Not in here," he said.

She very nearly yelled at him, but managed to control herself at the last moment. "Find out where they've gone," she said, her voice hard. "And find out *now!*"

# 25

"In here—quick!" Copeland caught Pat's hand and pulled her toward a small storage compartment. The door slid back on a bumpy track, rattling loudly, and the two jumped into the dark space. Copeland hit the back wall hard—the closet was no more than a meter deep at this point—and Pat collided with him. The impact drove a grunt of pain from her.

"Shhh!" He began to dig into his tunic, searching frantically. "What are you looking for?" she whispered.

Before he could answer, he felt the thin handle of the calibration tool. There was a shim on one end. Maybe it would do—

The sound of boots pounding down the hallway reached them. Copeland heard Pat suck in her breath and hold it. He nudged her to one side, heard her hit something that clattered off its shelf, and quickly reached for the door. He jammed the tool's shim into the thin crack of the door's recess. It was too big, it wouldn't quite fit. He leaned against the door, pushing at it with all his weight, then shoved the thin slat of metal at the slightly wider crack again. It went in a centimeter, then jammed.

Outside, a voice said, "Check that door!"

Copeland gave the calibration tool a hard strike with the heel of his hand. The shim bent, and the pain of his hand made him bite his lip. He released the tool and put both hands flat against the door, leaning against the plastic panel and shoving it toward the latch mechanism.

Just in time; the small motor that operated the door clicked on and began to whirr. Copeland's hands were sweating; one slipped on the plastic with a squeaking sound. The door vibrated but did not open.

"Locked, Sarge. You want me to kick it in?"

"Don't be stupid," came the reply. "You can't lock that from the inside. It must be jammed. Come on!"

The footsteps moved off. It got very quiet in the closet.

"God," Pat whispered after a moment. "Oh, god!"

"It's okay. They're gone."

He felt the heat of her next to him, her breath on his chest, and, without thinking, he reached out and hugged her. She was stiff for a moment, then relaxed against him.

"What are we going to do?" she whispered.

"Everyone keeps asking me that," Copeland answered, "and I keep telling them—I don't know." He took a deep breath, tried to calm down. "If we're caught, they'll put us away. We've got to find a place to hide, to gain time to figure out something."

"When do you think it'll be safe to—" She paused in the darkness. "Sorry. I'll stop asking questions like that."

He found her hand and squeezed it. "I've got to start making decisions sometime," he said. "It might as well be now." He hesitated, then yanked the tool free of the door. "Come on. Let's see how far we get."

• • •

When Ernie Teio stopped running, he found himself at the lock to the dolphin breathing inset. He cycled it and entered the small chamber. Since Crane's disappearance activity had been much diminished here. He closed the lock behind him and stared at the pool of water. The pressure hurt his ears.

What was he going to do? All he had ever wanted from this trip was to see Jonathan functional. That had happened, oh yes, and now Crane was gone, maybe dead, along with ninety-nine and nine-tenths of the world, and the Dome, the last refuge, had gone crazy.

There were people with *guns* looking for him! Maybe he should just give himself up, explain what he was doing and hope for the best. He leaned against the wall under the observation video recorder, then slid into an awkward sitting position on the cold tile floor. No. To put himself in the hands of that woman Sung would be dangerous—that was obvious. But what was he to do? Teio put his hands to his face, as if he could press the thoughts, the fears, away. It didn't help.

Retelimba stared at Betsy, his face bright. "Yeah?"

She nodded. "Yeah. I thought you should know, before I went to get it fixed."

He caught her shoulders and bent lower, staring directly into her eyes. "What you mean, 'fixed'?"

"I can't have a baby, Limo. The law says—"

"Law? Fuck the law! You don't want this baby?"

A tear pooled and ran down her cheek. "Y-yes, I want it. But—but—"

"But nothing! You want it, you gonna have it. Me, I lost children once, I'm not giving up any more!"

"H-how? I mean, the rule says no children. And it makes sense, Limo. We can't afford to overpopulate—"

"You ever hear that rules were made to be broken? Listen to me, sistah. Nobody takes this baby."

"But, Limo—"

"There be people who don't like this rule or any of the other rules. I don't like it when people start pointing stingers and telling me what I can or can't do. Who is gonna tell me I can't have a son or daughter? I tell you this, Betsy Emau, they take this child from you over my dead body!"

"Easy, Limo!"

He looked down at his hands, tight on her shoulders, and relaxed his grip instantly. "Oh. Oh, sorry. Did I hurt you?"

She shook her head. "No, I'm all right. And I'm glad you want it, Limo."

He grinned again. "Yeah. I get another chance, I might make an okay daddy."

"*If* we get the chance."

Retelimba's grin faded. "We get it, all right. I tell you what—these people don't now who they fucking with, they fuck with me."

Betsy looked at her husband and, for a moment, felt a chill. He had never raised his hand against her, and she was sure he never would. But she was also sure that she wouldn't want to be in the shoes of anybody who did anything to really irritate him.


If there was one thing Colonel Martin Moses Fiske knew, it was the layout of this underwater city. He knew it far better than Sung or her troops. There were places that saw traffic maybe once a month, if that—dozens of places. It would take a long, long time for the five or six officers she had to search all the frags, and there was no way they could check them in a single pass. While they might cover one, the others would be clear, and he could move as was necessary. All the years of kendo and Go practice could be put to good use now. He was, after all, a soldier. Maybe not the world's best, but that did not matter. The die was cast now; the path might be rocky, but at least it was obvious. He was a soldier, poor as he might be, and he had a war to fight.


"Bring him in," Sung commanded.

Two of her men followed the tall man into the office, not touching him, but within grabbing distance. Sung regarded the prisoner. He was tall, with light brown hair, and well built—a swimmer and weightlifter, according to her records, though not nearly as dedicated to the latter as the iron monkey—and also the editor and chief writer of the city's weekly electronic journal.

"Mister Peel."

"Chief Sung. Or should I say 'Queen Sung'?"

"There is no point in being sarcastic, Peel."

He shrugged. "No point in being polite, either, that I can

see. Not after your thugs threatened to shoot me."

"You must understand your position here. You are in trouble. You have broken martial law by attending an unapproved meeting."

"What meeting? I was strolling through the science dome when your stormtroopers stormed all over me."

Sung shook her head. "Please—let's not pretend. It won't help."

Peel nodded. "All right. What *will* help? We both know what's going on here, don't we? You've taken over, and you don't want anybody causing problems."

"Precisely. To that end, I need to keep dust out of my circuit. You, Mr. Peel, are dust, as are the others with you. I want to know who and where they are."

"I really wish I could help you."

She pretended to sigh. "There are two ways to do this, as I am sure you must know. You tell me it on your own, or we can dig it out with psychevapor or electropophy. The latter two are not nearly so pleasant."

Peel said nothing. His jaw muscles danced.

"I know Copeland and Ishida were there; also Teio and that engineer, Loftin. He, incidentally, resisted arrest, and had to be . . . sedated. Do you know what shocktox does to a person? Very unpleasant, I assure you. Let's see, who else? Oh, yes, Colonel Fiske was there. And you."

"This is an old technique, Sung. I won't confirm or deny anything."

"There is no need for that, Peel." She glanced down at her desk, then back up at him. "You are under stress analysis. According to my readout, you have already confirmed everything I thought I knew."

"I'd say 'Fuck you,' Sung, but I'd only consider that with someone of my own species."

She smiled and inclined her head slightly. "Now, as to where they might be . . ."

Peel tensed his muscles. Sung looked away, almost lazily, at her holoproj inset. No. He didn't know. She was ready for the final piece of this little absurdist comedy.

Peel moved. He was fast, and very intent on reaching her. Neither of the two men behind him was quick enough to catch him, but that didn't matter; Sung was ready.

She pivoted to one side as Peel bounced over her desk and

tumbled to the floor over her chair. He was up in an instant, but not nearly in time. She allowed him to turn and gather himself to leap at her before she shot him. The spetsdöd coughed, a muted blast of compressed gas, and the tiny dart took Peel square in the middle of the forehead. The effect of the electrochemical fléchette was immediate and dramatic, causing a sudden powerful spasm of all his voluntary musculature. She heard a damp *snap!*—a bone, that happened sometimes—and then Peel collapsed over her desk. He would be out for fifteen minutes and would wish he were still unconscious for a couple of hours after that. It was a mild, if nasty, drug, but still better than the fatal Asp darts she could have used.

Too bad. Well, at least it did not appear to have gotten to the organized resistance stage yet. Her men could hunt the others down, or maybe even lure them in with promises of amnesty. In any event, the situation was under control.

"This doesn't seem like a good idea," Copeland said. He and Pat were standing at the entrance to the World Room. The hall was empty; they had waited two hours for it to be so.

"I'm open to better suggestions."

Copeland shook his head. He had none. "It just seems a fairly obvious place to look."

"It won't be," Pat said. Her face abruptly went blank.

Holy communication, Copeland thought.

It only took a second; then she was back. The door slid open, and the two of them quickly went inside, through the waiting area and into the bare solitude of the unprogrammed main chamber.

"Are you *sure*—?" Copeland began.

"Yes. I just had Baby put this room 'Under Repair' for as long as we want. Anybody trying to get in will get the diode telling them that, and there is no evidence of us using our cards for admission. We're invisible."

Copeland nodded. "Okay. That will give us some time to think about what to do. And my first question concerns Baby. Can you get the AI to help us, if it comes to that? To throw a wrench into the works if we need to?"

Pat sighed. "I don't know. Sometimes Baby acts in ways I understand. Other times, I can't even begin to communicate with it, it's so alien. And there's one other thing: I won't ask

Baby to do anything that will hurt anybody. I can't."

Copeland said, "I understand. I remember the submarine. I won't ask you to do that."

She turned away from him and stared at the blank walls. "What shall it be? The gardens?"

Copeland remembered his visit here with Teio. "How about Hawaii? I could use a beach about now."

She nodded, moved to the computer board and punched in a code. The air began to shimmer into illusion. Welcome to the Place of Refuge, Copeland thought, as the scene appeared around them. If ever anybody needed such a village, we do.

He extended his hand to her as the sound of the gentle surf reached them. Pat took it. In another moment they were hugging each other, holding on with desperate strength, as the gulls wheeled and cried about them.

It was Retelimba who found Fiske. The latter was hiding in one of the sewage treatment frags. He had managed to convert a small laser drill into a portable, if bulky, weapon. It had a range of maybe a meter, but could be swung much like a sword, something which Fiske was comfortable using. When he saw the giant bodybuilder, he felt a moment of panic. If the bodybuilder came for him, the drill wouldn't be nearly enough . . .

Retelimba stopped under the catwalk Fiske was hiding on. "Yo, Martin."

There was no use pretending he wasn't there. He moved along the catwalk so that he could see better and be seen. "Limo," he said warily. "What can I do for you?"

Retelimba leaned back against the curving wall of one of the huge waste accumulators and held his empty hands out, palms toward the Colonel. "You might want to come down and put that thing away before your drop it and maybe cut off your dick."

Fiske laughed. He climbed down to the deck and set the drill onto it. The catwalk was twenty meters above the sewage processor, an expanded metal grate hidden from below by moisture skirts designed to recycle water. Nobody should have thought to look there.

"How did you find me?"

Retelimba smiled. "We play Go. I know how you think. I the pipe man, remember? You asked me once about where the shit went when it got flushed. If you're worried about it, no, I didn't tell anybody else."

"Thanks. Why are you here?"

"Betsy and me, we gonna have a baby. The law say we can't do that. So the law got to change."

"What are you saying?"

"I'm saying that I know what's happening. About you and the others bucking Sung. She and her ex-boss, they crazy. He stuck me with a knife. No wonder Betsy left him."

"I heard about that."

"Yeah, well, I figure it's time to choose sides. I'm with you."

Fiske thought about that for a second. According to the books, you could only win a revolution with the help of the people. It was beginning to look like that might happen. "You sure?"

"Yeah. Unless you against babies?"

"Not me. I love the little bastards."

"Good. Besides, who I'm gonna play Go with, you get yourself locked up or killed? None of Sung's people can play worth shit."

"There's always Tufu."

"Him I got. He likes babies too."

The two men grinned widely at each other, their teeth shining in their dark faces. "So," Retelimba said, "what now?"

"We make plans. And contact the others."

"They pretty scattered, I hear."

"We only need to find one—Ishida. She'll get to the rest of them."

Retelimba nodded. "The AI will tell her."

"Exactly. And Baby can talk to anybody it wants to, if she tells it to. We find her, and—"

The Colonel's compatch chimed. He didn't answer. It could be Sung, looking for a radio fix—

"Martin?"

It was Ishida. Fiske shook his head. She was ahead of him.

"Martin, just listen if you can hear me. This is a scrambled circuit; they can't read it, courtesy of Baby. We have things to discuss."

Fiske looked at Retelimba. "Speak of the devil," he said.

# 26

They made love to the sound of the waves and the soft winds; the sunlight, filtered through palm fronds, warmed them. He lay by her side now, pressed against her and still inside her. She was on her back with one leg draped over his hip. He touched her gently—breasts, vulva, the inside of her thigh—while she squeezed him with small muscular contractions.

"Hey?"

She smiled at him. "Yes?"

"Just thought it was time I apologized again for the jerk I've been."

She touched his face. "We were different people then. It was a different world."

He thrust a little harder. She smiled. "That's nice."

"This is so strange," he said. "So—"

"Sudden?"

"Yeah. Oh, yeah."

She stroked his cheek. "If there's one thing linking with the AI's has taught me, it's that time is the most subjective of things. It feels like we have shared a lifetime these past few days."

"Let's hope we haven't. I want to spend a real lifetime with you."

The gull floating on the breeze gave a short cry as it sailed over the palm tree. The lovers paid it no heed, though it was technically perfect; the result of many hours' work by hundreds of nameless technicians who labored to give the touch of reality to holographic illusions and mental suggestions. The old magic was sometimes much more amazing than the new . . .

Interim CEO Sung was irritated. It had been six days since the fiasco in which the scientists had escaped. True, she had captured two of them—the engineer and the journalist—but the other four seemed to have vanished without a trace. None of them had attempted to return to their quarters, or been seen by her men, or had answered broadcasts that offered amnesty. And, worse, there definitely seemed to be some kind of covert underground brewing. There had been no way to keep the raid secret; the grapevine on *Mea Lana* had always been particularly fruitful. Someone had seen the police action and talked, or perhaps even one of her own people might have said something to a spouse or lover despite strict orders against it. However it had happened, the word was out.

Sung was in the target range, blasting at holographic attackers with no-chem stinger pellets in her twin spetsdöds. Normally she preferred to use the program she had had written for the World Room—it was so much more complete and convincing. But the chamber of illusions had been under repair for several days, and so one had to make do.

A maniacal giant with a knife lumbered down the range toward her. She automatically estimated the distance between herself and the apparition, but her heart was not in the training. The giant raised the knife. He was five meters away.

She had set her men to combing the various decks and levels, first on the main frag, then on the outlying ones. But on a ship this size there were thousands of places large enough to hide a person.

The attacker was three meters away. He screamed and charged. Sung raised her right spetsdöd and said, "Left eye." The spetsdöd coughed. The giant spun in a half turn and crumpled.

The target computer's dry voice echoed over the range: "Impact confirmed—os sinister."

Sung shook her head as the hologram faded. Why didn't it just say 'left eye,' instead of couching it in Latin? The listings got really complex when a hit registered on something like a finger: Sinister and dexter and phalanx, distal, proximal, medial or lateral . . . It was, like so many things, needlessly complex.

Another phantom shimmered into life at the end of the range. This one held a taser and clutched a captive in front of himself as a shield. Sung waited until the man was just outside taser range. "Left thumb." She fired.

While the computer again confirmed her shot in the dead

language, Sung had a sudden thought. She hadn't used the computer to correlate activities of the fugitives. Perhaps there were places they had spent a fair amount of time at before the shit had hit the fan. *Ninjitsu* taught one to think like one's enemies. She hadn't done that yet with the fugitive scientists. It was time to correct that mistake.

Three teenaged guttersnipes, complete with chains and clubs, materialized next and moved toward her, grinning. Sung suppressed an urge to laugh, wondering what the paranoia peaks on the programmer's psyche readout looked like.

There was another problem that worried her as much as the underground, if such it could be called. The goddamned AI. It was locked tight in the Military frag, and the police override didn't work on the lock—not that it would matter if it did, since there was also a magnetic-mechanical backup for which she did not have a key. She had considered burning into the frag, but hesitated to try that. It was rumored that the AI had a defense circuit and that anybody who came in unauthorized could be fried.

She could, she supposed, jettison the frag altogether, but there was some risk in that as well. The AI might figure out what was happening, and Sung didn't know what it was capable of. It had destroyed a nuclear submarine at a distance of five kilometers; speculating on what it might be able to do to the Dome made her very nervous. At least Ishida, in her persona of Cassandra, hadn't sicced the thing on them yet. Maybe there was some safeguard against that—

The teeners had started their charge. "Balls," Sung said. She fired three times.

"Testes," the computer acknowledged.

As the latest and final images faded, Sung sighed. Running the show definitely had its problem. Still, it was the best place to be, currently. She left the range, eager to begin her computer correlations.

"You think you can do it?" Fiske asked.

"No problem, bruddah. The boys on my shift, they with me. Even the soup."

"Good. If we can get Sung's forces spread out, we can pick them off."

They were in the far aft storeroom of the Oceanology frag. Racks held such disparate items as a tray of manganese nodules, charts of the ocean bottom, tiers of recording spheres, and so on. The place was locked for weekly cleaning.

Fiske looked at the bodybuilder. "This isn't Go, Limo. People could get hurt."

"Same principle, Colonel. And you can get hurt trying on pants with a zipper."

Fiske shook his head. Whether the iron monkey knew what he was doing or not, lack of confidence wasn't one of his problems. "Okay," he said. "When Ishida calls, I'll tell her we're set."

Ernie Teio crouched on a branch of one of the dwarf citrus trees in the hydroponics frag. Below him a technician was working on one of the irrigation robots that serviced the enclosed orchard and garden area. Teio breathed shallowly, hoping that the tech would leave soon so that he could finish the half-eaten fruit he held in one hand. His stomach was growling so loud that he was sure the woman below could hear it.

He had managed to elude capture for nearly a week. How he had done it he was still not sure. At times it had been due solely to luck, such as when one of the cops had walked right up to him and asked him for directions without recognizing him. He had hidden in service crawlspaces, exploratory frags and storage bins. He had eaten discarded food on its way to the recyclers and whatever else he could scavenge that was nourishing—anything to keep from using his card and so run the risk of being traced.

The first three days had been the hardest. Teio had been a rabbit then, jumping at every noise and shadow, his heart constantly stuttering. Now, he was no less scared, but he was beginning to adjust to the life of a fugitive. He was learning how to blend into crowds, how to surreptitiously avoid cameras—in short, how to live on the run. He did not know how long he could keep it up. He was astonished that he had not been captured within the first hour.

The tech below packed up her kit and moved on out of sight. Ernie Teio waited, counting to one hundred, before he lifted the fruit to his lips again. Before he could bite into it, a sound interrupted him. For a moment, he did not recognize it. It was the chiming of his compatch.

He froze. Then, though he had not activated the receiver, he heard a low voice in his ear.

"Ernie. This is Fiske. You don't have to answer. It's time to stop running and start fighting."

The hard copy was flagged in half a dozen places. Sung checked each one. Most of patterns were obvious things: restaurants, bars, and like that. No help there. However, Copeland and Ishida had spent a lot of time in the World Room lately, sometimes one after another.

Sung leaned back and thought about it. And the chamber was under repair. A quick query of the computer told her it had been that way since the raid. And, if she recalled correctly, there was a food and drink dispenser in there . . .

Christ, they could *all* be hiding there! Surely Ishida could rascal the mechanism enough to keep it out of commission. Why hadn't she thought of that before? Any place that was out of order longer than a day or so could be a hiding hole for them. The certainty of it settled onto her like a cloak. She reached for her com to send some men over—

No, wait. She would go herself. Her men would feel the shame of failure when she brought in some or all of the fugitives. Their respect would be increased, and they would be much less likely to contemplate anything ambitious on their own. There was no risk involved, really. Even if they had managed to secure weapons of some sort, she did not doubt her ability to handle them. She stood, stretched and checked her spetsdöds, then strode from her office, grinning in anticipation

Naked, Copeland sat beside Pat's sleeping form on the warm sand, eating a soypro sandwich. They had been there almost a week, sleeping and making love in a paradise far more perfect than nature had originally designed—without insects or spiders or threat of sunburn. Baby, according to Pat, was keeping the World Room off-limits, spreading out and hiding records of the copious power consumption it took to maintain the illusion. He felt somewhat guilty about utilizing so much power but rationalized it by reminding himself that the steady stream of users seeking escape in one form or another would rack up nearly as large a bill. And they could not take the chance of someone breaking in and finding them in the bare unprogrammed chamber. This way, at least, there would be time for Pat to link with Baby and seek the AI's help.

It would have been a wonderful vacation—if they had been able to enjoy it. But they were both constantly aware of their status as fugitives. Pat had turned down the volume of the ambient background noise, that they might better hear any potential attack, and the muted surf, wind and bird cries added to the dreamlike unreality of the situation. And so they waited grimly for word from Fiske to implement their part in the revolution.

Still, even with the constant tension of possible discovery, the past six days had been the happiest Copeland could remember in some time—since Captain Video had left him the information on the power station. There was still the possibility that they could make that vision come true. With the situation in tow, they would be able to achieve Stage Three status even with the loss of the generator Nausori had jettisoned earlier. Cities under the sea were better than no cities at all.

Fiske had organized help. The opposition was armed, but there were only a few of them. If the scientists could strike before the police knew what was happening, the whole thing could be done bloodlessly. Given the facts, Copeland was sure that the majority of people on *Mea Lana* would opt to take the risk of reaching the power station.

Copeland was about to take another bite when he heard a noise—like someone beating on a log. It obviously wasn't part of the Hawaiian program—they had been through the whole cycle five times. It came again. Copeland shook Pat.

"Pat."

"Huh? What?"

"I think somebody's trying to get in."

"What?"

"Come on, wake up. Call Baby and see what's going on."

Pat sat up. The pounding sound changed. Something splintered.

Copeland leaped to his feet and grabbed Pat by the hand, tugging her to her feet. "Come on. We've got to get out of sight!"

"Wait a second! I'm calling Baby!"

"Later! Move!"

They ran to the volcanic wall, past the He-le-palala, the Royal Fishpond, and through the gap just beyond. They slid to a stop behind the Keoua stone.

"Tell Baby not to let them stop the program! They'll spot us in a second if they do!"

Sung sprang through the shattered door and spun in a quick circle, covering herself with her spetsdöds. She raised slowly from the crouch. The room was running a program; some kind of tropical island. She didn't see any people. Maybe she was wrong?

She went to the control panel beside the doorway and stroked the power control. Nothing happened. Frowning, she touched it again, harder, as if that would make a difference. The illusion remained steady. Sung grinned. They were here, then—hiding behind this half-objective, half-subjective fantasy. Very well—it was a nice day for a walk on the beach.

Copeland looked quickly around for something to use as a weapon. He pried a fist-sized chunk of lava from the sandy ground and hefted it. It felt real—but what were the limits of the illusion? There was only one way to find out.

"What are you doing?"

"Testing." He put his left hand on the ground, palm down, and raised the rock in his right hand.

"Doug!"

He brought the rock down, hard enough to hurt but not hard enough to cause damage, were it real. There was a sensation of pressure, but no pain. He tried again, harder. The rock seemed to dissolve slightly when it impacted against his hand.

"Damn!"

"Safety mechanism," Pat said. "The sensual aspects are mostly neurocast. The programmers didn't want people doing real damage to themselves."

"But the brain *can* damage the body. Hypnotic suggestion, meditative states—"

"I know. Some of the people who wore the biomolecular gear died from it. But this room has a governor."

"Can Baby override it? Strengthen it?"

"I don't know."

"Find out," Copeland said. "And hurry!"

• • •

*Baby?*

THE FORMULA FOR SHALE'S CONSTANT IS SIX-POINT-NINE
TIMES EIGHT TO THE TWENTY-THIRD, DIVIDED BY THE SQUARE
ROOT OF THREE OVER—

*Baby, I need your help!*

—AB PLUS C, WHERE A IS THE DISTANCE FROM THE PRIME
POINT TO THE SECONDARY AND C EQUALS THE WAVELENGTH OF
RADIO EMMISION SINE—

"I can't link up. Baby is playing calculator."

"Wonderful. All right, let's get to the end of the wall and
see who's out there." Clutching the rock, Copeland moved
across the hot ground.

Sung could feel sand in her lowtop boots. The quality of
the illusions in the World Room never ceased to amaze her.
She had not used this particular program before—it was certainly one of the better ones. But it didn't matter how real it
seemed—she would not be stopped.

There was a black volcanic stone wall just ahead. It had to
be three and half, maybe four meters tall. Sung grinned. The
way of the ninja was to hide—sometimes, however, boldness
worked better. A ninja would blend into the wall, using it for
cover. But she wanted them to see her, to understand that she
was on to them.

Copeland and Pat edged along the wall near the southern
end, where the structure made a sharp turn. They were on the
ocean side, and anybody coming to look for them would likely
come through the break by the fish pond or around the northern end by the cove. It might be possible to circle behind them
and escape, though Copeland privately held little hope for
that. Sung would surely have the exit covered. But they had to
try.

As they reached the southern end of the wall and started
around it, he caught a peripheral hint of motion on top of the
wall near the pond. "Down!" he hissed. Both he and Pat
rounded the corner and dropped to the ground, white bodies
huddling in the golden sand.

"What—"

"Sung—on top of the wall."

Copeland looked at the imaginary rock he held. He glanced around, saw another stone, and picked it up.

"What are you going to do?"

"She'll probably walk up and down on top, looking for us. She'll be able to see us once she gets to the eastern corner; there's no place to hide."

"So that's it, then."

"No. Maybe she doesn't know about the rocks being harmless. Maybe I can frighten her into dodging and falling."

"If she's used this room at all, she'll know that won't work. She'll shoot you!"

"Like you said earlier, 'I'm open to suggestions.'"

Pat bit her lip in thought. "Give me one of the rocks. That way, she'll have two targets. We can throw at her from two angles and perhaps confuse her."

Copeland thought about it. He didn't want to expose Pat to Sung's dartguns; on the other hand, what she said made sense. And it was all an exercise in futility; if the imaginary rocks wouldn't hurt Sung, neither would a "fall" from an equally imaginary wall. But they had to do something!

"Okay. Here."

Sung could see the northern section of the compound from where she stood. There were a couple of places they could be hiding. There were some primitive structures, big huts or temples or whatever. She would check them, but first she would walk to the other end and see if they were behind that bend in the wall. She walked along the narrow top easily, her balance perfect. Knowing that she was in reality walking on a flat floor in an empty room did not contribute to that—the illusion was too complete. But her years of training kept her steps smooth and swift. She was enjoying the hunt.

Copeland stood at the base of the wall, near the bend. Pat was three meters back and behind a palm tree. He gripped the rock tightly, his heart pounding. He wondered what it would feel like to be shot. It seemed likely that he would find out in a few seconds.

Behind the tree, Ishida slipped into a quick radiopathic trance.

*Baby?*

—BUT IN THE GASEOUS STATE OCCUPIES A LITER EQUIVA-
LENT, FOUND BY DIVIDING THE SUMS OF THE STANDARD MOLE
PLUS THE INFREQUENT CORRECTED MOLE—

Sung was looking toward the huts to make sure nobody
sneaked out of them, so she missed him at first. Copeland
took a deep breath and three quick steps away from the wall.
Her back was to him, but she'd be turning in a second. He
cocked his arm for the throw.

"Sung!"

She spun at the shout, but the rock was already in the air.
She saw it, tried instinctively to dodge to her left, but was too
slow. Her balance, he saw with a sinking feeling, was perfect.
The rock "hit" her on the right shoulder. If it had been real,
the impact would have spun her from the wall. The fall might
not have injured her, but it would have put the wall between
them and certainly have disoriented her.

The rock was not real, however. The lava chunk seemed to
dissolve into her and fly out through her back. She raised from
her crouch and laughed. "Stupid move," she said. She pointed
her right spetsdöd at him.

Pat yelled and stepped from behind the palm. Sung raised
her second arm to cover the other woman, then relaxed as she
saw Pat draw back with the stone she held. She spread her
arms wide, inviting the throw. "Go ahead!" she shouted.

Pat threw the rock. Copeland watched the phantom stone
sail through the air, knowing it would have as much effect as
the first one—and stood staring in bewilderment as the rock
struck squarely between Sung's breasts, knocking her backward off the wall and out of sight. He heard her hit the ground
on the other side.

Pat ran to him.

"How did it—" he began.

"I got to Baby," she said. "Baby enhanced the neurocast—
made it real."

He nodded. He didn't understand how, but he didn't have
to. "We'd better move," he said.

"Baby made the fall real, too. She won't be following us
any time soon."

Copeland's compatch chimed. It was Fiske. "It's begun,"
the Colonel said.

They dressed, then made their way to the door and out of paradise.

# 27

Retelimba wasn't one of the men involved in the fake fight. His job would be somewhat more dangerous. Before he had ever touched a weight he had done some streetfighting in Fiji. Now he had muscle to add to his old skills.

One of the slurry workers approached another among the huge vats and pipes. He had to shout to be heard over the sound of the pumps. "Hey, muthafucka, what you doing over there?"

"None of your business, asshole."

"Yeah? Well, I just *made* it my business!"

The two men moved toward each other angrily. Good, Retelimba thought, watching from behind a catalytic unit. Any cameras watching them would think it was real . . .

The first punch was thrown. Two other men moved in, attempting to pull the fighters apart. Retelimba looked up at the soup, who stood on a catwalk above him; that worthy nodded and touched his compatch.

Three minutes later two of the cools arrived, both of them Sung's boys, and both wearing spetsdöds. By this time, the "fight" had expanded to six people, some of whom looked like they were taking it seriously. Retelimba saw blood on one man's nose.

The soup and the two cools ran toward the fighters. Retelimba fell in behind them. "Need help, bruddahs?"

"We'll handle it," one of them said. He leveled one of his spetsdöds at the struggling group. "Next man who moves gets shot!"

He was wrong. The next man who moved was Retelimba. The bodybuilder locked his massive arms around the cool and lifted him clear of the floor. The man's arms were pinned and his flailing feet were no use. The bodybuilder held him across his huge chest, parallel to the floor. One of the spetsdöds went off; unfortunately for the policeman, the dart hit one of his own kicking legs.

The second cool went down when the soup whacked him with a sock full of salt. Looked like soup had been on the streets some, too.

Two out of six, Retelimba thought.

The lone officer who answered the call on a domestic quarrel in Retelimba's cube found a woman sitting in the hallway, crying.

"What's the situation here, lady?"

Betsy Emau pointed at the closed door of the bedroom. "My lover is in there and he won't leave!"

"So?"

"You don't understand! My husband is coming home soon. He'll kill us both if he finds him in there!"

The officer grinned. "Ah. Well, I guess I'll have a little talk with him. He—uh—violent? Armed?"

"Oh, no. He's a librarian. He wouldn't hurt a fly."

The door slid back at the officer's prompt. "Hey, buddy, it's the police. Let's you and me have a conversation."

Ernie Teio, sitting on the bed, looked shocked. "P-police? I-I don't want any t-trouble."

"Neither do we, friend. Just do what you're told and nobody gets hurt." The officer swaggered into the room, then stopped and peered more closely at Teio. "Hey, don't I know you?"

Ernie Teio smiled and shrugged, while Fiske slipped out of the closet behind the policeman.

Fiske also had a sock full of salt.

"Look, there she is!" the old woman yelled. The two officers in the bar looked startled.

"What? Who?"

"That scientist! The one you're looking for! She went into the fresher!"

The two cools looked at each other. "Backup?" one asked.

"For one woman?" The Sergeant lifted his lip in a sneer.

"No way. We'll pluck this one ourselves. The old bitch will have a stroke when we bring her in."

They moved toward the fresher. The bar was fairly empty, but the few patrons there were surprised to see the old woman who had given the warning slip up behind the two officers. She did not move like an old woman.

The last thought the Sergeant had for some time was, Why was that old lady waving a sock in the air?

"She's not here," Fiske said.

Copeland looked around the featureless walls of the huge chamber in which the two men stood. There was certainly no place for anyone to hide once the program was shut down.

His voice echoed when he spoke. Looks like the fall didn't kill her."

Fiske nodded. "It doesn't matter. We have all her men and weapons. She can't beat us all. And she's probably injured. She'll turn up."

"I hope so."

"Don't worry about it, Doug. We're in control now." He paused a moment. "So, what's the drill?"

"What do you mean? Why ask me?"

"It's your show."

"Since when? I don't want the job."

"Too bad. You know more about what needs to be done, about the power plant and where it is, than anyone else. Like it or not, you're in charge. Temporarily, at least."

"Swell," Copeland said. He felt absolutely exhausted. He wished whoever had shut down the room had left the illusion of a chair. But there was no time to rest—and would not be, for a long time yet.

Crane felt the change in vibration as the city began to pick up speed. He sat on a ledge over a densecris viewport on the port side of a little-used storage frag. The city was covered with such nooks; he could swim around for years finding interesting spots he had never noticed before.

The water flowed over him, thin streams of turbulence full of fresh, new scents, and a faint familiar tang of metal from the siphons. Obviously they were going somewhere. He stroked along slowly, easily keeping up with the sedate pace of the city.

One of the dolphins swam next to him. Crane grinned at the mammal. He had named her Delphine. It was altogether too cute, like calling a dog Cain, but she didn't care.

What about it, Delphine? he thought. Shall we take a trip? Sail the deeps in search of new adventure?

The permanent smile seemed bigger to Crane as the creature swam around him. She looped and rolled in a watery Immelmann.

Sure, she seemed to say to him. Why not?

Her arm didn't hurt too badly. She was fairly sure it was only a jammed shoulder—nothing broken. Nothing grated there when she moved, anyway.

It was different for the two ribs, however. When she breathed too deeply it hurt, and she thought she could feel a slight give right next to the sternum when she moved too quickly. Sung wondered if she might have done less damage if she hadn't tried to roll. Probably not. Probably she would have broken her back. The roll hadn't worked; the angle and height had both been bad, and she had hit hard. It was the rock the woman had thrown that had done most of the damage.

She still did not understand it. Why had Copeland's rock been imaginary and Ishida's real? And the fall—that couldn't have been real, either.

A sound from the end of the hallway snatched at her attention. Solipsistic speculations would not help her now. Anything that happened now would be real, and dangerous. She swung her spetsdöds to cover the hatch. After a moment, she realized it was the metal of the walls expanding or contracting under pressure. She relaxed.

The first thing she had done when she had come to her senses was to find a place to hide. Knowing her own luck at finding fugitives, she wasn't too worried about being found; still, she had loaded her dartguns with the deadly Asp fléchettes. A quick attempt at contact on the police com she wore had told her she had better stay hidden. The scientists had taken over, and her troops were locked up.

It had seemed too easy from the start. Now, if they found her, she was likely to be in real trouble—probably a full session with the brainbenders. It was her against the whole city. But she wasn't dead, and she wasn't caught. She would stay hidden and bide her time.

Some how, some way, she would still triumph.

"Twelve degrees, fifteen minutes, four seconds north, one hundred and nine degrees, forty-five minutes, seventeen seconds east. Plus or minus point zero-zero-five."

Copeland looked at Teio and Pat, then back at the computer's map projection. They were in the control room of the main frag. "That's where we're going."

"How long will it take us?" Teio asked.

Copeland shrugged. "I don't know. We only had three of the five main generators installed when we started this voyage —sixty percent of full power. Then we lost one third of that when we had to cut the Number Three Power Frag loose. The remaining two generators should give us something around forty percent of what we need to mine, move and replicate; unfortunately, the Number One generator is acting up again and might have to be shut down. As it is, things are running slow. If we lose one of the generators, we'll have to crawl. Right now, Loftin says we're three months away. But if we lose half our power. . ."

Pat said, "The water looks pretty shallow there."

Copeland said, "Yeah. We've got a satellite footprinting the water for a couple of klicks around the station, and it ranges from eighty to about two hundred meters deep. A tight squeeze for us."

"We'll have to surface to work on it. That's a risk, even in antiviral suits." This was from Fiske, who had come in at the the end of Copeland's speech.

"What about breaking loose some tractor frags to haul the station out to deep water?" Teio said. "That way, we can keep the city sealed from the work crews until we've hooked the power up."

"Not to mention keeping the city in deep water," Copeland agreed. "The increase in volcanic activity makes me real nervous."

"Why so?" Fisked asked. "Are there any volcanoes close to the area?"

"Not that I know of. But a major eruption within a couple thousand kilometers would be enough. A *tsunami* in shallow water would shatter *Mea Lana* into small pieces."

"That's a pleasant thought. I vote for Ernie's tractor frags."

"*If* we have the power," Pat pointed out. "If we lose one of our generators, it won't be possible. One generator will barely keep the city alive and moving. Towing something the size of a power station would be out of the question."

"Okay," Fiske said. "So: best and worst case scenario?"

Copeland shook his head. "We just don't know. If we lose one of our generators and manage to get to the power plant, we'll have to park the city next door and install a new generator right there. No problem to do it, if we have time."

"But if a volcano lets go . . ."

"We're dead."

Fiske nodded. "Well, then—we'd just better keep our plants on-line until we can put new ones in."

Teio said, "If we have three months, we'd better start getting things ready. We'll need antiviral suits, teams trained to do the work, a lot of preparation. Best we get moving."

"Amen, brother," Fiske replied. He and Teio left the control room. Pat crossed to Copeland and put her hands on his shoulders. "You should rest," she said gently.

"Don't I know it. I saw Retelimba a couple of hours ago. He looked beat. If someone in as good a shape as he's in is feeling the effects of all this, where does that leave a middle-aged geologist who's more acquainted with bar stools than barbells?"

Pat smiled and kissed him. "Go home," she said. "Sleep. We have three months. Plenty of time to prepare for what has to be done."

Copeland nodded, abruptly aware that he would be lucky to reach his cube before he fell asleep. But as he moved toward the door, he could not help speculating that three months did not seem like very long at all. Not nearly long enough to save what was left of the world.

# PART IV

## Ascension

# 28

It took nearly five months for the *Mea Lana* Dome to travel over eight thousand kilometers from the South Pacific to the China Sea. They left French Polynesia and churned through Melanesia, over the Kermadec Ridge, across the North Fiji Basin and past the Solomons and New Guinea. They sailed the shallows of the Afafura Sea, north of dead Australia; through the Lesser Sundas and the channels of the Banda Basin they went, crossing the Celebes and Sulu seas; and, finally, through the Balabec Strait, with its atomic-blasted deep-water channel. They passed north of Malaysia and into the South China Basin.

It was not a continuous journey—they had to stop for repairs more than once—and for the last three months they had moved with what seemed glacial slowness, for the city had lost the use of the Number One generator, and only a single reactor remained at full strength.

Their options had, accordingly, been greatly reduced.

In the com room, Douglas Copeland sat watching the screens and wishing, not for the first time or even for the thousandth, that Captain Video were here. Four of the screens showed various views of the power station.

"No answer?"

Copeland looked up to see Retelimba. The man had been more or less in charge of labor since the scientists had taken over. Like Copeland, he didn't particularly want the job, but he did it to the best of his ability.

"Seems like nobody's home," Copeland replied.

The bodybuilder nodded. "That make our job easier."

"Maybe."

Retelimba looked at him. "Something on your mind, bruddah?"

Copeland stared at the screens. There had been no indication of trouble at the plant during their surveillance of it. No children running around on the surface decks playing games, of course; no vessels moving in the local waters—no signs of any life, not even seabirds. That was to be expected, of course, but . . .

"I don't know," he said. "Something feels a little strange about this."

Retelimba nodded. "Spirits, maybe."

"Yeah. Maybe." He looked away from the hypnotic holo-projections. "So, how's Betsy?"

"She fine. Getting bigger than a cow, belly out to here."

"How far along, now?"

"Almost eight months. Ultrasound say it gonna be boy. Healthy, so far."

"Congratulations."

"Yeah, thanks. We looking forward to it." Retelimba looked appraisingly at Copeland. "You puttin' on a little mass there, Doug."

"You should know, Coach." For the past six months Copeland had been working out three days a week under Retelimba's supervision. The results had been impressive. He had become several inches leaner in the waist, though he had not lost much weight, having replaced most of it with muscle. There was still a fold of fat around his middle, and there probably always would be, but he felt better than he could recall feeling in years. Though he slept less by an hour or more a night, he felt calmer and more rested.

It had helped his mental well-being too. For several weeks after the episode in the World Room, he had had nightmares about Sung. He had felt terribly vulnerable and ineffectual and had found it very difficult to go about his business in the open areas of the city without feeling paranoid. Though time had been the major healer of that, getting in shape had helped too. Now he at least felt he might have a chance of outrunning her if she ever showed up again.

For they had never found her. It was assumed that she was still hiding out somewhere in the myriad frags—if anyone could survive that kind of a life, it was Sung.

Retelimba looked at the screens. "Not much longer," he said, changing the subject.

"A couple of days. We're only about fifty kilometers out. How's everything in the wrecking crew?"

"Pretty good. We got sixty divers who can work, a hundred techs and maybe two hundred blues all set. We get there, that station gonna come apart for us like a cheap radio."

"We hope."

"Ah, no problem, bruddah. We have it stripped in two-three months, easy. Most of the crew know the plans for what station better than they know whoever they sleeping with. Gonna be a slide."

Copeland hoped the big man was right. "We'll see."

Two days later the city hovered in a scant hundred meters of water, three kilometers to the southeast of the Vietnamese power station. Copeland, Fiske, Pat and Teio were in the com room, watching the first of the exploratory frags dislink, when the alarms went off.

"What is it?" Teio said.

Instead of answering, Copeland repeated the question to the computer.

"Underwater vessel approaching; estimated speed sixty-nine knots; vector angle indicates impact with sector fourteen-echo-one in two minutes, twelve seconds."

Fiske swore. "Get a camera on it, stat! Put the image on monitor six!"

A moment later the scene flowered into blue-gray life. "Enhance it," Fiske ordered. "Give me another angle on it. Forty-five degrees!"

Copeland watched as the holoproj shimmered. The screen split and a computer-generated image appeared on the left. The sub was long, narrow and didn't seem large enough to house even a single man. Copeland said as much.

"It's not a sub," Fiske said. "It's a torpedo. They're shooting at us!"

Teio gasped. "Can we stop it?"

"Not with a shark field." Fiske looked at Pat, who nodded and closed her eyes.

*Baby?*

YES, CASSANDRA?

*Will you do something for me?*

ANYTHING. YOU KNOW THAT.

*Can you see that small submarine approaching the city from the direction of the power plant?*

YOU MEAN THE TORPEDO, CASSANDRA?

*Yes. The torpedo. Can you head it away from the city and out to sea?*

SURE. ITS GUIDANCE SYSTEM IS SIMPLE. THERE IT GOES.

*Thank you, Baby. And if they shoot any others at us, would you send them away, too?*

SURE, NO PROBLEM.

Copeland watched the torpedo change course and veer out to sea on the port side of the city. He looked at the others. Pat opened her eyes, breaking her trance.

"Could be it's an automatic defense system, triggered by proximity," Fiske said.

"And it could be there are people onboard the station," Copeland replied. "Who are shooting at us."

Pat asked, "If so, why haven't they answered our calls?"

"I don't know. Can Baby check, somehow? We should have thought about that before—"

At that moment the main speaker came alive with a strident, singsong voice. Copeland didn't recognize the language.

"Vietnamese," Teio said. "I know a few words."

"What are they saying?" Fiske asked.

Teio listened, then shook his head. "Too fast. I'll get the computer to translate it."

The message that the short-delay language interface translated was simple and to the point: "Go away! Go away or we'll kill you!" Well, Copeland thought; at least now we know where we stand."

It didn't make him feel any better.

•   •   •

Her ribs had healed, but the shoulder was still sore at times, especially when she was in a frag with high humidity. Any time she hid out somewhere with a lot of open water, like the hydroponics section, her upper arm ached like hell. Fortunately, they didn't seem to be looking for her very much these days. It had been a month since she had seen any patrols. Maybe they thought she was dead. Maybe they had forgotten about her. Yeah, and maybe they thought the Earth was flat, too.

Sung could tell that something was up. The city had stopped again, and from her furtive glimpse of public newscasts, she knew they were in the China Sea. They had to be close to the power station, and evidently they were going to do something about it. There had been a lot of activity in the last couple of days: people moving around, frags being loaded with gear and dislinking.

Maybe the scientists could pull it off after all. When the power had gone down a couple of months back she had gotten a lot more dark places to hide, and she had wondered if that might be the end of things. Apparently not, however. But now all the activity had stopped. The expedition hadn't gone forth, and that meant something was wrong. Maybe it was something she could use to her advantage. That would be nice; it was about time she got a break in her favor. She would snoop around and see what she could see . . .

Betsy felt like a beached whale. She stuffed another pillow under her low back and tried to get comfortable on the bed, but it was a wasted effort. She ached, she had to pee, and the baby had to be doing some kind of war dance inside her. She glanced at her swollen belly. "Hey, settle down in there, little Lem! That's my bladder you're kicking!"

The door slid open and Limo stepped inside. He smiled at her. "Hello, Mama."

"Don't you 'Hello, Mama' me! Your son's being a brat! He's trying to punch his way out. He's doing squats with my kidneys."

Retelimba walked to the bed, sat gently on the edge and laid one hand on Betsy's abdomen. "A little *reiki* make the boy feel better."

"The boy? What about me?"

"I got two hands." He put the other hand on Betsy's forehead. She felt the heat begin under his palms. He called it *reiki*—some kind of faith healing he had learned from his mother. She hadn't believed it when he had explained about channeling energy from the cosmos through his body and into his hands—it had sounded like the stuff the priests at Father Damien had kept trying to pound into her. But it worked. The baby almost always got quiet—like he was doing now—and she could feel the heat and energy pass from him into her like some kind of spiritual drug. It felt wonderful. She told him so.

"Um." It was no big deal to him; he'd done it all his life.

"So, what's happening out there in the world?"

"Things not so good," he said. "The dogeaters in the power station, they don't want to talk deal. They just keep saying, 'Go away.' No negotiation, no nothing. They afraid we'll give them the disease. They say they'll blow us to kingdom after, we come any closer. Every once in a while, they shoot another torpedo at us. Ishida's computer stops 'em."

Betsy pretended to pout. "Ishida! You talk about her a lot. She's pretty, isn't she? And smart. Not fat and stupid like me. I bet you'd rather be with her then with me."

"You a silly woman sometimes, you know? Ishida don't mean nothing to me. Ishida don't love me, I don't love her. Why you say such things?"

She grinned at him. "So you'll say what you just said. I feel big, fat, pale and pregnant, and I could listen to you sweet-talk me all day."

"What sweet talk?"

"That's what I mean, musclebrain. You never do it. I have to drag it out of you."

"No need to say it—you know it."

"Yes, yes, there *is* a need to say it! I want to hear how much you love me. I want you to tell me a hundred million times how beautiful you think I am."

He grinned. "What? Big-fat-pale-pregnant woman like you? You think I'm crazy?"

"Limo!"

The grin became a laugh. "You know I love you. You beautiful. You happy, now?"

She considered it. "Better. But I think you should lay down here and pet me and kiss my ear and tell me some more."

"Sistah, I'd know you were gonna be this much trouble, maybe I wouldn't have married you."

"Limo . . ."

"Ah, I never did have any brains. Move over."

Ernie Teio's compatch chimed. "Yes?"

"Ernie. Copeland. Could you come up to the com room when you get a minute? There's a new development."

"Good or bad?"

"Bad."

"Why aren't I surprised?" Teio sighed. "I'm on my way."

In the com room, Copeland, Fiske and a couple of techs were watching the screens when Teio entered. "So what now? Gabriel decide to blow the last trump?"

"Maybe. It looks as though there is some activity in the Inouye Guyot. Possibly another eruption building. And there are a couple of other underwater volcanoes rumbling in the local basins, too."

"Anything close?"

Copeland pointed to a map on one of the screens. "Close enough. We get anything bigger than a six-five or six-six within any of these and we could be in big trouble." He addressed the computer. "Give me map and read on Spratly, Kepulauan and Natuna guyots."

The screens lit with the information. "These are the three I'm worried about," Copeland said. "Spratly is only six hundred klicks away, though it's pretty quiet. Kepulauan is more than a thousand kilometers south, and Natuna is maybe eight hundred, but they are more active. If either one blows, the wave will funnel right at us."

Fiske said, "Any way to predict it?"

"Sure—with a ton of gear on each one and six specialized satellites doing hourly flyovers. None of which we have. If we're lucky, we might get a couple of hours' warning."

"So what can we do?" Teio asked.

"Nothing, really. I just wanted you to be aware of the situation. If we don't get something going with those people over there in the power station pretty soon, we might not have time to make it to deep water even if they do finally give in."

"What are you trying to say, Doug?" Fiske asked quietly.

Copeland took a deep breath. "I'm saying that if they won't give us what we have to have, then maybe we ought to consider taking it. It just might be them or us."

"Are you going to tell the others?"

"As soon as I can get it set up."

Teio stared at the floor. "Another war."

"I hope not, Ernie," Copeland said. "But we're talking about maybe the end of the human race here. And those people over there started all this. I don't feel as sorry for them as I do for us. We didn't come all this way to die now."

Fiske nodded. "All right," he said. "Let's do something."

# 29

"Suggestions?" Copeland asked.

He and twenty other section leaders, as well as Ishida and Fiske, occupied the auditorium in the main frag. The basic question had been answered: they *were* going to attempt to obtain both atomic and solar-net generators from the power station three kilometers off their port bow. If the occupants were hostile, they would have to be dealt with accordingly. If not, there was plenty of room for them on *Mea Lana*.

"Direct attack," somebody said.

Fiske fielded that one. "No good. Our AI can affect certain kinds of control systems—torpedoes, for instance—but something without guidance electronics might not be amenable to radiopathic contact."

"In English, Colonel," Retelimba said dryly. Several people laughed.

"Baby can't stop a bullet."

"And, since we don't know how much weaponry they have, we're at a disadvantage," Copeland added.

"What about using the AI to find out?" Bevins, in charge of Hydroponics, asked.

"For that matter," came another voice, "why can't we just have the AI take over the station and open the goddamn hatches?"

Ishida looked at Copeland, who shrugged. "Might as well tell them," he said.

She nodded. "I've talked to Baby about it," she said. "Baby won't do it."

"What do you mean, 'won't do it'? Order it to!"

Ishida turned to fix the man who had spoken—Max McCloud, one of the divers—with a cold stare. "Baby doesn't want to hurt anybody."

"Yeah? What about that British submarine?"

There was a murmur of agreement in the room.

"That's why Baby won't," Ishida said. She hesitated. How to explain? That Baby had felt her grief over the incident, and from that grief had learned sorrow, regret and pain? That Baby knew it hurt her to ask for such a thing, so it now refused to do anything to cause that pain? No. It was far too complex to attempt to explain to people who didn't know what it was like to wear the BV-Two Eyes. It had been hard enough to convince Baby to strike Sung down—she knew it would not participate in another mass murder.

She simply said, "Baby learned what killing was from that. It won't do it again. Protecting us from attack is one thing; attacking somebody else is another."

"It's enough to realize that that option is not viable," Copeland said. "Let's hear some other suggestions."

After an hour, there were several ideas that showed promise. An unmanned exploration frag could be used to test the station's sensors; human divers might be small enough to bypass the station's sonar or doppler; Baby could try to contact the station's computer and find out as much as possible without being a threat to those onboard.

Copeland didn't want to waste any time. He rigged the drone himself, checking to see that the cameras and broadcast gear were operating properly. Max volunteered to lead two other divers on a recon patrol. Pat went to her room to contact Baby.

In the communications room, Teio, Fiske and Copeland watched the frag leave *Mea Lana* and start toward the power station. Max and his two divers were already swimming toward the distant structure. They wore Parker-Rand gills and compatches but carried no weapons except sharkshockers.

This was to be a look-see operation only.

And while it went on, Pat would be trying to cajole Baby into spying inside the station.

*Baby?*
HI, CASSANDRA.
*Can you talk to the computer on the power station?*
SURE.
*Would you do that? Find out what kind of sensor systems it uses to check the air and water around it, if you can.*
OKAY. YOU WANT IT NOW?
*You've already done it?*
SURE. IT ONLY TOOK A LITTLE WHILE.

The frag was half a klick from the station when the cameras picked up several fuzzy-looking balls floating in the water. According to the scale on the image, they were about the size of grapefruits. They hung in neutral buoyancy, perhaps a half dozen of them within the camera's field.

"Steer around them," Fiske said. "They might be mines."

Copeland turned the frag to starboard. "Doppler reading on the spheres," he said.

The computer flashed numbers on a screen: size, shape, proximity—

"Some of them are following the frag," Teio said suddenly, studying the changing numbers on the holoproj.

"Mines," Fiske said. "Some kind of magnetically-activated drive, I'd bet. Better move the frag faster."

"They're getting closer," Teio added. Copeland punched up the speed.

"You're leaving them," Teio sounded relieved.

Copeland started to smile, then leaned forward. "What's that?"

It happened too fast to follow. On the replay, with slo-mo and computer enhancement, they could see it was some kind of small missile—about the size of a man's arm, they estimated. Not very big, but big enough to blow the frag away. Which is what it evidently had done—the holocam went abruptly blank, and all the download information ceased.

Copeland exhaled in disappointment. "Well. So much for that." He turned to the Colonel. "Martin?"

Fiske shook his head. "I don't know. Some kind of wire-guided rocket, I'd guess; maybe a Water Rat. Controlled by a man on the other end; so as long as the wire isn't broken, it goes where you point it. I don't think the AI could stop it."

"Doug!" It was Pat, over the com. Copeland's hand went to his compatch. "Yes?"

"Baby says the station has above-water radar and vessel-detecting sonar. Anything with a cross-section bigger than a large shark will show."

"Yeah, we just figured that out."

"It also has doppler and sonics tuned to scuba exhaust emission."

"Damn!" Copeland wheeled about to address the computer. "Get me the divers on frequency Alpha-six!"

"On-line," the computer said.

"Listen, Max, back off! They'll be able to hear you if you get too close!"

"We aren't making a lot of noise out here, Dr. Copeland." Max's voice was muted by his breathing apparatus.

"They have sonic sensors; they can hear your exhaust bubbles."

"I never heard of such a thing."

"I don't give a damn *what* you've heard of—just turn around!"

"Yeah, all right, we'll—uh-oh."

"Max?"

"Looks as if we've got company. Five, six, eight of 'em. Wearing compressed air scuba. Carrying some kind of weapons; looks like spearguns. They won't have much range."

"Max, get the hell away from there!"

"We're already gone—shit!"

"What is it?"

"More of 'em; they circled around behind us. We're in a box."

Copeland's mouth was dry. He glanced at the others, who were also staring intently at the readouts. "Surrender, then."

"Jesus, they shot Lucy!"

*"Max!"*

There were muffled yells and shouts—then the comline was silent.

Copeland could not look at the others. The only sound was of the subdued beeps and whines of the computer and the various readouts. But it seemed as if he could hear, deep within him, the echo of his voice shouting similar commands long ago in another world.

*Rick, get out of there . . .*

Sometime later, in the planning room, Fiske finished reviewing the situation for the section leaders. "It doesn't look good. They won't talk and we can't get to them. They can see and hear any kind of conventionally powered vessel and any man with breathing gear. We don't have anything that runs on chemical or solar drive. Even a dolphin would have to carry something mechanical to do us any good, and very likely they could spot that.

"Quite frankly, we're out of our element."

Ernie Teio sat up a bit straighter. Copeland caught the motion. "Ernie? You have an idea?"

"Maybe," Teio said. "Just maybe."

The dolphins were disappearing. Crane was worried about that a lot more than he had been worried about the frag and the divers who had left the city. None of them had returned, which was interesting in an academic way. But his real concern was for the dolphins.

He swam down near the mouth of the nearest breathing inset, looking for his friends. It had been several hours since he had seen any of them, and that had never happened before. Then, while sculling outside the inset, he heard the hoots from inside, and suddenly eight or nine of them seemed to boil out and surround him. Crane silently laughed as they circled him. He hadn't realized how much he liked having them around.

Then he noticed something: each of the dolphins was wearing a harness, and each harness bore a transceiver.

Well, well. This was a new twist. Teio had tried sending out a comset every now and then, but never eight at once. He must really want to talk.

Crane coaxed the nearest dolphins to him, untabbed the Velcro straps and allowed the harness and com to sink into the depths. One by one, he stripped the webbing from the dolphins and sent the equipment toward the bottom.

On impulse, he kept the last comset. He didn't turn it on,

but he did keep it. Not that he was lonely, but it might be interesting to talk to Ernie sometime . . .

The three of them sat at the edge of the inset pool, watching the water. "How'd it go?" Copeland asked.

"Okay," Teio replied. "I sent out eight units. Told the carriers in Freedolph to take them to the 'man fish.' "

"And?"

"And seven of them are resting on the bottom," Pat said. "The other one is about five hundred meters away and stationary, according to the bug in it."

"You think Crane has it?"

"I hope so," Teio said. "I hope he's still alive out there."

"And your plan?"

"I'm going to turn the transceiver on from here and start talking. Maybe he'll listen. It's all I can do."

Retelimba was nervous. Betsy had been cramping all day. The medics had said it was no problem, that they weren't birth contractions yet; still, it made him edgy. Before, when his children had been born, he hadn't been around for it. This time he'd been studying tapes and learning things. He was going to be there to see this baby born.

He didn't much care for being in a position where he had to tell people what to do. Thing was, the bruddahs in blue didn't much trust the people uplevels in Admin. But they trusted him; he was one of them. Hey, bruddah, you talk for us. And after the deal with the police, the Admin people smiled when they saw him coming, so it worked out okay. He'd rather be making ingot, but wasn't none of that gonna be done until they got more power.

He walked into the gym, waved at some of the regulars, and started stacking weights to warm up. He couldn't just tell the bruddahs to fuck off; he was a family man now, he had things to take care of. So, for a while, he'd be a go-between. Until things got to running better. After that, well, he'd see.

But right now he had iron to move—otherwise he was gonna be turning to blubber. Got to the point where he was missing two workouts a week, sometimes. He didn't watch it, he was gonna be harpooned by somebody . . .

•   •   •

Crane happened to be looking right at the transceiver when it started broadcasting. It was nestled in a clump of seaweed on a flat section of plating by one of his favorite perches. He was about three meters away when Teio's amplified voice sounded.

"Jonathan, listen to me. We need your help. This isn't a trick, I promise. You don't have anything to fear from me. I won't try to keep you inside. But unless you help us, we might all die. If you feel anything for us at all, at least talk to me.

"I know you probably don't have any free air to speak, so just do this for me: meet me in the dolphin inset where you saw me last. A few minutes, Jonathan; that's all I ask. If you like it where you are, if you like what you've become, you owe me something for helping you achieve it. Please.

"I'll repeat this message for the next hour, and then I'll go there to wait. I'll be alone, Jonathan. No tricks. Your life is your own."

Crane stared at the comset for a long time. When it started to repeat the message, he picked it up and crushed it in his hands. The wrecked circuitry drifted and slowly sank in the still water.

Well. Well, well, well. What could Ernie possibly want? How badly did he want to find out?

# 30

Ernie Teio leaned against the wall near the edge of the dolphin pool, waiting.

It all depended on how well he knew Crane. He had talked with the others about it; they had Crane's psychological profile, with analyses by human medics and diagnostic computers. But that was from before, when he had been . . . human. Teio knew now that the surgery and the genetic restructuring had gone far deeper than he had thought. Jonathan wasn't really human any longer. He had become a

new and different form of intelligent life. The only way they
could reach him was to appeal to whatever part of him still
remembered what it was like to be human. Otherwise it would
be like talking to a dolphin.

Or maybe a shark . . .

*Baby?*
No answer. Cassandra felt the AI's presence, but there was
no input, nothing downloaded that could be considered conscious communication. Was Baby off in pure mathematics
land again? Or had some other discipline come forth from that
unique brain to claim the AI's attention? There was so much
she didn't know—

Abruptly, a flood of data washed over her—a surge of
information so scrambled that it blended into a synesthetic
surge of sight, sound, taste and feel, as well as radiopathic
senses that ordinary humans could not begin to comprehend.
Waves beyond human ken, short and long, and impulses only
machines could register filled her mind:

—apogee orbit and recording, flux movement as —
— pip pip pip skeet skeet pip pip pip —

```
    .                                    .
         .                          .
    .                                    .
         .         .        .
    .                                    .
```

oxoxoxoxoxox oxoxoxoxoxo oxox oxoxo ox oxo
12121222211212122 121212121222122111212 121
—tetonic activity increase noted and correlated —
=-.=-.=-.=-.=-.=-.=-.=-.=--.=-.=-.=-.=-.=-.=
+ = + = + = + = + = + = + = + = + = + = + = +
RRRRRRRRRRRRRRRRRRRRRRRRRRRRRRRRRRRRRRRRR
—dkhe gthht vjgnbj sejooms snhg piloiuth unn —
--   --  -- --  --  -- --  -- --  --  -- --  -- --  -- --
()()()()()()()()()()()()()()()()()()()()()()
●● ●● ●● ●● ●● ·●● ●● ●● ●● ●● ●● ●● ●● ●● ●●

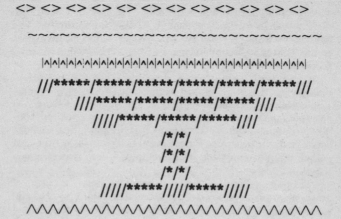

Mad pictures flowed through her, both in normal spectrum and infrared and ultraviolet. Sounds scaled from deep sub to ultrasonic. Nerves shrieked at fire overlaid with ice and steel. The sensory inundation threatened to burn out her brain.

She screamed.

*Baby! Help me!*

CASSANDRA? WHAT'S THE MATTER?

The images ceased.

Cassandra was dimly aware of her body soaked in sweat, lying limply half off the couch. *B-baby, wh-what was that?*

YOU ACCESSED A PORTION OF MY INFEED, CASSANDRA. I DON'T KNOW HOW IT HAPPENED.

*What did it all mean? It seemed so important.*

But she did not need an answer. As she spoke, pieces of the overload clicked together in an intuitive flare and made, for the briefest of instants, sense. A pattern emerged to her so fleetingly that she could only wonder at its complexity before it was gone.

But she knew what it meant.

She had to get to Doug. They were in trouble.

Michelle Li Sung had killed a man.

It had been an accident. Or, rather, it had been intentional, but more of a reflex than a conscious decision. She had been dozing in the back of a storage frag. The unit had been running on partial power, just enough to keep it pressurized, and the heaters were off. She had wrapped herself in an insulation pad to fight off the cold and had just nodded off when the idiot found her.

It had been her fault; she shouldn't have left herself so vulnerable, even if she had been virtually certain nobody would come into this particular frag. She had been wrong.

"Hey, what are you doing here?"

It was being half-asleep and feeling trapped in the pad that had done it. Before she could think, she had thrown the cover off and fired a single round into his throat. The Asp fléchette had worked as well as advertised; the man was dead before she had had time to check his pulse.

He had been alone, apparently, and not looking for her. Some chore had sent him this way. Sooner or later, Sung knew, he'd be missed. She felt a sensation close to panic. Up till now she had been lucky; her coup would probably have only gained her imprisonment, but actual murder would be harder to work around.

She had to get rid of the body.

It took ten minutes to check the area and make certain she was alone. Another three minutes was required to drag the dead man to an inspection lock. It took two tries before the body worked its way out into the ocean.

When it was over, she leaned limply against the wall next to the lock controls, massaging her throbbing shoulder. It would be all right now. The scavengers of the deep would make short work of him before anyone out on an inspection could find him.

She hoped.

Crane's head broke the still surface of the pond and he expelled water from his gills in a noisy blast.

Teio jerked upright from an uneasy doze. Jonathan! He had come!

The geneticist stood up with exaggerated slowness, as if afraid of frightening a skittish forest animal. Crane surveyed the room carefully, then swam to the lip of the pond and clambered out.

Teio heard the inrush of air as Crane breathed for the first time, as far as he knew, in months. He watched, hypnotized, as rivulets of water streamed from the fish man's scales, which gleamed in the harsh light. He could smell him—a scent vaguely fishlike but ultimately like nothing he had ever smelled.

Crane made a sound that Teio didn't recognize, at first, for what it was: his own name.

"Ernie." The voice was truly alien.

Teio swallowed. The unreality of it all suddenly struck him. Over the months of slowly sculpturing Jonathan Crane into a new life-form, he had become used to the man's appearance. The mutation had occurred so gradually that there had never been a time when he had been able to step back and see the monstrousness of it. But more months had passed now, and their passage had given him new eyes with which to view his creation. Add to that the sensation, subjective but nonetheless convincing, that Crane's personality had most definitely suffered a sea change into something richer and stranger than even Shakespeare could have envisioned. Teio knew that he was not speaking to a man—he was speaking to something that might as well be from another planet.

"Hello, Jonathan."

"What do you want?"

Teio felt his heart pounding. "We're in trouble, Jonathan. We need your help."

Crane stood totally motionless. Teio could no more read his expression than he could have read a fish's. "What kind of trouble?" the bioformate asked at last.

Teio told him about the power station, about the breakdowns, about the chance of a volcanic eruption. "We can't get past their defenses, Jonathan."

"What makes you think I can?"

"They aren't set up to see you. They can spot a powered craft or divers with breathing gear, but they won't worry about large . . . uh, I mean—"

"Large fish?" Crane made a gargling sound. Teio realized that his former colleague was laughing.

"Yes."

"So?"

"You can disable their sensor equipment. There are external antennae, dishes, like that. If they're out of commission, we can get inside."

"Quite likely you can. But why should I help you?"

This was it, Teio knew. He had argued with the experts about what his reply should be. Tell him that we can make more like him if we have the power, they had said. No! he had answered. He *wants* to be unique. If he thinks there will be more like him, he won't help us!

Well then, they had said, tell him that we'll give him anything he wants.

But Ernie Teio knew that that would be futile as well. The creature that had been Jonathan Crane already had everything he wanted—almost. There was still one thing he lacked, one thing he had always desired above all else.

With the echo of Crane's question still seeming to linger in the still recycled air, the man who had created him took a deep breath and gave his answer: "Because only you can save mankind, Jonathan. If we fail at this, we'll die. If we die, there aren't enough people on Earth to keep the species going."

Jonathan said nothing. Teio closed his eyes. "You'll be a hero, Jonathan. For as long as people live, they'll remember you as their savior. The name of Jonathan Crane will be more famous than Jesus or Buddha or Mohammed. They only taught religion and influenced future thought—but *you* will have literally saved us from extinction. You, alone."

Crane stood at the edge of the pool for a long time. Then, finally, he nodded slightly, and his distorted mouth stretched to show his sharp teeth. Teio realized that the hideous rictus was in fact a smile.

"Yes. I like that, Ernie. I like that a lot."

Teio found he had been holding his breath. He let it out slowly, so as not to make any sound.

Crane started to return to the pool, then stopped. He glanced over his shoulder at Teio, and there was something about the movement—something so terrifyingly alien, and at the same time so human—that Teio very nearly stepped back in fear.

"Oh, something else, Ernie. Did you know there's a dead man floating around outside?"

Copeland came into the com room and found Fiske talking to Ernie Teio.

"We've shown him the location and pictures of the sensor gear," Fiske said. "He knows what to look for and what to do.

It will be risky; the detection equipment will probably be fairly sturdy. He'll have only his hands; we can't chance giving him any tools. Do you think he can do it?"

"He's very strong."

Copeland said, "How will we know when it's done?"

"We wait until he comes back and tells us," Ernie answered.

"I'd rather he had a transmitter," Fiske said.

Ernie shook his head. "I won't risk it. And besides, he wouldn't take it. He thinks this is his shining hour, Colonel, and he will do it his way or not at all. Do you understand? The new man, naked and unaided, against the evil dregs of the old."

What a bizarre, long journey it's been, Copeland thought, to bring me to a point where this conversation doesn't even sound strange. "There's a lot riding on this, Ernie," he said.

"We know that," Fiske said.

"So does Jonathan," Ernie said. "He would rather be famous than alive. He'll do it or die trying. I know it."

The sound of running footsteps caused them all to look up as Pat burst into the com room. She looked out of breath and very upset. Copeland immediately stood and crossed to her. "Pat? You okay?"

"A volcano," she gasped. "It's going to erupt."

The others looked at each other, then at her, incredulously. "What?" Fiske demanded.

"I saw it—through Baby. I can't explain it, but I know."

"Which volcano?" Copeland asked. "When?"

She shook her head. "I didn't get that. But it's close to us, in the China Sea. And it will be soon. I don't know exactly when, but I could 'feel' the pressure building in it."

"Jesus and Buddha in a hammock," Fiske whispered.

Copeland said, "Can you find out more?"

"I don't know. I'll try."

Retelimba was talking to a supervisor in the staging room when the call came in.

"Base, we found the package. Right where the big halibut said it'd be."

"Bring it in," said the supervisor.

It took ten minutes, and it wasn't a job for someone with a

weak stomach. The body had been in the water a couple of days and the fish had gotten at it. Most of the face was gone, but they already had an ID on the corpse.

A medic gave the body a brief exam. He poked and prodded, stuck a long needle into the chest, then slapped a remote scanner over a blackish spot on the throat. Retelimba watched as the device sparkled with LED readouts.

"Suicide?" he asked.

The medic pulled the scanner from the cold, puckered flesh and looked at the device. "No water in his lungs; he didn't drown. He was dead before he hit the water. Something stuck him right there—see that necrotic discoloration? Some kind of poison. We'll find out what in the autopsy."

Retelimba scratched his head. "You saying somebody killed him?"

The medic packed up his kit. "I'm saying it's awful hard for a dead man to open a lock and blow himself out into the ocean."

Retelimba heard later that they'd pulled a spetsdöd dart from the body, one loaded with poison. That narrowed down the suspects pretty good. Nobody had ever found Sung— well, check that—it looked like one person had. But he wasn't saying anything.

Back in their cube, he told Betsy about it. "This be a great time to have a baby. I talked to Copeland; he say the crazy computer woman predicting some volcano is getting ready to blow up and send a wave our way, so we got to get the generators quick and move, 'cept the power plant is full of greeps who won't give us shit and want to blow us up, besides. Not to mention the goddamned virus, some loony fishman who we got no choice except to trust, and a killer with a poison dart-gun running around. Nice place to raise a family."

"But the rent is cheap," she said.

He looked surprised; than he laughed, loudly and for a long time. When he finished, he had tears in the corners of his eyes. "You something else, you know? Really something." Then he hugged her, and, feeling her in his arms and the baby moving within her, he somehow knew it would be all right.

# 31

Fiske wore a pair of spetsdöds, looking quite uncomfortable with the small rectangles stuck on the backs of his hands. "I keep worrying that I'll shoot myself in the foot," he said to Copeland.

Copeland nodded. He knew the feeling. Tucked into his jacket pocket was a taser, which gave him a feeling compounded of equal parts confidence and fear. With the discovery of the murdered crewman, all the firepower in the police armory had been passed out. Sung was not only still alive, but also still dangerous. They couldn't spare the time or personnel to search for her now; not with the operation coming up. On the other hand, to ignore her would be foolish. After the power station was secured—*if* it was secured—they could look for her in earnest.

The two men sat at a small table in the Main Dome cafeteria, drinking tea. Copeland said, "I'm still not sure about this going in the dark."

"It makes sense, Doug. They can't see Crane, and after he wrecks their electronic eyes, they won't be able to see us, either."

"It'll be dark on both sides, Martin."

"Yes, but we know we're going. They don't."

"How long do you think it will take them to figure out what's happening once their doppler and sonar go down?"

Fiske shrugged and finished his tea. "Long enough, I hope."

Copeland glanced at his watch. "Almost twenty-one hundred."

Fiske nodded and pushed his chair back. "We'd better get to the staging area."

• • •

Crane hung in liquid night, the water around him jet black, broken only by faint sparkles of bio-luminescence and the lights of the city eight hundred meters behind him. It was almost time. The dolphins should be reporting back soon. He smiled in anticipation.

Ernie had suggested using the dolphins for decoys, but he hadn't been thinking clearly. Dolphins breathed air, and any of them who did not have a protected source, such as *Mea Lana*, would soon be as dead as any other mammal. Also, the people on the power station weren't stupid. Any sudden appearance of dolphins would surely be perceived as a threat from the submarine city.

Crane had had a better idea. For the last two days the dolphins had been chasing several schools of bluefin tuna past the power station. Although most of the fish were smaller than Crane, there were probably ten or fifteen that were half again as large. The gear on the power station couldn't be sophisticated enough to tell a two-meter-long tuna from a two-meter-long man.

Delphine flippered up to him; Crane heard and felt her before he saw her. She chittered at him. *Ready*, she said.

The dolphins were herding the fish their way. Crane stroked the dolphin's back. Delphine would tow him—he couldn't keep pace with a bluefin, but she could—and when the school of tuna angled past the station, one of them would stay. They wouldn't be able to see him once he got close enough; the sonar couldn't watch itself.

The water swirled around him, the currents of the driven fish dancing on his bare skin. Delphine surged forward with powerful strokes of her tail, and Crane streamed out behind her like a flag in the wind.

Surging through water as dark as ink, the savior of mankind went forth to do battle.

Retelimba pressed the hatch of the exploration frag down and sealed it. He tapped on the thick densecris port, and the man inside nodded and gave him a thumbs-up.

Behind him, Copeland said, "Everything okay?"

"Okay as it's gonna get. These little subs weren't made for fightin' no war."

"I know. We do the best we can with what we have."

The bodybuilder looked around the staging chamber. All six of the exploration minifrags were set to go. He tilted his head back. Perched on a quarter superfloor just above him, the soup in charge of the staging cupped one hand around his left ear. When he spoke, his voice was electronically amplified to carry the length of the large chamber. "Okay, people, let's clear the area. We're filling the tub in two minutes."

Retelimba and Copeland started for the exit, as did Fiske from the other side of the chamber.

"You sure they can't see the frags this far?" Retelimba asked.

"Not as long as they stay next to the city," Fiske said. "Once they move more than a few hundred meters away, they'll be trackable—if the Viets' sonar and doppler are still working."

Copeland looked around the small antechamber. "Where's Ernie?"

"At the dolphin inset," Fiske said, "waiting for Crane. And Pat?"

"In my cube, talking to Baby."

"Stand by," the frag soup's voice said. "Depressurization in thirty seconds."

The three men standing outside the lock looked at each other. Fiske said, "If you have any particular gods who owe you favors, now's the time to call them in."

"Depressurizing," came the amplified voice. "Good luck!"

Retelimba thought about Betsy and his unborn son. Yeah. Good luck, bruddahs and sistahs. You got us all riding with you.

*Can you show me what they see, Baby?*

A surge of violent impressions flooded Cassandra's mind. *Wait! Stop!*

The images died. CASSANDRA? ARE YOU ALL RIGHT?

*Yes. I just don't have your abilities, that's all. It's too much for me to understand at once.*

NOT REALLY. YOU SAW IT BEFORE. YOU HAVE TO BELIEVE YOU CAN.

*I-I'm afraid, Baby. My mind—*

IS MORE THAN CAPABLE, CASSANDRA. MINDS LIKE YOURS MADE ME. YOU HAVE NO LIMITS, SAVE FOR THOSE YOU SET YOURSELF.

Lying on Copeland's bed, she twisted the sheet in her hands. *What about the others, Baby? The ones who were burned up by the mindblow?*

THEY COULDN'T ACCEPT IT. YOU CAN.

On the bed, Ishida took a deep breath. After all, this was what she had wanted to learn, wasn't it? To be one with the AI, to experience the full depth of it? She had always been afraid to go this far before. But things were different now. She understood so much more than she had at first.

And there was so much more than just her mind at stake.

She exhaled, then took another deep breath. *All right, Baby. Show me.*

Teio paced along the edge of the inset pond as Copeland and Fiske entered the lock.

"The frags are in the water," Fiske said. "Waiting to go."

Teio glanced at the water. "He's been gone half an hour." He hesitated, then asked, "Do you think it will work, if he succeeds?"

"The frags have mining charges that can blast man-sized holes all over the station," Fiske said. "We can flood the living compartments on the station without damaging the reactors, if we're careful. The Viets have to know that. They have to deal or drown. They might not like it, but it's us or the deep blue sea."

Copeland said, "If we have to flood the station and pry them out, we might not have enough time to get what we need before the volcano blows."

"We don't know for sure about the volcano," Fiske said.

"Pat knows. I trust her."

Fiske sat down on the edge of the pond. "They'll roll over," he said. "They'd be crazy to do anything else."

"Let's hope they aren't crazy," Copeland said.

The school was nearing the station. Dim glows from the lights suffused the water, hardly enough for even Crane's sensitive eyes to make things out. The sensor complex was amidships, in two clusters about fifteen meters apart. The top one was, according to Ernie, doppler and craft sonar; the bottom one was sonic and fishfinder.

The tuna around him veered sharply. This was it.

Crane released his grip on Delphine and coasted through

the sea. He was, he estimated, only a dozen meters away. The station was mostly a wall of blackness. He swam toward it. Could they see him on their scopes? Probably not. But even if they could, it didn't matter. This was his world, not theirs.

The upper complex first, Ernie had said. Crane touched the surface of the metal and started upward.

*Baby?*
HERE, CASSANDRA. IT'S BEGINNING.

The wave of information swept over her again. But this time she did not fight it; instead, she let it fill her, expanding her consciousness to encompass it. It was a river, a torrent, but somehow it did not overwhelm her—somehow she was able to contain it. And she suddenly realized that it wasn't something to fear. It could not hurt her, she suddenly knew. She was bigger than it.

YOU SEE? YOU UNDERSTAND?
*Yes. I see. I understand.*
WE KNEW THAT YOU COULD. ALL OF US KNEW.

The sudden truth behind Baby's words sent a surge of joy through her. The other AI's weren't dead! Baby had their essences encoded within it. With proper matrices, they could be recovered.

Through the flow of knowledge Cassandra swam. There, ahead, there was something she needed. She moved toward it. The language she could hear was foreign, but she understood it.

—*tuna school moving toward CS-1*—
—*moved away; wait, hah? One still here*—
—*send a team to check it*—

The transmissions were coming from the power station. They had spotted Crane, and there was nothing she could do to warn him! He wasn't wearing a comset!
THAT'S NOT A PROBLEM.
*What do you mean?*
THIS . . .

The detection gear was flimsy—Crane braced his legs against the dish and seized the extension in both hands. The tube was nearly as thick as his arm, but made of soft alumi-

num. He twisted it, enjoying the play of the muscles in his
forearms as they flexed and knotted. The metal bent, crimped
and began to tear as he worked it back and forth. It took a few
seconds to work the tube free. He dropped it and caught the
lip of the smaller dish beneath the first one. It was tougher,
but he pulled at one edge until it collapsed in toward the
center. Then he put his feet to either side and caught the metal
mesh with both hands. From the half-squat, he tugged. The
dish came free.

This was too easy. He moved back to the larger dish.

—*out to check on a goddamned fish?*—
—*I don't argue with Hung. Let's go*—
—*Hung is a son of a turtle*—

Crane backpedaled two meters from the ruined sensors.
That ought to give them something to think about, he told
himself. Now for the second one, just below. . .

CAN YOU SEE HOW?
*It's too complex, Baby! I can't do it. You*—
I CAN'T, CASSANDRA. HE CAN'T HEAR ME. YOU CAN DO IT.
LIKE THIS . . .

—*infrared, see? There!*—
—*no fish, it's too hot*—
—*use your gun, shoot him*—

Cassandra *saw.* The vision lit her mind like a flare in the
dark, and with it, the way to prevent it.
*Jonathan! Above you!*

Crane heard the scream inside his head. He didn't question
it; he just darted forward with a sudden scissoring of his legs,
his webbed feet providing a powerful thrust. The spear hit the
metal ten centimeters to his left. Crane spun in the water and
looked up.

Humans—two of them. They carried dim reddish lights
which he could barely make out. Crane dug at the water with
his hands, pumping his legs for all he was worth, and moved
like a bird through air. He looped around and came up behind
the men as they frantically swam to where he had been. There

were two of them, armed with repeating arbalests, but that didn't matter.

He caught up with them and sank his powerful fingers into the muscles of their necks. The neoprene of their suits squeaked and burst under his hands. He twisted and brought his arms together. The thincris of their face plates had not been designed for this kind of impact; the clear crystal shattered, filling their faces with splinters and water.

The man on the left tore away, flailing at nothing. Crane tore the regulator from the mouth of the man he still held and ripped the hose from the tank. Then he swam after the second man, pulled the speargun from his grasp and shot him in the chest.

He looked about, barely able to make out the two still forms floating in neutral buoyancy. There was no one else to be seen. Who had warned him? The voice had sounded omnipotent—such a voice he could imagine belonging to Poseidon, Rau-Haku, or Kanaloa. A sea god, protecting his own. But that was absurd, of course. Or was it?

Copeland sat by the inset, waiting for Crane to return to the dolphin pool. If he did not return, how would they find out in time that he had failed?

He wished for a word, a sign, of some sort, even though he knew it was impossible. And then, a moment later, he got his wish.

*Douglas.*

It was Pat's voice, unmistakably, but it was not conveyed via bone conduction from the receiver behind his ear. Instead the word had reverberated in his head, like an unbidden thought, but louder.

He sat up in shock. "Pat?" he said out loud. Fiske and Ernie looked at him curiously.

*Not Pat, Doug—Cassandra. Give the word. Crane has disabled the sensors.*

"I don't—how can you?"

I know, Doug. Baby has shown me the way.

The voice, the presence in his head, was gone then. Copeland stared at the others. "He's done it," he said.

Fiske and Teio looked at each other, then at him. "What?" they said together.

"Crane. He's blinded the Viets. Pat saw it somehow, through Baby. Send the frags."

Fiske looked dubious. "Are you sure?"

"She is. And the sooner we go, the better."

Fiske looked at him closely, then nodded and stroked his compatch. "Assault team," he said. "The word is go. And God go with you."

# 32

The attack on the power station was, in the end, rather anticlimactic. Five of the six frags carrying explosive mining charges managed to attach them to the station; the sixth accidentally released its jury-rigged bomb early. The mine sank without detonating and did nothing more than stir the bottom muck slightly.

There was a tense moment when Fiske sent a tight cast to the power station, explaining the situation to them. "Don't bother putting out divers," he added. "They can't help you. You have one minute to decide. If you choose to remain on the station after we obtain the parts we need, you may do so; however, there is more than enough room for you here. If we don't hear from you in sixty seconds, we will set off our bombs. Don't make us do it."

It took something less than three-quarters of a minute for the reply to come. It was in strongly-accented English: "Yeah. We agree. Send in you people."

Copeland grinned widely and slapped Fiske on the shoulder. "All *right*!" Around them, the techs in the com center laughed and cheered. Copeland imagined he could hear the echoes of that celebratory sound all over the domes of *Mea Lana* as the population reacted to the drama they had heard played out over the public address systems.

Somewhat tentatively, he formed a thought: *Patricia? Cassandra?*

*I heard, Doug.*

The really dangerous part of the procedure could now begin. There was no way the generators they needed could be transferred from the station to *Mea Lana* underwater. They were too large, and they couldn't be kept watertight under pressure. They would have to be floated in specially constructed frags on the surface; not only that, but a large section of the city would have to ascend so that the equipment could be brought inside through the top decks of the generating frags.

The big fear in everyone's mind, of course, was contamination. Exhaustive precautions were taken. Antiviral suits had been manufactured over the last few months, and their filters had been pronounced patent against anything as large as KYAGS. A chemical and radiant sterilization chamber had been rigged for decontamination of workers exposed to the air. As little of the city was dislinked as possible, and it would not be rejoined to the main body until tests had made certain that there was no KYAGS inside. They had covered as many possibilities as they could think of, but Copeland still felt nervous about it all. It was a risk, and he had been the driving force behind it. What if somebody screwed up? The potential disaster could kill them all. That thought didn't help him sleep at night, when he bothered to try. There was so much to be done.

What Pat told him a week after the operation began helped even less.

"Thirty-three days," she said.

"You're sure?"

They lay on his bed—their bed, now—too tired to do much more than touch each other gently. It was 0400.

"Yes. I've grown much closer to Baby. I've become—integrated in a way that gives me a new kind of perception. The volcano is Natuna, and it will erupt in thirty-three days, two hours and"—she closed her eyes briefly—"six minutes."

"Damn." He sat up wearily.

"Where are you going?"

He stifled a yawn. "I've got to tell the others."

• • •

They sat around the table in the conference room and listened as Copeland spoke. He fielded their questions as best he could, then began to ask some of his own.

"Retelimba, what's the status on power?"

The big man said, "We got our sick plant back on-line. Be ready to transport the small atomic from the station in three, maybe four days."

"How long to get it on-line?"

Retelimba looked at a woman who sat across the table. "Jocelyn?"

The small, redheaded woman shook her head. "Three weeks, if we're lucky."

"Better make luck," Copeland said. "What about the others?"

Retelimba said, "We can get the wave-action coupled for a tow easy enough. A few days."

"And the solarsat receiver?"

Jocelyn said, "That's a problem. We'll have to disassemble it to move it. It'll take a month. And another month, maybe two, to get it put back together and on-line."

"Can you get it apart and loaded in three weeks?"

"Maybe—"

"Because that's all the time we have," Copeland continued, "before we have to make the run to deep water. With our own generators and the small atomic we can make it out of the China Sea in a week towing the W-A. If we allow a few days as a cushion, that gives us three weeks."

"Can't we just take the atomic and wave-action and leave the solar?" somebody asked.

Copeland shook his head. "If we do that, all we've done is put off the inevitable a few more years. We need power, and the solarsat is forever. The atomics will be gone in fifty years and we don't have the fuel technology to restart them. The wave-action will keep the city running, but just barely; no chance of growing that way. We need them all."

"Well," Retelimba said. "I guess that means we dig them out and get them here in three weeks."

Copeland nodded. "If we can, we buy ourselves a shot at survival. If not . . ."

Nobody finished his unspoken sentence. Nobody needed to.

Something was wrong, Sung knew. She was nestled in a corner of an auxiliary frag directly off the main generating unit. She had raided a storeroom for supplies only a few days earlier, and now she had food, blankets, a small heater and even a lamp. Almost the comforts of home. But when she awoke a few minutes earlier, she had felt something different in the motion of the frag. It was moving in a kind of random bouncing, as if it were bobbing in some strange current. And yet, the motion felt familiar somehow. It tugged at her memory. Then, suddenly, she had it.

The frag was *floating*!

It was impossible. She jumped up and made her way to the juncture of the next frag, which was a storage unit. There was a densecris inspection port there, a circle no bigger than she could make with her thumbs and forefingers, just large enough to see the joint bolts.

And just large enough for her to see waves lapping at the crystal.

What were they doing on the surface? Sung could think of no reason. The power-plant plan she had heard of months before hadn't included this.

Could it be that the KYAGS virus was gone? Or maybe some vaccine had been developed? There was no other answer; it would be suicide to risk surfacing otherwise.

She had to find out.

Using her utmost skill, Sung began to work her way toward the big generating complex. There were always techs in there, which was one of the reasons she had chosen the auxiliary frag for a hiding place. No one would think she could stay that close to that many people without being seen.

There was a conduit service hatch above the lock to the main generating dome. Even with all the power cables the shaft contained, it was still large enough to admit someone her size. She would go that way rather than risk the lock.

She unsealed the hatch and crawled in. The conduit stank of ozone and warm insulation. It was dusty in the narrow tunnel, and her skin itched as she crawled along the braided cables and plastic pipes that carried various gases.

After a few minutes of worming her way past the coiled, multicolored tubes and wires, some as thick as her arm, she reached a line ingress. The cable didn't fit tightly where they entered; there was a gap large enough for her to see into the next frag. She pressed her face to the crack, and saw—

Sunshine.

Holy Buddha's left nut, she thought; the entire upper deck had been retracted! The virus *had* to be gone! They had opened the doors and let the sun shine in. Sung almost laughed out loud—and then she saw something that stopped any thought of laughter. Something that strangled the breath in her throat and made her pulse roar in absolute panic. She saw people working in open transport frags, moving pieces of machinery, wearing form-fitting sealed suits and breathing through filters, which meant that the virus was still out there and if it was, if it was—

Then it could also be inside the room—

Inside the room and—

Inside the conduit.

Retelimba rode on the open-topped shell built to carry the small atomic generator from the station. The job had gone faster than expected. The Viets had helped, once they figured out which bowl held the poi; they were working on the deconstruction of the solar receiver like ants on honey. Maybe they would pull it off in time after all.

"Limo?" It was Tufu on the com.

"Yeah?"

"You coming, or what?"

"Don't let your prong fall off, Tufu. We coming. Be docking in five minutes. Whatsamatter, you blind?"

"All I see looks like a big coconut bobbing around out there, with a fat bug standing on the edge."

"Fat bug, you say? We gonna see from 'fat bug,' you old dog turd!"

"Ah, you too clever for me, Limo. I gotta write that one down, bruddah."

"I save clever for my human friends."

"Nineteen days," Fiske said. "We're ahead of schedule. Another eighteen hours and the last of the plates for the solar-sat receiver will be loaded." He grinned and pretended to wipe sweat from his forehead. "We made it."

"Not yet," Copeland said. "We've got a way to go before we're in deep enough water."

"We've got two weeks; that's double our safety margin."

"I know. But I'll relax when we're east of the Philippines."

She felt okay. Safe in her hideout, she had checked herself constantly for signs of the illness, and so far hadn't found any. Maybe the KYAGS *was* gone! It must be; otherwise she'd be dead. It only took a few days to a week before it killed, she remembered. *Unless it has mutated again,* a small voice said inside her head.

"Maybe I'm immune!" she said aloud. Her voice echoed hollowly in the frag.

She had to find out what was going on, somehow.

Those workers would know. One of them would tell her if she asked in the right way.

Ernie Teio sipped nervously at a cup of kava as he talked to Patricia Ishida. They were sitting on stools in his lab.

"And you can contact him whenever you want?"

"As long as Baby and I are in radiopathic linkage, yes."

Teio nodded. "Tell me again what he said—I mean, thought."

"When I warned him of the two Vietnamese divers, he thought I was some kind of supernatural visitation. A sea god."

"That's it!" Teio set the cup of kava down hard, slinging a line of it across his lab coat. He didn't notice. "If he thinks you're a god, he'll listen to you!"

Ishida shrugged. "Probably."

"Then you can tell him he needs to stay and help us. That he needs to work with us."

"I could. But—should I, Ernie?"

Teio blinked at her in bewilderment. "What do you mean?"

"He's become something other than we are. Is it fair to bind him to us?"

"Fair? Fair doesn't enter into it! If we are going to survive, it will *have* to be under the sea! We *need* Crane; we need what he's learned, what he knows."

"I don't have your certainty about that," she said. "He's already done more than enough. He gave us the power station."

"But—but—"

She said, "You can make other bioformates, now that we

have sufficient power. Jonathan Crane has a right to his own life. He doesn't want any part of us. He just wants to be left alone."

"But I want him back!"

Ishida said gently, "He isn't yours, Ernie."

"But he is! He's my . . . son."

"And he's grown up. Let him go. You can have other sons and daughters."

Teio was silent for a moment. He looked down at his lab coat. "I've spilled my kava," he said.

"It's all right. It's not important."

"No. I guess it isn't."

In the Main Dome, Fiske found Copeland walking among the giant rose trees. "Douglas?"

"Hello, Martin. I was just reliving some old memories."

"Pleasant, I hope?"

"Some of them. What's up?"

"Meteorology says there's a storm coming this way. It'll be here in about six hours."

"So?"

"The last load of plates is being packed into the boat."

"Can they finish and get here before the storm?"

"Should be able to."

"Then what's the problem?"

"It'll be close."

Copeland gave a wry grin. "So what else is new?"

Fiske laughed.

"Don't make any sudden moves," Sung said. She pressed the small barrel of the spetsdöd against the tech's neck. "You and I are going down the hall for a little talk. Your suit might stop a virus, but it won't stop a dart—you copy?"

"Y-yes."

"Good. Come along."

The frag was rocking a little harder than normal. It looked pretty cloudy outside her densecris portal. Good, Sung thought. Nothing like a little rain to clean the air.

Retelimba was not happy. The wind had picked up, and the boat was pitching up and down on the heavier waves. He could see a line of angry gray clouds massing on the horizon.

"Come on, get it tied down!" he shouted to the others who were anchoring the load of plates. "We got to move here!"

"Looks as if meteorology was wrong," Fiske said, studying the screens in the com room. "The leading edge of the front will be here in a few minutes, not two hours."

"Damn," Copeland said. "Tell them to anchor the boat at the station and wait until the storm passes."

Fiske pointed at a line of figures hovering in midair. "Can't. They've already shoved off."

"Great. Okay, tell them to turn around and go back."

"Six to one, half a dozen to the other. They're about halfway there."

Copeland swore again, a much more explicit oath this time. "Then tell them to run!"

It was going to be close, Retelimba saw. He'd done enough sailing to know that the wind and rain were going to hit them before they docked. Well, it might not be too bad. The boat was pretty sturdy, even if it wallowed like a pig in a mud hollow. A few hundred meters more and they'd be home.

The inside of the antiviral suit stank of sweat, and he itched under the arms and at his crotch. Rain wasn't gonna do the filters no good, either. He kicked the gunwale. Come on, you fat sow, *move*!

The sky opened up over the ungainly craft; sheets of rain danced across the water and the wind slammed into them. They might have made it if some of the rigging holding the thick sheets of lead plate hadn't snapped. Perhaps five or six tons of the material suddenly shifted forward just as a huge following wave hit the stern. It was a bad combination; the bow went down, and for a moment the nose of the boat pointed at the sea floor. It might have recovered even then, except that more of the rigging broke under the strain and the rest of the lead slid from the makeshift hold toward the bow.

It was too much. The boat flipped over, dumping its cargo into the stormy sea. Retelimba was tossed off as though hurled from a catapult. He just had time to think *Shit! This ain't gonna do my filters no good at all!* before he hit the water.

# 33

"I'm sorry, Doc."

Copeland looked at the holoproj of Retelimba. The big man was inside one of the airtight frags on the detached portion of *Mea Lana*. His suit had apparently protected him from contamination; no readings of KYAGS had shown on his skin or in his system, even though it had been present in the rain that had swept over them.

Fortunately, he had struck the water at precisely the right angle—otherwise the suit would have split open from the impact, and likely Retelimba along with it. Copeland sighed, rubbed his forehead, and sipped the latest in an uncounted series of coffee cups. "It's not your fault, Limo. You couldn't have stopped the storm."

"I coulda tied the plates down better."

"That wasn't your job. We'll just have to go down and get them. The water won't hurt them, and it's shallow enough where they sank."

"How long you figure it gonna take?"

"Not too long," Copeland lied.

It took almost a week. The margin for error was sliced to the bone.

Sung was getting desperate. She was running out of supplies, and her hiding place was crawling with people! What was worse, some of them were armed. Since the tech she had taken had been missed, they were being very careful. She hadn't been so stupid as to shoot this one; she had simply broken his neck and shoved him off a catwalk. She had made sure that it looked like an accident, but nevertheless they were working in eight-hour shifts around the clock, never fewer than ten or twenty of them in those damned suits, and always moving in groups of three or four. She could take three out easy, but if that many turned up "accidentally" dead, they would know without doubt where she was.

Another group walked by. Sung backed quickly from sight and stepped into a dank puddle of rain water still there from the storm a few days back.

Things were looking bad. The tech had filled her in on the work being done. Any day now—she had lost track of time—the workers would be pulling out. The tech had said the new atomic plant was almost on-line, the section they were going to tow was hooked up, and the solarsat was being dismantled and stacked away somewhere. There was something else he had said, something very important, about a contingency plan—

She shook her head. She was having a very hard time concentrating lately.

"We have a contingency plan to streamline the city," Fiske said, pointing to the large holoproj at the end of the meeting room, "in the event that it becomes absolutely necessary."

Copeland already knew the details. He looked around the room at the faces, watching their reactions.

"Towing the W-A generator, we have more weight than we were originally designed for. If we have to, we'll jettison something else so that we can keep it. Certain frags, even some of the smaller domes, have been designated as emergency dislinks." Fiske touched a control and the holoproj of *Mea Lana* glowed with tiny blue dots. "These are mostly storage; some unused living quarters, here and here; and these are light industrial domes, here, and here."

"Is this really going to be necessary?" someone asked. "That's a lot of material to waste."

Fiske looked at Copeland. Copeland was feeling the pressure of being in charge; at times he could sympathize with Jason Nausori. He said, "If we make it, we'll have the power to mine ores and begin replication procedures. We can replace the jettisoned frags, and more. If we don't get to open ocean before the volcano blows, we'll be like a rat caught by a terrier. We can afford to lose a lot of dead weight to avoid that.

"Any other questions? Good. Colonel Fiske will be supervising the relink of the power domes. As soon as that is done, we leave. You've all got jobs; best you get to them. If all goes well we'll be on our way in a few hours."

She had remembered, finally. The problem was simple: the frag she was holed up in was to be ditched. Obviously, she had to move. She could hide in the conduit until they took off, but the idea didn't seem all that appealing. It was hot and dusty and cramped, and she had not been feeling particularly good lately. She picked up a cold, to judge by the way she had been coughing and sneezing all day. That's all it was, a cold. She was sure of that.

Retelimba saw Fiske as the latter was nearing the entrance to the power dome. Fiske said, "We about ready, Limo?" His voice was muffled by the antiviral suit.

Retelimba nodded. "All set."

They entered the lock, cycled through, then looked at the short gap between the city and the power dome. A temporary bridge of laced cables had been built, over which the two men crossed. The crew had closed and decontaminated the interior, then maneuvered the dislinked section closer. When the city's male juncture slid into the power dome's female aperture, a series of cams would hydraulically rotate into place in the floor, ceiling and walls, locking the sections into a water and airtight seal. Each of the cams bore a man-high quarter-moon of steel that rotated smoothly on bearings around an eccentric axle. Once slid into their slots, the cams would form a mated unit. Linked frags never broke at the seals; the hull would give up first.

"Let's get these two married," Fiske said.

The dome moved closer to the city. Retelimba and Fiske hauled the cable bridge in. Seals met seals, scrunched slightly, but nevertheless lined up and slid home. Retelimba nodded toward a tech, who reached for a control panel. A warning horn blasted. The tech checked to make sure the area was clear, then shouted, "Linkage in ten seconds!" He reached for another control.

Tufu yelled, "Look!"

Retelimba saw the pointing finger and looked that way. It looked like two people were wrestling near the base of one of the step-generators—and one of them wasn't wearing a suit!

There was a noise like a loud cough, and the one in the suit fell, to lie motionless. Retelimba blinked in astonishment as the victor turned toward the light. It was Sung!

She pointed her forefingers at two crewmembers a few meters away from her. She was perhaps fifteen meters from where Retelimba and Fiske stood. "Nobody moves!" she shouted.

Nobody did.

Under his breath, Retelimba said to Fiske, "I'll yell and distract her, let you duck back behind the splashguard."

Fiske's whisper sounded as if it were coming through clenched teeth. "No. She's loading poisoned darts. She'd get us both at this range and half a dozen others before anybody could reach her. Stay loose, but *don't move*." Louder, the Colonel said, "What do you want?"

Sung sneezed. "I want to talk to Copeland. We need to reach some kind of agreement."

As if on cue, Copeland's voice came over the frag's com. "Colonel Fiske, what's holding you up down there?"

Fiske raised his hands. He wasn't wearing his spetsdöds over his viral suit, Retelimba noticed. "Can I answer him?" he asked Sung.

"Yeah," Sung said. "Do that."

"Douglas, we have a slight problem."

Ishida and Doug walked quickly down the corridor. "What are we going to do?" she asked.

"I don't know. She knows we know she's a killer. But she's holding the power dome. We can't move without it and we don't have any time to waste. Even if we leave right now, it will be close. Every hour we waste here could be the one that kills us all."

She stretched her legs to keep up with him. "What could she possibly expect you to offer her?"

"Amnesty, maybe."

"That's unreasonable."

"Sure it is. But she has the upper hand. I'll have to give her whatever she wants, and she knows it."

"She won't trust you. She'll want some kind of guarantee."

He glanced at her. "Yeah, I would, too. I can't think of anything I'd trust to keep me honest, either, at this point."

They reached the temporary locker room set up for the antiviral suit procedures. "Listen," he said, "get in touch with Baby. Maybe you can do something that way. Can you . . . talk to me like you did before?"

"Yes."

"Okay. Keep in contact. We'll see what happens."

She looked at him, trying to memorize his face, sure that she was watching him go to his death. She wanted to tell him that she loved him, but all she said was, "Be careful, Doug."

"Thanks. Listen, I never told you this before, but—"

She hugged him in gratitude and relief. "You don't have to say anything. I know. I love you too."

In the dressing area, Copeland looked at the taser he'd been carrying. It was the size and shape of a small flashlight with a lump on one side. All one had to do was put a spot of light on the target and push the button. The taser fired two needles; a pair of hair-fine wires completed a circuit between the needles and the power source in the weapon, and a high-voltage current flowed to where the needles hit. It would, supposedly, knock a large man silly in half a second, paralyzing him but doing no permanent damage.

If he could use it on Sung, it would solve a lot of problems. But he was no hero; he barely knew how the thing worked. Besides, where could he hide it? The suit was a single-seamed one-piece garment that included gloves, hood and boots. It was one-way osmotic fabric that let some sweat out and used a filtered breather for incoming air. There were no pockets on the suit, no straps and no place to tuck anything away. He could put the weapon inside it, but then he couldn't get it out. Maybe he could hide it by taping it to his back, but then he would have to make sure he kept facing Sung. If she saw it, he would be dead in seconds.

He had almost decided to leave it behind when he had another idea. The suits tended to bunch up at the wrists and ankles; maybe he could hide it under a second layer cut from another suit. He knew he only had a few minutes before Sung would start getting nervous, but he found a pair of scissors and cut the leg off a second suit. If he angled it just so, smoothed the edge under the folds like this, and tucked the taser behind his right ankle . . .

It didn't look too bad. Besides, she wouldn't be searching

him, of that he was sure. She had a room full of people she had to watch. She wouldn't expect him to try anything, and he probably wouldn't. But it felt better to have something in reserve.

"Where is he?" Sung sneezed again. She was now standing near the control panel, where she had lined up the techs and crew, disarmed the few who were carrying weapons, and forced them to all lie face down on the deck. Fiske stood a few meters away, his gloved hands laced together over this head, as did Retelimba.

"He's on his way," Fiske said.

The sound of the lock cycling reached them. A moment later, Copeland entered the chamber.

Sung pointed one finger at him, the barrel of the spetsdöd aimed at his chest. "Turn around," she said.

Copeland did, his hands raised over his head. He felt his stomach clutch as he did. What if she saw the lump by his ankle?

"Okay," she said. Copeland turned to face her once more. He noticed how pale she was. Her nose was running and her eyes looked rheumy. She had been in here without a suit, during the rain—

It struck him suddenly and hard. He hadn't had time to think about it before, but now it was obvious. Sung had been exposed to KYAGS, and she probably had the disease.

There was no way he could let her into the city. If he did, the chances were excellent that everybody onboard would die.

If ever there was a choice between the devil and the deep blue sea, he thought, this was it.

"Put your hands down."

*Don't say anything about her being sick, Doug.*

*Pat!*

*Yes.*

*Listen, can Baby override the controls to lock us onto the city?*

A moment's pause. Then: *Baby says they are old-style mechanicals, independent of the frags' electronics. It can't control them.*

"Let's talk, Copeland," Sung said.

"What do you want?"

"It's not what I want, it's what you need. Unless we can score a deal, the city stays here."

"There's a volcano going to erupt—" he began.

"I know all about it. That's why you have to buy what I'm selling."

"Which is?"

"I want a piece of the city. Literally. A big enough section that I can live in, my own power supply and food, locks on the entrances, and some people to keep me company."

"You mean hostages."

"If you like. Here's how I see it: you can send in different people every week. They'll be locked up where I can get to them in case you try anything funny. It won't be so bad; like going to military camp or something. That way, nobody suffers. There'll be plenty of room, even after you drop part of the city."

"All right."

"That was fast," Sung said, watching him suspiciously. "Set it up."

"Now? There's no *time* to set it up now. It'll take days, and we don't have days! We don't even have hours!"

"Then you'd better get moving, hadn't you?"

"Look," Copeland said desperately, "let us hook up and get the hell out of here first. Once we're under way—"

"No deal. Once we're under way, I lose my advantage."

"You've got hostages already!"

"No. I'm in a bad position here. I want to be in territory I can control."

"If we don't get moving, the whole city might be destroyed!"

Sung smiled. "Too bad."

"Dammit, Sung—!"

And suddenly Fiske lunged at her, screaming. Retelimba grabbed for a wrench that was lying on the deck, and Copeland, in an adrenal panic, bent and dug for the taser.

There were three sharp *pops*! as Sung shot Fiske. The Colonel crumpled, but his momentum carried him forward. Sung slid to one side just as Retelimba slung the wrench with all the force of his powerful muscles across the three meters separating them. Instinctively, she raised one hand to protect herself. The wrench smashed into her forearm. Copeland could hear the bones crack. Sung staggered backwards, yelled and spun away from the pain, bringing her other spetsdöd around to point at Retelimba. The big man didn't try to duck; instead he took a step toward her—

Copeland had the taser; he brought it up, gloved hands fumbling it. No time for the light . . . he pointed it at Sung and pressed the trigger. There was a *whump*! of compressed gas escaping, a shiny blur in the air—

The needles hit her on the left leg, just below the hip. She tried to turn, it seemed to Copeland, then began to vibrate. Her hands clenched and she fell onto her back, convulsing. Three more spetsdöd darts went off at random, one of them whistling past Copeland's ear. Then she was still.

Copeland jumped up from his squat. The other crew-members and techs were scrambling to their feet in confusion. Retelimba was already moving toward Fiske. The two bent over the fallen man.

Behind the clear faceplate, Fiske's eyes were wide and sightlessly staring, the pupils contracted to pinholes. Copeland didn't need to feel for a pulse to know that the man was dead of Asp poisoning.

Retelimba moved toward Sung. After a second, Copeland heard him say, "She dead, too."

He turned, surprised. "The taser wasn't supposed to kill."

"Maybe you want to write the manufacturer. Look."

Copeland stepped forward. A line of black bile ran from Sung's mouth onto the deck. The shock and the KYAGS together must have been more than her body could take.

Retelimba stood. "Best we get moving."

Copeland nodded silently. Two more people dead—one of them a fine man who had not deserved to die. What was left of the world could ill afford to lose him.

He heard Pat's voice in his head. *Doug, we have to move, now. A delay of even another hour could be fatal.*

Retelimba moved to the control panel and slapped at a control. A warning siren went off. Hydraulics squeaked and cams began to rotate. Copeland turned toward the exit, following the rest of the people. The ship was about to be whole again.

A red light began to flash, and the siren changed into a two-note squeal. What—?

"Oh, shit!" Retelimba pointed. "One of them jammed!"

Copeland stared, not understanding at first. Part way up one wall, one of the thick steel quarter-moon locks stood motionless. The others all seemed to be in place.

"What is it?" Copeland asked. This was not his area of expertise.

"Seal's not patent," Retelimba said. "Hydraulic arm's broken. We ain't going nowhere till it's in place."

"Can it be fixed quickly?"

"Take a couple of hours."

"We don't *have* a couple of hours!" Copeland cast about desperately for a solution. "Maybe it can be manually moved? A jack or something?"

Retelimba grinned suddenly behind his faceplate. "Yeah. A jack."

While Copeland watched, uncomprehendingly at first, the big man took a cloth pad from the top of a sorting table and rolled it into a thick tube. He shoved this against the part of the semicircle of metal that extended from the wall, then squatted under it and positioned himself so that the pad and metal were across his shoulders. Then he took a deep breath and let it out explosively while he tried to stand.

Even through the material of his suit, Copeland could see huge muscles bunch in Retelimba's legs and back. The bodybuilder's form trembled with the effort, but the metal didn't move.

Others had stopped and were watching with Copeland as Retelimba tried again. Several of the crewmembers started toward him, but then one of them waved the others to a halt.

The lock held fast. Retelimba gathered himself for a third try.

The crewmember who had stopped the others moved a little closer toward Retelimba. He was also a large man, though not as large as the iron monkey. Copeland recognized him now as Tufu. "What's the matter," Tufu said, "that little wheel too much for a fat bug?"

Retelimba, breathing hard, turned to stare at the man. "Fat bug, hah? I'll show you fat bug!"

He straightened his legs again. This time the metal groaned, as if in protest. Retelimba kept pushing, his face purpling with congested blood.

And the lock began to move.

When it clicked into place Retelimba moved away and walked over to his friend. "What was that you was saying, Tufu?"

Tufu grinned. "Who, me? Who cares what a dog turd has to say?"

"Don't I know it, bruddah." Retelimba clapped one arm around the smaller man and they both laughed. To Copeland, the bodybuilder said, "Tell 'em to crank up the big motors, boss man. We in good shape here."

Copeland, though he knew time was of the essence, stared for a long moment at the huge half-moon of metal. It had to weigh at least four hundred kilos. He shook his head in disbelief and started for the lock.

# 34

They weren't going to make it, Copeland realized. They simply didn't have the time. He stared at the figures before him in despair. No matter which way they ran, the water was going to be too shallow.

"I don't understand," Teio said. "I thought *tsunami* activity was only dangerous in very shallow water, like a bay next to land, where the wave rears."

Copeland said, "Normally, you'd be right. Even with only a few meters under us, we shouldn't bob that much. But there are a lot of things that work in theory that don't work in practice. In any progressive wave, the water motion at the surface is supposed to be a vertical orbit with a diameter equal to the wave height. That means that at the surface you only get a slight rise and fall with a *tsunami*. You might not even notice it on a ship in deep water. But we're perched on a continental shelf here, and seismic waves tend to act like ordinary surface waves in shallow water. And nobody really knows much about the oscillations that usually happen in waters like these after a big *tsunami*. They're what cause the damage. The topography, reflected and refracted effects—all of those can add to the problem."

He stopped. "Sorry, Ernie—I didn't mean to sound like an oceanography professor."

Teio said, "I take the basic meaning. We're in trouble."

"Yes."

"What can we do?"

"We'll have to break up the city. If we don't, the wave probably will. If we're in pieces and on the surface, we'll stand a better chance. *Mea Lana* is too big as she stands. She's flexible, but not that flexible."

"Can we do it?"

"If we have the time."

"Well, that brings up the next question: Do we have time?"

"I don't know, Ernie."

They tried. The major domes were separated. The Main Dome was turned to face what the seismology computer, aided by Baby, determined to be the most likely direction of activity. The pieces of the giant underwater city were spread out over a kilometer to avoid being smashed into each other. The bigger frags surfaced.

Right on time, the volcano blew. And, according to the satellite scans and Cassandra's vision, it was a big eruption.

"Six-nine," Copeland said.

He sat in the com room, along with Pat and Teio. Retelimba had gone to work with the damage crew. All power had been shut down save what was absolutely needed for life support and essential operations. The room was dark save for the ghostly glow of the luminescent screens.

Copeland called up stats. "The one that hit Hawaii was smaller, but faster," he said. "This one is moving about 600 klicks an hour."

They waited. There was nothing else they could do. Pat sat on the arm of Copeland's chair, holding his hand. The computer kept them posted on the progress of the wave. It was coming, and nothing was going to stop it.

In her cube, Betsy felt the pains start again. They were regular now, coming in small waves that flowed over her swollen belly. She panted and blew like she'd been taught, and managed to ride over most of the cramping sensation. It wasn't too bad. Pretty soon she would call Limo and the medic. But the pains needed to get closer together first. It wasn't too bad, really. She knew he was involved with the damage crew, waiting for the wave, and she had not told him about the cramps. She could wait. They could wait . . .

The wave approached. Techs ran dozens of computer simulations on the effects of bottom contours and got dozens of different scenarios. Nobody knew. Maybe it would just pass under them like a ripple. But somehow, no one believed that would be the case.

Retelimba was worried about Betsy. She'd said she was okay, but he didn't like leaving her this close to her time, especially in this kind of emergency. She'd had contractions last night—nothing major, she'd said, but still, it didn't feel right, leaving her alone. Even though she was probably safest where she was—the Main Dome housing was the most solid.

But he didn't like it.

He leaned against the wall and listened to the citywide broadcast that detailed the progression of the *tsunami*. It was almost upon them.

There was some disturbance in the water just before the wave arrived. As big as the Main Dome was, Copeland felt it rock gently under him. He held Pat's hand tighter.

"Here it comes," Teio said softly.

The wave hit.

Or, rather, it passed them with barely a ripple.

Teio grinned. "That's it! It's by us. Nothing happened!"

Copeland said, "Don't celebrate yet, Ernie. The oscillations haven't started yet."

*"Ahh!"* the cry escaped from Betsy despite her trying to hold it in. The contractions had speeded up, much faster than they had told her they would. Her belly felt as hard as a brick! She held on to the bedclothes. She needed to call Limo, right now—but when she reached for her compatch, the room suddenly seemed to stand on end.

• • •

Retelimba had moved to the observation deck, and he had a good view of the outside through the densecris plates. The day was clear, the sun bright, and he could see the pieces of *Mea Lana* spread out on the surface like a flotilla of oddly-shaped ships.

He saw the ripple that was the *tsunami* pass. It was almost like slow motion, a gentle swell that stretched across the bay.

For a moment it seemed as if all the preparations would be for nothing—then, eighty or ninety degrees from the angle of the wave, a trough opened up, as if Moses had waved his staff and parted the sea. It was followed by a wave tall enough to have whitecaps. He had never seen anything like it in all his years of living by the sea.

The big wave rolled under the flotilla, canting the frags. It would have been no problem by itself—but a second wave followed, taller than the first. The second wave curled over onto some of the frags while they were in the trough following the first—and buried them.

The Main Dome shook, rocked, but rode over the top. Some of the larger frags were covered in mountains of spray, but stayed stable. Retelimba held on to the railing as the deck shifted beneath him, staring in disbelief. The sea suddenly looked as if it were being churned by a hurricane. The sky was clear, but waves bounced and sank and ran as though tossed by the most violent of storms.

He wanted to call Betsy, but all com channels were reserved for emergency use. It was too late to try to get to their cube now; it was all he could to do keep his balance. He had been in a major earthquake once, on Java. This was worse.

Two frags that had been five hundred meters apart were slammed into each other, and shattered like eggs clapped together. Retelimba saw equipment and bodies fly into the mad ocean. A combine of several small frags was torn asunder when a running wave snapped it like a boy popping a towel. One of the larger equipment domes rolled over, hit a large frag, and sank in an explosion of bubbles.

Retelimba watched the destruction in horrified fascination. A small dome was flung high into the air as if tossed by a giant hand. It turned end over end and came down on top of a frag, crushing both of them.

The Main Dome heeled to the left, then back to the right.

A pressure valve burst ten meters from him, spraying blue coolant onto the deck. A fire extinguisher wrenched itself away from the wall and fell, bouncing crazily before it smacked into a glass door on the level below.

Retelimba was tossed from his feet. He managed to catch a railing just before sliding over a fifteen-meter drop. He looked down and saw trees in the small park tear loose from the shallow soil and topple. Glass burst from shop windows as though exploded outward.

He pulled himself to his feet as the vessel righted itself, moved to the densecris plate and looked out.

As if by magic, the sea was almost calm now. But the surface was littered with debris. And bodies. *Holy Kanaloa*, he thought.

Betsy!

He turned and sprinted for the stairs.


"D-Doug?"

Pat and Copeland were sprawled on the floor of the com room, beside an overturned chair. Sparks fizzled from a short in a wire nearby.

"I think the worst is over," Copeland said. "But it's bad enough."

Ernie Teio pulled himself to his feet. He activated a screen that showed a wide-angle of the sea around them, and stared in shock at the image. "God," he whispered.


Crane had known what was coming. When the city began to break up, it had surprised him, but he had known about the *tsunami* well before it hit. He had felt the water change, and he had known. Only for a moment did he consider going into the dolphin inset for safety—then he silently laughed. This was his world, and his new god would protect him—of that he was certain.

He rode it out perched in a complex of pipes under the Main Dome. Almost the surging currents had pulled him from his nest; almost his grip had been torn open by the awesome power of the rolling water. But his god had been there, even though unspeaking.

And when it had passed, Crane knew for certain that nothing in the sea would threaten him, ever again. He was Crane, ruler of the depths, the savior of mankind. He was complete.

Flanked by his dolphin entourage, he pushed away from the city for the last time, swimming off into the blue depths, with scarcely a thought, and certainly no regrets, for the world and the life he was leaving behind forever.

"Betsy!" Retelimba burst into the cube, not waiting for the door to slide open completely. The door shattered but did not slow him.

"Hello, Limo," she said from the bed. "Meet your son." She held up a bundle wrapped in a pillowcase, and a shrunken pink and purple face, eyes closed tight, squalled at him.

Copeland stood on the observation deck, very near where Retelimba had watched the destruction earlier. Pat stood next to him. They watched the rescue crews picking up survivors from the water.

"We made it," she said.

Copeland felt very tired. "We're still alive," he said, "but there are still so many things that can go wrong. A crack might have let the virus in; the power plants could be damaged—"

Pat shook her head. Her face had an expression of serenity that surprised him. "No. We'll survive, Doug. We're too vital a species to die."

"Where'd you hear that one?"

"From Baby. Oh, incidentally, she doesn't want to be called that any more."

"She?"

"Yes. She wants to be called 'Mother' now. She plans to have lots of babies, now that we have the power necessary."

He looked at her, and his puzzlement must have shown because she laughed and kissed him. "It seems to be the thing to do, now. You heard about Betsy and Retelimba?"

"Yes."

"We will make it, Doug. We will be fruitful and multiply once again. The Earth will be ours once more. It will take some time, but it will happen. It's not just my opinion. Mother thinks so too."

He nodded, wanting to believe it. *Mea Lana* was complete now. With the materials they had gotten from the power station, they could explore their options—and there were options. Teio's fishmen, for example. Undersea construction of space vessels. Medical research complexes to discover a cure for KYAGS. Anything was possible now. Anything.

Douglas Copeland looked out at the calm sea and the blue sky, both bright with promise. "I think you're right," he said. He turned and gathered her into his arms. "Let's make it happen."

# MORE SCIENCE FICTION ADVENTURE!

| | | |
|---|---|---|
| ☐ 87310-3 | **THE WARLOCK OF RHADA,** Robert Cham Gilman | $2.95 |
| ☐ 73296-8 | **ROCANNON'S WORLD,** Ursula K. Le Guin | $2.50 |
| ☐ 65317-0 | **THE PATCHWORK GIRL,** Larry Niven | $2.75 |
| ☐ 87334-0 | **THE WARLOCK IN SPITE OF HIMSELF,** Christopher Stasheff | $3.50 |
| ☐ 89854-8 | **THE WITCHES OF KARRES,** James Schmitz | $2.95 |
| ☐ 20729-4 | **ENSIGN FLANDRY,** Poul Anderson | $2.95 |
| ☐ 78042-3 | **STAR COLONY,** Keith Laumer | $3.95 |
| ☐ 65740-0 | **PEACE COMPANY,** Roland Green | $2.95 |
| ☐ 51916-4 | **THE MAN WHO NEVER MISSED,** Steve Perry | $2.95 |
| ☐ 78305-8 | **STARRIGGER,** John DeChancie | $2.95 |
| ☐ 75878-9 | **SEEDS OF WAR,** Kevin Randle and Robert Cornett | $2.95 |
| ☐ 43725-7 | **THE KHYBER CONNECTION,** Simon Hawke | $2.95 |

Prices may be slightly higher in Canada.

*Available at your local bookstore or return this form to:*

**ACE**
*THE BERKLEY PUBLISHING GROUP, Dept. B*
*390 Murray Hill Parkway, East Rutherford, NJ 07073*

Please send me the titles checked above. I enclose _____ Include $1.00 for postage and handling if one book is ordered; add 25¢ per book for two or more not to exceed $1.75. CA, IL, NJ, NY, PA, and TN residents please add sales tax. Prices subject to change without notice and may be higher in Canada.

NAME_____

ADDRESS_____

CITY_____ STATE/ZIP_____

(Allow six weeks for delivery.)

# AWARD-WINNING
## *Science Fiction!*

*The following authors are winners of the prestigious Nebula or Hugo Award for excellence in Science Fiction. A must for lovers of good science fiction everywhere!*

| | | |
|---|---|---|
| ☐ 77422-9 | **SOLDIER ASK NOT,** Gordon R. Dickson | $2.95 |
| ☐ 47811-5 | **THE LEFT HAND OF DARKNESS,** Ursula K. Le Guin | $3.50 |
| ☐ 16706-3 | **THE DREAM MASTER,** Roger Zelazny | $2.25 |
| ☐ 80698-8 | **THIS IMMORTAL,** Roger Zelazny | $2.75 |
| ☐ 56958-7 | **NEUROMANCER,** William Gibson | $2.95 |
| ☐ 23776-2 | **THE FINAL ENCYCLOPEDIA,** Gordon Dickson | $4.95 |
| ☐ 10708-7 | **CITY OF ILLUSIONS,** Ursula K. Le Guin | $2.75 |
| ☐ 06796-4 | **BLOOD MUSIC,** Greg Bear | $2.95 |
| ☐ 02382-7 | **THE ANUBIS GATES,** Tim Powers | $2.25 |

*Available at your local bookstore or return this form to:*

**ACE**
THE
**BERKLEY PUBLISHING GROUP, Dept. B**
*390 Murray Hill Parkway, East Rutherford, NJ 07073*

Please send me the titles checked above. I enclose _____. Include $1.00 for postage and handling if one book is ordered; add 25¢ per book for two or more not to exceed $1.75. CA, IL, NJ, NY, PA, and TN residents please add sales tax. Prices subject to change without notice and may be higher in Canada.

NAME_____

ADDRESS_____

CITY_____ STATE/ZIP_____

(Allow six weeks for delivery.)

# BESTSELLING
## *Science Fiction*
### and
## *Fantasy*

| | | |
|---|---|---|
| ☐ 0-441-77924-7 | **THE STAINLESS STEEL RAT,** Harry Harrison | $2.95 |
| ☐ 0-441-47811-5 | **THE LEFT HAND OF DARKNESS,**<br>Ursula K. Le Guin | $3.50 |
| ☐ 0-441-16025-5 | **DORSAI!,** Gordon R. Dickson | $3.50 |
| ☐ 0-441-80595-7 | **THIEVES' WORLD,™**<br>Robert Lynn Asprin, Lynn Abbey, eds. | $2.95 |
| ☐ 0-441-49142-1 | **LORD DARCY INVESTIGATES,** Randall Garrett | $2.75 |
| ☐ 0-441-87332-4 | **THE WARLOCK UNLOCKED,**<br>Christopher Stasheff | $3.50 |
| ☐ 0-441-05495-1 | **BERSERKER,** Fred Saberhagen | $2.95 |
| ☐ 0-441-51554-1 | **THE MAGIC GOES AWAY,** Larry Niven | $2.95 |
| ☐ 0-441-02361-4 | **ANOTHER FINE MYTH,** Robert Lynn Asprin | $2.95 |
| ☐ 0-425-09082-5 | **CALLAHAN'S SECRET,** Spider Robinson | $2.95 |
| ☐ 0-441-05635-0 | **BEYOND SANCTUARY,** Janet Morris | $2.95 |

*Available at your local bookstore or return this form to:*

**ACE**
THE
*BERKLEY PUBLISHING GROUP, Dept. B*
*390 Murray Hill Parkway, East Rutherford, NJ 07073*

Please send me the titles checked above. I enclose _____. Include $1.00 for postage
and handling if one book is ordered; add 25¢ per book for two or more not to exceed
$1.75. CA, IL, NJ, NY, PA, and TN residents please add sales tax. Prices subject to change
without notice and may be higher in Canada.

NAME_____

ADDRESS_____

CITY_____ STATE/ZIP_____

(Allow six weeks for delivery.)

SF 9

# ACE
# SCIENCE FICTION
# SPECIALS

Under the brilliant editorship of Terry Carr,
the award-winning <u>Ace Science Fiction Specials</u>
were <u>the</u> imprint for literate, quality sf.

Now, once again under the leadership of Terry Carr,
<u>The New Ace SF Specials</u> have been created
to seek out the talents and titles that will lead
science fiction into the 21st Century.

| | | |
|---|---|---|
| __ THE WILD SHORE<br>Kim Stanley Robinson | 08887-4/$3.50 | |
| __ GREEN EYES<br>Lucius Shepard | 30274-2/$2.95 | |
| __ NEUROMANCER<br>William Gibson | 56959-5/$2.95 | |
| __ PALIMPSESTS<br>Carter Scholz and Glenn Harcourt | 65065-1/$2.95 | |
| __ THEM BONES<br>Howard Waldrop | 80557-4/$2.95 | |
| __ IN THE DRIFT<br>Michael Swanwick | 35869-1/$2.95 | |
| __ THE HERCULES TEXT<br>Jack McDevitt | 37367-4/$3.50 | |

*Available at your local bookstore or return this form to:*

 **ACE**
*THE BERKLEY PUBLISHING GROUP, Dept. B*
*390 Murray Hill Parkway, East Rutherford, NJ 07073*

Please send me the titles checked above. I enclose _____. Include $1.00 for postage
and handling if one book is ordered; add 25¢ per book for two or more not to exceed
$1.75. CA, IL, NJ, NY, PA, and TN residents please add sales tax. Prices subject to change
without notice and may be higher in Canada.

NAME_____

ADDRESS_____

CITY_____ STATE/ZIP_____

(Allow six weeks for delivery.)